TIME UNINCORPORATED

THE DOCTOR WHO FANZINE ARCHIVES

Vol. 3: Writings on the New Series

Des Moines, IA

Also available from Mad Norwegian Press...

Time, Unincorporated: The Doctor Who Fanzine Archives (Vol. 1: Lance Parkin)
Time, Unincorporated: The Doctor Who Fanzine Archives
(Vol. 2: Writings on the Classic Series)

Chicks Dig Time Lords: A Celebration of Doctor Who by the Women Who Love It

Whedonistas: A Celebration of the Worlds of Joss Whedon by the Women Who Love Them

Chicks Dig Comics (forthcoming)

Resurrection Code by Lyda Morehouse

Running Through Corridors: Rob and Toby's Marathon Watch of Doctor Who
(Vol. 1: The 60s) by Robert Shearman and Toby Hadoke
Running Through Corridors (Vol. 2: The 70s, forthcoming)

Wanting to Believe: A Critical Guide to The X-Files, Millennium and The Lone Gunmen by Robert Shearman

More Digressions: A New Collection of "But I Digress" Columns by Peter David

AHistory: An Unauthorized History of the Doctor Who Universe [Second Edition]
by Lance Parkin

THE ABOUT TIME SERIES
by Lawrence Miles and Tat Wood

About Time 1: The Unauthorized Guide to Doctor Who (Seasons 1 to 3)
About Time 2: The Unauthorized Guide to Doctor Who (Seasons 4 to 6)
About Time 3: The Unauthorized Guide to Doctor Who
(Seasons 7 to 11) [2nd Edition now available]
About Time 4: The Unauthorized Guide to Doctor Who (Seasons 12 to 17)
About Time 5: The Unauthorized Guide to Doctor Who (Seasons 18 to 21)
About Time 6: The Unauthorized Guide to Doctor Who
(Seasons 22 to 26, the TV Movie)
About Time 7 (forthcoming)

Jacket & interior design by Christa Dickson.

ISBN: 9781935234036
Printed in Illinois. First Edition: June 2011.

For Cadence, the best Goddaughter anyone can have, for all the Saturdays spent watching Doctor Who, *and much more*
GB

For Daniel Changer, for believing from the start, and ever since
RS?

TABLE OF CONTENTS

Introduction by Robert Shearman 9
Foreword by Graeme Burk and Robert Smith? 15

1. It's Back!

The Death of Doctor Who: Verdict Overturned by Dave Owen
(exclusive to this volume) 18
The Ebb and the Flow by Robert Smith?
(from *Enlightenment* #129, August / September 2005) 21
Where Old and New Do Not Converge by Adrian Loder
(from *The Doctor Who Ratings Guide*, October 2005) 25
What Does It Mean to be Doctorish? by Andrew Cartmel
(exclusive to this volume) 26
A Proposal to Bring Back Doctor Who by David T. Russell,
edited by James Downing
(from *Shockeye's Kitchen*, online version) 32

2. Trip of a Lifetime

Resurrection by Lloyd Rose
(from *Enlightenment* #129, August / September 2005) 38
It's Dangerous, I'm Loving It by Greg McElhatton
(from *Enlightenment* #128, June / July 2005) 40
We ♥ Chris by Robert Smith?
(from *Enlightenment* #131, December 2005) 43
D'you Wanna Come With Me? by Rob Matthews
(from *The Doctor Who Ratings Guide*, May 2006) 47
Boom Town Love by Robert Smith?
(from *Enlightenment* #133, April / May 2006) 60

Interlude: Journey's End - 1
by Scott Clarke
(from *Enlightenment* #154, October 2009) 65

3. Children of Earth

Was Davros Right? by Steve Lyons
(exclusive to this volume) 69
The Revolution Has Been Televised by Robert Smith?

(from *Enlightenment* #139, May 2007) ... 77
The Salt and the Sweet by Kate Orman
(exclusive to this volume) ... 81
Who Would Valiant Be by Wood Ingham
(from *Movement* #126, Summer 2007) ... 88
Neo Who Con by Ari Lipsey
(exclusive to this volume) ... 90
Queer as Who 2 by Scott Clarke
(from *Enlightenment* #135, October 2006) ... 95

4. Love in An Age of Squee

He Said, She Said by Deborah Stanish and Graeme Burk
(from *Enlightenment* #144, March 2008) ... 101
The Fan Wife's Survival Guide by Cheryl Twist
(from *Enlightenment* #143, December 2007) ... 109
The Shipping News by Deborah Stanish
(from *Enlightenment* #135, October 2006) ... 111
Personal Ads
(from *Enlightenment* #135, October 2006) ... 114
Choosing the Ship That's Right For You by Tammy Garrison
(exclusive to this volume) ... 115
Everybody's in the Play by Graeme Burk
(from *Enlightenment* #137, December 2006) ... 119
The Power of Cool by Jack Graham
(from *Shockeye's Kitchen* #17, Spring 2006) ... 122
A Fan's Life in Cardiff by Melissa Beattie
(exclusive to this volume) ... 126
The Downloading FAQ by Arnold T Blumberg
(exclusive to this volume) ... 132

5. Hooray!

Wasn't It Glorious? by Scott Clarke
(from *Enlightenment* #146, July 2008) ... 140
Reaching Total Dominance by Simon Kinnear
(from *Shockeye's Kitchen*, online edition, June 2005) ... 144
You Must Have Been Like God by Lloyd Rose
(exclusive to this volume) ... 146
Morality Play by Jonathan Blum
(exclusive to this volume) ... 149

6. Allons-y

Counting to Ten by Graeme Burk
(exclusive to this volume)........ 163
The Importance of Being Brilliant by Julie Chaston
(from *Enlightenment* #156, March 2010) 167
Savage Who by Scott Clarke
(from *Enlightenment* #134, July 2006) 170
Evolution of the Christmas Special by Robert Smith?
(from *Enlightenment* #144, March 2008) 173
How Do You Kill a Wasp? by Nina Kolunovsky
(from *Enlightenment* #147, October 2008)........ 177
Re-Mastered by Lloyd Rose
(from *Enlightenment* #141, October 2007)........ 180
Where to Next? by Richard Salter
(from *Enlightenment* #144, March 2008) 182
A Review of Planet of the Dead by Jim Mortimore
(exclusive to this volume)........ 186
Special Blend by Graeme Burk
(from *Enlightenment* #158, July 2010) 187

Interlude: Journey's End - 2
by Scott Clarke
(from *Enlightenment* #155, December 2009)........ 191

7. The 21st Century is When It All Happens...

Barrowmania by Richard Salter
(from *Enlightenment* #130, October / November 2005) 196
The Ten Commandments of Doctor Who Spinoffs
by Graeme Burk (from *Enlightenment* #143, December 2007)........ 200
Death, Corpses and Un-death in Torchwood
by Helen Kang (exclusive to this volume) 204
Camp Noir by Lynne M Thomas
(exclusive to this volume)........ 209
What Does It Take to Get Fired From Torchwood?
by Graeme Burk (from *Enlightenment* #125, Spring 2007;
revised December 2010) 215
Captain Jackass by Cameron Dixon
(from *Enlightenment* #149, December 2008 / January 2009) 217
What's the Point of a Spinoff? by Robert Smith?
(from *Enlightenment* #153, October 2009)........ 219
The Attic Inside Out by Jon Arnold
(exclusive to this volume)........ 223

8. Wibbly-Wobbly...

A Letter from Zog to Doctor Who Magazine by Paul Magrs
(from *Doctor Who Magazine* #375, November 2006) 230
A Tale of Two Writers by Scott Clarke
(from *Enlightenment* #152, August 2009; revised July 2010) 231
Whoniversal Translation by Melissa Beattie
(exclusive to this volume). 235
Like a Hovercraft by Graeme Burke
(from *Enlightenment* #141, October 2007). 242
Little Boys, Young Farmers and Gays by Dewi Evans
(from *The Tides of Time* #31, November 2005) 244
Just For Kids by Scott Clarke
(from *Enlightenment* #127, April / May 2005). 247
Death of the Planet by Robert Smith?
(from *Enlightenment* #151, June 2009). 250

Interlude: Journey's End - 3
by Scott Clarke
(from *Enlightenment* #156, March 2010) 255

9. Bowties Are Cool

First Eleven by Keith Topping
(exclusive to this volume). 261
What Kind of Doctor Who Producer Are You?
by Robert Smith?
(from *Enlightenment* #126, February / March 2005;
revised August 2010). 265
Dear Matt Smith by Graeme Burk
(from *Enlightenment* #149, December 2008 / January 2009) 271
A Madman With a Box by Mike Morris
(exclusive to this volume). 274
Squee-mendous by Robert Smith?
(from *Enlightenment* #158, July 2010; revised August 2010) 279
Visionary by Anthony Wilson
(exclusive to this volume). 282
It's Not You, It's Me by Deborah Stanish
(from *Enlightenment* #158, July 2010; revised August 2010) 286
Five by Five by Sean Twist
(exclusive to this volume). 288
Back to the Classic by Shaun Lyon
(exclusive to this volume). 293

INTRODUCTION

by Robert Shearman

I blame *Arc of Infinity*. After all, if you're looking for a scapegoat, that's as easy as anything else.

There was a time when my love for *Doctor Who* was so charmingly simple. The time I didn't know anything about it. And it lasted roughly three months; it stretched all the way through Peter Davison's first season of adventures in 1982. I'd never seen the show properly before. I'd been too scared of it, frankly. Even the theme music had sent me scurrying from the room; in fact, thinking hard, I think it was the blue, time-tunnel title sequence; in fact, thinking harder, I'm pretty sure that it was Tom Baker's face. Tom Baker had a face designed for nightmares. The way it came out of the tunnel straight at you, he looked so stern and unsmiling. (They missed a trick there, didn't they? They could have had him grin at us so winningly. They could have had him *wink*.)

I caught the odd moment of Tom Baker. My sister liked *Doctor Who*, after all, and she seemed to survive with her nerves intact each Saturday. I had to be made of tougher stuff than her, as I was (a) older and (b) male. So, once in a while, I'd grit my teeth, I'd get out a cushion to hide behind and I'd sit down beside her. I never lasted for long. I remember the moment in *The Sun Makers* when the Collector turns into a blob; that was so horrid an image, I didn't dare return to the TV set at all for weeks. My sister pointed out that that bit wasn't even supposed to be frightening; that was the bit where the Doctor won. Yeah. With that nightmare face of his.

I didn't go back to *Doctor Who* until scary Tom had left. I was by now 11. That seems shockingly old actually; most of my classmates at school were growing out of the show at about the time I got sucked in. Sid Sutton's title sequence of stars and neon tubing wasn't scary; nor was Peter Davison's shimmering face. I loved *Castrovalva;* I think partly, looking back, because there were no sequences in it where anyone turned into a blob and there weren't even any monsters, only genial old men dressed up as monsters for a little while. I decided I liked *Doctor Who. Doctor Who* was easy. I could take *Doctor Who* on.

By the time the monsters did appear, I was ready for them. I'd read the

Target books, even the one with the disgusting mutant eye on the cover. When I watched the Cybermen gun down troopers on a big spaceship a couple of months later – in the sort of story I'd always imagined *Doctor Who* would show and precisely the sort of story that had made me avoid the programme in the first place – I was thoroughly bloodthirsty. I bought Jean-Marc Lofficier's *Programme Guide* and loved to read all about the epic adventures I had yet to see. *The Space Museum*! *Underworld*! How good did they sound!

I even liked *Time-Flight*. Oh, *Time-Flight*. Last story of my innocence.

By the time the next round of adventures started, a whole Christmas away, I had memorised each and every one of the titles in *The Programme Guide* (complete with production codes and guest-star credits). I had joined the Doctor Who Appreciation Society. I had been to my first convention. And I had started a fanzine.

*

Actually, I didn't start the fanzine. *Cloister Bell* was the brainchild of Owen Bywater. Owen was three years older than I was, and the laws of the playground would have normally dictated that we could therefore never have been friends. But he loved *Doctor Who*, he was making his own magazine all about it and I so wanted to be a part of that, I just had to be.

Owen was dubious. I was a 12-year-old kid with a stammer, acne and a wide array of antisocial tics. He told me I could write a review of the season opener if I liked, to see if I was any good. So when *Arc of Infinity* was transmitted, I watched with the newly beaded eyes of a critic.

I decided I didn't like *Arc of Infinity*. I now knew that Omega's design was wrong, he wasn't supposed to look like that at all. And that they'd hired altogether the wrong actor to play him; they'd cast someone from *The Time Monster* and not *The Three Doctors*. And that the explanation for *Earthshock*'s continuity error that allowed weapons to be fired in the TARDIS was somewhat glib. And I couldn't work out the two occasions previously in Time Lord history that the recall device had been used. (I still can't, actually.)

I soon learned it was very easy to write bad reviews. Owen asked if I'd like to take a pop at *The King's Demons* as well. Boy, would I! I hated *The King's Demons*. I'd had an argument with my Mum right before transmission, which had put me in a bad mood.

Cloister Bell was awful. It's hard to exaggerate just how awful it really was. We filled each issue with reviews that largely sneered at the episodes we so breathlessly watched and listened back to on our audio tape recordings often enough that we knew the dialogue by heart. And when we ran out of stories that we'd already seen, we wrote reviews of the stories we hadn't. There was a regular section at the back we called *The Doctor Who Encyclopaedia,* in which we set ourselves the task of critiquing each and every adventure ever broadcast... in order! One issue I was given *The Smugglers,* another *Fury from the Deep*. Neither had been broadcast in my lifetime, of course, and both had been long erased from the BBC archives. But I knew all about them from the paragraph synopses in *The Programme Guide*, so I decided they were a bit rubbish and said so.

What I need to stress, though, is that *Cloister Bell* was by no means the worst fanzine out there. Hey, it wasn't even the worst fanzine in my school. (That would be *Time Key,* edited by one half of the *Little Britain* duo and by a boy who now specialises in directing social-history documentaries for the BBC. Sorry, chaps, but I have your first issue preserved in my attic and, let me tell you, it's rank.) The pages of my DWAS newsletters were choked with ads for fanzines; at conventions, the dealers' room was overflowing with them. And mostly they all did the same thing we'd done. Reviews of recent stories. Reviews of stories from long ago. No comedy. No insight. Precious little fanfic – that would have seemed dangerously imaginative – and what there was usually served only to provide continuity explanations the TV shows had had the gall to leave out.

Ours wasn't the worst. Ours was typeset.

I remember my Dad reading through one of the issues and asking me why I was wasting my time on a hobby like *Doctor Who.* On something that was just fed to me from the television, something I never had to work for, something that was so passive. I wished I could have said that doing the zine was honing my critical skills in preparation for literature studies later at university. Or that it was broadening my imagination, that wallowing in this rush of different stories of different styles and different settings was going to make me a writer one day; yes, one day, I would do it for a living! But I wouldn't have been able to have said any of that, even had I had the wit to do so. Because Dad was right. There was no value to what we wrote. There was no analysis. Nor, crucially, was there any self-analysis; here we were, deliriously in love with a television programme and we expressed that best by routinely carping at it. We spent most of our energies coming up with ingenious word-search puzzles that would include the names of all the black and white Dalek adventures, or the surnames of all the actors credited in *The Seeds of Doom.*

The best part was the celebrity interviews. The first one we conducted was with Lis Sladen at a pizzeria in Covent Garden. I sat there shyly whilst Owen did most of the talking – and, once in a while, I'd break into the conversation to ask something inappropriate. I remember I hadn't been able to find the Target novelisation of *The Android Invasion* in any bookshop, so didn't know what had happened in it; could Lis then please tell me what the story was about? She seemed bemused by that. She felt sorry for us, I think, and paid for our pizzas. That night, I wrote a love letter to Lis Sladen, asking her to leave her husband Brian Miller and run off with me. It later dawned on me that we'd given Lis a free copy of our most recent issue featuring a review of *Snakedance*, in which we told the fan world just how terrible Brian Miller's performance had been in that story. I like to think that was the reason Lis never wrote back.

I don't think we ever published a single challenging article, anything that didn't reinforce all the popular beliefs and opinions of the time. We loved *The Daemons*; we hated *The Gunfighters*. We mocked the entire work of Graham Williams, though I hadn't at that point seen a single story he'd produced; there was no need to, I reasoned: they were Graham Williams stories! Our final issue was No. 12, boasting Alexei Sayle on the cover; we told our faithful readers we'd be back after the 18-month hiatus imposed by Michael Grade. We promised them. We promised ourselves. We wouldn't let our enthusiasm wane. We lied.

*

Lars Pearson had heard I'd once co-edited a fanzine, and asked if I had anything that was worth republishing in *Time, Unincorporated*. I nearly bust a gut laughing.

And, of course, I see now that there were good fanzines produced in the eighties; ones that were questing, and inspired, and bright. It was just hard to find them. The signal to noise ratio was that great.

Something wonderful happened to *Doctor Who* in 1989. It was cancelled. Suddenly, the fanzine world changed. Fanzines were allowed to become something different. No longer could they merely show breathless excitement for the future (and all-too-breathy disappointment in the present). Instead, they were forced to look at new ways of writing about the old, to begin a process where the programme could be seen as a complete whole and reassessed accordingly. Where – let's be honest – it could be mocked, but mocked affectionately. Mocked as something that was nostalgic and for what that nostalgia said about us. Once we'd done that, we realised that *Doctor Who* was best written about when it really was about us; that all this analysis of Sontarans and Zarbi and the different interpretations of the Valeyard was actually an analysis of why we'd ever cared. We began to look ever inwards. Inwards, into why we were fans in the first place, into why we'd let that define us, why years later we were still worshipping at the altar of a cancelled children's series. Because it was worship, it was, no matter how ironic was all the kowtowing. We'd learned to celebrate the eccentricity of who we were. That's what fanzines became: little pieces of joy, revelling in the fact we had a common bond in something weird and silly.

Weird, silly and safely dead.

And then.

The series was revived. Remarkably. I never thought it would be. (I never thought I'd be one of those writers kicking at the dead horse either, but that's another story.) The fanzine world didn't sink back into the unthinking mush of *Cloister Bell* and its ilk. The way in which fans discussed the series had matured; just as the series itself – now written by, produced by and starring those fans – was in some ways a more knowing development of the show we'd enjoyed in the past, so were the fanzines.

It's not a point I want to labour, but the spirit of the new fanzine lives on through those early days on the "new" *Doctor Who. The Unquiet Dead* was written by the comedian who'd sent up the history of the show as a single pitch on *Doctor Who Night; The Empty Child* by the chap whose Comic Relief parody was written with such honest love that it didn't deride the programme as all other parodies had done, but called for its resurrection. When I was invited by Russell T Davies to contribute to the fun, I emailed him a thank you. In his response, he told me that I mustn't blame him if we both got stuck in a Welsh field in the middle of the night filming the exploits of the Taran Wood Beast. The whole grammar of what *Doctor Who* was and could be had been irrevocably altered by the fact it had been off the air for 15 years; if we were to keep our affection for it alive, we had to learn to laugh at it and not feel personally threatened by its shortcomings. We had to embrace those shortcomings, because they were just as much *Doctor Who* as anything else.

Of course, there aren't so many fanzines out there. That's the internet for you. Some will say that's a bad thing, but I'm really not so sure it is. The internet allows us all to air our kneejerk reactions to anything from *The End of Time* to the redesign of the Daleks; we can go into public forums, or start a blog and we'll have the same instant rush of unthinking self-expression that were the trademark of my reviews in *Cloister Bell.* But that means that if something is to reach print, then it has to be more considered than ever before. The quality of the articles published in this book, I think, represents a high water mark of fanzine content for that very reason. There's wit here, and reflection, and the idea that *Doctor*

Who isn't the sole reason for writing but a happy launchpad for it. Nothing passive, as my father would have thought. Instead, something creative and artistic in its own right.

*

When I wrote *Doctor Who* for the telly, all nice and proper, I named a character after my co-editor, Owen Bywater. I had a Dalek exterminate him. It was a tribute to an old, dear friend. And something else entirely.

*

I've nothing against my 12-year-old self. He was a nice kid. He never meant anyone any harm. Except, quite possibly, Brian Miller.

But I'm often asked what my young fan self would have made of the fact that, decades later, he'd have written for his favourite show. And I say the usual guff, that he'd have been flabbergasted, over the moon, that it'd be like he'd won a golden ticket to Willy Wonka's chocolate factory. In truth, though, I think he would have been horrified. He'd have hated the fact the new Doctor Who wore a leather jacket. He'd have hated the fact there was no on-screen regeneration. He'd have hated the colloquial feel of it and the way the show was more in touch with its emotions than he ever was.

And he'd have hated my episode. Oh God, yes. The way I sentimentalised that Dalek. The fact that I referred to Davros, but wouldn't mention him by name. That I gave the sink plunger an entirely new function; if a Dalek could do that, why hadn't it done it in *Day of the Daleks*, why hadn't it done it in *The Chase*, what the hell did I think I was playing at?

He'd have hated the fact we'd have been allowed to add to the ongoing story of *Doctor Who*, because *Doctor Who* was something to be observed and criticised, not to be engaged with directly. He'd have hated it because, deep down, he'd have thought none of us deserved it.

Good. I'm glad you hate the idea, Rob. Because, yeah, you're a nice kid. But you come from a time before fandom grew up, and took the fanzines with it. I've long learned that there is nothing more staid and reactionary and piss-poor lazy than the stuff you wrote for *Cloister Bell* – and I don't blame you for loving *Doctor Who* with such obsession, but that you did it in such a gutless way. To make *Doctor Who* work, I think, you look back at all that my 12-year-old self wanted. Let him point it out to you in every detail. Nod politely. And then do the exact reverse.

In all things. Except, of course, in the matter of giving *Arc of Infinity* a good kicking. Because, let's face it, *Arc of Infinity* is pants.

FOREWORD

In the previous volume of *Time, Unincorporated,* we talked about how probably the biggest controversy in coming up with this series of anthologies was the subtitle "The Doctor Who Fanzine Archive", as a great deal of Volume Two featured essays that either didn't appear in fanzines or were specially commissioned for the volume.

Simply put, there are hardly any *Doctor Who* fanzines out there any more. That's not to say the medium is completely dead. Over the past year or so, there has been something of a minor resurgence of the print fanzine, which we're pleased to see. In many respects, this new vanguard of zines harkens back to their original purpose: publishing as a means of building a community of fans. As such, these new fanzines tend toward the short and pithy, featuring capsule reviews, fiction, graphics and humour. This doesn't really fit with our remit for longer-form criticism but, nonetheless, we would recommend you look up *Panic Moon, Blue Box, Fish Fingers and Custard* and others.

As to why there are fewer fanzines fulfilling the promise demonstrated in our second volume of *Time, Unincorporated,* there is a simple reason for this: the internet happened. The sort of ongoing debate that a fanzine engendered across multiple issues over several months in the 1980s or 1990s now happens in accelerated fashion over a matter of days, if not hours, on online forums such as Gallifrey Base. Thoughtful opinion is found less and less in actual zines and more and more in blogs, LiveJournal postings, podcasts and comment threads on websites.

We obviously feel there is still a place for print criticism and analysis of *Doctor Who* in this post-2005 world, or we wouldn't have spent the time editing this collection. There is something about the print form that encourages careful writing and discerning reading, and we're proud to be keeping that tradition alive in a small way.

There are a number of venerable fanzines we did reprint essays from; we would have used an even broader sampling but several zines now have publishing deals of their own. We also increased the number of original commissions in this volume. Almost half of the volume is exclusive to this edition, and written by a combination of the leading lights of the *Doctor Who* literary world, some of the most thoughtful writers in *Doctor Who* fandom and a number of talented newcomers to the world of

Doctor Who writing. We're so grateful to everyone who took part in this bold venture.

This is the final volume of *Time, Unincorporated,* though we are confident that that the celebration of articulate fan thought will continue in other publications in the future. We are, frankly, happy to be closing out this series with Mad Norwegian Press on a high. We feel the writing in this volume is a testament to the diversity of thought in *Doctor Who* fandom since the new series debuted in 2005. The influx of new voices and new perspectives have only enhanced the capacity of one of the most thoughtful, most articulate, most compelling collection of enthusiasts ever assembled.

Doctor Who, probably more than any other television series, has long been an "open source" fandom in that it encourages fans to go beyond what's happening on screen and to appreciate the inner workings and dramatic techniques used to create it. It's this open-source quality that brought fans to write for television. In 1999, Lance Parkin was interviewed by *Doctor Who Magazine* and asked if *Doctor Who* could come back. Lance answered, "I firmly believe that, in a few years' time, a group of BBC execs will say, 'Someone wants to bring back *Doctor Who,* isn't that a stupid idea?' And the others will turn around and say, 'No, actually we all started out writing The New Adventures'."

That day happened, almost precisely as predicted, with Russell T Davies. May this open-source fandom – in all its complexity, barminess and wonderful, passionate love – inspire the next generation to create, perform and write *Doctor Who* in the decades to come.

IT'S BACK!

Life is often full of instances of do-you-remember-where-you-were-when? Famous deaths. Huge global events. Big, earthshaking, news.

For the long-time *Doctor Who* fan, one such moment was 25th September, 2003, when, out of the blue, BBC Controller Lorraine Heggessey announced that *Doctor Who* would return to British television in 2005 in a series written and produced by Russell T Davies.

No one saw it coming. The series had been dead for almost 14 years by that point. The 40th anniversary of the series saw its fandom – or what was left of it – factionalised by their loyalty to their particular brand of tie-in product. There were entire cottage industries based around a time-travelling voodoo cult that had appeared in the background of a few BBC novels. Two guest characters who once appeared in a novella span off into their own universe, populated by a series of seventies monsters whose copyright had expired. Audio adventures starring actors who hadn't worked in years were all the rage. The *Bernice Summerfield* line became a spinoff of a spinoff of a spinoff. The biggest new thing was a webcast cartoon featuring Richard E Grant as the Doctor.

But then the news came. There was cheering, crying and parading in basements everywhere. We tried to anticipate who the new Doctor would be: Bill Nighy or Alan Davies?

Then came the other do-you-remember-where-you-were-when moments: 18 March 2004: Christopher Eccleston is cast; 19 July: the debut of Eccleston in costume (a leather jacket!?) and the first public bit of location filming (the new TARDIS! Autons!); 6 March 2005: a viewing copy of *Rose* is leaked online; 26 March 2005: the new series debuts on BBC1.

These milestones trace the route of long-time fans' anticipation leading up to the debut of the new series. And when it came, the series had to live up to both that and the glorious 26-year past it had on television prior. Would it live up to the anticipation and those halcyon days? Did it deserve to be resurrected? How did this new series connect to the old one; not just in terms of continuity but in terms of what can only be defined, nebulously, as the spirit of the programme.

What follows are some of the answers some fans found to those questions. Though, really, what any of us really cared about was that finally, wonderfully, it was back. And it was about time.

The Death of Doctor Who: Verdict Overturned

by Dave Owen

By the turn of the century, secure in the knowledge that *Doctor Who* was never, ever, going to be produced on television again, it was easy to complete the television series' post-mortem. The report went something like this...

Having begun as a blank canvas, *Doctor Who,* like the Doctor himself, was an enigma, defined more by what it was not than what it was. New viewers were chaperoned into the world of the Doctor by figures such as schoolteachers, secretaries, pipers and soldiers who were just as bewildered as they. However, the series gradually acquired a tangible myth, along with its own history and geography; this was exemplified by the Time Lords, and the emerging rules about what the Doctor could and could not do. However, the Doctor continued to encounter individuals who would need to have explained to them what the viewer had already been told, and such explanations served as reminders to any hypothetical latecomers. The usability model, if you like, for the series was more akin to continuous drama, like soaps, rather than today's finite serials, prefacing their installments with "Previously on..." revision crammers. The only reminder you'd get would be a reprise of the previous episode's crescendo, of more use to a loyal viewer who missed a week than to a potential new follower. It was the responsibility of the programme makers to respect incoming viewers by starting with a fresh situation every few weeks, and pepper it with a few introductions – "I'm the Doctor, and this is my friend Sarah Jane; we're travellers" – but not so many as to be offputting.

There'd be a few rewards for the faithful, of course. Old friends and foes would come back, but this would diverge from the soap-opera model, where the surprise return of an old face, and its on-screen impact would not form the crux of the drama. At the end of *The Sontaran Experiment* episode one, a section of the audience might be thrilled to share Sarah Jane's belief that Linx has returned, but a considerably larger remainder would simply be excited by the simple appearance of a monster. These overlapping viewing modes did not, crucially, interfere with one another.

It didn't start to get messy until the 1980s. This was when organised *Doctor Who* fans, feeling that the series of the late 70s had ignored their priorities, were able to sit up and praise a programme which now appeared to be made with them in mind. Linked umbrella arcs of adventures, the return of the Master and of the Doctor's changing face were all a delight to patient, longstanding viewers. None of these might alienate the less devout, but a significant indication of the series' priorities comes with the fifth Doctor's first adventure, screened an unprecedented nine months after his predecessor's swansong. Rather than being a relaunch, fresh start or jumping-on point, it continues that previous adventure without missing a beat, commencing with two episodes which are blatantly the middle of a continuing story rather than the beginning of a new one. To fans, who might have been patiently waiting to find out what happened next, this may have given the impression of a programme being made just for them. For anyone else, it must have seemed very odd indeed; or, as people were just beginning to say in 1982, not very user-friendly.

More noticeably, *Doctor Who* became hooked on its own history, never resisting a resurrection or spurning a second coming. While doubtless stimulating whatever gland of long-term fans which responds to seeing childhood happiness sustained into and beyond adolescence, this would inevitably alienate less-attentive or long-term viewers. Imagine a friend who keeps going on about people he used to have a whale of a time with before you came along, and vocally celebrates every time they return to his circle. How fantastic the gang used to be in the old days! You might put up with it if your friend was worth it, but otherwise you'd likely move on and leave him to his incessant, exclusive nostalgia.

Doctor Who, our hypothetical post-mortem might conclude, cut off its own life support by becoming a closed shop, adopting its own mythic language and rituals, and serving a tiny subset of its potential audience. It was not merely cavalier but, at times, downright hostile to potential new viewers. Case closed. Oh, and reopened briefly in 1996, following a temporary disinterment, which confirmed earlier findings, and added "Fans are the last people on Earth for whom television legends should be made, let alone made by, because they'll get all the minutiae right but neglect to include what made them legends in the first place."

By the year 2000, it was very easy to maintain the stance that someone could make *Doctor Who* to please fans, but they'd only be shifting a few thousand units of books or CDs at most; alternatively, they could make it for a wider viewing public, but would have to cut the fans off and present the public a series which was very much what they thought they remembered *Doctor Who* as being like. If – and it was a very big *if* – it ever came back, then the Doctor would be a Victorian adventurer, he'd have an assistant (in the same way as a magician) and the Daleks would be nasty robots. Whichever path you chose, you couldn't choose both.

Another way to look at it was that, by the early twenty-first century, *Doctor Who* had evolved into two separate species, like Wells' Morlocks and Eloi. The best-known was a fondly remembered childhood adventure, a homogeneous commodity often referenced in comedy produced by the children who had grown up with it. This was the *Doctor Who* celebrated in BBC2's *Doctor Who Night* in 1999, safe to watch with peers amid occasional coos of "Oh, I remember that." But beneath the ground was a still-developing culture where *Doctor Who* remained in the present tense, becoming ever more ornate, clever and exclusive. The traveller would venture down here at his peril – for the prescribed route was three decades long – and find *Doctor Who* for grown-ups, being told away from the TV screen and taking for granted the foreknowledge that three-decade path ought to have inscribed. The two were genetically incompatible, it seemed.

Wrong. Wrong. Wrong.

A decade later, miraculous miscegenation has given birth to a series which diverts millions without spurning fundamentalists. Post-mortem overruled. *Doctor Who* is British television's biggest success, despite still serving the vocal minority who kept the flame. It doesn't merely avoid offending such zealots by blaspheming against their orthodoxy, but actively embraces it, invoking the mythos at every turn.

That should not be a surprise. As Gary Gillatt discusses in *The Sheer Brilliance of Doctor Who* (*DWM* #400), the climate now favours series requiring more attention from their viewers. Domestic technology such as the PVR and DVD season boxed-set make it easier to embark on a relationship with a series. It's hard to imagine *Lost*, *Six Feet Under* or *Life on Mars* sustaining the viewer commitment needed to keep going in the nineteen-eighties.

There's some evidence, too, that the new production team have deliberately followed the path of the original series, by beginning with an enigma and gradually fleshing it out with a tangible framework. It's significant, probably, that the Doctor doesn't name the Autons in *Rose*, but is swift to identify the Macra two years later, in *Gridlock*. But don't confuse the trick with simply acknowledging events of the twentieth century series. It's to do with the ongoing mythos, the continuing tapestry for committed fans of the twenty-first. How are the presence of interwoven strands such as the Face of Boe, the Time War or Pete's World any less alienating than, say, Peri alluding to Dalek time corridors or recognising a picture of Jo Grant?

Simply put, the new series handles its own on-screen PR far better than the old did. It actively markets its continuing identity with proven tactics, such as aligning on- and off-screen events. Billie Piper's departure was big news in the press, which chimed with the Doctor's continuing remorse at Rose's absence. If it's helpful to know what's happened before, rather than being awkwardly told it, we're shown it, either within the characters' experience (all the Bad Wolf flashbacks) or by establishing montage at the start of the episode (almost every episode two). There's a subtle but distinct line between alluding to a wider scope of events than those in the immediate 42 minutes, so that it appears enticing, and smothering one's storytelling in masonic winks and nods.

So what can popular-cultural pathologists take from this? Mythos, if used in moderation and taken at narrative mealtimes, may not innately shorten your series' life. It's safe to feed the fans, and indeed their diet may become more widely popular. And, specifically, that pandering to perceived fan taste wasn't what did for the series in the eighties. Those fans can now stand acquitted, at least knowing that they aren't guilty – by association at least – of the old series' downfall after all.

The Ebb and the Flow

by Robert Smith?

From Enlightenment #129, August / September 2005

Here's a game you can play at home: watch *Survival*, the TV Movie and *Rose* back to back. Three Doctors, three companions, even three different TARDIS props. Snapshots from the eighties, nineties and 2000s. Made in England, Canada and Wales. You can't imagine three consecutive *Doctor Who* stories this different. At least, not if you weren't there for the *Cat's Cradle* arc in the New Adventures novels of the 1990s.

And yet, spaced out over 15 years, the through-line from Season Twenty-Six to *The Parting of the Ways* isn't that hard to follow. The leap from the TV Movie to *Rose* is particularly short. Both feature note-perfect reconstructions of scenes from *Spearhead from Space*. Both feature a Doctor who establishes himself entirely within his first hour of screen time – which turns out to be fortunate, as both Doctors would end up with minimal overall television exposure. The TV Movie and the new series feature major companions in Grace, Rose and Captain Jack, but both also feature supporting companions, such as Chang Lee, Jackie, Mickey and Adam. The supporting companion is an idea the original series barely dabbled in and only then because the Doctor was actually trapped on Earth for most of the early seventies. Ace's "old friends" in *Survival* are brand new, never even mentioned before... although you get the feeling that Season Twenty-Six was edging towards this idea and would have loved to have run with it.

It's funny to remember that early edition of *Doctor Who Confidential* where Russell T Davies talks about the TV Movie, saying that a) he had no problem with the kiss, none whatsoever and b) regenerating the Doctor at the beginning was a mistake. Davies posits that having Paul McGann appear in the opening of Rose and then becoming Eccleston wouldn't work, as the casual viewer would have no reason to care about the loss of the original leading man. Instead, Russell says, the ideal time for a regeneration is at the end of the first season when you've come to know this new Doctor and then his regeneration means something. Those comments have a lot more resonance now than they did back in April.

Mind you, the Doctor kissing Rose in *The Parting of the Ways* is a lot more meaningful than the Doctor kissing Grace. Not only does it have a season of buildup (the subtext to their relationship is almost text as early as *The Unquiet Dead*, and anyone who missed the dancing subtext in *The Doctor Dances* is watching the wrong show), but it also understands its audience. By giving us a passionate kiss that's nevertheless explicitly there as a way for the Doctor to save Rose (those beams of TARDIS energy flow out of her eyes as well as her mouth), it allows fans who simply hate that sort of thing to be at least partially satisfied. Bonus points for the Doctor and Jack's earlier kiss too. Anyone who gets upset at that doesn't deserve to be watching *Doctor Who* and should head off for the very safe, very heterosexual and very cancelled *Star Trek*.

Then there's the TARDIS materialisation effect, which is almost beat-for-beat the same as the TV Movie's. It helps that the windiness makes a lot of sense when you think about it, and also that every TARDIS materialisation is subtly different. The console room, on the other hand, would be a lot more effective if the TV Movie hadn't got there first, and better. The rationale for the new console room – that the Doctor has spent so long wandering the universe that he's been lashing it together with spare parts and bicycle pumps – is a great one and something every one of us can intellectually appreciate... but it just doesn't have the same emotional impact as previous console rooms. Although given that this one probably cost about 1% of what the TV Movie's cost, maybe that's fair enough.

Of course, what the series discards is just as important as what it retains. The ninth Doctor's costume, a black jumper and black leather-jacket, might yet be the single most brilliant thing about the 2005 revival. The tenth Doctor's costume doesn't have nearly the same spark of outrageous, mind-bending simplicity to it. And it suits Eccleston down to the ground: a protective shell for a creature who's hard on the outside, but immensely vulnerable on the inside. Remind you of any exterminating monsters you might be familiar with?

Like the costume, the new series rewrote the rules on what was and wasn't essential to *Doctor Who*. From the accent to the sexuality, Eccleston proved that what was fundamental about the Doctor didn't have to look, talk or act like an Oxford professor. For a man fleeing the scholarly society of the Time Lords, this actually makes even more sense than the original, once we finally wrap our collective brains around the concept. Previous Doctors' costumes, manner of speaking and lack of sexuality were all leftover elements dictated by the confines of 1960s television, only they got stuck in that shape for decades. The new series realises this, even if the rest of us never did.

One thing that *Survival*, the TV Movie and Rose all share is the concept of the Doctor-as-inspiration. The bulk of the original series had focussed on the Doctor-as-hero, so much so that when he isn't it feels odd, despite that fact that he was originally designed as an anti-hero anyway. Season Twenty-Six saw a more distant Doctor than before, one who often sat back and let his companion figure out what he'd known all along. The climax of the TV Movie sees the Doctor in chains, while it's up to Grace to stop the Master. A running theme of the new series is the Doctor's effect on those he encounters, inspiring them to greater things. *The Long Game* is a case in point, contrasting the rise to heroism of Cathica with the descent of Adam. It even has the Doctor (and Rose) in chains for good measure.

Which leads into the next point, the companions. Originally created to be the viewer-identification characters, they were quickly supplanted by the Doctor himself and relegated to plot ciphers, with a few notable exceptions. The late eighties overturned this with Ace, finally giving us a companion whose story seemed at least as important as that of the Doctor. This caused something of an uproar at the time, which is rather amusing to think about now. Ace's story arc saw her move from troubled delinquent to independent young woman, inspired by the Doctor's mentoring. The TV Movie charts Grace's progress in embracing life's options, thanks to the life-affirming example of the Doctor – so much so that's she's even able to stand free of the Doctor by the end.

The new series sees Rose grow from her mundane life to someone capable of saving the universe and even the Doctor from his own failings. What's remarkable about Rose, however, is how much she remains her own person. With the exceptions of Tegan and Grace, previous companions were content to throw themselves into the Doctor's world entirely, with barely a mention of family or friends while they travelled the universe. Which seems like the fantasy we'd all like to indulge in – who wouldn't want to embrace the Doctor's lifestyle if it came along? –

but the reality would be very different. One of the running themes of the new series is exploring what it would actually mean to live in the Doctor's world and Rose exemplifies this. She keeps a foot in each world, refusing to choose one totally above the other and having to live with the consequences of that.

Boom Town deals with this in considerable detail, wrapping itself around all manner of the season's consequences. There's the Doctor-as-killer, whereupon a simple dinner date conversation is turned into riveting viewing as you realise just how terrifying the Doctor actually is. Then there's Rose's treatment of Mickey and the way throwaway moments throughout the season have led to her current situation, clearly attracted to three men and unable to choose between them. Not to mention a considerable amount of foreshadowing in the episode, which is pretty impressive given that there were only two episodes to go. *Boom Town* is quite, quite brilliant, sure to be rediscovered (along with *The Long Game*) in ten years' time.

Graham Williams used to say that you could maintain consistency in *Doctor Who* by changing about 15% of what you had the year before. He was referring to a series in continual production, so the rule doesn't really apply to Season Twenty-Six, the TV Movie and the Eccleston series. But it's not all that far off either. At the very least, if you took Season Twenty-Six and changed 15% of it every year for seven years, conceivably you might get something like the TV Movie. But if you kept changing the series by 15% increments for a further nine years, it's highly unlikely you'd have anything even remotely like what we just watched. The current series is new, yes, which is as it should be, but it also understands that what went before might have something to offer an audience in 2005. Which, frankly, is probably more than any of us were hoping, let alone expecting.

All this is the new series doing what it does best: taking what works from the old series and discarding the rest. *Doctor Who* used to do that with the pop-classics of film and literature, now it's doing the same, only to its previous selves. Think about the mind-blowing implications of exactly what that means for a moment. *Doctor Who* hasn't so much returned, as it has continued where it left off. What a great time it is to be a fan...

Where Old and New Do Not Converge

by Adrian Loder
From The Doctor Who Ratings Guide, October 2005

In the old days, *Doctor Who* was definitely story-based. Characters were fleshed out over a series of episodes and, in the case of the leads, over the course of seasons. Evolution was slower and more gradual, but also more lifelike and subtle. With the primary focus on plot, characters are not defined through lengthy emotional interaction, but by the way they react to others, the events around them or the actions they take in response to others' actions. We are not told how a character is, but rather we are shown how the character is through the unfolding of the plot. In this way, characters are not shoved into pre-fabricated roles that they expound on at length in constant emotional heart-to-hearts; instead, they gradually reveal themselves, in a slow and subtle way.

Aside from being superior simply in terms of not hitting people over the head with things, story-based drama is also better when the actors and actresses are not exactly Oscar material. This is not a jab at the fine men and women who have worked on *Doctor Who,* but rather an acknowledgement that then, as now, sometimes people aren't up to snuff. When you put someone like this into a position where they have to do one of the most difficult things in all acting – to realistically and powerfully portray deep emotion and feeling without being trite, maudlin or hyperbolic – and that person doesn't have the capacity to perform, you get disaster. Or, more specifically, you get Rose's mother.

The new show is far more of a character-based affair than the show was in the past, and the problem is that very few in the cast have the chops to justify it. Chris Eccleston is able to pull it off, and John Barrowman isn't too bad, but no one else is that strong. This isn't to knock them; as mentioned earlier, being able to consistently pull this sort of thing off is very tough.

Furthermore, you can only work with what you're given, and the fact of the matter is that the writing in a character-based drama also has to be stronger on the emotional front and capable of real, sincere emotion and words that ring true. Crafting a tight plot is difficult, but in a different way. It's tempting to ask Russell Davies to try stories like that. Sure, the ratings might drop – although audiences were just as "common" in the sixties, seventies and eighties, and *Doctor Who* had several periods of multi-year ratings awesomeness – but the stories might improve.

Davies has been acclaimed for his writing on other melodramatic shows, but frankly I have to wonder if this stems from the same folks who now fail to see that most of the new series' supporting cast, insofar as emotional depth is concerned, are not up to the task. I felt that Paul Cornell and Steven Moffat actually did the best in welding a greater, but sincere, emotional element to what has been forged into what we know as *Doctor Who* over the previous 40 years. This is not to say that Davies is horrible; there are good moments, and it is my emphasis on the good that allows me to still see the *Doctor Who* in this and embrace it as a continuation of the past.

There is no doubt whatsoever in my mind, however, that the weaknesses that exist are largely due to this change from story-based to character-based drama. If you're going to do the latter you'd best have the absolute finest actors and writers money can buy lest you risk unintentionally make fun of yourself. That the spirit of *Doctor Who* lives on even within this is a testament to its staying power.

Perhaps I emphasise the good elements in *Who* a bit too strongly – if I were to rate *The Web Planet*, I'm thinking I might give it as a high as a 7 out of 10 – though, unlike someone's suggestion that people who like everything have no taste, I do not enjoy everything equally.

Perhaps, were I not so desperate for the dead old Doctors' adventures to continue, I would not view the new series as still retaining the breath of the original 26 seasons. I don't think that's the case, however; I think both sides of this argument are exaggerated, and that if this matter of character-based storytelling were remedied, we would see an appropriate uptick in the quality of the programme.

What Does It Mean To Be Doctorish?

By Andrew Cartmel

The announcement of a new actor to play the lead role in *Doctor Who* always occasions a rush of speculation. When I heard that the honour had been conferred on a certain Matt Smith, I fell naturally to wondering what kind of Doctor he'd be, and pondering yet again just what constitutes a Doctorish Doctor.

I think I first heard this term from John Nathan-Turner when he was producing *Doctor Who*, and I had just started work on the show as the script editor. Of course, he was referring to the special quality that makes the character of the Doctor distinctive, what makes him what he is.

Some Doctors had it aplenty. Some lacked it severely. The irony was that John, who had such a firm grasp of what constituted Doctorish behaviour, presided over some of the least Doctorish incarnations in the show's long history.

Whatever happens with Matt Smith, he is following on the red-Converse-All-Star-clad heels of one the more Doctorish Doctors of recent times, in the shape of David Tennant. In some ways, Tennant was the epitome of what a Doctor should be. As the tenth Doctor, he was simultaneously likeable and odd, strange and familiar, alien and inviting. He was scruffy and disrespectful of authority, while himself projecting great authority. Whether it was taking the situation in his stride when he found himself in a hospital transported to the moon (*Smith and Jones*) or calmly introducing himself to the outlandish occupants of a sequence of vehicles as he moves briskly through an eternal alien traffic jam (*Gridlock*), Tennant distinguished himself and embodied many of the best aspects of a Doctor. Matt Smith has a tough act to follow, and a very long and varied one if all the previous Doctors are taken into account. (Well, all the accepted ones. Sorry, Peter Cushing, you'll have to wait for another day.) Only time will tell, appropriately enough, how Doctorish the eleventh Doctor will prove to be.

But what does it mean to be Doctorish in the first place? Well, it's a sort of phase / space of behaviour, charted by the accumulative adventures of all the previous Doctors at their optimum and most choicely characteristic.

The first Doctor was at his best when he was spooky and mysteriously powerful, and seemed to be holding all the cards. He managed to suggest the sort of vistas of dangerous wonder and dark adventure that can send a shiver down your spine. As in *Planet of the Giants*, when the prospect of a conflagration prompts Susan to remark, "It will be just like that air raid, Grandfather. Do you remember?" And William Hartnell replies, "Yes, very well. What infernal machines those zeppelins were." Hartnell was definitely not Doctorish when he was being querulous or tiresomely crotchety as in *The Dalek Invasion of Earth*, where he threatens Susan with a spanking for being too adventurous. Yet the same story shows him being casually fascinated by the menacing wasteland London has become under Dalek rule and eagerly admiring the technology of a Dalek flying saucer.

This kind of attitude was picked up and turbo charged by Patrick Troughton. When the second Doctor watches the TARDIS being engulfed by lava on the planet Dulkis at the beginning of *The Mind Robber*, his reaction is, "What a wonderful sight!" He was also adroit at flinging himself forward, into the thick of the narrative even when surrounded by people pointing guns at him, as in *The Tomb of the Cybermen*. In this respect, he is very similar to Tennant as the tenth Doctor. Like Sherlock Holmes, the Doctor is always constructing what is going on in the story. Here, he hurries to a dead body lying outside the eponymous tomb and concludes, "He appears to have been electrocuted. Trying to open these doors, perhaps."

But the second Doctor was at his absolute best when he embodied that crucial aspect of the Doctor's character: his relationship with authority. This is key to being the Doctor, and it must never be a servile relationship. Quite the opposite. As in *The War Games*, when he is confronted by the brutality of military "justice". Troughton stands up against the court martial with impressive power and that essential Doctorish defiance. "This is all just a mockery," he thunders.

The corollary of all this defiance and insubordination is that the Doctor can effortlessly assume authority himself. As in the same story when he pretends to be an examiner from the war office ("You were expecting us, surely?"). Claiming that he has come to inspect the military prisons, he browbeats the commanding officer into submission ("You send no car to meet us on our arrival!"). This scene also displays the Doctor's resourceful pragmatism. By presenting himself as an inspector of prisons, he can set about finding his imprisoned companion Jamie. Importantly, such a scene also evokes the otherwordly power of the Doctor.

When Troughton gave way to Jon Pertwee, it seemed initially that a less otherworldy, more conventional (and therefore less Doctorish) characterisation beckoned. Exuberant, dashing and physically heroic, yes. Mysterious, powerful and strange, perhaps not. However, soon enough, the third Doctor was displaying his alienness in clever counterpoint to the staid military normality of UNIT.

Admittedly, some of these attempts to appear alien were somewhat perfunctory and silly, as in the use of "Venusian karate" in *Inferno* et al. But there are other, superb moments of Doctorish behaviour in the same story when Pertwee confronts the monstrous, menacing Primord. "There's nothing to be frightened of, old chap," he says! This kind of cool, amusing reversal of expectation is the Doctor *par excellence*. The crucial disrespect for authority comes through from Pertwee loud and clear in his insolent attitude to Professor Stahlman, who is in charge of things and whose ooze created the Primord. We see this even more emphatically with Pertwee in *Carnival of Monsters* when the Doctor escapes the miniscope and confronts the Minorians. He stands up to these officious bullies so fearlessly that they end up dangerously close to admiration of his audacity, calling to mind again that intimidated commanding officer in *The War Games*.

As someone has written (and it might have been me), "The Doctor's unflinching, bold assertiveness in the face of authority has now become one of the beloved riffs of the show."

As the fourth Doctor, Tom Baker echoed the best aspects of Pertwee. In *The Talons of Weng-Chiang*, when he is confronted by a ghostly apparition in a theatre (which causes the fellow accompanying him to faint), the Doctor greets it with delight. Exactly the attitude of someone who could address a Primord on such familiar terms. *Weng-Chiang* also features the magnificent moment when the Doctor confronts the villainous Magnus Greel. Establishing his own credentials as a time traveller, the Doctor says, "I was with the Filipino army at the final advance on Reykjavik." It's a brilliant, resonant line from writer Robert Holmes, a tip-of-the-ice-berg line suggesting a whole surging, turbulent world of the future.

But Tom Baker went further, a lot further, than his predecessors in the direction of creating a strange, amusing and eccentric Doctor. Indeed, he went too far for John Nathan-Turner. John was said to be disenchanted with Baker's portrayal because, as he related to Howe and Walker for *The Television Companion*, Baker's "assured and flippant interpretation made the character seem too dominant and invulnerable". This may be why, under John's aegis, the fifth Doctor went too far the other way in compensation. Peter Davison was a handsome, charming young chap whose summery white outfit suggested a lighter and more temperate character after the dark eccentricity of Tom Baker. Not even a stick of celery jutting from his pocket could save him from bright normality. And when, in *The Caves of Androzani* he reprimands Peri for her Americanisms ("Try and speak English"), he seems to be harking back to the least agreeable, and least desirable, aspects of Hartnell.

Not that Peter Davison was devoid of Doctorish moments. In *Mawdryn Undead,* Turlough infiltrates the TARDIS and there is a prime Doctorish moment when Davison hurries in and find him sneaking around in there. The Doctor initially just doesn't pay him any attention. As if to say, "You're not a threat, or even a surprise. How could you be? I'm the Doctor."

But then he reacts in a more conventional way and the spell is broken. Davison is a talented actor and an effective leading man, but his portrayal of the Doctor was seldom strange enough or spooky enough. To emphasise what was lacking, one need look no further than Mark Strickson, who played Turlough. Strickson had an introverted, alien quality which might have made for a very interesting Doctor. Enigmatic and not always reassuring, he might have been just what the Doctor ordered.

But during John Nathan-Turner's tenure, the clean-cut, handsome and not-too-eccentric leading man approach to the Doctor held sway. Ironically, John's understanding what it meant to be Doctorish was chiefly directed at exterminating any of its vivid appearances in the character.

Peter Davison's successor, Colin Baker, was soon developing in a far from Doctorish way, and indeed moving fast in the other direction by the time of *Vengeance on Varos,* when he sends two guards plunging into a lethal acid bath (one inadvertently, one culpably less so). And as the sixth Doctor watches their horrible painful demise, he utters the line, "Forgive me if I don't join you." The cold-blooded callousness of this jape is what we'd expect from James Bond or an Arnold Schwarzenegger action hero, not the Doctor. I suppose Tom Baker might just about have carried it off, with a suitably ambiguous bug-eye look. But Troughton or Pertwee would have saved the guard from falling into the acid bath.

In some ways, though, the sixth Doctor was a move in the right direction. After the amiable, sunny blandness of the Davison Doctor, there was a conscious desire on the part of John and his then-script-editor Eric Saward to present a more acerbic and quirky characterisation. But there were crucial elements missing in their formula. All too often, the Doctor is allowed to fumble around and become a victim of events, when he should be taking control and assuming stature.

Taking control and assuming stature were two of the things I had most clearly in mind when I set about retooling the characterisation of the seventh Doctor, with John's blessing and the assistance of a team of crack writers. In our pursuit of this ideal, we unknowingly played our own variation on *The War Games'* examiner from the war office. In Ian Briggs' *The Curse of Fenric,* Sylvester McCoy cheekily borrows a typewriter and types himself an official letter authorising his presence on the military base, signing it ambidextrously with a flourish. This scene, which was evolved in careful discussions between Ian and myself, achieved a number of Doctorish things at once. It asserted authority while presenting weirdness and, as a bonus, it was amusing. This was the kind of approach we'd arrived at by my third season on *Doctor Who.*

But the (unwitting) attempts to create a Doctorish Doctor extended back to my earliest work on the show. One of my first tasks on being hired (working in a drafty office overlooking Shepherds' Bush during a freezing January) was to write an audition piece to be acted out by prospective candidates to play the seventh Doctor. This fragment of script was my own homage to Dr Manhattan from Alan Moore's *Watchmen,* with his kaleidoscopic view of time. I had the Doctor talking about days like crazy paving and so on. I was aiming at creating a sense of wonder in the character and, I must admit, hoping for a small shiver down the spine.

By great good fortune, I'd hit upon a Doctorish approach. And one that Sylvester McCoy liked so much that he insisted on using the material in the show proper. Hence Ian Briggs being prevailed upon to crowbar a lot of the dialogue into his script for *Dragonfire*.

Sylvester McCoy was a return to the Doctorish style of protagonist and it looked as though the trend might continue with the eighth incarnation. Paul McGann's Doctor was agreeably Doctorish. Like Davison (and like Matt Smith), he was a very young Doctor. But unlike Davison (and hopefully like Smith), McGann avoided the image of a nice, normal chap. In spite of a less-than-brilliant script, McGann was convincingly the Doctor. He was offbeat, alien yet likeable, and vividly conveys the sense of a stranger in a strange land. You can ask more of a Doctor than that, but it's a damned good start.

As it happened, McGann's start was also his finish. The ninth Doctor would also have a distressingly brief run, though consider longer than McGann's. Christopher Eccleston was quite different from the whole sequence of earlier Doctors, although his Byronic brooding quality and unconventional good looks had some parallels in McGann. That same brooding, introverted aspect also usefully suggested the alien. Eccleston was youthful yet capable of being grimly serious. Crucially, he had authority.

To me, it seems that Matt Smith is in a similar mould. He is younger still, of course, and it is always hazardous to move the Doctor too far in the young-leading-man direction. But, on the promising side, he is like Tom Baker, Paul McGann or Christopher Eccleston in being unconventional looking and rather plausibly alien. Indeed, he looks like David Bowie in *The Man Who Fell to Earth*.

What kind of Doctor will Matt Smith be? Well, his performances in recent BBC dramas like *Moses Jones* bode well for him as an actor. And with Steven Moffat at the helm of the next season of *Doctor Who*, there is a good chance he'll be given the right kind of writing, which is just as important as the right kind of acting and always plays a crucial factor in creating a Doctorish Doctor.

Time will tell.

A Proposal to Bring Back Doctor Who

by David T. Russell (edited by James Downing)
From Shockeye's Kitchen (online version)

It should be obvious, even to the morons at the BBC, that *Doctor Who* should be back on television. I mean, come on! You make crap "drama" like *Spooks, State of Play* and *Casanova,* and waste millions on boring wildlife documentaries like *The Blue Planet* – but so what? Just because they win industry awards and are watched by many millions of brainless idiots, doesn't make them worthwhile television programmes!

It's time the BBC woke up and smelled the coffee: the only programme that deserves to be on television is *Doctor Who*, and the only audience you need to satisfy is the hardcore *Doctor Who* fan.

(And I don't mean the so-called-fans who buy a DVD once in a while; I'm talking about true fans! Fans who know the difference between Season Seven UNIT uniforms and all the UNIT uniforms that came after – and they'd spot the alternate-universe UNIT uniforms from *Inferno*!)

The 200-page document that follows outlines the only proper way to bring *Doctor Who* back to BBC1. It is colour-coded for easy access (e.g. the sections in light yellow deal with the first [pre-Davros] Dalek timeline, and the sections in dark yellow obviously deal with the Dalek timeline after *Genesis of the Daleks*) and has 34 Appendices (see Index). Lastly, there is a petition to ensure that I am the producer, signed by all seven members of the East Swindon *Doctor Who* Group.

Let's get straight to the important stuff.

The Continuity

The fiction of the Doctor has got 40 years of backstory...

Which we'll worship. In detail.

Of all the things that a new series of *Doctor Who* needs to get right, continuity is absolutely the most important. In fact, the very reason *Doctor Who* needs to be back on television is to finally get the continuity right; something that should have been done all along, if only previous producers actually cared about the series when they were making it (which they obviously didn't!) For example, one of the first stories that should be made is *Return to Karn,* in which the Doctor finds the body of the Morbius creature, revives it and has another mind-bending duel with it. Then we'll reveal that all those faces seen in The *Brain of Morbius* really do belong to Morbius, as I've said all along, and that will shut Philip

Hinchcliffe up once and for all!

To ensure that continuity is treated with the respect – nay, reverence! – it deserves, the new series will have six "Continuity Advisors" (all members of the East Swindon Local Group), though as producer, I'll have the final say on everything (e.g. Katarina is not a proper companion, no matter how much my friend Gareth Wilbury-Smith insists that she is!)

The Second Most Important Thing!

The end titles will credit the lead character as "The Doctor" and absolutely, definitely not "Doctor Who"!!!!!! Only kids and the general public call him Doctor Who, and they're stupid and don't count.

In fact, now I think about it, we must have a story in which the Doctor meets WOTAN again, and learns that the Master had programmed the computer to say "Doctor Who is required". Enraged, the Doctor smashes the computer to bits and goes on to list all the evidence relating to why he's most certainly called the Doctor, no question about it! (I'll supply all the evidence, which I have stored on a database on my laptop and which is also colour-coded.)

Tagline

"*Doctor Who*: A Continuity of Hard Sci-Fi Adventures in Time and Space (and Alternate Universes), Which Definitely Isn't for Girls or Kids."

The Doctor (1)

We pick up from the end of the appalling *TV Movie*, which mucked-up continuity so badly that we're going to have to fix a lot of things. The Doctor, played by Paul McGann (who absolutely must return, even if he says he doesn't want to; we can take him to court, or something), is in his eighth incarnation.

He wears eccentric, nineteenth-century-style clothing, has long girlie hair, speaks in a posh accent and uses lots of long, confusing words, as all aliens must do.

Adventures in Deep Space

If the Zogs on planet Zog are having trouble with the Zog-monster... then I'm interested.

I don't give a toss about ordinary humans and their boring, "beans on toast in front of *EastEnders*" lives and neither does the Doctor, who views these pathetic people with contempt. In fact, during an "Earth is invaded" story, the Doctor won't bother to save these types of people; he'll let them die, and save better people (sci-fi fans) instead.

If true fans switch on *Doctor Who* when it comes back on and the first scene they see is a guy in a black cloak with a beard in front of a pink sky with three suns, making some kind of death threat, then they will love it. If it's set in the "real" world of pubs and mortgages, then the fans will hate it, and rightly so.

Bringing back Gallifrey will ensure that the Time Lords appear in the majority of the stories; it's a guarantee that old men in silly hats are going to turn up. In my view, I don't think we can have enough of them.

The Stories

Fifty-two episodes should be enough, for the first year, at least. From Year Two, we'll consider having 104 episodes, broadcast on Saturday and Sunday nights at 10:30pm.

And the stories should be fanwanky. Well, obviously. But I mean unashamedly continuity-heavy, and utterly devoid of any feeling or emotion. This programme's going to be dark, gritty and watched by a few thousand *Doctor Who* fans, so there should be nothing to grab a new viewer. We don't want them. Especially girls or kids.

Hard sci-fi ideas, cardboard characters and no emotions. Simple as that.

The Episodes

The plots have been worked out in excruciating detail, to ensure that the continuity is correct and the sci-fi ideas are clichéd and utterly uninteresting to anybody except true fans. These outlines give a good example of the continuity, the grittiness, the darkness and the absolute lack of any kind of fun.

Story 1 (Special: 2 x 2hr episodes)

"*The Dark Legends of Rassilon and the Time Lords of Gallifrey.*" The Doctor travels back to Earth, to visit his companion Ace (so we finally find out what happened to her). Unfortunately, the Doctor discovers he's in an Alternate Universe and Ace believes that the Doctor "died" in his seventh incarnation (this clears up that *Death Comes to Time* travesty). The Doctor realises that this is the reason why he stupidly believes he is (I can barely bring myself to type this) half-human, and also why the Master is a snake-thing and why the Daleks sound like Smurfs!

The Doctor travels back along his own time-stream and meets the seventh Doctor (Sylvester McCoy). Together (and taking Ace with them), they travel to Gallifrey, home planet of the Time Lords, to sort out the continuity nightmare they are in.

After meeting Romana, Leela, Andred and K9, the Doctors explore

Gallifrey, and discover that the Time Lords have erected Thirteen Giant Statues of the Doctor, each statue representing one of the Doctor's incarnations! The eighth Doctor uses his sonic screwdriver to activate the first six statues. A door opens in the statues... and out step the first six Doctors!

(Doctors 4, 5 and 6 are played by the original actors. They explain that the Time Lords are rubbish at art, which explains why they all look like old, fat, balding blokes. For Doctors 1-3, see Appendix 3: CGI Technology and Jon Culshaw.)

The first Doctor says, "Hmmm, so that's what I've become, is it? A clown, a dandy, a bohemian who walks in eternity, a feckless innocent, a burly bloke who shouts a lot, a player of chess on a thousand chess boards who also plays the spoons, a dishy Mr Darcy type, and..." (he mumbles the rest of the thirteen, so we don't actually hear any clear descriptions, except for a vague reference to the Valeyard)!

Anyway, after a lengthy flashback sequence (see Appendix 11: Readily Prepared Flashback Sequences), all eight Doctors, Ace, Romana, Leela, Andred and K9 enter into the Time Lord Matrix, where they discover alternate Doctors and companions (this explains, amongst other things, the arseing Peter Cushing movies, *Curse of Fatal Death,* the blasphemous Big Finish "Unbounds" and all those stupid, not-at-all-like-*Doctor-Who* New Adventures / BBC Eighth Doctor books). Each proper Doctor takes it in turn to say just how crap these other Doctors and adventures are, and how they're not proper *Who* at all.

(This would mean that any true fans would burn their copies of these silly adventures, and would start to toe the line, continuitywise – and I would have won every argument I ever had with a so-called fan.)

We end on a cliffhanger. The Master reveals himself! He shoots the eighth Doctor with his Tissue Compression Eliminator, and the Doctor regenerates...

Part Two

The Doctor regenerates into Richard E. Grant! Immediately realising that this is a terrible idea that will never work (he's a cartoon, for God's sake!), the "new" Doctor deliberately taunts the Master into shooting him again, triggering another regeneration...

The new "new" Doctor sets everything to rights (see Appendix 21: The Absolute Avoidance of *deus ex machina* Endings, Except in Countless Classic Stories, Particularly Those Written by Robert Holmes) and leaves Gallifrey to travel the universe.

The Doctor (2)
Your worst nightmare. A gruff, mysterious character, who speaks like Shakespeare, or someone clever like that. He's dressed in a long, flowing cloak, top hat and German lederhosen, and wears a stinging nettle on his lapel (the nettle is the only plant that grows on Gallifrey). He should be played by Adam Rickett.

Story 2 "The End of The World"
The TARDIS takes the Doctor to Peladon, where he gains his new companions, Alpha Centauri and Erato, the Creature from the Pit...

(Editor's note: It was at this point that the BBC got on the telephone to Russell T Davies...)

TRIP OF A LIFETIME

It may be the greatest ad for *Doctor Who*, ever: Christopher Eccleston as the Doctor in the new TARDIS set, facing the camera (on 35mm film, no less) telling the viewer with charismatic bluntness, "D'you wanna come with me? Because if you do, then I should warn you..."

We just get goose pimples remembering it.

The Doctor then tells us the viewer will meet ghosts from the past, aliens from the future, the day the Earth is consumed by flame – although he neglects to mention the farting aliens, the space pig or the burping wheelie bin. However, by this point, we don't care. We'd follow this Doctor there, to the end of the universe and, if necessary, to a Manchester United football match.

2005 was the year *Doctor Who* came back. Everything was fresh: new Doctor (with a leather jacket and a northern accent), new companion (with a mum and a boyfriend), new Daleks (that can actually do things, like frighten people) and a new format (what was this thing called a "four-part story"?). It was so exciting.

It's hard to believe, but nobody knew if it would work. *Doctor Who* authors working on the final Eighth Doctor Adventures novels were told to leave some wriggle room in their manuscripts in case the new series didn't take off. There were fears of the show being taken off after three weeks and being bumped to a death slot on Friday evenings at 9pm. The plan – to have a 13 episode science-fiction adventure drama for the whole family on Saturday nights on the BBC's flagship channel – was now so unconventional that parsing this very sentence could merit several essays alone.

But it worked. Of course it did.

Here now is a snapshot of the fan reaction to 2005's *Doctor Who*: revelry in the moment; love letters to Christopher Eccleston; cool, detached analysis on whether it was doing what it should. People cheering, people bewildered that it's *Doctor Who* at all. And ten million people watching.

What did the Doctor say in that ad? "It won't be quiet, it won't be safe, and it won't be calm. But I'll tell you what it will be..."

Resurrection

by Lloyd Rose

From Enlightenment #129, August / September 2005

I'd figured the best to be hoped for was that the new *Doctor Who* wouldn't be too embarrassing, until I saw the publicity photo of the ninth Doctor struggling with the Auton; the one where Eccleston is all teeth, passionate and furious. Whatever else the new show was, it was clearly intense. Intense turned out to be the least of it. Fans who take *Doctor Who* seriously – who appreciate its peculiar blend of horror, humour and moral seriousness – have always had to grab at small moments of authenticity. The show's dreamy, frightening implications were more powerful than anything that made it to the screen; yet they wouldn't have been there without the surface-silly stuff that actually did make it. Russell T Davies, a fan grown up, understood this and deliberately aimed for a mix of genuine emotion and fantastical nonsense. As a result, his *Doctor Who* is to the previous series as *The Empire Strikes Back* is to the *Star Wars* movies: more affecting than it has any aesthetic right to be.

Sure, the show can stumble. Eccleston takes a couple of episodes to find his feet. Jokes that should explode fizzle. Sometimes the storyline is obvious and sometimes the story doesn't quite make sense. The Doctor blows up a department store building right after closing time, when the sidewalks would be full of people leaving work, yet no one is crushed by falling concrete. There are strange plot misfires: in the climactic episode, the Doctor's last, when he ought to get a heroic send-off, Rose is the one who saves the day. (It's a tribute to Davies' writing skill that the story barrels along so confidently that you hardly register this lapse.) We say a poignant farewell to the last remaining Dalek only to find out later that, oops, there are a few million still out there. And so on. Who cares? Anyone who defines a television show by its blunders should probably just stop watching television.

People who priggishly insist Davies is the program's weakest writer miss the obvious: he's the author of the whole show. He hired those writers "better" than him (and I think they produced two classic episodes: *Dalek* and *The Empty Child / The Doctor Dances*), he conceived the new Doctor's character, found the actors, defined the design (a perfect mixture of high-tech and down-at-heels), chose the composer, approved the music, and set up and guided the season's hurtling, 13-chapter story.

That story reveals itself gradually. At first, we just seem to be moving through self-contained episodes. The new Doctor is charming, goofy, impulsive and fast-moving. Very quick. Then we get that first mention that Gallifrey is gone; then discover that the Doctor is responsible (when in doubt in *Doctor Who,* have him destroy Gallifrey is what I always say); then begin to recognise his tortured survivor's guilt, that he moves so fast because his past is at his heels like one of those billowing special-effects fires in action movies, ready to burn him alive. Finally – and it's done with delicate understatement – we realise that, in an unmelodramatic way, he's ready to die. In the first episode, a character warns that the Doctor brings death in his wake. Who would guess he'd brought it to his own people? All this in what is primarily a show for kids. Plus jokes.

Somehow, Davies has made radical changes to the show without betraying its spirit. In spite of the kiss in the TV Movie, the Doctor traditionally has the sex life of a stone. Is he asexual? Repressed? Uninterested in shagging aliens? Maybe he's just very, very discreet. These questions don't come up with the ninth Doctor, although other ones (such as: what exactly is going on?) do. Davies and Eccleston have been provokingly unforthcoming about the character's sexuality. He flirts. He can be adolescently jealous. He shows off in front of Rose. Nothing actually happens (and when Captain Jack kisses him farewell, the camera carefully shows only the Doctor's back). Still, what a departure! Imagine any other Doctor inspiring Rose to mutter about "testosterone". Hormones? The Doctor? All that biological stuff used to stop at the disclosure that he had two hearts. (The most subversive joke in the show is that the hero of a children's programme looks like rough trade.)

Genre fans have to get used to movies and television shows in which the principals aren't particularly talented but nonetheless become the characters (there were sequels to the original *Star Trek,* not attempts to remake it). It's a nice shock to be reminded what a real actor can bring to pulp. All the implications in the material suddenly deepen and manifest. Eccleston, uninterestingly good in previous roles, is electric here, ferociously committed to the role. You don't often see this kind of go-for-broke, unprotected acting, particularly in television.

Not that the Doctor is necessarily an acting role. It's beside the point, for example, to debate whether Tom Baker's performance is good or bad. Whatever he's doing (incarnating? thinking about jam?) is mesmerising. No matter what you think of Baker, he remains the iconic Doctor. Aside from his splendidly eccentric appearance, he had whimsy, surprise, force, uncanniness and presence. Plus two qualities no one else in the part had till Eccleston: authority and threat.

Baker was commanding (lordly, so to speak) and, though he never did anything that wasn't heroic, virtuous, etc, he was always a little scary. Eccleston has authority and threat in spades (one English reviewer referred to his "often frightening alien goofiness"). He's big and intimidating (the coat gives him some needed bulk, disguising the fact that he's something of a beanpole). But Baker's aloof detachment has gone. There's nothing remote about Eccleston's performance. He's fiercely involved; something even more radical than the sexual hints. The character was previously beyond passion; like a mage, he transcended fear and hope. But his ninth incarnation has both feet firmly on the ground; in the dirt even, the grim mess of life. Experience has scarred this Doctor; like Oppenheimer, he's known sin: "I am become Death, the destroyer of worlds." (In a typically Whovian mix of joke and pain, the TARDIS console has so many improbable objects as levers because there's no longer any place to get proper replacements.)

Eccleston, and the whole season, would seem to be an impossible act to follow. But if Davies could create a Doctor who brought out Eccleston, he'll do the same for Tennant. The show is his, not the lead actor's. Tennant's stage reviews are mostly raves; aside from being nominated for an Olivier award, he's played everything from Shakespeare's Benedick to Osbourne's Jimmy Porter in *Look Back In Anger*; arguably twentieth century drama's biggest asshole. Last year, in *Pillowman*, he was a children's book author who murders his brother. This is, to put it mildly, quite a range.

Tennant can appear cuddly-handsome in pictures, but just as often he looks odd, as if his features weren't positioned quite as they should be. His entrance at the end of the final episode, grinning fanatically and intrigued by his teeth, slightly alarmed me, which was reassuring. But my response could be completely off target; it was only a glimpse. On the other hand, Tennant knew that a) this was his Big Entrance and b) as drama it wasn't a patch on Eccleston's, so it's a safe bet he put all he had into those few seconds.

What the Christmas special is going to be like I really cannot imagine.

It's Dangerous, I'm Loving It

by Greg McElhatton
From Enlightenment #128, June / July 2005

The second episode of a television show is, in many ways, more important than the first. Certainly, the first one matters, don't get me wrong. If you've got a bad first episode, your show is on rough footing from day one. It's the second episode, though, that's critical, because you need to convince your audience that the quality that made them stick around for a second viewing isn't going away any time soon. There's nothing worse than having a really promising debut promptly lose everything good about the show in its second week.

Instantly, *The End of the World* is off to a good start, with a roller coaster recap of *Rose*, letting the excitement level build as the Doctor takes Rose on the proverbial trip of a lifetime. What struck me almost immediately about the pre-credits sequence was how well director Euros Lyn and score composer Murray Gold worked together here, making the story more frantic with each passing second until the TARDIS lands at its final destination – and suddenly everything's still, a very serious moment as Rose discovers where they are. The music is soft and respectful, and Christopher Eccleston and Billie Piper have shed their wink-and-grin attitude to help Lyn bring Russell T Davies' script across to the viewers: it's not all fun and games, and this truly is the end of the world.

It's a mixture of frivolity and seriousness that runs through the entire episode, and with great effect. The Doctor and Rose are surrounded by jokes and laugh-inducing moments as the different alien races are introduced but, despite all of the humour in the scene, there's still a great deal of seriousness on display as well, with Rose unable to cope with such a new and different range of stimuli in such a short period of time. It's one of the big differences between *The End of the World* and just about any other episode of *Doctor Who* where the new companion is removed from familiar surroundings. In *Planet of Fire*, the story might as well have been set entirely in Lanzarote based on Peri's reactions to suddenly being transplanted to an alien world. In *The End of the World*, we get a perfect range of emotion: wonder and amazement, unease and confusion, fear and confrontation, and finally acceptance and enjoyment. It's a thoughtful and careful approach to Rose's new life as a time traveller, and it really emphasises that the character of Rose is one of the stars of the show in her own right.

The plot structure of *The End of the World* will certainly be familiar to *Doctor Who* fans: a classic, closed-environment whodunnit. It's got all the familiar tropes on display: a multitude of colourful suspects, red herrings to pull the viewer off-course, and a body count that steadily rises. The main plot, about the destruction of Earth even as a killer is disposing of everyone on board the space station Platform One, is surprisingly the weakest part of *The End of the World*. It's too standard, too ordinary, even down to the secondary character deaths who might as well have targets painted on their foreheads. Given the choice of watching either a ludicrous "must get the switch" sequence that looks like it was written specifically for a videogame (because all emergency override switches are put in a place that's almost physically impossible to get to, right?) or the Doctor's emotional reaction to a personal tragedy that's just been revealed to the viewers, it's easy to see which part is the more interesting.

Instead, *The End of the World* gets its strength from the character moments peppered throughout it. Hints about the recent history of the Doctor and his status in the universe build steadily through the story until a revelation that will no doubt shock some long-time fans is delivered, but the important part is really how the Doctor reacts and what it says about this new incarnation's character. Eccleston brings the scene to life beautifully, and it's one of the few times that a television show has made me breathless as a scene played out. Some viewers might get hung up on the usage of Britney Spears' "Toxic", but if so they're missing how perfectly the lyrics connect with Rose's inner struggle about travelling with the Doctor, and her attraction to the danger that threatens to end her journey before it's even really begun. It's another wonderful character moment, one that pays off brilliantly in Rose's ultimate decision to continue her travels with the Doctor.

Mind you, this sort of thing wouldn't work nearly as well if it wasn't for the cast. Christopher Eccleston and Billie Piper continue to be a breath of fresh air in the show, both bringing their characters to life in such a short period of time. Eccleston's enough of a veteran actor that his strengths here aren't a shock, but Piper's newness to drama meant that it was a pleasant surprise how easily she slips into the role of the working-class girl who suddenly gets the chance to travel throughout space in time. Watching her move across the screen, it's hard to forget that it's an actress and not an actual person named Rose Tyler who's struggling to adjust to this strange, fantastic journey. The rest of the supporting cast helps seal the deal here, all excellent in their own right. Zoë Wanamaker's voice work as Cassandra – the bigoted, self-proclaimed last human – is a dead-on satirical masterpiece, able to bring a fine mix of menace and humour to the screen. Simon Day's turn as the Steward is so comfortable, you'll find yourself playing the "Do I know him from somewhere?" game. Last but not least, Yasmin Bannerman as Jabe has so much instant charisma that you find yourself hoping that she'll be joining the TARDIS crew at the end of the story, impracticalities of having a living tree as a companion aside.

I was really impressed that, in making Jabe a "tree", production didn't just put some twigs behind Bannerman's ears and call it a day. This is a full-blown transformation, with Bannerman's bark-coloured skin transforming into chunks of wood atop her head, complete with leaves sprouting on top. This is movie-calibre makeup, and it's almost startling to see the amount of care put into a character to show up in a single, 45-minute story. There's a lot of nice visual work elsewhere in the show, especially with the exterior view of Platform One, which is quite possibly one of the most realistic space stations to ever appear on *Doctor Who*. You get a real sense of how massive the area is and the computer graphics look fantastic here. The only time the effects really fall down is when they've got to show massive fan blades spinning over a catwalk; they don't look terribly good in the long shots, and when the Doctor is digitally inserted into the scene it's almost cringeworthy how fake they look. It's a surprising mis-step in an episode that takes so many things into account, even down to the computer fonts and the musical cues.

Ultimately, *The End of the World* is a rousing success. Even where the show makes slight mis-steps, they're easily drowned out by everything that works so well. The new "all over in 45 minutes" format works perfectly here, Davies ruthlessly cutting out all padding to instead plunge the viewers directly into the story. There's no need to spend 22 minutes watching the Doctor and companion wander a vacant space station when they can discover their new location in a matter of seconds and proceed from there. With *The End of the World,* Davies has raised the stakes of the show; Rose is out of her element, in life-threatening situations and even the Doctor is proven to be extremely vulnerable. And yet, in the end, they're victorious and stronger from their experiences. To use the ninth Doctor's favourite adjective, it's fantastic. If *The End of the World* doesn't make viewers want to come back for more, nothing will.

We ♥ Chris

by Robert Smith?
From Enlightenment #131, December 2005

Dear Chris,

I remember the moment when I first knew. No, it wasn't that opening scene of Rose ("Run!"), magical though it is. You did a fine job, sure, but the power of that opening is fairly and squarely due to Russell's writing, I think we can all acknowledge that. It's not that scene where you take Billie's hand and talk about the spinning of the Earth as though you're drunk, despite the fact that that scene got all the airplay on every documentary imaginable in those first few weeks. You were good, sure, but I still wasn't convinced.

Oh yes, I had my doubts. Some of it wasn't your fault, some of it couldn't be helped. The costume, the accent, the hair... it's as though they'd stripped you down to the bare essentials and asked you to create a Doctor without any of the usual trappings the others had to fall back on. What a challenge that must have been... but it's one I didn't think you –

or anyone – was up to. I mean, I tried to imagine Tom Baker with a shaved head, dressed in jeans and a T-shirt and talking in a thick Liverpudlian accent and I just had to lie down for a while. I wondered about Sylvester McCoy facing down Davros in a pair of shorts and those round spectacles while putting on a broad Australian accent, and suddenly the master of a thousand chessboards didn't seem so impressive. I thought about the third Doctor, as played by Jon Pertwee if he didn't bother to do any acting – and it wasn't that different, really.

But I digress.

No, the moment I first knew was when you have to explain what a police box is to Billie. It's that scene that every other Doctor has played straight, taking that fundamental conceit at the heart of the series as seriously as possible and simply pretending that of course everyone knows what a police box is, decades after the last one was removed. It's the look in your eyes and the lilt in your voice as you proclaim "It's a disguise!" as though it really were the cleverest disguise in history. It's a plot point you have to get across to new viewers, it's a nod to the series' history for long-time viewers, it's a character point about the Doctor and it's a really funny joke, all rolled into one. And you pull that off magnificently.

That was the moment when I first knew you were the Doctor.

And not just a Doctor, but *my* Doctor. I've been a fan for longer than Billie Piper has been alive, but suddenly you made me feel ten years old again, staring at the screen with wide eyes and a grin on my face and that's when I knew that not only was *Doctor Who* back, but the Doctor was too. You know how *The Unfolding Text* spends about 40 pages academically dissecting the three words "similar, but different" when tracing through the origins of the first story and its relationship to the pop-culture paradigm from which it was born? Well, you probably don't, but trust me, it made a big semiotic impression on my 12-year-old self.

But those words describe my impression of what you achieved perfectly. Sure, *Doctor Who* was back and, as difficult a logistical behind-the-scenes process as that was, it was just a technical procedure. The real test was whether someone could step into the role and convince me that the show really was back. And even that wasn't too hard: Paul McGann managed it in the nineties and he only had about 60 minutes of screen-time and some well-fitting shoes to do it in. No, what was really tough was to take that concept and that character and make it into something that was like what came before, yet was also new and innovative. Similar, but different.

And so, about 30 minutes into *Rose*, you had me.

But best of all, it didn't end there. From episode to episode, you continued to impress. Your revelation at the conclusion of *The End of the*

World, where you and Billie are firing on all cylinders, had me glued to the screen. The sudden, easy authority you exhibited just before the cliffhanger of *Aliens of London*. The timed-to-perfection jokes in *World War Three*. The "narrows it down" scene. All great stuff, all pushed even further than the material required.

Then along came *Dalek*. In among the action-movie staging of the gunfights, the battles and the return of the scariest monster ever to glide across a studio set, you stood out as the highlight of the episode. From the sheer depth of emotion in the "Why don't you just die?" speech to the pained and damaged Doctor you played at the conclusion, awkwardly holding that gun, but saying "They're all dead, Rose" like you were a little boy lost. Episode by episode, beat by beat, your acting choices were spot on, shading the Doctor's character with subtlety and emotion... when I'd never really thought the Doctor was the type of character that needed that sort of thing. He'd always struck me as an archetype, rather than a type, but you turned my expectations upside down and forced me to reevaluate a character I thought I knew back to front.

In your speech to the Editor, which is really a speech to Cathica, you take the Doctor from what appears to be a position of weakness, captured and manacled, and create what is almost a mission statement for the ninth Doctor's character. He's the one who inspires others to be better than they are. You turn that position of weakness into one of strength, so we understand that the manacles are irrelevant. The panic you show when you find the TARDIS interior gone in *Father's Day* is wonderfully unsettling, to say nothing of the way you salvage the "Who says you're not important?" scene from the cliché it could so easily have been.

The Empty Child sees you range from bewildered standup comedy to unbridled curiosity at Jamie's true nature, coupled with the child-like rapport you have with the homeless kids at the dining table. In *The Doctor Dances*, you make the "bananas are good" scene completely your own, sounding more like you'd ad-libbed the entire thing than learned it from a script. Then there's the way you bring out the subtextual jealousy while resonating concrete and the sheer, almost panicked, joy you express at the possibility of winning. It's an interpretation that so many others could have taken the other way, given that the Doctor almost always wins, but you play it with a pained desperation that tells us so much about this intricate and complex character.

In *Boom Town*, you show us the Doctor's darker side. In a story that's taking apart the Doctor to see what makes him tick, you're the perfect vehicle for conveying multiple levels of meaning at once. Whether it's your distaste at taking Margaret to face the death penalty, but willingness to do it anyway, or the magical "dinner and bondage" scene where you answer her charges but tell us, the audience, that they all have some merit nonetheless.

And then there's the final two-parter, which is your tour-de-force, but best highlighted by *Bad Wolf*'s conclusion. What makes it delicious is the way you scowl and tug your jacket down just before having to face the Daleks, as though you're about to stand up to the school principal. And then your "I'm coming to rescue you, Rose" speech is riveting television. Only on later viewings did I realise that the entire cast swung around as one to face you the moment you pronounced "No." I missed that entirely, so captivated was I by the power of your delivery.

The Parting of the Ways sees your character become so focussed that he even contemplates the unthinkable... but you convey this with utter conviction, so much so that I thought you might even go through with it. Until, finally, your realisation that there's only one answer to the "killer or coward" dilemma, which you act as though relieved at the prospect of death. It's a note-perfect climax to a perfect season.

And, naturally, I was devastated when I found out you were leaving. My disappointment only grew as the season continued. But, by its conclusion, part of that disappointment was tempered by the realisation that your arc couldn't have played out more perfectly. The sheer range of emotions you shared with us brought more out of the ninth Doctor in one season than other Doctors in three, five or seven seasons. The small touches and undercurrents you shaded the character with forced me to see that there was so much more to my favourite time traveller than I'd ever conceived.

So I want to say thank you. You opened my eyes to the wonder of the Doctor again... but "again" is the wrong word, because you showed me a side to the Doctor I'd never seen and for that I'll always be grateful. Episode after episode, scene after scene, you took your lines and actions and made them something greater and more powerful than they were intended.

I like to think you had me convinced from that "disguise" scene. However, that was just the moment when my cynicism and pre-expectations melted away and I was able to open myself up to the magic of what you had to offer.

Really, you had me at "Run!"

D'you Wanna Come With Me?

by Rob Matthews
From The Doctor Who Ratings Guide, May 2006
(revised October 2009)

It may not in the future be remembered as part of the season proper, but in the trailer for the 2005 *Doctor Who* series, Christopher Eccleston walked about the TARDIS set promising us "The trip of a lifetime."

That, as it turns out, was not merely a bit of nice-sounding sloganeering. It turns out to be somewhat of a key phrase for the 2005 season; indeed, I think it's just as apt an umbrella title for the season as *The Key to Time* was for Season Sixteen, or *The Trial of a Time Lord* was for Season Twenty-Three. The beauty of the *Who* format lies largely in its capacity for continual (cyclical, perhaps) reinvention, and the preoccupation with "life" or, perhaps more specifically, "a lifetime" was what constituted the main shift in emphasis in the 2005 season from those before.

Of course, *Doctor Who* has always been in one way or another about the subjects of life and death; the Doctor, after all, is a bloke who goes around the universe saving people's lives and defeating those who want to kill. But, more often than not in the TV show, "life" is a possession, something which belongs to you that bad guys threaten to steal, something that you might heroically surrender for the sake of others. Or it's "life" as an essence, a huge breathtaking panoply of gumblejacks and bumblebees to be regarded with awe and humility. Life, Drathro, life. It's indomitable, indomitable.

But life as it is lived, life as the day-to-day interaction of who one is with what one does, life as an accumulation of experiences, values, prejudices, perspectives... that's not something which has ever in any thorough way been part of the *Who* formula on TV, at least not with any consistency or conviction. In fact, you could more or less guarantee that if one of the Doctor's companions started talking at any length about their own life and what they wanted to do with it, it was because they were either leaving the show (Jo in *The Green Death*) or joining it (Peri in *Planet of Fire*). Characterisation, you'd be forgiven for thinking, was something that *Who* production teams only paid attention to in emergencies. Occasionally, in the case of certain companion characters, like Nyssa and Mel, this inattention became glaring. Usually, though, it was more a matter of plot taking precedence over character, and in the main certainly wasn't a problem as such.

Doctor Who, in its original run, was never something that could be described as a "character driven" show. Indeed, for many fans in the run-up to the broadcast of the new series, the idea that it might end up becoming one was anathema; this was a show built to explore ideas, not characters; it was sci-fi, not soap opera. A few continued to make this argument once it finally arrived on air and Rose Tyler turned out, pretty much as expected, to be a character who nabbed a far greater slice of narrative attention each week than the majority – if not all – of her "companion" predecessors. And, unlike all of them, she even dragged her mother and boyfriend into the series with her! At least Tegan's auntie Vanessa had the decency to get herself killed by the Master as soon as humanly possible...

So far as one can tell, this was, and is, based on the fear of a horrifying feminisation of a show whose most hardcore fanbase consists of blokes, dammit, geeky blokes. Because, you know, blokes don't like mushy stuff as it detracts from action and explosions and car chases and shit, and geeks don't like mushy stuff because it detracts from spaceships and federations and concepts and attempts to build a "continuity" and shit. So there's a kind of double-strength resistance there.

I don't have that much sympathy for anyone whose unwillingness to engage with the new show arises from prejudice of this ilk. Not because I don't share the blokey disdain for shows where people just blather on about girly matters (oh, believe me, I do) but because I recognise that *Doctor Who* the television series – whether this one or the one that, say, Philip Hinchcliffe produced – is not made for an exclusive audience of geeky blokes.

Indeed, one surprisingly refreshing thing about reaction to the new series is how little our niche fannish opinions actually matter now. When us fan reviewer types are discussing the merits or demerits of the show, we have to bear in mind (although many of us don't) that it's a completely different animal from the *Who* we fans have been enjoying in the years since the old series went off air. Different in that it's no longer something aimed directly at us. In reviewing, for example, a Virgin or BBC book, you'd likely have some idea of what fan consensus is on certain subjects, or of how fandom might react to, say, Lawrence Miles murdering the third Doctor in *Interference*, or Gary Russell deciding to write the sixth Doctor's swansong adventure. You might look at them with these things in mind, even if offering an opinion differing from what you perceive as the fan consensus.

But now, that fan consensus itself is not the be all and end all of opinion on the show anyway. To the audience for whom New *Who* is intended, *Spiral Scratch, Zagreus, The Tomorrow Windows* and *Fear Itself* are simply not a context, and the show can't be talked about wholly in terms of satisfying our expectations, since that is not primarily what it's built to do. *Doctor Who* stories are being reviewed in, like, actual newspapers now, not just on fan websites, and you can bet your arse that no columnist in the *Times* is going to take issue with, say, *Father's Day* because its treatment of time paradoxes differs from that depicted in *Day of the Daleks* or *No Future*. No one in *The Independent* is dissing *The End of the World* for showing a different "end of the world" from that suggested in *The Trial of a Time Lord* or *Frontios* or what have you. They're able, instantly, without all our silly baggage, to see the show as it is.

I'm constantly surprised at how often this goes unacknowledged in online fandom: this series is not just for me, and it's not just for you, either. It's a show that's for everyone. In the case of the original series, it was a programme made primarily for kids but built for the enjoyment of families too, evolving to incorporate more and more elements for adults as time went on. In the case of this new one, it's more overtly a case of being made simply for the whole damn BBC audience, anyone who might happen to tune in, and hence is as suitable for kids as anyone else. I mentioned Philip Hinchcliffe there; even he – rightly the most venerated of producers by fans – considered *Doctor Who* to be a show that fits into the "light entertainment" bracket. And that's just the context for which the new series is being made. You can't just ignore what the show is: a big, expensive, license-funded, Saturday evening family entertainment programme starring an acclaimed actor and an ex-pop star, and was an enormous gamble for the BBC.

And that's not me merely making excuses for the introduction of intrusive soap opera elements to our precious, finely honed, perfectly oiled, needs-no-tinkering cult franchise, by the way. Nope, because the "soap opera" criticisms that have popped up in certain corners of fandom are exaggerated in the extreme. There were a negligible amount of genuinely soap-operatic scenarios in the 2005 season; in fact, one admittedly very tedious argument between Rose and Mickey in *Boom Town* about covers it, and you couldn't fill even five minutes of *Family Affairs* with that. Rather, the underlying objection seems to be that Rose – a mere "companion"! – has been fleshed out with a history and a life, and is essentially being portrayed as a human being rather than a formula-serving cutout ala Tegan, Peri or Mel. This, I can only surmise in bewilderment, is taken as a betrayal or a misunderstanding of a tried and true formula.

If so, I think it's an unimaginative viewpoint. Classic *Doctor Who* sagged whenever the people making it treated it as merely formulaic; all the best periods of the show came as a result of the makers of the show taking a step back, looking at how the show was working, how they themselves wanted it to work, making changes of emphasis and commissioning or accepting scripts that worked for their own visions.

The use of Rose Tyler – the idea of her as part of the central dynamic of the series – demonstrates care, thoughtfulness and just plain old-fashioned professional competence on the part of the show's lead writer. The very opposite of the laziness or betrayal or selling out that's implied in some of the criticism I've read. Davies has evidently asked himself the simple question of just what it is about the show that he finds so appealing. At its very barest bones, what is the single great idea that propels the show? Is it the alien do-gooder travelling through time and space? Nah... it's the idea of an ordinary person like you or me, going on an extraordinary journey with the alien do-gooder who travels through time and space.

That is the starting point of RTD's vision for the series, and that is the idea he has actually succeeded in communicating to a mass audience. He hasn't made it successful all on his tod, of course; everyone who's been involved in the series has had their part to play, and it wouldn't have been a success without the acting, the up-to-date FX work, the other contributing writers; ideas originated by Paul Cornell and Robert Shearman, in particular, appear to have contributed significantly to the overall flow. Nevertheless, all evidence points to that convivial Welshman being the one who gave it that all-important sense of focus. He's the one who had the Doctor sneer "You could fill your life with work and food and sleep" to Rose in episode one, and gave us Mickey's quietly aggrieved response "It's what the rest of us do" in episode thirteen.

Oh dear, there I go complimenting Russell T Davies on a job well done. How gauche. A hefty swathe of fandom seems to think some kind of conspiracy exists to shower Davies in excessive praise. Yet, so far as I can see, fan consensus has rarely risen above "grudging respect" – and certainly fulsome praise has been a rarity in our elite little ghetto.

Doctor Who's capacity for reinvention is a real necessity this time round, with the show having been off the air for 16 years. You couldn't reasonably deny that the 2005 season qualifies as a new start. I don't think the old series would ever have dared to destroy Gallifrey off screen in a between-seasons time war, for example, and usually the status quo at the end of one season would carry across to the beginning of the next; even the fact that Colin Baker refused to appear in *Time and the Rani*, for example, didn't stop an ersatz "sixth Doctor" appearing in the prologue to that story anyway. And, just from a production point of view, there's no carry-over here from the last televised season in terms of cast and crew. Not to mention that this new series is not the under-budgeted, neglected (by them upstairs) show the old one was when last on air.

Unlike arguably every other season of *Doctor Who* before it, this one could not assume a basic carry-over of audience from the previous year's run. Philip Hinchcliffe is a name that, again, springs to mind when you think of people who've given the show an overhaul, but he didn't do that all at once, or within the same context. Hinchcliffe inherited a healthy, popular show from Barry Letts and, able to assume a certain level of "built-in" devotion on the part of its core kiddie audience, went on to develop the show in a way that would bring in more adult viewers as well. Russell T Davies' *Doctor Who*, on the other hand, was the risky resurrection of a defunct show with a caricatured reputation for "wobbliness", and whose only remaining fans were a minority of weirdos who do odd, mad things like sitting here drafting and re-drafting this article for hours even though I've been sitting in the same hunched-over position at work all day and my back's bloody aching.

The important point is that this was a show built primarily for people who had never seen *Doctor Who* before; people who don't know what a TARDIS is, or who the Doctor is, what he does, where he's from, etc. Even though a good part of its audience undoubtedly were people who had seen it before, they were not the audience to whom it was *a priori* addressed. *Doctor Who* 2005 is, in practical terms, a new show; one that, if viewed in a vacuum, with no prior knowledge of the franchise, stands up as a self-contained piece of entertainment.

Russell T Davies' explanation (to fans, mark you) of why he decided against any regeneration sequence to introduce the ninth Doctor speaks volumes about the clarity of his approach. He pointed out that, without the establishment of any emotional investment in the character, a scene which showed the Doctor changing his face would merely be an odd, irrelevant event. No one would have thought that about showing the Doctor's rushed pre-credits regeneration in *Time and the Rani*, because that was a new series of a continuing show, and the emotional investment could be assumed to have carried over from the previous season. This, on the other hand, has been in every important way a new show.

There is another layer to it, though. Watching the 2005 season, I'm convinced that we're seeing something that Russell T Davies had thought about for an awfully long time, the fruition of something long-nurtured. Rose and her council estate were always meant to be a part of his *Doctor Who*; you can even spot the seeds of them in his New Adventure, *Damaged Goods*; you can see the Roses and Tylers in his other shows. The Time War felt inevitable; the Time Lords and the Daleks were always meant to have destroyed each other by now; hints that they'd ultimately go to war appeared in two of the 80s Dalek stories and the Big Finish audios, of which Russell is a fan. The phrase "last of the Time Lords", first spoken in *The End of the World*, had haunted fandom since the early 90s, when it was the title of one of the many mooted *Doctor Who* movie projects. Clearly, these things had been absorbed and gestated over time.

The season is light on specific continuity references (amusingly, there's no reference to "Davros" or "Gallifrey" where there might legitimately be some, yet there are two references to *The Web Planet*), but RTD's sense of the legend of *Who* goes much deeper than superficial namechecks. The idea of the damaged post-Time-War Doctor is an extrapolation of the old series as much as it's a clever, clean-slate way of launching the new one. We know that Russell's a fan, and that *Doctor Who* hasn't been away for him, just as it hasn't for many of us. It's been living in his head alongside his own vision for its comeback, the story of the Doctor and Rose Tyler. And that makes the season feel rich and large, and helps it pull off the trick of being a new show for a new audience while still being, fundamentally, the *Doctor Who* of old.

Mind you, one rather interesting and rewarding thing about watching the new show with fan eyes as opposed to normal-folk ones is that with the first broadcast of *Rose*, we were suddenly able to see with clarity just how much popular television has changed in the years between 1989 and 2005. No matter that we may have been watching the box all along, *Doctor Who*'s been out of it for 15 years – give or take a telemovie – and when, more in hope than expectation, we pondered the idea of a new *Doctor Who* television series, it perhaps became more and more difficult to envision what that would look like and how it would play. Then, with a rapid title sequence, a zoom-in on Earth, England and then London from space, an alarm clock, a council estate, breakbeaty music, Trafalgar Square, a boyfriend, a shop... suddenly, here it was. *Doctor Who*, as a mainstream show, on television as it is today. A perhaps-unnerving thing to see when you've been used to enjoying *Who* as a "cult" thing and have for years been cultivating a healthy, aloof loathing of the crass mainstream. To me, just as a casual TV viewer, *Rose* represented a fairly hopeful 45 minutes (all the moreso when the ratings came in and the announcement of a second series was made), because it appeared that the tide was turning away from "reality" and "celebrity" bullshit and that people wanted to see television that told stories, that was imaginative and inspiring. Television that says something a bit more worthwhile than "clean your curtains" or "buy some new clothes". But, conceivably, there were also fans out there seeing the other side of the coin; not mainstream television being improved by the presence of *Doctor Who*, but *Doctor Who* being degraded by becoming part of mainstream television.

To my mind, the first moment of greatness in the 2005 season is the scene at the very end of the second episode. "She's lucky to be alive", Jackie Tyler babbled down the phone in episode one, but in this wonderful moment with the Doctor and Rose standing unmoving in a bustling metropolitan street, *Doctor Who* 2005 says that and means it: Rose is lucky to be alive. Life, simply living and breathing and experiencing, is the most precious, amazing thing of all. And what, if anything, gives it meaning, is truly knowing that it's going to be gone one day. It strikes just the right bittersweet tone, this scene: those joyless, dour "chips" from episode one suddenly becoming things of beauty, just as joyless dour routine life can all of a sudden be recognised anew as a thing of beauty. That sense of looking at things from a renewed, unexpected perspective... well, that's the joy of taking a trip in the TARDIS, part of the essential lure of the show. Here, in episode two of the new run, is something important the nineties telemovie overlooked. Soul, I think you'd call it.

"Have a fantastic life. Do that for me, Rose."

If you've seen the series, it's hopefully quite unnecessary for me to spell out how these concerns come to a head in *The Parting of the Ways*. But if that scene on the street is the first great scene of *Doctor Who* 2005, then Rose sitting with Jackie and Mickey in that café in episode thirteen is – nearly – the last.

Actually, the last, which I adore more each time I see it again, comes at the climax as Bad Wolf Rose unravels the Daleks. Direction, performance and music all combine to make her simple line "Everything must come to dust; all things; everything dies" truly extraordinary. It harks back to that scene in *The End of the World* with a sense of having now proved its point. The bleakest, most terrible truth of all is made beautiful and affirmative.

So, yeah, *Doctor Who* – this *Doctor Who* – is explicitly about life, and its quality. It's also, as Russell T Davies points out, "about death, really". Which sounds like a contradiction, but of course, isn't when you think about it. Life is all the more precious in the Doctor's universe precisely because it's a place where you can witness death at every turn. I mean, who'd have thought Jabe would have died in *The End of the World*? In a manner surprisingly similar to the vision of 80s script editor Eric Saward, 2000s *Who* gives us a brutal universe where death is not the simple matter of "just deserts" one might expect from escapist storytelling. In the context of recent history, I doubt the larger part of the audience finds the notion of arbitrary atrocity at all questionable.

Not that they should anyway, but it seems that people generally are unable to quite believe that non-recent history actually happened; like those crass voices in the media suddenly questioning the existence of a benevolent god after the Asian tsunami; Stalinist Russia or Hitler's Germany apparently having never tarnished their confidence in this matter.

Still, though, this probably speaks of a shallow and forgetful media which only debates these timeless arguments in the same faddish, transitory sort of way it might discuss the merits of the latest single from the Sugababes. *Doctor Who* has frequently been at its best when addressing the prevalent anxieties of its time. And it's been even better when doing this in a subtle way that will outlast that particular stretch of time.

Whether *Who* 2005, with its glib Iraq references and *Big Brother / Weakest Link* parodies, will do so remains to be seen. I'd guess some of it will and some of it won't. *The End of the World*, for example, seems a timeless sort of tale. But it's clear enough that RTD and company have looked outwards in their conception of this incarnation of *Doctor Who*. It's obvious enough which chord that scene of Big Ben getting smashed in by a spaceship was meant to strike. Ditto the Daleks chanting about blasphemy – and, incidentally, if you didn't know the Daleks had existed before, you'd be forgiven for thinking their name had been recently invented, comprising all the consonant sounds of al-Qaeda.

Did I just say death can be found at every turn in this universe? Well look, it's even right there behind that console, death with a goofy grin on its face, a Mancunian accent and a battered leather jacket that's seen a lot of action. At the risk of appearing pseudo-something-or-other, I think one thing worth noting about the Doctor's world is his status as the last of his people, survivor and orphan of an all-consuming war. That gives him a different edge that even us old-guard fans can fully appreciate as new. He's been a mysterious mischievous space hobo before, and he's been an exile from his own august super-civilisation, then a wandering rebel who purposefully rejected his own deeply corrupt pseudo-benevolent people, and for a while he was a possibly godlike being just pretending to be a mischievous space hobo. This time, he's both victor and victim: as last man standing after the time war, he has technically won, while at the same time having lost everything; his attitude to this somewhat pyrrhic victory being first revealed in Robert Shearman's *Dalek*.

Two factors are very pertinent in establishing this new bipolar role for the Doctor: firstly his culpability, the fact that it was, so to speak, his hand on the trigger that ended the war in which the Daleks and the Time Lords "burned together", making sense of his determination to exist only in the moment ("This is me, right here and right now") and perhaps excusing a little that moment of self-importance in *World War Three*. The other factor, only revealed after *Dalek*, is that the homeworld the Doctor lost wasn't the country club of some decaying oligarchy comprised of time-policing rotten old bastards. It was, the Doctor seems to genuinely believe in *Father's Day*, a truly benevolent civilisation and, importantly, as suggested in the same episode, it was a place where the Doctor had family that he actually cared about. Including, *The Empty Child* goes on to very strongly imply, children and grandchildren.

I think that's worth noting in this particular fannish context, since it's the kind of thing we sometimes overlook when it doesn't fit in with our – occasionally almost unconscious – continuity theories and assumptions. If we're thinking the planet the Doctor lost was the corrupt Robert Holmes Gallifrey and his only relatives there were the grotesque Cousins of the NAs, we're not quite seeing the character that's being presented. He's a man who's lost his loved ones and is constantly trying to escape from his own feeling of guilt, from himself. He is, if I may employ a dull cliché to describe an engaging and nicely layered performance, a man on the edge.

And in light of this conception of the character, a few complaints about the overall narrative of the season dissolve; most obviously, the criticisms of Eccleston's occasional bouts of forced cheeriness in the role miss by a mile the fact that the Doctor is the one forcing the cheeriness. Look at when he bops about a bit to "Tainted Love"; that doesn't look like a man who's actually enjoying himself, and it's not meant to. There's far more genuine cheer in his observation that "That's not supposed to happen" when he scents trouble later on.

More controversially, there's his Doctor being obviously in love with Rose. This never once felt like a problem for me the way it did for some; perhaps surprisingly, given that I didn't at all like the romance with Grace in the McGann telemovie. In retrospect, and in the face of compelling new evidence, I'd say my objection was less to the idea of the Doctor getting a bit now and then, than a reaction to its being so obviously contrived, tacked on just so that the foppishly dressed Doctor wouldn't look too gay to people in the midwest. But also because the telemovie was so much of a mishmash, a bunch of sound and fury in search of a clear identity it never quite established.

Doctor Who 2005, on the other hand, does have a clear identity, and the Doctor-Rose relationship has not just been shoved onto an existing formula like some kind of sexy elastoplast. On the contrary, it's a crucial part of the formula here: the cumulative story of the season is the love story of the Doctor and Rose. And, though some of that may come across as strong stuff to those of us accustomed to an asexual, spoddy Doctor, let's not forget that by the standards of most TV series it's fairly subtle and chaste; hell, the Doctor only finally kisses her to save her life. He's not exactly a lothario.

Still, that he loves Rose is quite clear. And, cut him some slack, why not? She's his shot at redemption. Here's a 900-year-old man who's travelled the universe and seen planets die and civilisations fall, including his own. Here's a man who states with suppressed anger that he did not survive the Time War by choice, a man who actually appears to feel a beatific sense of relief when he's told that he's about to die. And here's Rose, a sparky girl stuck in a rut on Earth, someone who's probably seen nothing of the world, maybe even nothing outside of London. Someone who will see the universe with the fresh, innocent, wondering eyes the Doctor has long since lost and thinks he'll never get back, while still being a bit handy in a fight. Given this, I find their relationship quite beautiful, and utterly plausible. Rose might not be the first "stupid ape" he's hung out with, but it's a friendship that takes on a new importance and a greater emotional investment when you see it as the only thing the Doctor has left. Given this context, those occasional displays of petulant jealousy aren't as jarring as is sometimes suggested. Having lost everything, the Doctor doesn't want to lose Rose too.

Thirdly, there's the, let's say, "finality" of the Time War. I've noticed fans occasionally expressing dismay that dribs and drabs of Daleks, who were supposed to have completely perished in said war suddenly turn up out of nowhere. The complaint being that the series blithely contradicts the backstory it's set up for itself just for the convenience of the episode at hand.

Look at who's making the claim that the war has ended and no one but him survived: it's a man who desperately wants to believe that it's all over. The Doctor, as we finally discover, had been clinging on to a belief that the annihilation of his own people had a silver lining, that they had taken down with them the biggest force for evil in his universe. The idea that the enemy could have even in some small form survived is not one he wants to acknowledge.

If the Doctor is linked with death, well then, I guess it's Rose who represents life. You know, the kind of life he's never had.

"Who says you're not important?"

Despite that annoying recent effect where the newest thing is always considered to be the best and anything from the past becomes simplistically caricatured, Rose Tyler is not an exceptional *Doctor Who* companion. Tabloids tell us that she's "feisty" (ungghhh...) compared to the screamers of the past, in much the same way as broadsheets tell us RTD's *Who* is far, far better than the old show ever was. But, of course, both assertions are total bollocks (the mainstream media might be able to recognise the virtues of the new show, but it still has fuck all clue about those of the old). The attention lavished on characterisation in the scripting makes her feel more special than most but, divorced of that, Rose is an emphatically average companion for the Doctor. She's not "all instinct and intuition" like Leela; not tenacious and out to prove herself like Sarah Jane;

not super-smart like Romana, Nyssa or Liz Shaw; and, while admittedly fairly gorgeous, she's not unbelievably beautiful like Romana I or Peri. She's an everygirl. A bit braver than some – she did get the bronze! – but she's basically Ordinary with a capital O.

But as New *Who* tells us with every breath in its body, that's important. Even an ordinary life is an extraordinary life because that's all there really is, an ordinary life multiplied by billions. The ordinary lives throughout this season are given a level of attention that's rarely been seen in television *Who* before. Which is why Rose's ordinary life has a "mythology" too. The "legend" of her father's death as inculcated in her by her mother, leaving school for Jimmy whatsisface, a casually volatile relationship with her mother and a boyfriend she's seemingly stayed with out of habit. Rose is the focal point of the entire season, and I'd go so far as to say that the hints of the Doctor's backstory in this first episode are flat and unconvincing by comparison. All that "I couldn't save your world, I couldn't save any of them!" stuff fails to really hit any emotional note (not helped by the lack of musical accompaniment in that scene), and the bit where Eccleston yells "I am talking!" at the Nestene Consciousness is frankly no more or less convincing than when Sylvester McCoy attempted to convey innate power by suddenly shouting. This imbalance is, however, redressed in the next episode, with the Doctor-Jabe scenes beautifully bringing out the inner turmoil of his character. And isn't that single tear far more effective than any "woe is me" speech?

Is a *Doctor Who* that's primarily focussed on its central duo, that's structured as a love story, "soap opera"? I certainly don't believe so. In terms of form, soap operas by their nature have no beginning, middle or end, whereas the 2005 season does. In terms of content, soap operas are about the domestic and emotional lives of a wide assortment of characters. In a soap you'll see 13 extra-marital affairs and two drunken kitchen punch-ups a week, whereas in *Doctor Who* you'll see one life-saving kiss and one "emotional" argument scene that doesn't really come off per series. Plus four attempted alien invasions. And, as suddenly became clear to me in the festive context of *The Christmas Invasion*, the Sarf-East London council-estate dahn-the-market milieu of Rose's home life owes far more to *Only Fools and Horses* than *EastEnders*.

Interesting to recall that those "soap!" accusations are not wholly new; funny to think of it now, but the same remarks were made quite a few times about Season Nineteen in the early eighties as well. They're just as off the mark now, but in a different way.

The fundamental thing, I think, which sums up the difference between old and new *Who*, the thing that gives this season its distinctive character and its appeal to adults who would previously never have conceived of watching such a show, is awareness of mortality. That awareness is a great leveller. It's the one thing the new series possesses consistently which the original run only had in individual stories, here and there. The "trip of a lifetime" is a re-learning of the innate worth of life, and the forging of values. And not just for Rose either; throughout the season, we see the Doctor continually inspiring others to take a stand, become heroic (like Jabe, Gwyneth, Harriet Jones, Captain Jack, Mickey and even, finally, Jackie Tyler).

When Rose, in that café, tried inarticulately but powerfully to express the "better life" the Doctor had shown her, I felt – not for the first time during the season – such a sense of triumph that *Doctor Who* was back. The season might not have demonstrated every single solitary strength of the old show's run, but – and I've said it all along – it was never, ever reasonable to expect it to do so. What is has done is recreate the show for a whole new audience, stimulated the imagination of a new generation of kids and adults alike, and successfully reignited the fire in the belly of the old. "You take a stand, you say no, you have the guts to do what's right!" may not sound profound divorced of context and Billie Piper's excellent performance, but in an arena where attention-seeking idiots seek empty fame by entering a spartan house full of cameras for a couple of months, or where some hunchbacked little shrew rakes through fat people's shit and berates them because it doesn't smell of jasmine and gardenias, or where statuesque actresses stand next to picket fences looking over the road and wondering "As long as they sort through their mail and park their cars nicely, how much do we really want to know about our neighbours?" like they're performing *Hamlet*... well, it's very, very welcome. Us fans are accustomed to *Doctor Who*, to its imagination, its fun and its sense of morality. Now a whole bunch of other people have the chance to see that too.

As a literal journey, mind you, the season had a far stronger sense of volition during its first five episodes than at any point later (excepting, perhaps, the thrilling denouement). In terms of where they went and what they did, these five episodes got the series off to a more or less perfect start, pseudo-farting or no: *Rose* saw an ordinary girl's ordinary life turned upside down by the arrival of the alien time-travelling Doctor; *The End of the World* took us to the far future and introduced an assortment of alien races and thought-provoking concepts while expanding importantly on something momentous that happened during that war mentioned in episode one; *The Unquiet Dead* took us back in time and clarified that the Doctor's life can sometimes involve scary monsters and famous historical personages; and *Aliens of London* and *World War Three* gave us a contemporary invasion-of-Earth story more developed than the earlier Nestene one, while at the same time expanding on Clive's discussion of the Doctor's appearances throughout Earth's history. (He was, apparently, involved with something called a United Nations Intelligence Taskforce...)

All great. Forwards in time, backwards in time, back home with Rose to pick up some clothes and a toothbrush, and now the real journey begins. The Doctor's showing off what this ship of his can do, a ship that can go anywhere... next stop has got to be an alien planet, yeah?

Um. Well, no. No, next place we saw was a bunker under Utah. But there was a dirty great Dalek there, and it was more badass than the Daleks had been in years, if rather emotionally brittle, so that successfully papered over the slight sense of disappointment at being back on Earth again. Then the next week... well, at least it wasn't Earth. It was a space station. Erm, orbiting Earth. A bit like the one in *The End of the World*. Okay. What about the next week then? Oh, back to Earth again. But at Rose's request, I guess, and what a good episode it was.

And then... oh great, an alien weapon! And it's heading for the centre of... London. Oh, for fuck's sake. Where the hell are we going to go next, back to sodding Cardiff?!

Ah.

Time and space, Mr Davies. You've omitted one of them, and it's an absence even the normal people are starting to notice! No way round it, this was one of the major disappointments of the season. It simply didn't live up to the Doctor's original promise of a ship that can go anywhere and at the same time it cut us off somewhat from Rose Tyler as our point of identification. Let's not kid ourselves; even outside of the Pertwee era, the show has always spent an inordinate amount of time on Earth. *The Web Planet* was, as noted on its recent DVD release, the last *Who* story to feature a supporting cast with no humans in it. But Earth has never before been the only bloody place the show takes us to week in, week out, and it's starting to get claustrophobic. A little sprinkling of the exotic goes a long way and, it's worth repeating, to not bother with Rose's first steps on an alien world was a simply staggering omission.

Davies has indicated in interviews that he's only interested in stories set on alien planets if there's a human element there to keep the emotional connection with the audience, i.e. colonists from Earth on a hostile new world or something. Hopefully the 2005 season's establishment of a vast (and suspiciously NAish) Earth Empire in the future will provide him enough scope for this. I understand we're finally going to see at least one new planet in 2006, so we're getting there in baby steps.

Still, you'd be hard-pushed to deny that this stands up as one of the more consistently good *Who* seasons. If – and this is arguable – it hasn't quite scaled the greatest heights of the old (for all its flaws, *The Daleks* is far more daring television than anything in *Who* 2005; ditto *Inferno, Deadly Assassin, The Robots of Death, Ghost Light* and others), it hasn't dipped anywhere remotely near its lows either.

Doctor Who can, as some of us like to say, be anything. So when it chooses to be something, just one thing – when it's Christopher Eccleston and Billie Piper, Slitheen, Gelth and Daleks and frequent visits back to Cardiff, Satellite Five and a council estate – we start to lament all the things it could have been, what we would have made it had we been in charge. It's a show with limitless possibilities, so of course it's always going to feel like there's some avenue not being explored.

That should not, however, stop us appreciating what it is here and now, in this moment. *Doctor Who* can indeed be anything and, to prove it, here it is as a popular TV show. It's been a success without sacrificing the intelligence, frivolity, anti-authoritarianism and morality that make *Who* what it is, and that's heartening.

No. That's fantastic.

Boom Town Love

by Robert Smith?

From Enlightenment #133, April / May 2006

"Boom Town *is quite, quite brilliant sure to be rediscovered [...] in ten years' time."*

—Robert Smith?, *Enlightenment* #129

Let's do it now.

I think I've finally figured out why so many *Doctor Who* fans don't like *Boom Town*. It's because we don't like consequences.

I'm not talking about continuity, we love that like the trivia-obsessed nerds we are. But we, like the Doctor, don't actually want to deal with the consequences of our hero's actions. Because they're... well... they're not actually very pleasant. Continuity is small and we fans always love the small stuff. We love finding the secret background knowledge or the hints about what's truly going on. Fandom, in a very fundamental way, is all about what's happening around the edges. But we're not so comfortable with the big stuff.

"I spent years wincing at Buffy and her mates talking to each other with breezy, self-referential smugness, and the first five minutes of Boom Town *nearly had me in the foetal position in fear that Joss Whedon had taken over Russell T Davies' brain."*

—Graeme Burk, *Back to the Vortex.*

Boom Town has been described, by both its fans and detractors, as *Buffy*-esque and I think there's more to that than meets the eye. *Buffy* had its share of breezy, self-referential smugness, but it also wasn't afraid to deal with the consequences of what it would actually mean to be a vampire-slaying teenager. Often in a very real and painful way. *Boom Town* is a lot like that: it's hip, it's smart, it mixes comedy buckets with deep moral questions... and it also takes the time to truly examine what it would mean to be the Doctor, or to be his companion. Or even his enemy.

"But the major error that Boom Town *makes is this – it presumes that the entire world getting torn apart and everybody dying, just because one alien is getting a bit of cabin fever, is less important than having a bit of a chat about how the Doctor does things. And it presumes in turn that the questioning of the Doctor is less important than showing us that travelling through time and space can lead to you having a tiff with your boyfriend."*

—Mike Morris, *The Doctor Who Ratings Guide*

Boom Town gives equal weight to its three plotlines: the Cardiff rift, the dinner date, and Rose and Mickey's relationship. It doesn't actually put them in a hierarchy, but you can see why fans, especially male fans, think that it does. We're used to world-threatening dangers erupting from strange technobabble devices and mad aliens. That's comfortable, familiar ground for *Doctor Who. Boom Town* isn't about that plotline, so it's little wonder it isn't given a particularly original spin. It's just there to kick off the action and provide the "ticking clock" to hang the rest of the drama on.

"And then there's Mickey's and Rose's interactions in the story. Rose has chosen to leave him, not once, but twice – she's not in love with Mickey – so why does she want to see him here? That bit makes no sense and just makes the whole episode feel like a waste of time."

—Robert Franks, *Back to the Vortex*

We've occasionally seen actual relationships in *Doctor Who...* but since all our previous views have been within this one season, it still takes some getting used to. Of course the fanboys hate this aspect of the new show. There'd be something seriously wrong if they didn't. Not that the new show shouldn't hold plenty of appeal for such fans – indeed, it goes out of its way far more than it has any need to, in order to accommodate this niche of the audience – but they're not the whole demographic. They're not even the majority.

"This is the closest to domestic the Doctor has ever got."

—John Anderson, *Enlightenment* #128

Not only has *Doctor Who* been an amazing success with the mainstream audience, single-handedly reviving the "family drama" timeslot not seen since its death in the early eighties, but – incredibly – it's gained a female following as well. You can't do that with technobabble and made-up science and explosions alone. The great thing – the truly great thing – about the new series is that it hasn't just grafted soapish relationships and interactions onto the series, it's actually incorporated them into the ethos of the show. This really is what it would be like to have a partner who went off with a captivating alien to travel in time and space, and that's actually a fascinating concept to examine. Once upon a time, we thought that *Doctor Who* had done everything it was possible to do; now we see that it had barely scratched the surface.

"It doesn't really feel like it resolves the issue of the Doctor's destructive lifestyle or his culpability for the damage he causes. Not that there is probably a sufficient answer, but the questions RTD asks are ones not really considered prior to this series. He paints the Doctor as a man who almost murders through intent to interfere who then rushes before the dust falls. We see very little evidence of that in the show so it does seem a rather odd proposal."

—James McLean, *Outpost Gallifrey*

However, the most shocking part of *Boom Town* is also its most successful: the Doctor's morality. Here, it's ruthlessly dissected and the answers aren't comfortable. Our Doctor, whether we like it or not, is a killer. He always has been, he always will be. In the name of justice, perhaps, but a killer nonetheless. And yet, one of the things that makes him so fascinating, and so accessible, is his inability to face that. He almost never gets his hands dirty and talks a big line about the sanctity of life and so on... while nevertheless dispatching villains with a cold morality that would be shocking if he ever acted directly.

Boom Town's genius is to take all this and bring it to the surface. No wonder it's so strongly disliked by some fans. It's a bit like going to therapy and discovering that you're actually not a very nice person.

"The reliance on the TARDIS to solve the story is annoying and looks like lazy writing. However I am prepared to be proved wrong about this if Davis [sic] is, as I suspect setting up the mysterious properties of the TARDIS for a future story line."

—Kenneth Baxter, *Outpost Gallifrey*

Then there's the ending, which is so reviled by fans. After all, even the writer admits that it's a *deus ex machina* (in an episode of *Doctor Who Confidential*). Handy power that, right inside the TARDIS, there for the Doctor to use whenever he wanted. What was Russell thinking?

For one thing, the ending doesn't seem nearly so random, given what happens at the end of the season. Sure, the Doctor could open up the TARDIS and use this incredible power whenever he wanted. Assuming, of course, that he landed on a planet-shattering rift, or kept an enormous tow truck about his person, which might be a little impractical. And opening the TARDIS might be fun, so long as he was prepared to revert to an egg, become the bad wolf or regenerate every other story. Could be a short series.

Then there's the fact that dodgy endings abound in *Doctor Who*, even in classic stories. *The Evil of the Daleks* (whoops, forgot he wasn't human!), *The Talons of Weng-Chiang* (handy of Mr Sin to suddenly start shooting from that very convenient laser), *The Seeds of Doom* (get UNIT to blow everything up), *Pyramids of Mars* (that radio signal thing is incredibly dodgy for someone with a time machine), *Genesis of the Daleks* (let's basically do nothing about the Daleks, but oh look, here's an explosion), *Kinda* (the Doctor fights evil every week; why doesn't he just carry a bunch of mirrors around all the time?) and most of the Hartnell historicals (let's just leave in the TARDIS). *Doctor Who* has almost never been about its endings.

"Look, for God's sake, can we have some baddies who are just plain bad? We've already had to deal with a lonely Nestene and a tearful Dalek (though, admittedly, that was well done). Now, we have to understand the isolation and painful upbringing of yet another slavering killer alien."

—Antony Tomlinson, *The Doctor Who Ratings Guide*

I've also figured out another reason some fans don't like the new series, when so much of the mainstream audience does. It's because we don't like *Doctor Who* to collide with the real world.

So many fans talk of the appeal of the series as escapism, which strikes me as a particularly odd thing to say about it. It's hard to see what you're escaping from if your escape involves lots of death and killing and cold justice and intangible fear every Saturday night. No, what I think people mean when they talk about escapism is actually the unreality of the show. In all senses of that word. We like the show because it isn't the real world. And the reason we don't like the real world is that, secretly, we think we're better than that.

"And can we please have a ban on cell-phones in future seasons?! It's bad enough that the damn things exist in reality, let alone in fantasy..."

—Ben Hakala, *Enlightenment* #129

So when *Doctor Who* not only meets the real world, but actually embraces it, we have the bizarre outcome of the fans decrying the series in droves, with the general public simultaneously loving it. I mean, honestly, if I'd travelled back in time to 2002 and told you that would be the reaction, you'd have laughed in my face. We became so used to the series belonging to us and being "special" in the same way we were "special" (read: unloved by the mainstream) that when reality actually intruded on it, we weren't exactly pleased.

"And while I love spaceships and monsters and intergalactic wars, the simplicity of this episode makes it, just sometimes, when the wind's in the right direction, my favourite."

—Russell T Davies, *Doctor Who: The Shooting Scripts*

Boom Town is many things. It's funny, it's clever, it's probably the deepest character examination of our hero ever shown on screen, it deals with a realistic response to a realistic relationship – in the context of a time-travel fantasy series no less! – and it deconstructs the fundamentals of our favourite show. Partly to see how it works, and partly to see what made it so great in the first place. It should be easy to love; indeed, it should be greatness personified. That it's generally perceived not to be tells us far more about ourselves than perhaps we'd like to realise.

And if that isn't what television should be all about, I don't know what is.

INTERLUDE

Journey's End - 1

by Scott Clarke
From Enlightenment #154, October 2009

The end of time draws ever closer. Whenever I talk on my cell phone I can hear a cloister bell in the background (I must speak to my telecom provider about that). And recently I saw the ghostly figure of my editor standing across the street from my apartment building.

"Is it time?" I bellow. "Is this my final Enlightenment *article due?" My editor gives me that look that says "At the rate you're going, we'll be through the end of Moffat's first season before we go to print."*

And so it seems appropriate, as I conclude ten years of writing articles for Enlightenment, *to explore three of the cornerstone elements of the new series thus far as the Russell T Davies era draws to a close, examining the essential elements in re-imagined* Who *whether it be in its prevalence or its absence.*

The end is near...

Part One: Emotion

While *Rose* may have been the first episode of Russell T Davies' *Doctor Who, The End of the World* was the episode that truly established the template for the next five years. The pop music, the contemporary vernacular, the absurd aliens, the perfunctory plot – and of course a new depth of emotion that the series had never really known in its past. Sure, we had moments with Barbara breaking through the first Doctor's crusty exterior, the third Doctor riding off into a melancholy sunset after the departure of Jo, and Tegan's brief weepy on the fourth Doctor's shoulder after her aunt was reduced to a Dapol action figure. But these were more aberrations than essential ingredients, rarely lasted long and never went particularly deep. Although I would be remiss not to mention that, towards the end of the show's original run, much was done to explore the emotional life of the character of Ace. Season Twenty-Six saw an unparalleled focus on a *Doctor Who* companion up to that point. The character of the Doctor, however, would remain an enigma.

But television evolved between 1989 and 2005. Expectations from a viewing audience changed; they demanded something more challenging (Captain Picard got an episode to recover from the Borg, Buffy took a year to get over death). And yes, the alternative media such as the Virgin books, Big Finish audios and BBC books certainly opened up the possibilities of how *Doctor Who* could be peopled and aliened with characters who dealt with the consequences of their actions; let us inside their skin, scales and titanium alloy.

But the medium of television moves like lightning and, for a family drama with fantasy elements to tell a story in 45 minutes, writers and producers have to be very clear on what their priorities are.

Russell T Davies was quite clear that characters came first in his version of *Doctor Who* (with sheer entertainment value coming a close second). So let's dissect *The End of the World* for a moment. What's really going on there? A worldly, exotic man has taken his new friend – a young, inexperienced, adventure-starved woman – on a trip abroad. They really don't know each other and, quite naturally, she starts to experience culture shock. The rest is about lowering the barriers, working out the bugs and peeling back the skin. Okay, that's the plot, but *The End of the World* is all about Rose and the Doctor learning to trust each other.

Platform One is populated by all sorts of bizarre aliens with poetic names like the Face of Boe from the Silver Devastation, Trees, the Adherents of the Repeated Meme, and then the deliciously banal Mr and Mrs Pakoo. Inspired by Douglas Adams, Davies disorients the viewer, constantly keeping us off balance. We laugh at the jukebox that we know isn't an iPod, but then we catch a passing reference of Cassandra referring to herself as a little boy. Characters are spitting and blowing on each other and the Earth is going to blow up in half an hour! But, in all this craziness, Davies takes the luxury of establishing the emotional temperature of his characters. Rose is unnerved and flees the spectacle of the Manchester Suite for the quiet solitude of the only thing that makes sense to her: her home, planet Earth, below her. It's a beautiful image that sets up her conversation with the Doctor perfectly. We really feel Rose's discomfort and her dawning realisation that she knows nothing about the Doctor. He's a complete stranger and she's billions of years from home. She's potentially frakked (and I thought I had it bad when I drove to London, Ontario, one time to a party full of people I didn't know, just because of the excitement I felt for a guy I barely knew).

Even an element that old-time viewers have come to see as part of the magic of *Doctor Who*, the TARDIS translating languages inside traveller's heads, is suddenly shaped into something invasive and dangerous. Rose is scared and frustrated, and she doesn't know what she's gotten herself into. It's one of the central scenes of the episode. *The End of the World* isn't the doomed planet below, it's everything Rose has known to be true up until that moment. But, even as amazing as that is, it's the Doctor's reaction that marks a revolution. The Doctor gets right into it. Instead of telling Rose they have to get back to the plot (such as it is), he gets angry at her probing. "This is who I am, right here, right now, all right? All that counts is here and now, and this is me!" It's like he's hiding behind a coda of everything the character has been to that point. That line is the razor's edge between old *Who* and new.

But the Doctor isn't ready to lower his defenses to Rose (in terms of "emotional plot", that will be forestalled for the climax). The character of Jabe eases the Doctor into that position. Davies needed a character who could engage with the Doctor more as an equal, but could also draw out his emotional life. Jabe had to be very good, because drawing out emotion in a character as mythical and iconic as the Doctor is an act of delicate hearts surgery. Expose too much and the audience will cry foul, rolling their eyes and reaching for the remotes.

The real mystery of the story is not who is sabotaging Platform One (a rhesus monkey with a degenerative brain condition could figure that one out), but rather what has happened to our favourite Time Lord. Clues are dropped and Jabe gently probes the Doctor. Davies holds back and then lets a little of the story leak out in the brilliantly touching scene where Jabe puts her hand on the Doctor's and consoles him, "I'm so sorry." And the Doctor accepts her consolation and the look in Eccleston's eyes is heartbreaking.

Everything that happens after is underlined by that moment of trust. When Jabe emits her "creeper" to retrieve the robotic spider, she's exposing a part of herself that she's not supposed to. There is a warmness, a closeness between the two that feels very real and earned, so that by the time Jabe sacrifices herself it is truly wrenching. Davies is so adept at building up to these moments of consequence.

By the end of her experiences on Platform One, Rose has been through a hell of a lot. Lost in a whole new world, almost frying, presented with a twisted example of future humanity and then the end of the Earth. The Doctor has saved her life and offered her the ability to communicate with her mother through a jerry-rigged cell phone. Both characters are battered by loss and uncertainty. Davies (and the Doctor) takes us and Rose home. Jostling crowds, *The Big Issue* and chips. We're all safe, everything is back to normal.

Except it's not.

The Doctor decides to trust Rose. He bares his soul. He's all alone; his world is gone and his people are all dead. Suddenly the reason for the trip to the "end of the world" takes on a new meaning. He's trying to connect with Rose; trying to share his pain; trying to find a way to share his experience of a lost home. And the Doctor doesn't want to be alone anymore. The end of the episode was game changing.

The 2005 season was defined by the effects of the time war on the Doctor and by Rose growing up, learning to take her first steps into a larger world. And of course it was about learning to trust each other. *Dalek* pushed the Doctor to a dark place, when he was confronted by a mortal enemy that was also alone. We saw him lose control by the end of the episode and Rose has to draw him back with her act of compassion. Who could ever have predicted that a story featuring the monotone nasties would turn out to be one of the most emotional episodes ever for the Doctor? Later, in *Father's Day*, the carefully built trust between the Doctor and Rose is severely tested by Rose's betrayal; by the end of the series, the Doctor finds cartharsis in his newly rediscovered compassion. The entire arc of the season is about "emotional plotting".

And Davies was only gathering steam. The 2006 season was about Rose and the newly regenerated Doctor growing closer and having their relationship being tested by the past (*School Reunion*), infatuation (*The Girl in the Fireplace*) and the future (*The Impossible Planet*) before the devastating separation they experience at the end of the season.

The 2007 season was about unrequited love (Martha) and loneliness (the Doctor). Casting the Doctor as the last of the Time Lords is probably one of the most inspired ideas that Davies has had. How else do you give an emotional arc to a character so all-knowing and godlike? Episodes like *The Runaway Bride, Turn Left* and *The Waters of Mars* illustrate only too well the essentialness of having that anchoring bond with a companion. Conversely, new story elements like the fixed / fluid dichotomy of time, as illustrated in *The Fires of Pompeii,* unveil the weight of the Doctor's decisions on his soul (only hinted at in such classic stories as *Genesis of the Daleks*).

But the end of time draws near and, while the tenth Doctor's final stories look fraught with emotional weight and consequence, one can only speculate at what regeneration will bring. Steven Moffat certainly seems committed to exploring similar emotional beats in the *Doctor Who* universe. Most of his episodes to date have pushed our understanding of the hearts beating under the Doctor's skin. His relationship with Madame de Pompadour was like nothing we'd ever seen before, and the jury is still out on the significance of River Song. At this point, I don't believe there is any going back: televised *Doctor Who* has changed forever.

Emotion is now a fixed point in *Doctor Who*.

CHILDREN OF EARTH

In the previous volume of *Time, Unincorporated*, we pointed out that the beauty of the *Doctor Who* format was that its politics were, well, flexible. Mostly, they existed to aid the telling of a good story.

That's still mostly true. But what happened with the advent of the new series was Russell T Davies.

With Davies came a more cohesive authorial voice in *Doctor Who*. And Russell T Davies was already known for being political. The man put gays and atheism in prime time in a big way with *Queer as Folk* and *The Second Coming*. In many ways, the biggest surprise about Davies' *Doctor Who* was how unpolemical it was compared to his past work. Even so, Davies understood that part of the fun of the *Doctor Who* format was that it could satirise and comment on real-world issues without reverting to grim realism. *Aliens of London, Gridlock* and *Planet of the Ood* follow the same glorious tradition of *The Sun Makers, Vengeance on Varos* and *Doctor Who and the Silurians*, to poke fun and provoke thought.

As the following essays attest, there is a lot of thoughtful response to Davies' politics in new *Doctor Who*. Some say it's too radical, some say it's too reactionary. Some quibble with the contradictory moral stances, others revel in the ambiguity.

Doctor Who still hasn't moved the goalposts substantially when it comes to politics in the new series. The politics of *Doctor Who* are ultimately the politics of good storytelling: telling a tale that engages, excites and incites its audience. Judging by the response here, it's obviously succeeded admirably.

Was Davros Right?

by Steve Lyons

Well... was he?

About the Doctor, I mean. "The man who abhors violence," he calls our hero in *Journey's End*, "never carrying a gun. But this is the truth, Doctor. You take ordinary people and you fashion them into weapons."

We even get a flashback sequence, ostensibly of people who have died in the Doctor's name. Some of the faces therein are misplaced (you can't blame the deaths of the LINDA gang on the Doctor, he wasn't there – and Ursula survived anyway), but still there are enough to build a case.

Jabe burns in *The End of the World* so that the Doctor can save Platform One. Sir Robert sacrifices himself to buy the Doctor time in *Tooth and Claw*, the Face of Boe to give him power in *Gridlock*. Luke Rattigan and River Song carry out suicide missions in his place in *The Poison Sky* and *Forest of the Dead* respectively, while Jenny takes a bullet for him in *The Doctor's Daughter*.

Perhaps most memorably of all, we have Astrid Peth: the last of a succession of characters to hurl themselves into fiery pits in *Voyage of the Damned* in order to save the Doctor from having to lift a finger.

And what of *Journey's End* itself? What about the events that have prompted Davros' accusation?

First of all, there's Martha Jones. Martha has a plan, you see. A measure of last resort. She can save the imminently doomed universe by destroying her own world. Logical enough, you might think. Indeed, when it comes to sacrificing the few to save the many, the Doctor has a recent track record. This week, however, he seems to have forgotten his actions in Pompeii. Martha's plan is vetoed as "never an option".

Fortunately, Sarah Jane and Captain Jack have a plan too. Thanks to some convenient lethal jewellery, they can save the universe by blowing up the Daleks' flagship, and this time only a handful of innocents have to die. The Doctor's verdict? "You can't!" he cries.

That's because Davros is wrong. This is the Doctor. And the Doctor is our hero precisely because he doesn't compromise his principles. Why would he have to? He can always find another way, a better way, to do things. The right way.

Can't he?

*

It's not easy being a liberal hero. Not at the best of times – and certainly not when you live in the fictional *Doctor Who* universe.

In the *Doctor Who* universe, absolute evil exists.

There are whole races out there that are beyond redemption. You can't reason with a Cyberman, much as we might admire a man who tries from time to time. Likewise, the Sontarans are never going to see the error of their ways. This is true of the majority of *Doctor Who* monsters. It also happens to be the very antithesis of the liberal values that the show is reputed to portray.

In the *Doctor Who* universe, you can't do things the way we do them in the real world. Famously, the real-life United Nations were upset by the series' suggestion that they could have a military wing taking a proactive approach to alien threats. We all know, though, that UNIT could never spend 12 years trying to reason with its enemies. Not only would it do them no good, but said enemies always have weapons of mass destruction and are always ready to deploy them within 45 minutes.

The only way to deal with a *Doctor Who* monster is by direct confrontation. More often than not, this means by violent confrontation. And this is something that, from the time of his first visit to Skaro, the Doctor has generally accepted.

Even in the old series – back when he sometimes demonstrated his intellect rather than just boasting about it – it's rare for the Doctor to find a non-violent solution to a monster problem. Sure, he might occasionally trap an invasion force in a time loop or some such – but he's far more likely to just blow the buggers up.

And, as fans, we accepted this – on the whole – because we knew there was usually no other choice. It was kill or be killed. And because the Doctor fought monsters, mockeries of life. (It's probably no coincidence that it was the Ice Warriors, the only natural-bred of the classic recurring monster races, who were ultimately rehabilitated.)

Still, there were limits. In 1984, we found a fifth Doctor repeatedly helpless in the face of a rising body count – and, in *Resurrection of the Daleks,* debating the morality of taking Davros' life before he can kill again. He can't do it, of course, but, the following year, a more pragmatic Doctor is happier to take a gun to the Cyber-Controller, kill his enemies on Varos with a poison-vine trap and press a cyanide-soaked pad to Shockeye's face. And how we hated it!

The point being made was that sometimes even the Doctor has to choose between two evils. Too often during Season Twenty-Two, however, he doesn't seem to have tried all that hard to come up with a third option. "There should have been another way." Yes, Doctor, and *you should have thought of it*!

But if the sight of the sixth Doctor gunning down the Cyber-Controller was too much for some fans, then what do we make of his successor's premeditated act of genocide in *Remembrance of the Daleks*? Not to mention his similar actions in *Silver Nemesis*? Do we excuse him because, on those occasions, he was able to manipulate somebody else into pulling the trigger for him?

*

This uncomfortable question looms large at the heart of new *Doctor Who*.

The tenth Doctor, we are told, believes in "no second chances" – and, given the world in which he lives, this seems a practical philosophy. It's an acknowledgement that, sometimes, fire is needed to fight fire, a declaration of his willingness to choose the lesser of those evils when he must.

And it's just as well. Because, let's make no bones about this, if the Doctor orders Captain Jack to go out there and start shooting, he is every bit as responsible for each ensuing Dalek death as is the gun-wielder himself. The same goes for Jackson Lake; we might refer to his weapons of choice as "info-stamps", but if it quacks like a gun and it kills like a gun...

It's the Doctor who plots to burn the Krillitane in *School Reunion*, even if somebody else does it for him. It's the Doctor who calls down a missile strike on the Slitheen in *World War Three*, even if somebody else does it for him. It's the Doctor who suggests tearing the Abzorbaloff apart in *Love & Monsters*, even if...

There's a telling moment in *Utopia*, when the Doctor stops Captain Jack from defending him with a gun, only to happily accept the protection of an armed guard a moment later. "He's not my responsibility," he explains. And so, the Doctor hypocritically relies on the violent actions of others to keep him alive while at the same time condemning those actions.

What right does he have, then, to be quite so rude to Colonel Mace in *The Sontaran Stratagem*? "I don't like people with guns hanging around me, all right?" he growls, before deciding (in *The Poison Sky*) that the only way to handle the Sontaran threat is with a suicide bombing. This time, to be fair, the Doctor almost carries out the act himself; although, thanks to the timely intervention of another willing martyr, we'll never know if he could have gone through with it.

It is, however, the Doctor who washes all those Racnoss babies down the plughole in *The Runaway Bride*. With his own two hands. It's the Doctor who kills the werewolf in *Tooth and Claw*, albeit at its own request. It's the Doctor who sends the Sycorax Leader plummeting to his doom with a satsuma and who finally murders Richard Lazarus on his third attempt.

Oh, and it's the Doctor who zaps a bunch of Cybermen with a piece of the TARDIS in *The Age of Steel*. That's our liberal hero, right there, carrying and using a gun. That's exactly what he's doing. All the rest is mere semantics.

*

Crucially, though, "no second chances" tells us that the Doctor will always offer his foes a first chance. This is important because, in new *Doctor Who,* even a Dalek can undergo a change of heart. Witness Sec and Caan, not to mention the unnamed Dalek in *Dalek* who only needed the touch of a good woman to change him.

So, when the Doctor despatches the Sycorax Leader in *The Christmas Invasion,* it's only after the alien has spurned the chance to leave quietly. We're also shown the flip side of this coin, as he brings down Harriet Jones – and forestalls the United Kingdom's Golden Age – for the crime of slaughtering the remaining Sycorax after they have (unusually) taken the hint and run.

Sometimes, however, the Doctor's methods can backfire. When an unknown force takes over bus passenger Sky in *Midnight,* everybody but the Doctor wants to hurl her overboard. The Doctor wants to give the entity within Sky a chance – and who would argue that he is wrong to do so? Unfortunately, the net result of his intervention – and, once again, his failure to suggest a single other way of dealing with the problem – is that Sky gets thrown off the bus anyway, and the Hostess dies too.

Nor is this the only time that his scruples have made things worse. In *Human Nature* and *The Family of Blood,* the Doctor goes to frankly insane lengths to avoid his enemies because he's "being kind" to them. This kindness to the guilty results in the slaughter of the innocent. And, sure, it's all very noble of the Doctor to give the Sontarans the choice between surrender and death in *The Poison Sky,* but did he really expect them to take it? Was that futile gesture worth another life?

His actions in *Evolution of the Daleks* are a bit suspect, too. Held at gunpoint the Doctor may be, but still he has surprisingly few qualms about helping Dalek Sec turn a batch of living-dead human beings into his new breed of Daleks, based on the merest chance that this breed may turn out less evil than the last. He also allows Dalek Caan to escape – which brings us right back to *Journey's End.*

*

In *Journey's End,* the stakes are as high as they can possibly be. Davros and the Daleks are threatening the whole of reality – and haven't they both used up more than their fair share of chances? Indeed, it's the Doctor's squeamishness in New York that has indirectly brought the universe to this crisis point.

So, what exactly is his problem with his companions' plans?

Is it that they both entail the genocide of the Dalek race (or so we're told; let's overlook the fact that there are millions of them alive and well in the Void)? The Doctor's subsequent words and actions suggest as much, as does his earlier leniency toward Dalek Caan. ("I've just seen one genocide. I won't cause another.")

Echoes, you might think, of the classic "Have I the right?" scene in *Genesis of the Daleks*, but... well, no, not really. The Doctor's objections to wiping out his arch-foes in that story were twofold: (1) the effect it might have on other worlds, and (2) the fact that he was in the past, and that the Daleks hadn't yet become monsters.

And, let's face it, it's certainly not concern for individual Dalek lives that is the motivating factor here. The Doctor is perfectly happy to engineer the deaths of three of the last four Daleks, through the usual army of second parties; it's only when it comes to finishing the job that he flinches.

Likewise, those Racnoss babies are fair game, so long as Mummy Racnoss is left alive. For a few seconds, anyway. Technically, it's the Doctor's favourite scapegoats, the military, who commit the genocidal act by shooting her down. So, our hero's conscience is clear. Right?

Rose Tyler, too, commits genocide in *The Parting of the Ways*, dividing "every single atom of [the Daleks'] existence". So, why not a word of protest from her travelling companion? Instead, he tells her she's "fantastic".

Like his predecessor circa Season Twenty-Five, it seems that the new-series Doctor has no real problem with genocide at all, so long as he can pretend that it's "not my responsibility". At least the seventh Doctor could argue that he was giving the Daleks and the Cybermen enough rope to hang themselves; not so the ninth or tenth.

And if you were expecting a lesson to be learned – if you were expecting Davros' stinging rebuke to have the slightest effect – then the very next story, in which the Doctor engineers the destruction of every last living Cyberman through the intermediary of Miss Hartigan, certainly puts paid to that.

*

When the Doctor climbs onto his moral high horse in *Journey's End*, then, it is in contradiction to his actions in both earlier and later new-series episodes. It is not, however, the only time we have seen him paralysed by self-doubt.

In *Boom Town*, the ninth Doctor is adamant that he can't take Margaret Slitheen home to face the death penalty; even though he can be sure that, if he sets her free, she will carry on killing. The first thing to note about this dilemma is that the tenth Doctor will, in *Smith and Jones*, hand the Plasmavore Florence over to the Judoon for execution without the slightest hesitation. The second is that it isn't really a dilemma at all. With his supposedly gargantuan brain and the whole of space and time to roam, surely the Doctor can think of somewhere to take his farting foe where she won't do any harm? Instead, all he can do is stand and wait for matters to be taken out of his hands by one of the series' more literal *dei ex machinis*.

Similarly, in *The Parting of the Ways*, the Doctor is unable to destroy the Daleks because it would mean destroying Earth too. The fact that the Daleks are, at that very moment, engaged in the destruction of Earth doesn't seem to have registered with him. He has the means to save the universe at his fingertips, and he declines to use it. It takes another outrageous twist of fate to do the job for him.

Just as Astrid Peth has to save Earth for him in *Voyage of the Damned*; because what does the Doctor actually do to combat the threat of Max Capricorn? Just as the Hostess has to save everyone on the bus in *Midnight*. Just as Cathica has to deal with the Jagrafess in *The Long Game*.

And just as it's left to Donna to kill the Vespiform in *The Unicorn and the Wasp*; the Doctor disapproves of her actions but, again, what was his plan exactly?

*

It should be noted that the Doctor rarely asks somebody else to act for him; sometimes quite the opposite. Somehow, though, it just keeps on happening. His presence alone, it seems, is enough to turn those who meet him into heroes; or at least (in the cases of Sir Robert, Luke, etc) makes them suddenly keen to give their lives in atonement for their mistakes.

There are two ways of looking at this phenomenon. One is that the Doctor, whether intentionally or not, inspires those around him into becoming the best they can be. If we accept this, though, then we must also accept that the Doctor is responsible for those people's actions. After all, he's the one who winds them up and points them at his problems without offering so much as a suggestion of a non-violent – or indeed, in many cases, a non-fatal – solution to them.

And this would mean that Davros was right. But the alternative...?

The alternative is that the Doctor, for all his bravado, for all his boastfulness... rarely makes a difference at all.

*

If ever there was a time for the new-series Doctor to prove himself, to show once and for all that the terms "liberal" and "hero" aren't mutually exclusive, then *Journey's End* is it. Instead, with Davros' accusations ringing in his ears and the whole of reality dependent upon him, what does he do?

He yells at Davros: "Just stop!"

And that's it. That's his plan.

Thank goodness, then, for that handy, once-in-an-eternity, human / Time Lord metacrisis that comes along at just the right moment to save everyone's bacon. It's left to the Doctor-Donna to defuse the Daleks' reality bomb – and to the clone Doctor to deal with the Daleks, who, as he rightly says, are still an enormous threat.

As for the real Doctor... well, unfortunately, wringing his hands while other people save the day has become a habit for him. You'd think, though, that he might at least show a bit of gratitude toward those who acted in his stead. Not a bit of it.

The clone Doctor, you see, may have saved the universe, but he also committed genocide. Sort of. Never mind that he did it in order to prevent the genocide of every other race in the universe. "He's too dangerous," sniffs the Doctor, "to be left on his own." And that means summary exile to a parallel Earth, where the clone can be "made better" by... er, Rose.

That would be Rose Tyler, then. Who has also been guilty of a little genocide in her time. Against the same race, in fact. I wonder if, when the Daleks return as they inevitably will some day, the clone Doctor will be forgiven?

It is, of course, nice to see these issues raised in *Doctor Who*, to be able to examine the moral greys of the Doctor's chosen lifestyle. And, okay, we can forgive him if he doesn't have all the answers yet. As we have seen, though, his approach to similar situations in the new series has been wildly inconsistent. Not only that, but when the Doctor has made a difference, it has all too often been by sacrificing his principles – and when he has held on to his principles, it has all too often rendered him ineffectual.

Maybe that's the point. It really isn't easy being a liberal hero.

But if anyone should be able to show us how, then surely it's the Doctor.

Right now, I fear he's failing on both counts.

The Revolution Has Been Televised

by Robert Smith?
From Enlightenment #139, May 2007

There's a term in cultural studies called "homonormativity". It's a witty shorthand that encapsulates a complex phenomenon. It describes the ascendance of gay subculture into the mainstream: whereas being gay used to be something that had to be hidden away, with organised resistance conducted in secret, now being gay is almost mainstream. We have gay marriage, adoption, *Will and Grace,* Abercrombie and Fitch. In essence, the term describes how, by emerging into the light, gay subculture is becoming subsumed into mainstream consumer culture. Mainstream society couldn't eliminate gayness when it took it on, so instead it absorbed it into itself, thus neutralising the threat entirely. Homonormativity is about what happens when you take something rebellious and furious and radical and actually give it what it wants, thus creating a toothless white-picket-fenced niche, that fits into society perfectly well and won't frighten the horses. And as a result, gay resistance is largely rendered impotent, by virtue of achieving the majority of its goals.

Don't get me wrong: these goals are entirely laudable. Only the most heartless or ignorant would argue that giving people the choice to be with who they want and to embrace the kind of lifestyle they choose – even if, it seems, most people are embracing exactly the kind of thing their parents did (marriage, kids, house in the suburbs, overconsumptive shopping) – is wrong. It's just a shame that the once-furious gay movement is now so whitebread that it's now basically ineffectual. Perhaps this was inevitable: put the revolutionaries in power and they can't be revolutionary any more.

So what does this have to do with *Doctor Who*?

"If you'd told me five years ago that *Doctor Who* would be on telly / huge ratings / Christmas specials / critical and popular success / an actor the calibre of Christopher Eccleston / multiple spinoff series / arc words / new generation of fans / old monsters / Autons / Sarah Jane Smith / Daleks / Cybermen / K9 / Saturday night on the BBC / oh my god, my girlfriend likes it / squee!"

It's doing very well.

New *Doctor Who* is an astonishing success. For those of us who lived through the wilderness years, this is – quite literally – everything we dreamed of. Never, in a million years, did we expect to see what we're seeing now. Sure, we all hoped it might come back. But we assumed it'd go one of two ways: either a) it'd be just another mainstream show, designed with a mainstream audience in mind, that didn't understand the concept and was just cashing in on the brand (see also the Telemovie) or b) it'd be clever, fannish and wonderful, with an audience of about 16 people, who nevertheless loved it into the ground and took on all comers (see also The New Adventures). There's no way we expected the best of both worlds.

And that's what 2005 gave us. Eccleston's season pulled out all the stops: *Doctor Who* stripped down to its component elements (mysterious man in a blue box, time and space, Daleks, adventure), reinvented for the modern audience (Rose, the Powell estate, sexual tension), but with brilliant, subtle bits for fans to get their claws into (Bad Wolf, the Time War, the damaged Doctor). It had an actual arc (not just le Mal Loup, but the story of the Doctor's redemption and literal rebirth), developing characterisation (encapsulated in the fish and chips scene in *The Parting of the Ways*) and, most importantly, it packed an emotional punch. This was truly great television.

And subversive too. It takes on media, the Iraq war, gasbag politicians, reality TV and even, dangerously, the idea of the Doctor as terrorist. This got subdued in the directing, but watch the early scenes in *Rose* and tell me you don't get a shiver at the idea of this man who blows up buildings for his own agenda. This is television doing what television should, but so rarely does: challenging our assumptions, making us question what life is truly about and imploring us to take a stand against the mainstream and say no.

A lot can change in a year.

Look at the Christmas specials, then and now. Last year we had an almost Doctorless story, but one that's still playing with fire. The Doctor actually brings down the British government! This is astonishingly brave: like all genre entertainment, *Doctor Who* simply doesn't interact directly with the real world. Remember that episode of *The Dead Zone* called "The Hunt for Osama"? No? Well, it's no surprise, because the networks pulled it from the schedule at the time of the Iraq invasion, changed the title to "The Hunt" and deleted all references to bin Laden. Instead, the guy with the superpowers helps the army out for a bit, uses his superpowers to keep them out of a trap and then concludes that he isn't cut out for this sort of work. Basically, you can't have Superman trying to catch Osama, because then you're stuck with trying to figure out why he wouldn't.

The Christmas Invasion also has the mythic elements of the series coming to the fore, but not too grandly. The sound of the TARDIS drawing Jackie and Mickey out of their humdrum lives is good, the Doctor's awakening via the translation unit is excellent, but Harriet Jones going on TV to plead for the Doctor's help is heartbreakingly compelling. By this point, the Doctor is almost a force of nature, one whose power is virtually unlimited. He dispatches the Sycorax in a matter of minutes and duly calls the PM on humanity's monstrousness. In part, this is backed up by the weight of the historical allegory: Margaret Thatcher's troops sinking a fleeing battleship in the Falklands war already showed us that the monsters were ourselves, but it takes something as wide-reaching as television to make the lesson stick.

Fast-forward to *The Runaway Bride*, skipping over an entire season of mediocrity, where – with one exception – the series swapped its subversiveness for mainstream appeal, making the subtle gratuitous (Torchwood, the Doctor's "anger" at injustices, his relationship with Rose), the edginess safe (Lumic, the mortgage, the Olympic torch) and fundamentally misunderstanding what it was that made the series so powerful but throwing in references anyway (Cybermen, the TV Tower, the entirety of *School Reunion*). This Christmas, things look superficially similar: robot Santas, using the series' mythology to try and be epic ("Its name lives on"), an attempt at showing the darker side of the Doctor (calm amid the flames) and a life-affirming message ("Be magnificent"). Yet, somehow, it doesn't have nearly the same resonance.

For one thing, the life-affirming message undercuts everything the Eccleston season stood for. "Be magnificent" really means "try and make the best of things, but don't rock the boat". This isn't about fighting the system for what's right, it's about becoming a good citizen. A good consumer. The robot Santas are there for one reason only: because they were in it last time and that's what everyone expects. No, they weren't explained last time either, but at least then they were mysterious, rather than gratuitous.

The Doctor's darkness doesn't go nearly far enough: how much better would it have been to have Donna utterly horrified by what she saw, unable to look this monster in the eye and bringing the sheer horror of what it means to be the Doctor home to us? You can understand why they might not do that in a fluffy episode of televised Christmas cheer... but that's exactly the problem. *Doctor Who* has become safe.

Then there's the mythology. Dealing with the aftereffects of Rose's departure is actually better than the long-awaited uttering of the word "Gallifrey", because at least that makes sense within the context. The Doctor should be dealing with the ramifications of losing her, so this plays out reasonably well. The word "Gallifrey" means nothing to the non-fan... except that we're all fans now, aren't we? So even though whole generations never heard the word on TV before, by now they know enough about *Doctor Who* to be at least passingly familiar with his backstory. It's not that the barbarians are at the gates; rather the gates are at the barbarians.

When the newly regenerated tenth Doctor brings down the British government with six words, it's a shockingly powerful mission statement and an unheard-of intersection between *Doctor Who* and real-world politics. When the newly Rose-less tenth Doctor brings down the Empress with one word, it's a gimmick. It shows that we're now expected to take the Doctor on faith. He's proved himself, so why shouldn't we?

And this is exactly the issue: *Doctor Who*'s return did everything it set out to do and it did it all within the first nine months. It met all our expectations and blew them out of the water. It was loud and brave and angry and it overthrew every assumption we thought we had about the show itself, about television today and about the intersection of fandom and the mainstream. The problem is, it had to live with the aftermath and that's not as simple as it looks. Little wonder the 2006 season didn't seem to know where it was going. Consider the issues it tries to address: the demands of the healthcare system, watching loved ones grow old and die, mobile phones as a means of pacifying the population, television as a destroyer of original thought, faith vs science, protecting our borders from the alien. These are great issues, worthy of allegorical exploration, but there's only one that isn't approached half-heartedly and that's the second. Mainly because they flip-flop the theme across otherwise disconnected episodes. The only story that's actually furious and kicking is the glorious *Love & Monsters*, which is loud and angry and powerful and caused apoplexy in about half of fandom. Thank goodness.

So, is it too late for the series to regain its edge? I have no idea, but I'm holding out a glimmer of hope that there's subversive life in the old show yet. For one thing, the 2007 season has to introduce a new companion and it has to do it in a way that doesn't repeat what happened with Rose. I think the producers know this, so I'm looking forward to seeing how they rise to the challenge, because it isn't an easy one. Having Tennant be the experienced one and the companion a novice might be a better arrangement than the setup of the 2006 season. But, fundamentally, what the next season needs to do is to strike out on its own. It needs its own defining monster, it needs to not rest on its laurels and, crucially, it needs to be about something.

Whichever way it goes, I'll definitely be watching. It's not that *Doctor Who* is bad; indeed, part of the problem is that it isn't. It's playing it straight and narrow and not taking risks, so naturally it's mostly successful. Like putting all your investments in a huge and stately bank, rather than risking it all on a hunch, the returns are pretty much what you'd expect: steady and profitable, but there's no roller coaster of excitement from the risk that might fail or the windfall from a gamble that paid off, against all odds.

This is what *Doctor Who* has become: a mainstream success, with scenes where children in the back of cars cheer the Doctor's success, while their parents are comically ignorant. It's a show just like any other. A very good show, unquestionably, but not the show we were watching just two years back, let alone the angry voice in the wilderness that we fought for with every fibre of our being, back in the nineties. The revolution has already been televised.

And you know the worst part? I quite liked *The Runaway Bride*. It's witty and moves at a fair clip, with some decent moments and a reasonable sense of internal logic. It's a fairly good episode of a fairly good TV show. Expect a lot more like it, because our dreams and nightmares have come true simultaneously. We've reached Whomonormativity.

The Salt and the Sweet

by Kate Orman

If you haven't experienced the craving to see yourself reflected on the TV screen, it can be hard to describe, but I suspect most of us have felt it at least a little. Thanks to lazy writers and nervous sponsors, TV has a long, bad history of mostly leaving out great chunks of the watching audience.

TV is, in the words of researcher Sarita Malik, "the primary site where the nation is imagined and imagines itself". The shows, the characters, the settings are shared by millions of people, creating a common experience, a picture of what the world is like. Where that picture is distorted, a powerful message is sent to thousands or millions of viewers: *you don't exist*, or *you don't matter*, or *you're a freak*.

Even if you're white, straight, middle-class and male, like most characters on television, you can still feel left out of the picture. Perhaps the new *Doctor Who* has nodded to you – if you're a redhead, or tubby, or geeky, or wear glasses, or have a Northern accent. If those moments have meant something to you, then you have a glimmer of the craving I'm describing.

Seeing yourself reflected in the distorting mirror of stereotypes is no cure for the craving; more like salt water when you're already parched with thirst. Even when TV began to include more kinds of people in bigger roles, at first it was mostly as clichés, or as some kind of problem or issue.

Despite many advances, TV is still waking up from its history of excluding, marginalising and misrepresenting large parts of the viewing public. How much is *Doctor Who* contributing to the wake-up call? How well is it quenching that powerful thirst everyone has – to see ourselves clearly reflected?

*

People aren't numbers, but numbers are easy, so let's start with those. At the last census in 2001, Britain was about 7.9% non-white. 4% of Britons were desi (ie of Indian, Pakistani, or other south Asian ancestry) and 2% were black. In the new *Who* (up to and including *The Next Doctor*), 18.5% of the supporting cast is non-white: 3% are desi, 1.5% are Asian and 14% are black. See online appendix, available at:
http://seeingred.livejournal.com/42748.html

The show includes a larger proportion of non-white characters than the population of Britain contains non-white people. That's a good start, but right away it raises some questions. If the aim is to roughly mirror the racial makeup of the UK, why are the vast majority of non-white characters black, rather than desi? Is this in an attempt to appeal to overseas audiences, particularly in the US? Perhaps, but if so, wouldn't there be more east Asian characters? (Britain's population is less than 1% Asian, compared to about 5% for the US.) Is there an unconscious assumption that "not white" equals "black", a sort of lumping together of everyone who isn't white? (This could be partly the influence of shows imported from the US, which tend to over-represent whites and blacks while under-representing other minorities, such as Latinos / Latinas and Native Americans.)

What's more, the racial diversity of Britain varies depending on where you are. For example, two in five Britons in London identify themselves as other than "White British". To a Londoner, then, the show must look on average about half as diverse as what they see out their window every day.

It gets even more complicated when we look at the setting of individual stories. Most shows don't visit a different setting almost every week. It's not unreasonable to have a mostly white cast in certain settings: World War II London, Victorian Scotland, or an English mansion in the twenties (or deep in rural Wales). But, equally, the show could visit times and places which dictate a mostly non-white cast without straying from settings which the audience will find familiar. Perhaps a trip to Darjeeling during the Raj, or to Liverpool's nineteenth century Chinatown, or to Montmartre in the 1920s.

Interestingly, in the original series of *Doctor Who*, the past is more white and the future is less white. In *Inferno*, shown in 1970 but set in a near future, black male and female scientists can be seen in the background of the Inferno Project, but are conspicuously absent from its fascist alternative universe counterpart. The futures of *The Mutants*, *The Robots of Death*, and *Resurrection of the Daleks* all include non-white characters (albeit minor or stereotyped ones) where present-day settings mostly exclude them. This might reflect the influence of *Star Trek*, but I think it also suggests a positive assumption that, far from the "rivers of blood" predicted by politicians such as Enoch Powell, racial integration was natural and inevitable. (In *Torchwood*'s *To The Last Man*, we and Gwen know she has returned from a vision of the past when she sees a black foreman.)

But of course, the past isn't all white, and the new show has made a point of the presence of black men and women in historical Britain and Europe, in *The Shakespeare Code* (which explicitly addresses it), *The Girl in the Fireplace* and *The Next Doctor*. (Similar casting in the *Casanova* mini-series suggests this might in fact be a Russell T Davies-ism.) On the other hand, the effortless racial harmony of Hooverville in *Daleks in Manhattan* is unconvincing: rather than easing racial tensions, the Great Depression exacerbated them, as resentful whites found themselves competing with non-whites for scarce jobs.

There are fascinating historical people of colour whose lives would provide fantastic and fresh material for stories: determined nurse Mary Seacole's hotel for British soldiers in the Crimea, Dean Mahomed's baths and coffee house in eighteenth century London, Song Ling Whang's extraordinary walk from China to Britain in the early twentieth century. I'd love to see the show do much more in this area; to quote Lenny Henry, this would be treating diversity "as an asset, not a problem".

*

Everyone knows the cliché of horror and action movies in which the token black guy is the first to die. *Doctor Who* has always had a high body count; in the new show, 38% of all supporting characters die. Are characters of colour more likely to perish? This question, at least, is simple to answer: no. The white mortality rate is 37%, the non-white rate is 43%; the difference between these numbers is too small to have any statistical significance. See online appendix, available at:
http://seeingred.livejournal.com/42748.html

If we consider just black male characters, though, the mortality rate looks worse: it's 50%. However, there's a mathematical problem. With only 28 black male characters in total, the sample size is too small to tell us whether that's actually a meaningful difference or a blip, because even a few more characters can easily send the numbers up and down. (Add Lou and Barclay from *Planet of the Dead*, and it's already dropped to 47%.) So let's turn now from the numbers to more complicated questions.

*

In *School Reunion*, Mickey Smith is a bit of a fool, and is picked on by the Doctor, but proves himself to be brave and resourceful. If we compare him to the other characters in the story, we see this is true for all of them: Rose and Sarah indulge in silly jealousy over the Doctor, but soon laugh it away, at his expense; similarly, Mickey gets to tease both the Doctor and Rose. Even Kenny the feckless schoolboy, sneered at by the Doctor (in a scene cut for time), ends up being instrumental in saving the day. So, looked at in this internal way, Mickey is treated about the same as any other character; and he fits the pattern seen throughout the show, of ordinary people inspired to heroism by their encounters with the Doctor's world.

But consider this: not all audience members will look at the episode in this *intratextual* way; rather, they'll look at the portrayal of Mickey in an *intertextual* way, by comparing him with characters in other SF shows, as well as other genres of TV, plus movies, comic books and so on. For example, some black viewers might see him as just the latest in a long parade of black male sidekicks there to be the butt of jokes.

That Mickey is the first black regular TV character in the long history of *Doctor Who* can only add to that disappointment. The smaller the pool of characters, the more significant each one of them becomes. This is partly why, I think, fans sometimes overestimate the mortality rate of non-white characters: those characters are fewer, therefore more conspicuous, therefore those characters – and their fates – tend to stick in the mind. It's the same quirk of psychology that makes people greatly overestimate the percentage of people of colour in their country's population. Although an online friend, asim, pointed out another possible explanation: "The two most critical *Doctor Who* characters of colour end up in some ways as tag-alongs to, well, Rose's story. And that frustration is part of why we look critically upon other portrayals of characters of colour in the show. A show that treats main characters of colour in unhealthy ways is, one must acknowledge, likely to treat secondary characters of colour in unhealthy ways, as well."

The scripts for the new *Doctor Who* tend not to specify the race or ethnicity of supporting characters. The *Rose* script makes no mention of Mickey's race, and Noel Clarke won the part by auditioning. Similarly, Freema Agyeman was cast because, as casting director Andy Pryor told *Doctor Who Magazine,* "We'd had our eye on Freema ever since she auditioned for the part of Sally in *The Christmas Invasion,* and [RTD] was watching the rushes [for *Army of Ghosts*], thought she was great, and we thought that we could make this work." Executive producer Piers Wenger told the *Daily Telegraph* that Matt Smith was only one of about a dozen actors who auditioned as the eleventh Doctor: "Some of them black. There was never any resistance to the idea of a black Doctor."

Of course, having cast an actor of colour, the showmakers can and should return to the script to address any unintentional implications. Sometimes, though, this might damage the story: think of *Midnight* without the death of the Hostess, the story's one redeeming human act. In such cases, should they cast a white actor instead? I think the answer is probably no; it would be better to cast people of colour in as wide a variety of roles as possible, without squeamishness. Perhaps other ways can be found to compensate for any unintentional messages; for example, casting a second black actress whose character does survive, as Dee Dee does in *Midnight.*

On the other hand, there's always the danger of overcompensation. Unlike every other companion of the new series, Martha Jones didn't have to find her inner hero, but arrived ready-made as one in *Smith and Jones*: intelligent, resourceful, self-reliant and resilient, all but taking their arrival on the moon in her stride. It's a positive portrayal, certainly, but it left little room for the character to develop – and made it seem a bit odd that the Doctor didn't fall for such a flawless woman.

Despite disappointments for some viewers, Martha and Mickey are major black characters in a leading TV show, both of whom survive and succeed. In 2007, Freeman Agyeman told *The Toronto Star*: "I get letters from black children, saying, 'I really want to be like you.' That is quite something. I mean, it's nice to have a role model that all children can look up to, that non-white children can also identify with." Again, in my opinion, it's much better for the show to try and not completely succeed than it would be to not try at all.

*

Talking about "people of colour" or "non-white characters" carries the danger of forgetting the enormous diversity of the larger part of the human race: of blurring together the experiences of different ethnic groups in different times and places. Racism manifests itself in similar ways in different times and places, but different countries still have different histories – and these cultural differences can create confused messages.

Consider the disparate experiences of the UK and the US. Slaves had been restricted to British colonies (any slave brought to England was automatically freed), and their emancipation predated that of US slaves by 25 years. Large-scale immigration to Britain from Africa, the Caribbean and south Asia only began after World War II. So Britain's non-white population is smaller and more recent as well as having a different makeup.

Early British TV either cast people of colour in very small roles (including American maids, of which more later), even resorting to makeup and prosthetics to place white actors in major roles. Later, non-white actors were most likely to appear in stereotypical roles (criminals, nurses, mechanics, etc) and / or in dramas about the "issue" of race. This is similar to what happened in US television, but took place more recently and more quickly. In the late eighties and early nineties, British TV finally began to reflect the diversity of the modern UK.

As a very long-running series, *Doctor Who* is a record of these changes. When it comes to race, the original show's lowest moment is paradoxically one of its most popular stories, *The Talons of Weng-Chiang* (1977), a checklist of pulp clichés: fanatical tong members, poison, opium, imperiled white women, etc. (Sadly, three decades later, *Turn Left* fell into similar stereotyping, with its brief visit to an exotic "Chino-planet" complete with cunning "dragon lady".) On the whole, though, the original *Doctor Who* was more likely to simply leave out non-white characters altogether. Numerous stories from the sixties to the eighties had all-white casts, although the last couple of seasons reflect how UK television was changing. The far more diverse casting of the new show reflects the continuing effort of people of colour to change the face of British television. Of which, more in a moment.

Seeing Martha and her mother and sister obliged to dress as maids was painful to some African American women, a reminder of a long history of constricted roles for black women , both on TV and in real life. (Famously, a young Whoopi Goldberg exclaimed of *Star Trek*'s Lieutenant Uhura: "I just saw a black woman on television; and she ain't no maid!") The stereotype is so well known in the States that black maids have largely vanished from television. But in the UK, the image of black-woman-as-domestic doesn't have quite the same long and painful history. I think this explains why the showmakers could include that image without realising the reaction it might receive across the pond. (Perhaps another example is Martha's mum, Francine Jones; to British viewers, she may only look like another of the show's cranky "mothers-in-law", but for US viewers she may invoke the stereotype of an aggressive, emasculating black woman.)

Also vulnerable to miscommunication is New *Who*'s inclusion of numerous interracial couples, beginning with Rose and Mickey. In the UK, this reflects everyday experience: in 1997, half of black men in a relationship had a white partner, as did a third of black women. This is unsurprising when we recall the very small percentage of black Britons. Given the long history of interracial romance being forbidden on American screens (the UK, too, has been timid about it), you might imagine this would be received by American viewers as an unqualified plus. However, interracial dating and marriage is a controversial topic for African Americans. In the 1990 US census, only 8% of black husbands and 4% of black wives between 25 and 34 years of age had white spouses. Those percentages have been increasing for decades; some African Americans welcome this trend, while some decry it as disloyal, and implying that black people aren't good enough to marry, particularly black women. (This implication also comes through in the media: Hollywood's tendency to pair both black and white leading men with white or Latina love interests, the near-absence of black women from US bridal magazines, and so on.) So you can understand why this was a sore point for some when it came to Martha's relationship with the Doctor, which was defined by another RTD-ism: unrequited love.

Given this context, the show's interracial couples may look very different from a US perspective. Persistently pairing non-white with white characters may suggest that white people are particularly desirable, and that a black man or woman's great ambition is to have a white partner. Francine Jones losing her man to a young blonde woman may have unpleasant connotations for an African American woman watching the show, although this may be ameliorated somewhat by the couple's apparent reunion. Similarly, perhaps the fact that it's Mickey who dumps Rose (in *Boom Town*; he sees her searching for him and walks away) and Martha who dumps the Doctor, helps address the implications of their storylines by making them the ones who choose.

*

Returning to researcher Sarita Malik: in 2008, she remarked in her *Guardian* blog that focusing on proportional representation in BBC shows was a distraction from the "real issues": the people behind the scenes. Criticised in 2007 by writer Jimmy McGovern for a lack of diversity *behind* the camera ("You do see lots of black faces in the BBC. But you see them in the canteen. You do not see them in positions of power."), the Beeb pointed irrelevantly to the diversity *in front of* the camera – including Freema Agyeman in *Doctor Who*.

Malik joined comedian Lenny Henry and BBC director Samir Shah in criticising the lack of non-white Britons behind the scenes at the Beeb, especially in influential or powerful positions. (Despite a target of 7%, only 4.3% of BBC management in 2008 were members of ethnic minorities.) Shah, a member of the BBC's board of directors, says that the Corporation has sometimes overcompensated with plentiful but unrealistic characters of colour: "The plain fact is that this tick-box approach to equal opportunities has led to an inauthentic representation of who we are: a world of deracinated coloured people flickering across our screens – to the irritation of many viewers and the embarrassment of the very people such actions are meant to appease."

What affects the BBC as a whole will of course affect *Doctor Who*. It's hard to be certain, but from what we've seen from behind the scenes, the makers of the show are almost entirely white. If so, then they're less diverse than their audience, whether in the UK or around the world. And that runs the risk of the showrunners missing nuances and implications that audiences of colour will notice.

*

These are the thoughts of a white, middle-class Australian woman. I mention this, reader, because what you think of how the new show handles race depends profoundly on who you are and where you are. Maybe, like me, you can't feel in your gut the same delight or disappointment felt by fans from different background. But maybe, like me, you can make the imaginative leap needed to see why it's so important, to so many thousands of thirsty viewers, to see themselves clearly reflected by the TV screen. Not just one of Britain's leading shows, but in their favourite show.

Who Would Valiant Be

by Wood Ingham

From Movement #126, Summer 2007

Like many, I remain an avid follower of *Doctor Who*. Now, the good Doctor is no stranger to religious themes, but this year they came up quite a bit. And they were... muddled. Confusing.

Take *Gridlock*, the third episode. So you have these people trapped beneath the beautiful city of New New York, they're on the motorway, and they're going round and round and round in this eternal traffic jam, hoping that one day they'll find the exit, except there isn't one. The police can be called, but never answer. The people sing hymns (sentimental favourite "The Old Rugged Cross") and live for the hope that the authorities above are looking out for them. The Doctor realises that they aren't. There's just the motorway. Tell me that isn't a metaphor for the apparent pointlessness of religion.

Except, it turns out that, up above, those people are being watched by the "textbook enigmatic" Face of Boe, a big inscrutable, er, face with awesome powers, a wholly benevolent attitude and billions of years of unexplored backstory. The Face of Boe, at the end, sacrifices himself, Christ-like, to give the people access to the wonderful world of promise above.

Only, the Face of Boe doesn't remotely resemble the benevolent overseeing force the people believe in, because the authorities everyone thinks are there are in fact all dead. Then there's that whole issue of the Face of Boe turning out to be pansexual action man Captain Jack in a few million years' time. I don't know what they were thinking there.

In every episode, the word "valiant" came up, which is one of those words that's rare enough that you prick up your ears when you hear it. By the episode *Human Nature*, boys in a provincial public school are heard to sing Bunyan's Pilgrim hymn: "He who would valiant be / 'Gainst all disaster / Let him in constancy / Follow the Master". A mate of mine once confided in me that when they sang that hymn in primary school (this would have been about 25 years ago now) he always used to substitute the word "Doctor" for "Master". Aww, bless.

Anyway, maybe that's why, when the Doctor's arch-enemy appeared and made his nasty, world-conquering HQ on a clone of Captain Scarlet's Cloudbase called the *Valiant*, I wasn't surprised. It was just a play on words. Wasn't it?

The Master's plans for world conquest depended on him stealing the future human race from Heaven (namely, this perfect planet at the end of time to which they retreated) and getting them to slaughter their ancestors in a big, messy paradox. You see, the promise of the new world at the end of everything was a lie: Heaven was Hell, and the human race went nuts and became disembodied heads floating in vicious little ball-shaped things. Oooh-kay. Subversion of the idea of an afterlife. Got you. Subverted stuff I can deal with.

So they help the Master take over, along with this big, vaguely hypnotic, psychic mobile phone network thing, scorching the Earth and reducing the Doctor to a wizened, helpless creature. But Martha, the Doctor's lovelorn companion, walks the Earth as a travelling evangelist, spreading the word of the Doctor and getting everyone to pray for him to save them at the precise moment of evil's victory. And lo, the Doctor is resurrected in power and glory, the Master is defeated, and the Doctor comes to him and says "I forgive you."

And if that isn't a religious image, I don't know what is.

Except, it's not really any more than that. It's just an image. Divorced from its original meaning, the picture of the Christ-Doctor doesn't actually make a lot of sense. He forgives the Master, but he still intends to imprison him. His answer to prayer is a wish-fulfillment. His salvation still involves blowing stuff up.

It makes my head hurt.

Maybe I shouldn't think about it so much.

Neo Who Con

by Ari Lipsey

In an interview for *The Sunday Times, Doctor Who* showrunner Russell T Davies mused that he'd love to do a "crossover" with *Doctor Who* and *Star Trek*. "Landing the TARDIS on board the Enterprise would have been magnificent." I hope the comment was a joke the reporter didn't quite get, because if the TARDIS did materialise in the middle of the Federation's galactic 'hood, Captain Picard might cast our beloved Doctor as a villain. *Star Trek,* like *Doctor Who,* has an ethos and a moral universe where tragic consequences await those who break the rules. In *Star Trek,* it's best to follow the Prime Directive: don't get involved in the internal affairs of other worlds.

At times, a character's morals or desires come into conflict with this principle, and what follows is usually disastrous. There's the episode *The Outcast,* where Commander Riker, Picard's second-in-command, falls in love with an alien from a strictly androgynous species who has the misfortune to exhibit "heterosexual tendencies". The allusions to the gay movement abound, Riker implants some rebellious thoughts in her head that there's nothing wrong with the way she is, and that it's her society that is ignorant and parochial. The tale ends with the pitiable alien refusing to leave with the planet with Riker, because she's undergone some type of therapy, and feels she has been "cured" from her sexual "illness". One assumes the story isn't meant as a celebration of attempts to "cure homosexuality", but rather illustrating our society's treatment of homosexuals, and the unfair stigma attached to a biological orientation. But the ending of *The Outcast* reaffirms the Trek ethos: sure, it's unfortunate that this woman isn't accepted within her society, but Riker's attempts at imposing Federation (or the viewers') morals and opinions onto that society leads to a sad conclusion.

Now, cast a similar set of circumstances in the *Doctor Who* universe. First, the androgynous society would be ruled by a family of giant, slimy earthworms. But, monsters aside, the ending would have changed the entire society, ushering in a new era where everyone's sexual preferences were celebrated. *Doctor Who*, with rare exceptions, makes judgements on entire societies and has its alien antagonist become instrumental in changing them. *Star Trek*, particularly in its post-original-series form, is openly contemptible of such notions.

The classic-series story that establishes the ethos of *Doctor Who* is *The Daleks*. Here we have two alien races at war on an alien planet, one clearly good and one clearly evil. The Daleks have yet to evolve into the galactic-faring, time-travelling race we've come to anticipate season finale appearances over, but are just a bunch of angry fascists who live in a domed city. And yet, the Doctor and his companions get involved and fight for one side in what is, essentially, a civil war. The first season is fascinating because the show has still not quite developed the underpinnings of its moral universe: it's reluctant to make a judgement on human sacrifice in *The Aztecs*, and flat out refuses to do so with the caste system of the Sensorites. But *The Sensorites* is an aberration, not a template, for the 25 seasons that followed, while *The Aztecs* is a "historical", a subgenre later abandoned by the production team. Two stories after the last historical (*The Highlanders*), in *The Moonbase*, the Doctor takes a moment to impart to his companion Polly the nature of the universe:

"There are some corners of the universe that have bred the most terrible things. Things which act against everything we believe in. They must be fought..."

As Patrick Troughton's tenure ends, the Doctor returns to his home planet and is put on trial for breaking the Time Lords' version of *Star Trek*'s Prime Directive. Earlier in the story, he explained to his companions his original motives for leaving: he was bored with the uneventful lifestyle. However, he defends his decision to the Time Lords by citing the Cybermen, the Daleks and the Quarks: if someone doesn't get involved, the villains have their way with the universe. The Time Lords aren't wrong because they're boring, but because they're neutral.

But surely there are times when *Star Trek*'s Federation "gets involved"? Don't they have their enemies, like the Romulans, the Dominion and the Borg? They do, but in *Trek*, the evil races must interfere or attack the Federation. The Borg are evil because of what they do in *Star Trek*; namely, assimilate other cultures into their collective by force. But if the Borg popped into the *Doctor Who* universe, they would still be an enemy of the Doctor even if they only assimilated people from their home planet. It would be their collectivism, not their expansionism, at issue.

To say that *Doctor Who* has something in common with the politics of Che Guevara, who, though an Argentinean, fought for the Cuban, Congolese and Bolivian resistance movements, and believed interference was a moral duty, is perhaps not particularly unsettling to fans. It's been said by many a fan with a political slant that *Doctor Who* fans tend to lean leftward, and would no doubt have some sympathies for Guevara's politics, though perhaps not his more bloodier methods. But Guevara's lasting impression on our culture is as a fashion symbol and, in today's geopolitical climate, the political ideology that most closely aligns with the universe of *Doctor Who* is one which most fans would find unpalatable: the neo-Conservative movement. They agree with the second Doctor's speech, that great power (e.g. America) must be used to fight against dictators. And yet, you're unlikely to find much sympathy from *Doctor Who* fans for the like of Paul Wolfowitz, Irving Crystal or John Bolton.

For many of us, our politics are integral to who we are and we assume that our enjoyment of this programme is naturally complementary, even though our politics tended to evolve after we acquired a fondness for the programme. In an average Year 3 classroom in 1975, were there more *Doctor Who* fans or organised labour sympathisers? Most of us fell in love with *Doctor Who* not because of the allegory underlying episodes like *The Sun Makers* but because episodes like *The Sun Makers* had monsters, futuristic technology and didn't take place within the confines of contemporary Earth. We'd rather travel from spaceship to alien planet than from home to school. Nevertheless, there's a continuous attempt to shoehorn beliefs that fans acquire later in life, such as pacifism or realism, into the fabric of the show. And that's a shame, because politics should be irrelevant to enjoyment. It would be absurd to suggest that a reader could like the *Lord of the Rings* series, or the Narnia chronicles, but certainly not both, on account that the former was written as critical response to the latter. Likewise, you can be a fan of *Star Trek* and *Doctor Who* regardless of the fact that their politics are diametrically opposed. But *Doctor Who* is clear about its politics throughout its tenure. Like the theories of the neo-Conservatives, it believes that interference is a moral obligation.

Enjoying the programme is possible without subscribing to its politics, but does the same hold true if you're writing for it? One writer who's clearly not enthralled with the Bush cadre is none other than Mr Davies himself. He has Prime Minister Harriet Jones make a crack about the

American President "starting another war", and goes all out in *The Sound of Drums* by presenting a brash and arrogant American President. So far, so good. It's all in good fun, and these cracks don't necessarily affect the narrative. I personally think that Davies is responsible for the best episode of each of the seasons he has produced, but his major missteps, particularly in the 2005 season, tend to come about when he tries to work against the programme's ethos.

The 2005 season has two *deus ex machina* endings. The first is in *Boom Town*, where the Doctor attempts to have compassion for a Slitheen, only to find that it betrays him, takes his companions hostage and almost destroys Cardiff. There was so much potential for dramatic exploration here, the Doctor having to come to terms with the fact that evil will use his sympathies to its advantage. The Doctor refuses to become a "killer", so he relies on what can only be described as a "Care Bear stare" coming out of the TARDIS to resolve the episode.

The second such ending happens during *The Parting of the Ways*, when the Doctor is given a similar choice: kill off the Daleks to save the universe, but at the expense of killing the innocents on the Earth. The setup itself is fascinating for *Doctor Who*. The Doctor is used to having to kill the Daleks, and innocents always die in the process, but this time he'll be killing faceless innocents to save other faceless innocents. It's an unfair choice, but the Doctor relates the consequences if he doesn't do it: a Dalek-run universe. Sadly, the resolution comes about by turning Rose into a god. This resolution works slightly better than the one in *Boom Town*. The Doctor makes a selfish choice to save Rose, but Rose has realised that "there is another way of living", and fights her way back to the battlefield.

Some have argued that the Doctor is making these selfish decisions because of the trauma of the Time War (though there's no proof of that in Davies' narrative), and the Doctor not wanting to be a killer is set up earlier in the season in *Dalek*, where the Doctor is seen brandishing a blockbuster-sized gun and Rose telling him he's become as bad as the Dalek he's fighting. But the difference in *Dalek* is that the Dalek itself has changed. The Daleks of *The Parting of the Ways* haven't. Rose defeats them by sheer chance, not premeditated cunning. She didn't plan on "staring into the time vortex" to become all-powerful. *Doctor Who* is a universe of mighty villains, and it's usually the Doctor who has to make the decisions that lead to the resolution, even if he uses an assailant. Rose is simply not strong enough to defeat the entire Dalek fleet without some TARDIS magic, and the TARDIS magic is only necessary because the Doctor refuses to live by the ethics he outlines at the end of *The War Games*.

When *deus ex machina* is deployed because the writer wants a happy ending that the confines of the narrative have made impossible, the results are always unsatisfying. When the original series made use of the device, it was usually in service to some of the show's more sombre endings. In *The War Games*, the Time Lords arrive and sort out a mess that even the Doctor can't fix, but the Doctor is the one who contacted them for help, and not without much hesitancy. He has to give up his freedom to do the right thing. It's used again in *Mindwarp*. The Time Lords pull the Doctor out of the events because they believe his interference has lead to irreversible evil. He claims that had they not, he would have been able to save the day. This time, the choice is not his to make, and the resolution sees his companion seemingly killed. The one redeeming feature to the conclusion of *The Parting of the Ways* is the part we almost didn't get: the ninth Doctor's regeneration. This is the one price that is to be paid, but it too comes out of nowhere (as it inevitably had to, given the uncertainty of Christopher Eccleston's return). And its celebratory tone ("You were fantastic and... so was I") makes it difficult to jive with the context of the narrative.

It's worth comparing the events of *The Parting of the Ways* with the "do I have the right" speech in *Genesis of the Daleks*, where the Doctor has a similar choice and even muses whether this act of genocide will turn him into what he wishes to destroy. And, as in *The Parting of the Ways*, he's stopped from having to make a decision by the appearance of another character. However, in *Genesis*, the Doctor witnesses the consequences of his decision and, at the moment of safety, chooses to go back to the front lines to reverse his mistake. In the conclusion to *Genesis*, the Doctor claims that the mission was not a failure because "out of their evil, must come something good". The good he's referring to is those who are brave enough to fight and, to use a strong word, kill them. In contrast, in *The Parting of the Ways*, the Doctor proudly boasts to preferring cowardice over murder, unleashing a galactic suicide. Davies discusses the links between *Genesis of the Daleks* and his mythology in an episode of *Doctor Who Confidential*. As he saw it, the Time Lords started the Time War with the events of *Genesis*. Is that how it's supposed to be interpreted? Or is it, as the Time Lord at the beginning of the episode implies, that the very nature of the Daleks necessitates war?

But a Doctor unable to make hard choices would find it difficult to get top-billing in the large epics Davies is partial to. In *Doomsday*, there's a huge army of Cybermen and later an army of Daleks that the Doctor has to defeat, but it comes at a cost of losing his friends. But he does it. How much less dramatic would it have been if Mickey had suddenly obtained handy abilities at the last minute, or Rose achieved powers to slip through the void and reunite with the Doctor? He sacrifices K9 in *School Reunion* to stop the Krillitanes. *The Family of Blood* has him taking on the eponymous family by giving up on a quiet life with love.

In *Doctor Who*, characters need to fight their tendencies to avoid conflict with antagonists. In *Star Trek*, the characters have to work against their intuitive morals to avoid catastrophe. You can judge for yourself which one of these more realistically depicts the human condition, or, for that matter, the position of the average politically minded *Doctor Who* fan on certain geopolitical issues of the day. Having both of these in the same narrative, however, would be a disastrous. In the *Sunday Times* interview, Davies lamented it could never be done, though he said the same thing about a multiple Doctor story and the Master popping up. One hopes, however, that the *Star Trek / Doctor Who* crossover remains safely in the realm of harmless fan-fiction. That doesn't preclude a tongue-and-cheek allusion that, like Davies' political cracks, doesn't adversely affect the narrative. How about this one? If the Time Lords ever return, the new leader of the High Council should be played by Patrick Stewart.

Queer As Who 2

by Scott Clarke
From Enlightenment #135, October 2006

"You're so gay."

—Rose to the Doctor, *Aliens of London*

Well, not really.

When *Doctor Who* first returned to our screens last year, there was considerable speculation on what Russell T Davies would bring to the reinvention and updating of the programme. Some feared that the creator of *Queer as Folk* and *Bob and Rose* (and author of the Virgin New Adventure *Damaged Goods*) would use the programme as a soap box for gay issues or that the TARDIS would be "pinked up".

After all, since 1989, there have been tremendous steps forward for GLBT people in many countries in terms of rights and visibility. In the US, Ellen came out; in the UK, *This Life* and Davies' own *Queer as Folk* pushed the boundaries of what is presentable on television in terms of queer reality. And in Canada, gay folk can now spend unbelievable amounts of money and express significant lapses of taste at the altar, just like straight people.

I suspected these fears would be unfounded, though. Like the current Archbishop of Canterbury, Rowan Williams (who was quite radical before he took office but has subsequently plotted a middle course for the Anglican Church worldwide), Davies has decided to take a more conciliatory and mainstream approach to the programme. He's made nods to the fans, but is very much aware that *Doctor Who* is for a new generation of mainstream British families.

Davies' approach to the programme is to treat sexuality as a non-issue. Everybody has it (including the Doctor, as we discover), but it's seen as more of a fluid continuum, as evidenced by the character of Captain Jack. Jack seems to show no discrimination with regards to sexual preference. Is he bisexual or omni-sexual or pan-sexual? He has certainly expressed no particular identity as bisexual.

Back in February of 2002, I wrote an article in *Enlightenment* entitled, "Queer as Who" (included in *Time, Unincorporated* Volume 2) that examined the attraction of *Doctor Who* for queer viewers. I speculated that the programme offered special resonance for queer viewers who might be feeling isolated and alone in a mainstream society that shunned and misunderstood them. With a central character who was himself a misfit in his own society, his adventures were set against a universe of colour, whimsy and camp. And the Doctor's sexuality was all but invisible, leaving plenty of space for speculation. Much has transpired since those days and I thought this would be an excellent opportunity to revisit the subject.

Overall, it's been my observation that *Doctor Who* has become less "gay" in a number of key respects.

Sure, things began much as they'd been, with a mysterious, enigmatic Time Lord who wasn't quite human, and a companion who very much wanted to escape her dreary existence. By the second episode, we even had the surgically challenged diva, Cassandra, dishing out zingers in a camp extravaganza. But as the relationship between Rose and the Doctor developed, a shift occurred, and their relationship was put squarely in the forefront.

Narratively speaking, this was good. It provided much more emotional weight than the previous version of the programme could ever muster. But with all gain, there is loss. There is less ambiguity in terms of the Doctor's sexual preferences, a distinct absence of camp, and in tying the narrative arc to Rose's family on Earth, the programme doesn't explore themes of isolation and escape as explicitly.

In the first 26 years of the programme, the absence of sexuality in the character of the Doctor (with the exception of Susan's presence or some harmless flirting with Cameca) left much more room for gay viewers to identify with him or at least created more imaginative space. The Doctor was a mystery, an outcast, forced to leave his home because he couldn't conform to a place with no space outside the norm. To his companions, he was somewhat aloof, even when he established strong bonds with them. Sure, there was the second Romana holding hands through Paris, but that's in the same story where the Doctor says, "You're a beautiful woman, probably." A gay viewer (particularly an adolescent) would pick up on that sense of being the outsider and holding back a part of yourself. We would identify with them.

Flash forward to 2005-2006 and the return of *Doctor Who* to our screens. Arguably, the relationship between the ninth Doctor and Rose is closer than any previous Doctor / companion and, although this in itself is not reinforcement of the Doctor's heterosexuality, by *The Doctor Dances* a clear subtext has emerged around the Doctor's sexuality. Dancing becomes a metaphor for sex, with the Doctor, Rose and Jack in a triangle of sorts. Of course, one could argue that the Doctor is quite open to Jack's flirtations, but this merely confirms that he's comfortable with his own sexual identity, not that he has designs on the flyboy.

In *Bad Wolf* and *Parting of the Ways*, it is quite clear that the Doctor feels a special affection for Lynda with a "y". Within the structure of the story, this is intended as a foil to Rose's own relationship with him, but it does, if only subtly, reinforce a sense of the Doctor's heterosexuality.

With the arrival of David Tennant's tenth Doctor, things become even less ambiguous, as the Doctor's relationships with Sarah Jane, Madame de Pompadour and, of course, Rose are explored in greater depth. I'll avoid more explanation at the risk of spoilers; suffice it to say, there is little doubt as to which side the Doctor butters his bread.

Then there's the camp factor, or rather the lack of it. There has been much discourse as to the actual meaning of camp, but I prefer to subscribe to Christopher Isherwood's take in his 1954 novel *The World in the Evening*, where he comments: "You can't camp about something you don't take seriously. You're not making fun of it; you're making fun *out* of it. You're expressing what's basically serious to you in terms of fun and artifice and elegance." What I hear in that statement is a sense of creativity born of an attempt to celebrate something we truly love. *Doctor Who* was used to being the bastard child of the BBC, constantly striving for approval from executives who just didn't take it seriously. There was never enough money to realise many of its lofty ambitions in terms of monsters or alien worlds. Thus the production team was left to "make fun *out* of it." The word camp originates from French slang "camper", meaning to pose in an exaggerated fashion. *Doctor Who* turned this approach into a strength, offering up Art Deco robots, meglomanical cacti and cybernetic pirates.

Doctor Who in the new millennium is no longer the outcast or the pariah. It's lavished with as much time and resources as the BBC can muster. A wheelie bin can now trap and consume a man in a – depending on your level of acceptance of CGI – fairly realistic fashion. The whimsy, fun and childlike exuberance are still there, but I would argue that the sense of camp has all but vanished. There are glimpses in the Slitheen and Victor Kennedy (in *Love & Monsters*), but they seem to be kept to a minimum.

And what of the central audience identification: the companion? From the moment she answers the Doctor's call to join her in the TARDIS, Rose chooses to escape a life that has left her wanting. And then Russell T Davies does something revolutionary in *Aliens of London*: he brings Rose back home to deal with the consequences of her departure. He breaks the "fourth wall" of escapism. Dramatically speaking, this is a stroke of brilliance and takes its lead from the direction of the Virgin novels of the nineties. Ultimately, all of us, whether straight or gay, have to live up to the consequences of our actions. It's a more conflicted escapism. Rose has one foot in the fantastical and the other in the mundane world of playing lotto and eating chips. Russell T Davies has tapped into something much more universal for the entire audience: the chasm that exists between who we are and who we'd like to be. It's no longer something aimed solely at the outsider, but at everyone.

It doesn't matter if you're Rose, Mickey, Jackie or even the perpetually resurrected Pete Tyler, we can all escape to a better life. The queer experience ceases to be gay or lesbian or bisexual or transgendered, but universal.

Which is not surprising when one considers Davies' work in *Bob and Rose* and *The Second Coming*. In the former, he deconstructs gay identity and gay prejudice to expose the fluidity of human relationships. One suspects that Davies sees such labels as "gay" or "bisexual" as merely training wheels to help us cope until we come to our senses about the expansiveness of love and sexual experience. Similarly, in *The Second Coming*, the writer challenges his audience to look beyond the particulars of religion to a broader sense of humanity.

The difficulty arises when one acknowledges that we do still live in a heterosexist world. Queer viewers do still look to see themselves mirrored in the stories of our society. It is gratifying to see Jack hit on a man and a woman in the same breath, but there is a part of me that feels somewhat sad and outside the circle to observe a Doctor who clearly shows more of a preference for the females he encounters than the males. Take Mickey "the idiot" for example, or Adam. Both could be aptly described as spare parts, and the Doctor doesn't truly give either of them much of a chance. Mickey in particular is just as changed as Rose by the experiences he undergoes, with a fraction of the nurturing that Rose receives from the Doctor. And did the Doctor even give a second thought to discover Jack's fate at the end of *The Parting of the Ways*?

In the end though, I can still celebrate Davies' prophetic nod to a future where the universality of human experience celebrates a myriad of sexual expression. Until then, I will still speculate as to what exactly the Sisters of Plentitude get up to in their off-duty time...

LOVE IN AN AGE OF SQUEE

A funny thing happened in 2005: new fans came to *Doctor Who*.

This is an unbelievably facile statement, and yet it changed everything. As a living show, suddenly its fandom was living once more, and these new fans brought with them all the interests and foci that came from other TV fandom fiefdoms.

It was a shock to the thoughtful, curious breed of fan who had stuck it out since the series went off the air in 1989. All these new people with their interests in shipping, in cosplay, in recaps, in saying "Squee!", in being interested in the in-universe developments onscreen rather than the behind-the-scenes machinations offscreen. Suddenly, there were teenage girls not only in our fandom, but dressing up in a feminised, renaissance reinterpretation of Colin Baker's costume, despite the fact that they hadn't been born when his episodes were being broadcast.

But the great thing about *Doctor Who* fandom is that it was already really diverse: a show that had lasted 26 years with seven lead actors and multiple changes in production and tone couldn't help but be. It's often been joked that if you put two *Doctor Who* fans in a room there would be three opinions. What's one more fan, then?

Over the past five years, old-time fans have, hopefully, caught some of the excitement of experiencing developments as they happen on screen and care about the character relationships a little more. New fans, hopefully, have learned form the old-timers a sense of *Doctor Who*'s history and a sense of perspective about the constant change in *Doctor Who* that, by its very nature, foil things like One True Pairings.

As new *Doctor Who* enters its sixth season, the "new" and "old" fan monikers are increasingly meaningless. We're all fans, with different interests and approaches, watching our favourite show. Squee!

He Said, She Said

by Deborah Stanish and Graeme Burk
From Enlightenment #144, March 2008

What happens when a veteran fan and new-school shipper try to bridge the gap across the fandom void? Let's find out in these letters between Enlightenment *editor Graeme Burk and columnist Deborah Stanish...*

Letter #1

Dear Deb,

Okay, this is something that's been puzzling me about "the new fandom" for a while. (Don't you find the term "new fandom" a bit specious? It sounds like "New Coke": same thing, just slightly and imperceptibly different but it draws proportionately more notice.) I guess I'll say it by way of a story...

I'm sitting watching a panel on *Torchwood* at a convention. Hey, I've done more embarrassing things in my life. Someone asks why Captain Jack is different in *Torchwood* than in *Doctor Who*. A woman of the shipping persuasion says: "Jack's had to live on Earth for 150 years waiting for the Doctor to arrive and he's incomplete without him."

I say: "It's because Chris Chibnall isn't a very good writer and somewhere along the way the production team wanted to have him emulate Angel in order to fit in with the darker tone. Furthermore, they were constrained by Jack's origins on a kid's show to have him be overtly sexual."

Do you see the difference here? One way looks at it in terms of story, in terms of character, in terms of ongoing arcs. The other looks at it in terms of the mechanics of making television.

In this respect, I am perhaps the most old-school of *Doctor Who* fans. From the day I bought my copy of *The Programme Guide* (an episode guide to a British series written by a Frenchman living in America), I've known *Doctor Who* to be a television programme, written by writers, directed by directors, script edited by script editors, performed by actors and publicised by producers. I loved finding out what happened behind the scenes and getting all the minutiae: like the fact that the first episode of *The Mind Robber* was written by a script editor when the previous story had to be scaled back an episode, or that Tom Baker insisted that Time Lord blood was blue, necessitating reshoots during the making of *State of Decay*. This is an inherent part of *Who*: no other television programme made today would have a 45-minute documentary about the making of the 45-minute episode just broadcast 45 minutes ago. And it's why I suspect so many fans of it went on to work in British television.

So when I get to the new fans (shippers? what do I call you?) talking about how Jack was deliberately angsty because he missed the Doctor... it strikes me in my set-in-my-ways, old-school male fandomness as, well, making excuses for bad scripting and characterisation. Do I think in a million years Russell Davies, Chris Chibnall or Richard Stokes had this in mind when they made *Torchwood* Series One? Hell, no.

There are times where I feel there's a different story being watched to the one I'm watching. Once, for my considerable sins, I sat on a panel on *Doctor Who* and sexuality. Now, I think there is a greater degree of romance in the series, including with the Doctor, and tons of jokes about Captain Jack's multiple orientations. On all that I can agree. But, sitting on this panel, you'd think the programme was being shown at 11pm. The opening remark was "Well, as we can see, *Doctor Who* is more adult than ever, so of course it's more sexual." To which I pointed out the programme was in fact, still being broadcast at before the watershed to a family audience. But the meta-narrative constructed from their reactions to what they watched holds more for them than what's actually broadcast on BBC1 at 7pm on a Saturday.

On the one hand, I love story, I love watching the way things unfold, I love the way characters interact with each other and the relationships they form. I could really go for most of what shipping stands for even if I can't stand the word "Squee!" But, for me, I think there's an emphasis on a meta-story; not necessarily a story that's on TV, but a story fans construct for themselves based on the nuances in the narrative – and even the large flaws within them. And maybe, in that respect, *Doctor Who* fandom is getting the type of modern-day television viewer that's been a part of any other genre television fandom.

But I can't help but greet it with mild suspicion. I think characters and relationships are important, but so is appreciating television drama for what it is. I guess my question is this: what am I missing? Or have I just become too damn curmudgeonly in my dotage?

Best,
Graeme

Letter #2

Dear Graeme,

As a proud member of the new fandom cabal, I can say without a doubt that we are specious. Obnoxious and loud, to boot. And you have my utmost apologies. As someone who has been with *Torchwood* since the bitter, grinding beginning, I find myself pounding my cane on the internet floor as the new "*Torchwood* via James Marsters" fans come barging in, flipping off continuity and declaring all that came before just doesn't matter. These people have not paid their dues. Where's the respect? But I'll lay my cane down for now and tackle your not-so-curmudgeonly questions.

First, we need to clarify terminology. We may all be "new fans," but only a subset of us are "shippers" and within the shipper group there are the One True Pairing or "OTP" crowd – those who have a favoured pairing – and the more general shippers: those who look for the emotional connection between any of the characters. The OTP crowd tends to be a bit militant. I can almost guarantee that the woman in your example is an OTP shipper.

However, the issue at hand, how to interpret what we see on screen and how much do you let the offscreen noise affect the story, isn't new. People have been arguing the Doylist (outside the universe of the story) versus Watsonian (inside the universe of the story) approach to interpreting text since, well, Sir Arthur Conan Doyle wrote Sherlock Holmes. While it isn't specific to *Doctor Who*, it may be more of a girl fan / boy fan issue. (You can stop rolling your eyes now!)

Again, this is a very broad brush but, in my very first column for *Enlightenment* (reprinted later in this chapter), I said that *Doctor Who* fans of the male persuasion seemed to look at their show much like a sporting event; all stats and players. It's like fantasy baseball. You guys love the minutiae of fandom. Don't get me wrong, girl fans love it as well, but it's the icing rather than the cake. And the girls love the cake. We even squee over it a little. In this case, the cake is the emotional story, whether it be romantic or not. We care just as much, if not more, about those connections as we do the gizmos, gadgets and aliens that help propel it forward.

The one thing that has helped make the new series so attractive to new viewers, particularly women, is the fact that New *Who* is serving up the cake on a silver platter. We know this, you know this and Russell T Davies is counting on this. He pushed the emotional storyline of the Doctor and Rose as far as he possibly could without breaking long-established tradition. He's said it was a love story and played it as such, knowing full well what the modern viewer would assume and how the fans would run with the concept. Shippers, in particular, are experts at constructing universes from a shared glance, a casual touch and a piece of gum; Davies gave us a lot of material to work with.

Does that make it fact? No. It doesn't even make it fanon, but it is part of the age-old practice of fans appropriating the material and making it their own. The source is the mothership and what is extrapolated from that is far more personal. I'll stop now before I start quoting Henry Jenkins.

This is a skill that serves us well when dealing with the *Torchwood* inconsistencies that you mention. Of course Chibnall is pants when it comes to characterization, and if you peer behind the curtain you can see that the Wizard was trying far too hard to make *Torchwood* cutting edge, but all that is incidental. The story is the thing and however that story came about is inconsequential to what we're watching on the screen. It has to stand on its own, or else you risk turning the show into a multimedia sort of event with the story being a by-product rather than the intent.

I really wouldn't call it making excuses, it's really more of a case of making lemonade out of lemons. How can we make sense of something that doesn't fit into the established universe that we've been given? Smoothing the rough edges of a bit of story or characterisation and making it work, also known as "fanwanking", is the modern television viewer's specialty. It's our version of retconning but, you know, with a bit more creativity.

I don't think one way is necessarily better than the other, but they are both certainly valid. There is nothing more frustrating than being told "you are doing it wrong". And whether the creators or other fans like it, once the text is released into the wild, it will become what the viewer makes of it. How long has Ray Bradbury been arguing that *Fahrenheit 451* isn't about censorship?

I don't think it's a matter of missing anything, I think it's a matter of how people choose to watch television. Genre television has always been far more personal. It engages fans in ways that sitcoms and procedural dramas fail to do. It's only reasonable to assume that it will be interpreted on a more personal basis as well.

Now, here's a question for you. Do you think that Russell T Davies has written himself into a corner by making the companion such a focal point of the story? And, further, by starting the new series off on a love story? He set Rose up to be the companion to beat, so does that mean that all future companions will be judged by that standard? It was certainly the case in the 2007 season and, in my opinion, made Martha's story weaker for it. Or am I just having a hard time taking off my shipper goggles?

Regards,
Deb

Letter #3

Dear Deb,

I feel like Vond-Ah in *Superman The Movie* when she tells Jor-El "I do not dispute your data, merely your conclusions". Mind you, Jor-El was right and the planet blew up about 20 minutes later...

I broadly agree with your assessment of the differences between guy and girl fans. But I don't think you do the male view complete justice. Yes, guys do have a way of reducing things to pure statistics and minutiae, but with baseball I think it's a manifestation of the enthusiasm of what happens on the field; with *Doctor Who,* I think there's a healthy appreciation of what's on screen in terms of relationships on the part of men. I cheered when Jack said "You too, huh?" to Martha in *The Sound of Drums* and cheered even louder (well, I did when I saw it on my own) when Martha said "This is me, moving on" an episode later. And I sighed with the final scenes in *Smith and Jones* where Russell Davies, David Tennant, Freema Agyeman and Charles Palmer wrested every single ounce of romance out of it.

But do you see what I did there? I liked it for the cake and the icing. I loved the scene and appreciated what happened behind the scenes that made it.

I guess that's what frustrates me so about the sort of shipping outlook we're discussing: I find it so very uncritical. I love Henry Jenkins as much as the next fan who's done any reading and I appreciate the notion that we create new texts out of the primary text we watch on TV. But I think at least one of the texts we create should be a critique of what makes good television.

To use another *Torchwood* example, the notion that Jack hooks up with the bloke who previously swore he'd kill him (and reiterated his disgust toward Jack on more than one occasion) without any on-screen development is bad storytelling. It's bad television writing. It's bad characterisation. It's sloppy and stupid. What astounds me though is that when I've talked to (admittedly very passionate) shippers about this they haven't seen it as a problem. Apparently, because Jack wants to be whole and Ianto is missing his girlfriend, it makes sense. But it doesn't.

This bothers me way more than it should. Perhaps because old-school fandom taught me that admitting what you love has flaws is okay and it's okay to think critically while watching. I feel the rush to use bailing wire and gum to make bad mistakes in storytelling seem okay does everyone a disservice.

Jeez, I really need to lighten up. Come on Graeme, it's a *TV show with monsters and funny accents.*

You asked me if I thought Russell T Davies wrote himself in a corner by having the setup of the new series be about the relationship – romance, essentially – between the Doctor and Rose. Yeah, I suppose he did. But I think one of the most important things Russell did was to acknowledge that the whole of television drama is about relationships nowadays. Crime procedurals, science fiction, mob-family sagas, political intrigues, historicals, medical shows... they're all undergirded by relationships. In order for *Doctor Who* to be a show for people to watch, it needed to have a real, full-blooded relationship at its core to be a part of the television landscape. Fighting with that – which I think would have been what every old school fan might well have done – would have made the series a museum piece at the outset.

But this approach does paint you in a corner when, as is the case with *Doctor Who*'s format, actors depart regularly. You can't just have the Doctor restarting intense relationships with romantic overtones every time. In some ways, perhaps they should have just gone with what I think they're going with Donna: a witty relationship which doesn't have to be romantic. Or maybe they should have had Rose be like Martha and have the relationship an unreciprocated crush.

Which is, I think, a valid reading of the text of the first two seasons of the new series. I guess my question is: would shippers be open to that? I mean, there's nothing to say that the Doctor ever really reciprocated Rose's obvious feelings toward the Doctor. The Doctor would do anything for her and cared deeply, but he does the same for Donna and Martha. True, he does seem to grieve her loss profoundly, but is that the same as loving her? There's an ambiguity to writing the Doctor romantically that's delightfully nuanced in the new series: he's more sexual, has more passionate feelings, but is also remarkably detached. Russell doesn't even have the Doctor say he loves her.

Oh, but there's me again: mixing my interest in the relationship with my interest in the making of the show and suggesting that conclusions are not necessarily what they seem. I'll stop before I bore everyone!

Best,
Graeme

PS: Shippers, OTPers... how the hell do you keep track of each other? Badges?

Letter #4

Dear Graeme,

If only fandom were as simple as Superman... Wait, bad analogy.

I think we can agree that it is a very broad assessment in the differences between guy and girl fans, but at least it's a plank in the bridge. And, just when I was going to be all smug about it, you have to bring up *Torchwood*. Series One of *Torchwood* was bad writing, bad characterisation and bad storytelling. But it was addictive. It was like really cracky, pixie-stick-fueled fanfic with a big budget. On a whole, it worked, but, when you looked too closely, the straw man fell apart.

So, how do you reconcile something you like, even if somewhat shamefacedly, with those elements of bad television that you mention? Bailing wire and gum is one way, extrapolating tiny bits of dialogue and body language to explain the inexplicable if you're desperate – and, of course, the age-old tradition of fanfic. I don't think the shippers are necessarily dismissing all the valid criticisms – there isn't one *Torchwood* fan I've bumped into who's said *Torchwood* is good television – but they've agreed it's captivating television. I guess you could liken it to having a really homely child whom you love dearly. Of course you'd try to build up their positives while blithely ignoring the more unfortunate aspects and fiercely defending that child against all detractors. Again, I don't think the shippers are naive, just selective. Does it do the show a disservice? Hmmm... I'm not sure. Having a supportive and positive fanbase is always good, but if the powers that be ignore all the grumblings underneath (and I don't care what Russell Davies says, they are in tune to what fandom blathers about), then they run a risk of pandering and that's even worse television.

But you are right, sometimes the shippers can make astounding leaps of faith that even boggle those of us who understand the mentality. Then we're put in a position of explaining the behaviour of those who are explaining the behaviour of the characters themselves. Personally, I think the reason that the out-of-the-blue Jack / Ianto relationship has caught fire in *Torchwood* fandom is that for the first time we're seeing a slash relationship played out on television. For the slashers (the legion of fangirls who favour a male / male relationship), it's like being fed 100-proof alcohol. After years of having to dwell in subtext, the text is smacking them in the face and they are positively giddy. Giddy enough to ignore the huge storytelling leap it took to get to the relationship.

Interestingly, in a conversation where we're discussing how the shippers can ignore all the smoke and mirrors that go on behind the screen, we can talk about the one area where the shippers have taken some of that smoke – authorial intent, to be exact – and run it into the ground. Specifically, the love story between the Doctor and Rose. What we see on screen is a very caring relationship but one that has been described by the writers, the actors and the public as "a love story". Add that intent to the relationship-driven story we saw in the 2005 and 2006 *Doctor Who* seasons, and you have a shippers' dream. Now, I find authorial intent to be a dodgy standard but considering how little most shippers need to construct their own version of the text, it was like a beautifully wrapped present.

However, I also think it created an unintentional conflict, both on screen and off. I get that *Doctor Who* fans can be, umm, a bit contentious, but, by setting up Rose as the companion to beat, there are now "companion battles" in a vein that were once reserved for which version of the Doctor was preferred. I agree that moving the show forward by focusing more on the relationship was necessary to modernise the format, but I think it went too far in making that relationship a romantic one. Or a failed romantic one, as the case may be. I have great hopes that a witty relationship like that promised with Donna will help move the franchise away from a focus on romantic love and back to a platonic love.

Not that it will matter to the shippers, of course. We delight in subtext and can find it anywhere.

Regardless of our position, it's amazing that a "TV show with monsters and funny accents" can stimulate such passion and debate across the board. I think we new fans can thank you old schoolers for creating such a deep and rich fandom legacy, and for letting us specious new folks into the party.

Regards,
Deb

PS: Badges and secret handshakes. Fandom is serious business!

The Fan Wife's Survival Guide

by Cheryl Twist

From Enlightenment #143, December 2007

Editor's Note: Enlightenment *FanLife columnist Sean Twist's deadline problems provided Sean's wife Cheryl with an opportunity to step in and guest-write his column and give her side of the story...*

Stepping into this column feels much like having invaded the boys' bathroom for the first time back in school. It was alien space; somewhere I didn't belong. There were strange devices and the feeling that I was being very bad. At least this time I have an invitation.

The temptation is, of course, to use this chance to vent years of snark, reveal embarrassing secrets about the author of the *FanLife* column and generally take the piss. I am the quintessential long-suffering wife, a victim of two decades of passive *Doctor Who* viewing, the Doctor et al invading my brain the way second-hand smoke pervades the lungs. Not that I harbour bad feelings about it. (That did sound snarky. I guess I'm not good with temptation.)

But I make it sound like I haven't had fun. To be fair, since I first laid eyes on *Kinda* and *Mawdryn Undead,* I was kind of hooked. And yes, I did notice the gleam in my husband's eye when he realised he had me. Thus began my indoctrination. (I had to do it. Not sorry.) It was tough going sometimes, but here I am now, rabid with anticipation for new episodes and enjoying *Torchwood.*

So, as a veteran companion, here is my advice for fans and their girlfriends. (I know I am making an assumption here, and if you are a female fan reading this who got into *Doctor Who* on your steam, and not roped in by your boyfriend, the queue for special commendations is down the corridor.)

First up, the fans that are trying to get their girlfriends interested. In *Doctor Who.*

Tip One: Pick your battles. The capacity to watch any airing at any time of any episode, no matter how often you've seen it and regardless of its actual merit, is likely not shared by your mate. Do not ask her to stay up until four a.m. to view episode two of *Timelash.* Just don't.

Tip One, Part Two: Positive Reinforcement. Do, however, choose an outstanding first episode she hasn't seen yet. Start it up while she is either bored or doing something tedious from which she can be easily and gratefully distracted. Once her attention is engaged, offer chocolate and a chair. If she asks for episode two, you owe her dinner. If she watches all four episodes... figure something out. Eventually, the show's quality will be reward in itself. But you are still on the hook for chocolate. Your girlfriend is smarter than your dog (I hope) and will know how to work you for treats.

Tip Two: Do not underestimate the power of pretty. Be sure she is watching the current series because, like it or not, Eccleston is dead sexy. If he's not her type then Tennant should do the trick, and let us not forget Barrowman and Simm. Use them to your advantage.

Tip Three: It's unwise to go on too long about Zoe's tight, sparkly catsuit or Billie Piper's latest project. Unless your girlfriend is heroically indulgent, less is best. You might wonder why it's all right for the women to get all wibbly wobbly over Captain Jack and you've got to shut it. You might think it seems like a double standard. You'd be right. It changes nothing.

Aside to the ladies: Does anyone else feel that Billie Piper as Rose wore too much mascara? Was it intentional? Could Rose not have made use of some future cosmetic technology? Something that didn't make her look as though she'd gone bobbing for apples in a bucket of tar? No? It was so... distracting. It was *The End of the World* and the only thing on my mind was why her eyelashes weren't melting. Where was I?

Right, time for the girlfriends.

Tip One: Do not nit-pick the female companions in his presence (the above rant as an example). It doesn't matter that you are right. Or that it is extremely satisfying. He won't have noticed the thing that was bothering you, and won't care once he does. You will only be frustrated if you go after Sarah Jane. Adric, however, is fair game.

Tip Two: Do feel free to point out continuity issues. It will allow him to practice the favourite pastime of *Doctor Who* fans: justifying, prevaricating, supposing and equivocating. They call it retroactive continuity, retconning for short. It is both cursed and revered. The advantage to you, if you're wondering, is that it is a useful tool of misdirection. It can be employed at any time (not merely during viewing) and it is guaranteed to distract him from whatever you don't want him thinking about. Even having read this, he won't be able to resist the urge once baited. Save Dalek and Cyberman topics for emergencies.

Tip Three: Enjoy yourself. Have fun. It really is a good show. Snarking and gender satire aside, the ups outweigh the downs by a wide margin. And when it's up, it's truly fantastic.

The Shipping News

by Deborah Stanish

From Enlightenment #135, October 2006

When the BBC announced Billie Piper's departure from *Doctor Who* towards the end of the original broadcast of the 2006 season, the reaction was mixed. Long-time fans continued munching their toast and speculated who would be travelling in the TARDIS next. But for the new crop of *Doctor Who* fans, the news reverberated through fandom like a gunshot. It was a devastating blow to the fans who had become invested in the relationship between the Doctor and Rose, so the remaining episodes were viewed with a sense of impending doom.

Everyone even remotely aware of the *Doctor Who* mythology realised that the Doctor regenerates and companions leave but, for new fans, Rose Tyler was much more than a companion. She was the co-star of the show and not just a human tagalong. More importantly, Rose Tyler was the gateway into the dense world of *Doctor Who.*

From the moment Rose ran across our screens in episode one, she asked the questions that the novice viewer was thinking. She gently led viewers into the story and was the perfect character to introduce a new generation to *Doctor Who* without overwhelming them with a complicated backstory. As Russell T Davies explained in the BBC Radio programme *Project Who,* he did not want to flood the programme with dry explanations. Davies stated that he wanted the story to be about the Doctor and Rose, alone together, which ultimately is a much more emotional story. Because we understand Rose, it is through her eyes that we slowly begin to understand who and what the Doctor is.

While the emphasis on Rose's character caused some fans to cry foul, it was a calculated move on the part of Davies to engage the new viewers. By developing the relationship between the Doctor and Rose, the show acknowledged that there was a new type of fan out there and the BBC was going to bring them into the fold.

Traditionally, sci-fi is seen as the male domain. While that may be painting fandom with a very broad brush, it is fair to say that the boys had a different viewing sensibility than women. They tended to keep count of planets visited, alien races encountered and how complicated storylines and arcs fit within their show. Think of it like baseball statistics with ray guns and alien tribunals rather than RBI's and homers.

But it is a whole new sci-fi world out there today. The girls are not content to let the boys have all the fun and have squeezed their way onto the couch in greater numbers than ever before. Women have always been interested in sci-fi, but shows such as *Star Trek: The Next Generation* and paranormal shows such as *Buffy the Vampire Slayer* have recognised that female fans bring different expectations to the table.

While the fangirls like the gizmos and gadgets and watching stuff blow up as much as the next guy, they also like their stories to engage them on an emotional level. They want a story with a personal undertone. The accusation that the fangirls are looking for a soap with a sonic screwdriver may have a ring of truth, but they also want good storytelling, exciting action, wit and humour.

With *Doctor Who,* the relationship between the Doctor and Rose presented all that on a silver platter. Their chemistry drew the viewers deeply into their world. This wasn't just a story about the Doctor and his TARDIS saving the universe; it was a story about the Doctor and Rose, so the fangirls ate it up with a spoon. The fangirls primarily interested in the Doctor / Rose relationship proudly wore their "shipper" badge. For them, the emotional arc became the primary story throughout 2005 and 2006.

While not every fangirl is a shipper, nearly every shipper is a fangirl. It's an overwhelmingly girl thing and they have own scorecard that's a bit more complicated than the boys' because it often relies on subtext, intent and plain old wishful thinking. Some shippers paddle in the "unconsummated love" waters while others are firmly in the "shagging like bunnies" camp. Casual glances and off-hand remarks are analysed and debated with the same seriousness as the Looms and how the Big Finish audios fit into the televised timeline.

The desperate hug at the end of *Dalek*? Shagging like bunnies. The mirrored body language in *Fear Her*? Shagging like bunnies. The Doctor's casual grip around Rose's waist in *Army of Ghosts*? Shagging like bunnies. The Doctor and Rose's absence during *Love & Monsters*? They were very busy... *shagging like bunnies*!

Of course, the internet has proven fertile ground for the shippers and fangirls. Websites and blogs have sprouted; fanfic of varying degrees of skill and taste are flooding fanfiction.net and archives such as *A Teaspoon and an Open Mind*. Fanvids, music mixes, fan art and graphics are all mixed in with serious, frivolous and often compelling discussion. Fandom has been swamped by a tsunami of fangirls and they're even storming the venerable gates of Outpost Gallifrey.

But, make no mistake, for every fangirl and shipper who gushes over David Tennant's floppy hair, there are ten more who are bringing thoughtful, intelligent and analytical discussion to the forum. They may be looking for something different in the show than the traditional fan, but they are just as committed.

But the question remains: what do the fangirls and shippers do once the emotional arc has been torn asunder? Do they rend their garments and shake tiny fists to the heavens, vowing to never to love again or do they pick up the pieces and move on?

As Davies intended, Rose served her purpose as the gateway character into *Doctor Who* and the relationship kept the fangirls and shippers watching but, somewhere along the line, a curious thing happened: the new viewers wanted more. Thanks to little bites of trivia doled about by the *Doctor Who* writing staff, the fangirls and shippers began working their way backwards. Who were the Daleks? When did the Doctor become acquainted with UNIT? Who were his past companions and what was up with Gallifrey?

While treading the waters of 40 years' worth of storytelling is a daunting task, a recent poll on the Doctor / Rose shipper's blog, Time and Chips, showed that, of the more than 200 people who responded to the question, 74% said that watching the new series caused them delve into the classic series. The previously televised episodes as well as the novels and audio adventures have seen a resurgence of interest.

So, while the fangirls and shippers may have lost the relationship that initially drew them into the show, it's been replaced by something deeper and more meaningful: a passion for *Doctor Who* and all that it entails. The show has captured their hearts and, regardless of whose hand the Doctor is holding, the fangirls are along for the ride.

Relationships

WHAT WILL BECOME OF US?

WANDERING LORD OF TIME with possible God-complex and no fixed abode seeks travelling companion to share adventure and fun with sonic screwdriver. Must have an inquisitive mind, good lungs and strong ankles. Note: Appearance of Time Lord is subject to change without notice.

BORED SHOPGIRL with a nose for trouble looking for unrequited love and adventure with older stranger. Must have a big heart, preferably two.

LAST HUMAN seeks pure partner for mutual blood bleaching and body swapping. Must use moisturizer, enjoy trampolining and find skinny girls attractive. Digihumans, quasi-humans or humanish need not apply. Box 51040

SINGLE, MATURE FEMALE JOURNALIST seeks new travelling companion for exciting adventures in Croydon. Enigmatic and larger than life man preferred, with own means of transportation. Must love dogs. Box 25178

BABY-FACED MEMBER of large family seeks big beautiful man or woman for dressup fun and much shaking of booty. Must be person of moderate influence or power. Owners of comfortable apartments preferred. Personal hygiene issues unimportant, unless you eat pickles. Fun times guaranteed: It'll be a gas! Box 39847

LOOKING FOR A TREE HUGGER. Mature sapling from the Forest of Cheem seeks same for germination. Will not show liana in public...but in private is a different matter. Box 59336

BEAUTIFUL FRENCH COURTESAN in search of the man who fixed her fireplace as a child. Am I destined to walk the slow path alone? Box 1749

ARE YOU MY MUMMY? Mummy, is that you? Are you my mummy? Mummmmy mummmmy mummmy... Box 89071

IMPRESSIVE IMPERIAL IMPRESSARIO seeks peerless premiere professor of pathology to form Holmesian Double Act. By dash me optics, this could be an apriori alliterative association! Box 89071

SINGLE-MINDED CLONE from proud warrior race seeks same for destroying Rutans, making military conquests and achieving prime objectives. Contact Box 77777

LET THE GENIE OUT OF THE BOTTLE - Evil Since the Dawn of Time quietly waiting for the right wolf of Fenric to come along to assist with my release, play some chess. No emotional cripples or people with mother-issues. Box 666

LONELY HEXAPOD from Alpha Centauri has spent too much time dithering and panicking about nothing of consequence. Wants to settle down with another hermaphrodite hexapod, preferably one that wears a shower curtain for modesty sake. Box 14345

SPLINTERED ACROSS TIME BUT LOOKING FOR COMPANIONSHIP - collector and connoisseur seeks companion for sham marriage spent playing with Chinese Puzzle boxes, enjoying fine art at the Louvre and summers at the ancestral Italian Villa. Separate rooms - I'm the last of the Jagaroth. Box 19792

PITY THE GELTH. Gaseous entity wants to cross the rift that separates us. We want to stand tall. To feel the sunlight. To live again. Would you help us? We love recycling. Willing to move to Cardiff if necessary. Box 65234

DO YOU CLAIM GREATER KNOWLEDGE? Former CEO of Geocomtex struggles to regain memories after living as a junkie in San Diego, Sacramento, Seattle...something beginning with S. Can you rekindle my spark? Box 23411

FLYBOY GOES IN ANY DIRECTION. Dashing and gorgeous Captain seeks guy or gal or...well anything really, to ride his tribophysical waveform macrokinetic extrapolator to the stars and back. Must be breathing with a pulse and, er, that's pretty much all that's necessary. Box 21135

DIFFERENTLY ABLED GENIUS requires the ultimate upgrade in the form of a camp associate willing to accomodate delusions of grandeur and plans that make no sense. Must have a high tolerance for pain and an affinity for steel. If interested, please contact John FROM BEYOND THE GRAVE. Box 51040

I HAVE A DOOR IN MY HEAD BUT YOU CAN UNLOCK MY HEART... Boy nerd still living with parents seeks open-minded bleach blonde. No travelling to anywhere exotic. Or anything terribly exciting at all. Contact Adam at box 19313.

OLD SOLDIERS DON'T NEED TO FADE. Former Brigadier and maths teacher seeks adventure, excitement and an opportunity to at least get seven out of ten. Box 10007

MAD GOD EMPEROR seeks to escape loneliness and boredom of centuries in the dark spaces for extermination and casual worship. Only 1 cell in a million will be harvested. Box 51040

LONELY AZTEC SPINSTER still looking for man she became betrothed to in cocoa ceremony. Why did you disappear with Yetaxa? Did you only want me for my plans of the aqueducts? We could be happy. Box 51040

I HAVE A BADGE FOR MATHEMATICAL EXCELLENCE and I just want to be understood. Why won't anyone listen to me? Will you? Box 82453

FUN-LOVING ZARBI seeks same. Must love Venom Grubs. Box 39847

Employment Opportunities

WANTED: EDITOR OF LARGE, MULTI-PLANETARY NEWS SERVICE. Must be able to work under pressure, hold hands of underlings and not mind it when your boss goes into a slathering rage above you. Employment opportunities offer (extremely) long-term prospects. Our motto is: "we don't just report the news, we are the news". Bleach-blond goatees a plus. Experience working with the undead a necessity (note: applicants with FOX NEWS experience do not need to provide further evidence for this requirement). Address all enquiries to the Mighty Jagrafess of the Holy Hadrojassic Maxarodenfoe, Satellite Five, Floor 500

INEXPERIENCED? INCOMPETENT? SELFISH BEYOND BELIEF? The Torchwood Institute are looking for suitable candidates to belong to a Top Secret organization, skulking about Cardiff killing aliens. Intelligent, stable people need not apply. Contact J. Harkness, Torchwood Institute, Cardiff, Wales. Good looking people preferred.

Items for Sale or Trade

CHULA AMBULANCE for sale. Never been used before. Is utterly empty except for the million or so nanogenes inside (and provided you're not a nearly dead child wearing a gas mask you should be fine). Comes with alarm clock for Volcano Days. Contact J. Harkness, Torchwood Institute, Cardiff, Wales

Choosing the Ship That's Right For You

by Tammy Garrison

"Do you enjoy a bit of summer romance, or the occasional hot hookup in your science-fiction television programs? Even if the show doesn't actually support them? Perhaps you find yourself gravitating toward forbidden love, or the relationship that will never be, and only hope that the spaceships, time travel and explosions will help those two (or three!) characters realise that their love is meant to be. If so, then talk to your Doctor about Shipping. You and your Doctor can decide which Ship is right for you."

I am not a doctor; I don't even play one on TV. But I'd like to talk to you about Shipping in New *Who*. And there's a Ship for everybody, well, unless you don't like Shipping. And if you don't, why are you reading this? Well, maybe you're Ship-curious? That's okay, I suppose. Every once in a while, we all get these unexplainable feelings...

Perhaps I can interest you in a nice, series-reinforced relationship, with Amy and Rory? That's safe. They're married, after all.

First, they're adorable together, even when Amy's being a little mean to Rory. But I secretly believe he enjoys it. Otherwise he'd have walked away from the crazy chick with "Doctor" issues ages ago and not looked back.

While their relationship is complex – and it was complicated further by Amy running off with the Doctor and planting a kiss on his clueless, alien lips – Amy decided she'd rather live in no world at all, than a world without Rory in it, whereas Rory was willing to wait nearly two thousand years for her, just to keep her safe.

Beyond the grand romantic gestures, there is a normalcy to their relationship that one doesn't find when zipping through time and space; humans meet and fall in love every day, in every corner of the world. Companions are always representative of us, so they're like us even in this most basic way.

They're an easy relationship to get behind and be fans of. They're cute together, they're obviously devoted, and they've managed the very simple and human thing of falling in love.

Maybe it's all too easy. After all, the show has already explored their relationship; there's not a tonne of fodder for debate or speculative fan fiction on the internet, if you tie it up in a big bow like that! How's about a relationship that's implied by the show, such as the Doctor and Rose?

She obviously dug him and, for his part, he really seemed to have his heart ripped out when they were separated at the end of *Doomsday*. If you were so inclined, you could go so far as to surmise that they were the One True Pairing (OTP). The love that would endure all things and would never die. A lot of fan communities are quite fond of this pairing, *A Teaspoon and an Open Mind* being a prime example of fans getting behind the idea of a Doctor / Rose relationship.

Which is why I'd like to talk to about shipping the first Doctor and Rose.

The first Doctor and Rose, I say? What sort of madness is this? If we remove all the reasons why this can't work – she's in another dimension, surely the ninth Doctor would have remembered meeting her before – let's look at why it would. If the Doctor and Rose are the One True Pairing, she will love him in any form, even if he's old, takes frequent naps and occasionally suffers from bouts of incontinence. And he will love her despite her dropped consonants and affinity for tracksuits. Just think of all of the glorious, wonderful, sometimes-awkward smut that would ensue!

Don't look at me like that. It's possible. She'd have to see past the obvious "elderly grandfather" look that the first Doctor was sporting back then, not to mention the curmudgeonly attitude that he had going, but he is her One True Love, right? And a less mature Doctor who puts all of his stock in science, education and correct Queen's English could certainly see past the flaws in Rose Tyler's upbringing to love her with the type of love that burns up a star just to say goodbye, right? I believe it could happen. Let me have my dreams.

Okay, maybe that isn't your thing. Perhaps I could interest you in something that has not even been hinted at in the television show. Possibly you would like something that crosses over between characters on spinoff programs like Sarah Jane / Captain Jack? I see you're interested. She's an older lady with needs and Jack's technically an older fellow. Let's put it this way: he certainly has the benefits of experience and the added advantages of physical youth. I think he could provide Sarah Jane adequate... assistance in certain areas.

Aside from Sarah Jane being a mature lady who knows what she wants, and Jack's ability and willingness to provide, they have other areas of common interest. Even if the relationship is not hot and steamy, they still have enough to bond over to make for comforting, interesting times.

They were both left behind by the Doctor and had to pick up the pieces of their lives and move on. I think even if Jack wasn't showing Sarah Jane his extensive... repertoire, they'd still have enough similar life experiences to have a fulfilling friendship with plenty of late-night conversations about the universe, the Doctor and the meaning of it all. Even though there's little-to-nothing in the television series to actually support this, it certainly would be fun to imagine the possibilities every time the two encounter or reference each other onscreen. A quick glance during *Journey's End* or a brief mention of Torchwood in *The Sarah Jane Adventures* is enough to set imaginations and hearts into motion, thinking of the many wonderful possibilities, from hot, desperate sex between two lonely, mature people to friends capable of holding each other's deepest secrets.

And yes, it's okay to be a fan of a friendship-based relationship as well! You may be more comfortable with this in the beginning and it may be easier than moving directly to pondering just what excuse Sarah Jane will use to get Luke out of the house on the nights Jack is driving all the way from Cardiff for some... grownup time.

Or maybe you've mastered the friendship-ship, and the non-implied ship. For those who have moved on past the OTP, I present to you: the OT3. Yes, the One True Threesome. Probably the most common OT3 to be a fan of is the Doctor / Jack / Rose, but there's nothing common about you, right? That's why, in my back room, I have something so magnificent it exists only in our hearts and minds (and possibly in some dark corner of fanfiction.net): Doctor / Owen Harper / Jackie Tyler.

Yes, you read that right. The Doctor and Owen Harper and Jackie Tyler. Why, dear God, why? Why not! Sure, the most likely scenario for getting this unlikely group into the sack together involves Alien Sex Pollen and Torchwood's pheromone spray, but think about it. First, it's not been explored in the show, which is a strong attractant for some people. Next, it's also a rare enough gem to not have been explored ad nauseam at the usual fan-fiction sites. Again, for some people, this is important.

It's also a grouping of three incredibly strong-willed people. The Doctor is almost a force of nature, with his ability to plow through situations and turn them around with the snap of a finger. Jackie raised a daughter on her own and is not afraid to stand up to an alien like the Doctor when she thinks he's wrong. As for Owen, he's quite capable of getting his own way and fulfilling his own desires, as seen in his relentless pursuits of Gwen Cooper in *Torchwood*'s first season.

The Doctor comes off as prickly enough to not be interested in sexual dalliances, but he has shown interest in such relationships: he did nearly marry an Aztec noblewoman, flirt pretty heavily with Madame de Pompadour and, if nothing else, seemed at least comfortable with the idea of Jack and other humans "dancing" their way across the universe.

While Jackie has disdain for the Doctor, largely for taking her daughter away for an entire year, Jackie was initially attracted to the ninth Doctor when he entered her bedroom in *Rose*. She's also proven that she is open to the idea of being in a relationship with a younger man, as evidenced by her flirting interest in Elton from *Love & Monsters*. While it may take a little outside... inspiration (read: sex pollen, booze, or other inhibition-lowering substance) to get Jackie into a compromising position with the Doctor and Owen, it's not outside the realm of possibility.

Owen Harper is a wounded creature (aren't they all?), but he is capable of both love (Diane) and lust (Gwen), and obviously doesn't mind the occasional same-sex or threesome encounter, even if it is aided by pheromone spray (*Everything Changes*). Would he be willing to explore such a situation with the Doctor and Jackie? As far as we know, they are strangers to him. They'd probably have about the same odds as anyone else of getting Owen in a compromising position.

We have here two guys who are equally self-involved and self-flagellating, and possibly the one woman in the Whoniverse who can bring them down a peg and who would be more than happy to abuse them so that they would not have to abuse themselves. Sure, the first time might be due to that old standby of Alien Sex Pollen, but subsequent encounters might not need any such assistance! There'd be drama, there'd be comedy and there'd be awkward conversations as they attempted to explain things to Jack and Rose!

We've looked at a lot of "ships" already. Friend-ships, romantic relation-ships, series-supported, series-implied, OTP, OT3, and "dear God, what were you thinking?" ships. It's quite a range of options. But perhaps you've tried all of these, and none have been your perfect shipper-fit. How's about a crossover pairing?

Yes, that's right. If none of the usual (or unusual) pairings strike your fancy, you can always look to outside sources for inspiration. What about the ninth Doctor and Daniel Jackson from *Stargate SG-1*? The ninth Doctor's a grumpy immortal with Post-Traumatic Stress Disorder, Daniel's been resurrected so many times he's practically immortal and he has his own baggage to bring on this jolly trip. They're both explorers (insert innuendo here) and each could certainly hold his own in the other's world.

Logic and our own personal interpretations of characters' behaviour or sexuality aside, enough people take this particular crossover relationship seriously that there are at least two LiveJournal communities dedicated to the proposition of an Air Force archeologist and a time-travelling alien getting together, having adventures and sometimes having hot, steamy sex.

Of course, Internet Rule #34 applies to everything I have mentioned above: if you can think of it, not only is there smut for it, but there's a LiveJournal community dedicated to fan fiction for it somewhere.

Don't wait; ask your Doctor if Shipping is right for you.

Shipping side-effects include lost time surfing the internet for fanfic, long discussions about minutiae, loss of bodily control at the sight of confirmation of a Ship's viability, occasional arguments with otherwise sane and rational people who just won't acknowledge that your Ship is the only logical one in this circumstance, dry mouth and anal leakage. Talk to your Doctor today.

Everybody's in the Play

by Graeme Burk

From Enlightenment #137, December 2006

This is the story about how I got to know Russell T Davies. Well, except that I've never met Russell T Davies. Aside from a couple of emails, the most substantial of which was about *Bob & Rose*, I've hardly spoken to him. I doubt I've ever made more than the most cursory impressions of cursory impressions on him, if any impression at all.

And yet, Russell T Davies knows me. I know it. He made a *Doctor Who* story just for me.

It's called *Love & Monsters* (note the subversive, style-manual-busting ampersand) and it's funny and heartfelt and honest and sad and true; often all at the same time. *Love & Monsters* is utterly brilliant. No *Doctor Who* story this season – and believe me, I've really enjoyed everything this season – has etched itself so firmly on my psyche.

But before I talk about that, I want to talk about me. Because I'm a fan, and it's the fannish thing to insert one's self into the story. I am the Mary Sue of this review, if you will. My name is Graeme. I'm 37 years old. I became a fan of *Doctor Who* when I was 14 and I watched an episode of the Tom Baker story *Pyramids of Mars*. It was the smartest, funniest, most exciting thing I had ever seen on television. I loved it like no other show.

Within two months, I was incessantly calling my best friend for information about the show. Within six, I owned a copy of the *Programme Guide* and was answering my best friend's questions. When I turned 26, I attended my first convention and it was a wonderful, liberating experience as I discovered how amazing it was to be with people who loved *Doctor Who* like I did. People who knew all the jokes and had opinions on all the controversies. When I was 31, I became editor of *Enlightenment* and have been doing this for six years. At the same time, we started a monthly Tavern gathering of fans in Toronto and that has given me something to look forward to every month for almost seven years.

I know what you're thinking. "This is hugely conceited. When is he going to stop talking about himself and start reviewing *Love & Monsters*?" Believe me, I understand; I hate it when Vinay Menon does the same thing in *The Toronto Star*. But my life isn't that different from a lot of fans and not so different from Elton Pope, the lead character of *Love & Monsters*. Elton is an ordinary guy with an interest in the Doctor that stems from an event that happened in his childhood. Elton starts attending a monthly meeting with others who are also, if you will, fans of the Doctor. They get together to talk about their opinions on the Doctor and share their artwork, and gradually they become friends.

You would think from the delightfully comedic tone of the episode that Russell T Davies would want to mock fans of *Doctor Who.* And yet, he doesn't. The fans on display here are eccentrics, but the sort of eccentrics that everyone is, in their own way. They're people with rich inner lives with worlds of pain, hope and imagination. I know these people. And I know Victor Kennedy, the mysterious man who comes into this little group of Doctor fans and organises them into a proper information-gathering squadron to find information on the Doctor and Rose; or, at least, fans like him who take their hobby just a little too seriously and spoil the fun of it for everyone. (And this is true for any type of fan, whether of a TV show or a sports team or a musician.) All these people are some of my best friends and some of my worst enemies, but they seem true to life nonetheless.

But that's not why *Love & Monsters* is so great. You see, I'm not only a fan of *Doctor Who,* I'm a fan of Russell T Davies. I've been a fan of his since I was given *Damaged Goods* as a birthday present (along with a crocheted TARDIS bookmark) by my friends Steve and Tuffy in 1996. I know the moment I became a fan of Russell: it was when a local thug inexplicably immolates himself in the middle of a council estate, is taken to hospital and commits suicide in casualty, then resurrects in the graveyard, just as two people are cottaging. What's more, the prose was as audacious as the ideas. I believed then that *Damaged Goods* was the best *Doctor Who* story of the 1990s. And I followed Russell's career, getting bootlegged copies of *Queer as Folk* and watching them before they ever aired on Canadian TV. Then I watched *Bob & Rose* and *The Second Coming* and anything else of his I could get my hands on.

Because I think Russell is a genius when it comes to writing. He grasps the modern television medium like no other. Scenes are fast paced and the characterisation is honest and stripped down to its most emotional core. There's a toughness to his stories; I'll never forget Stuart's defiant proclamation that he's gay in *Queer as Folk II* (undermined and played for comedy in the American version). Russell's characters are quirky but fully rounded people and you feel connected to them in a very real way. But what I love most about his work is how poetic it is, how fluidly it moves. The ending of *Bob & Rose* may be the most satisfying conclusion I have ever seen of a TV series as it uses a stunning montage of quick cuts and gorgeous dialogue. I had honestly assumed it had been made in editing, like the ending of *American Beauty*, but it was exactly as scripted.

As good as Russell's *Doctor Who* has been (and is), I was always disappointed we couldn't have a story that really showcased the genius of Russell's non-*Who* writing in *Doctor Who*. *Love & Monsters* is that story. With the Doctor and Rose's presence in this story minimal at best, there was really nothing else he could do. And so Russell pulls the rip-cord and gives us a story with narration, talking (literally) to the camera, flashback, flashforward and melancholy, tough but gorgeous character pieces and funny gags all at breakneck pace. I'm greatly disappointed there isn't a script book for this season (yet) as I really want to see the script. I'm sure I'll be amazed to find yet again that, as good a director as Dan Zeff seemed to be, Russell had the rapid editing for it all in his head right from the start. But that's just gloss that tells a story that's both uplifting and heartbreaking. A story with an achingly real theme appropriate for a story set in a fandom of sorts: the thing we're most obsessed with is often the best and worst thing in our lives, and the best and worst thing about ourselves. That's just so perceptive.

As fans, we've all fancied ourselves to be Elton Pope at one time or another: sweet, innocent, not totally sharp but happy to dance around the apartment to ELO (or another band) and most himself when with fellow fans who understand his passions better than anyone. Marc Warren's performance in what is, in fact, the de facto lead, is brilliant. Playing the part in a slightly exaggerated way, I think, only helps the "everyfan" connection. Shirley Henderson is also quite funny as well.

And then there's Camille Coduri, who is an absolute revelation here. Without Rose to dominate, we get to see Jackie at her best – she's confident, flirtatious, funny, dominant – and at her most vulnerable. Russell Davies finally shows us what's inside Jackie's head, how she copes without Rose and how she'll defend her to the death, and Coduri makes the most of the opportunity.

My only real quibble with the episode is with Peter Kay, who is brilliant while he's Victor Kennedy but less so when his true villainy is revealed. The story is written in a slightly exaggerated way, with everyone just a touch off the ground. Kay, however, soars into the stratosphere. And yet, as with the exaggerated way the story is told, that might be deliberate as well. That's the great thing about *Love & Monsters*: there are any number of ways you can look at the story, all of them rewarding.

This story should never have worked; I mean, it was made without the regular cast and it featured a monster that won a contest on *Blue Peter*. But what Russell did instead was create a story that is to *Doctor Who* what *Jose Chung's From Outer Space* was to *The X-Files* or *The Trouble With Tribbles* was to the original *Star Trek*: the episode that eschews everything and turns the very premise of the series on its head and has a load of fun doing it. And, just as those stories have their detractors, so does this. People who don't like the comic tone. People who can't stand the *Scooby Doo* gag. People who don't get the ELO. People who think the Doctor and Rose need to be in a *Doctor Who* story for it to be a *Doctor Who* story.

Philistines all, I say. Fie on them. (Well, at least until I have a pint with them next week.) *Love & Monsters* proves that *Doctor Who* can do anything it wants to do and that my favourite television series is indomitable. Furthermore, it proves that Russell Davies is one of the great geniuses working in television. But then, I always knew that. I'm a fan. And Russell wrote a *Doctor Who* story just for me.

The Power of Cool

by Jack Graham

From Shockeye's Kitchen #17 (Spring 2006)

I want to tell you about the day when I "came out". I was at University. I was sick of hiding my true nature from my friends. I decided to trust to their broad-mindedness. I waited until they were all together and, my heart pounding, I just blurted it out.

"Guys," I announced, "I'm a *Doctor Who* fan."

They were all totally cool about it.

Okay, so it wasn't really like that, but you know what I mean. Back in the old days (before Russell T Davies' *annus mirabilis)*, being an outed fan was, sometimes, a risky social move. People tended to look for your anorak.

Of course, these days, mention *An Unearthly Child* to someone in passing and they're liable (as I know from bittersweet personal experience) to say something like: "Oh yeah, that was the one with Victor Meldrew in, wasn't it?" before repeatedly asking you if you'd happen, by any chance, to be their Mummy.

With non-fans, this is only natural. The new series is fresh in their minds. The old series is the stuff of hazy childhood memories, associated with all the cultural bric-a-brac of a childhood in the 60s, 70s or 80s, the sort of thing that Phil Jupitus is professionally mocking on nostalgia documentaries. As fans, we have a familiarity with the old series that separates us from the wider public perception of *Doctor Who*. To non-fans, "old" *Doctor Who* is – at best – a jumbled collage of long scarves, giant maggots, jelly babies and green, budgie-faced monsters in string vests. At worst, these memories have been spoiled by a thousand wobbly-sets and Daleks-can't-go-upstairs gags. For us, both the old and new series are parts of one living text. To non-fans, the new series is... well, a new series – and a pretty cool one, according to some.

So, if new *Doctor Who* is "cool", does that mean that old *Doctor Who* has also been touched by the same cultural pixie dust? Richard and Judy have interviewed rock stars; does that make them cool? Cool by association doesn't really work.

It certainly doesn't work for us fans. People might not immediately look for the anorak anymore, but the old stereotypes still live on. Being a fan, a fan of anything, is still decidedly uncool. Enthusiasm – especially for a minority interest – is inimical to "cool". The only things that buck this trend do so because they are colossally profitable. Football, for example, generates vast profits for players, agents, teams and investors, for the people who sell trainers and sports equipment, for the agencies that broker sponsorship deals, for the companies that the star players endorse, for the newspapers and magazines that trade gossip about celebrity footballers. Football is big money, which is why the media foster the idea that it represents a norm of masculinity and imbue it with "cool" (mediaspeak for profitable).

Football is one thing. Old sci-fi TV shows that never made much coin for anybody except the BBC are a different matter. But perhaps, now that *Doctor Who* is once again a success, now that remote control Daleks are gliding off the shelves of Toys-R-Us in their thousands, now that the show (via its hip writer and stars) is helping to sell celeb gossip mags... perhaps, now, "cool" and *Doctor Who* may be mentioned in the same sentence.

After all, the new series didn't star a little clown known chiefly for musically adapted cutlery and trouserial ferrets. The new series starred that credible Northern thesp Chris Eccleston, acclaimed star of gritty dramas, arthouse flicks, cult hits and big movies alike. And he wore a hard-as-nails leather jacket, not a coat that looked like Timmy Mallett designed it during an acid flashback. No foppish tresses were flopped around; he sported a no-nonsense buzzcut. Looking at him in costume, you can imagine him staggering out of a nightclub into a limo (stepping over the paparazzo he's just decked), a blonde on each arm. The new Doctor looked like a hellraiser, a debauched celeb at a premiere bash.

And he didn't share a screen with the girl from *Corners*, he shared it with Billie Piper, a bona fide pop star, a lad's mag photoshoot veteran, a regular in FHM's 100 Sexiest Women listings and, to top it off, a mate of boozy and clothes-shunning tabloid darling Charlotte Church.

It didn't hurt the *Doctor Who* publicity machine that Billie and her equally famous hubby (zillionaire presenter and media mogul Chris Evans) were entering the final stages of their much-publicised connubial apocalypse at the time she was cast. Nor did it hurt that, as filming commenced, media speculation (unfounded, natch) about Billie and her co-star became rife. No wonder the celeb glossies were interested. Gossip and glamour. A source close to Billie said this, a friend of Billie's said that.

But does all this mean that *Doctor Who* (old, new or both) is now cool? The glib answer is that if it ain't cool now, it probably never will be. *Doctor Who,* in relation to cool, is currently in perihelion. This is as close to cool as our show gets. Oh, I know all about Dalekmania, but that was the Daleks not the show as a whole... and that brief craze was far more to do with playground popularity than with the kind of cultural caché implied by "cool". If the Daleks were "cool" during Dalekmania, then so were the Teletubbies during their brief heyday.

The new series has certainly gone to town trying to shake off *Doctor Who*'s naff image and connect with modern reality. Rose was conceived as a real person of today's world. She is recognisable and her life is recognisable. She lives with her mum in a boxy flat crammed with knick-knacks, paperbacks and News 24. The Doctor finds a copy of *Heat* magazine in the Tyler residence. (Modern *Doctor Who* seems to have a cosy, mutually referencing relationship with *Heat.*) From the iPod to Big Brother, the new series went out of its way to connect with contemporary media culture, to reference the experiences and tastes of today's young, from *Blue-Peter*-watching kids up to *What-Not-To-Wear*-watching nearlythirtysomethings.

Doctor Who Confidential got in on the act too, dubbing pop music under their clips, using everything from Orbital to Snow Patrol.

At times, the determination to reek of "now" was – like Cassandra – horribly overstretched. The blast of Britney in *The End of the World* smacked of the archetypal "trendy" Geography teacher (I can almost see the jacket with the patches on the elbows now) who tries to impress his pupils by telling them he likes "Lincoln Park" and "Limp Biscuit". The "Toxic" slip up was especially embarrassing as the show had already revealed its real soul with a snatch of Soft Cell: the epitome of camp retro.

Nevertheless, the overall effect was a contemporary feel permeating each episode. It made *Doctor Who*'s return seem very relevant, very real, very "now", very... cool?

Well, what is "cool" anyway? I've seen the word "cool" be applied, by different people, to Marilyn Manson and Westlife, to Eminem and the Fonz, to *Reservoir Dogs* and Harry Potter. Ask ten people, picked at random, to define "cool" and you'll get ten different answers. "Cool" is a totally subjective word for a totally subjective concept. More than that, its meanings are so manifold and diffuse as to make the word itself almost empty. Pick up any style magazine these days and you'll find acres of copy about what's hot and what's not, what's in and what's out, and what's the new black this week. It's gibberish dreamt up by people operating within the fake worlds of advertising, promotion and media imagery, and then foisted on the rest of us to make us buy stuff.

As a word, "cool" is an example of something that we *Doctor Who* fans are quite familiar with: bafflegab, technobabble or, in this instance, culturebabble. It fulfils the same basic function as "I've reversed the polarity of the neutron flow". It is used as a substitute for a concept too fundamentally unreal to be explained.

On a day-to-day level, "cool" is usually used as an emphatic way of saying "I like this!" But the word also implies the caveat "and so should you!" There's always that slight totalitarian undercurrent to it, as anyone who's ever been to school will know. Being "cool" is a way of conforming, of obeying media messages and social pressure. Fashion has a little more in common with fascism than just alliteration.

How often do you think Damien Hirst and Tracey Emin discuss *Doctor Who* down at the Groucho Club? When the chemical generation cheered Orbital's version of the theme tune, were they paying tribute to the genius of Grainer and Derbyshire... or was it just ironic nostalgia for their childhood TV? Slipknot are supposedly into *Doctor Who* aren't they? It was even rumoured at one point that they'd be doing the new title music. (What a choice: Satanic thrash rock or Murray Gold!) But, in all honesty, do you reckon Slipknot hang round Outpost Gallifrey discussing the continuity problems raised by *Mawdryn Undead*? And, no matter how much the kids might have loved the new series, are the actual playground fans really going to be above mockery forever?

I remember having to keep pretty quiet about *Doctor Who* when I was at school, back in the dying days of the classic series when *Who* was the height of "gay". "Gay" was a generic insult at my school. If you didn't like someone's coat, it was "gay". If you hated a particular teacher, you called him "gay". But more than that: "gay" carried connotations of utter out-of-touchness. *Doctor Who*, back then (circa *Delta and the Bannermen*), was the apotheosis of "gay". Talking about it was as likely to get you beaten up as wearing jeans with turn-ups on mufti day or smelling of fish. (I don't mind telling you I got an uncomfortable feeling when, in *Aliens of London*, Rose told the Doctor "you're so gay!")

As *Doctor Who* languished in televisual limbo, I sometimes thought about what I'd do with it if, somehow, I was the producer of a new series. I suppose most of us did. My ideas changed drastically over the course of 16 years, but one thing remained constant: the Doctor would be played by a serious actor in dark clothes. Great minds obviously think alike. (Unless Russell T Davies has a machine for reading my mind... in which case, well done for not taking me up on 99% of my ideas, Russ!) Now, at last, the Doctor has been played by a serious actor in dark clothes. And it was pretty good. But, strangely, I now have a perverse longing for a Doctor as hopelessly uncool as me. I suppose the clunky, awkward, lonely teenage me could empathise with the wally in the silly clothes, could feel validated by the idea that a geek could be a hero. Don't get me wrong, I wouldn't want the new series to dust off the question-mark pullover... yet there is a part of me – the part of me that will always be a teenage outsider – that misses it, that wishes the Doctor was a geek again, that wishes "cool" wasn't an issue.

But let's face it: in its soul, *Doctor Who* isn't cool. Cool is about elitism, complacency, profit, media doublespeak, vanity and conformity. *Doctor Who* is, fundamentally, about fighting evil... evil that, very often, involves elitism, complacency, profiteering, media doublespeak, vanity and conformity. Think about those soulless, plastic dummies in designer clothes. Think about that vain, bitchy trampoline, committing murder for profit. Think about the Editor, manipulating populations with a carefully chosen word. Think about the sheep-like denizens of the Gamestation. The celeb mags might not notice, but *Doctor Who* is as anti-establishment, anti-acceptance and anti-cool now as it ever was.

Cool, huh?

A Fan's Life in Cardiff

by Melissa Beattie

It was one of those sudden realisations you have when lying in bed at about two a.m.

Torchwood exists to fight aliens in Cardiff.

I'm a foreign national living in Cardiff.

I'm an alien in Cardiff!

Cue theme song.

Right. Well, my impending capture aside, this is quite a normal expression for the often surreal feeling of living in Cardiff as a fan of *Doctor*

Who, Torchwood and *The Sarah Jane Adventures.* I remember arriving here in late September 2007; according to *The Writer's Tale,* the exact day Steven Moffat agreed to be Russell T Davies' successor, and a year to the day after I'd got myself hooked on *Doctor Who.* Scary, no? Immediately, I realised, in a jet-lagged way, that I was standing quite near where Gwen had seen Emma off in *Out of Time.* Taking a taxi to my new student halls, I saw that I was passing several vaguely familiar places, though the exhaustion, flight and disbelief that I was actually in Cardiff made everything kind of blurry and strange anyway. Once I'd managed a decent night's sleep, I awoke to meet one of my new flatmates, who promptly took me to the City Centre.

Shouldn't Abaddon be stomping on that building there?

This is where the Autons attacked Jackie!

ACK! Living statue that looks uncannily like a Weeping Angel!

And so on.

This wasn't so much culture shock as reality shock; I'd gone through the same thing visiting Vancouver and seeing various filming locations for the various *Stargate* series. In a strange way, though, it's also a bit like coming home. Now, I should preface that by saying I'd lived in nearby Bristol (about an hour to the east, though firmly in England) for about a year before living in Cardiff, with a year back in the US in between. In fact, I started watching *Doctor Who* because I was homesick for the UK. Even so, with all that kept in mind, Cardiff itself was so familiar to me, it was like I'd been here before. I think it's because I'd been so immersed in the sights and sounds of the city through my television set, entering into and interacting with the *Doctor Who* universe that way, so there was that sense of my trans-Atlantic move being a return not just to the UK, where I'd lived before, but to Cardiff, where I'd never properly visited. The TV show, like the past, is just another country.

Because so much of the city is used as either London or itself, however, everywhere you turn can be "someplace else". You get used to it quite quickly – I've walked past everything from Cyberman-esque street performers to giant handbags without batting an eye – but it does affect your thinking, if only for your own amusement.

I walk from my house in Roath (south / central Cardiff) down to Mermaid Quay three times a week. One day, whilst walking down Lloyd George Avenue, I noticed a sign saying "Silurian Place". My first thought: "Don't tell the Brigadier!" (*Doctor Who and the Silurians,* if you've missed the reference.) The next thought was that it had something to do with the Rift, which is a very convenient excuse for things. If I can't find my keys, my shoes, or that vitally important piece of paperwork, clearly it was taken by the Rift.

A funny thing happens to me sometimes when I open my mouth. I'm an American ex-pat living in Cardiff doing a postgraduate degree, and my voice reflects that. Before *Doctor Who* really took off (and before *Torchwood* or *The Sarah Jane Adventures* had begun), I would invariably get the comment (admittedly, in Bristol) about how I certainly wasn't a local. In Cardiff, I almost never get that. I'm not sure if it's the increase in tourism or just being used to hearing Captain Jack's accent and associating him with Cardiff, but it's rare that anyone even asks. What's more, when I do get asked, if I quip that I'm actually an ex-Time-Agent from the fifty-first century (don't tell anyone), it doesn't always need explanation. Even the casual fan gets the reference, rather than just the die-hard, con-going fans (in which group I am proud to claim membership).

Of course, the accidental and random stuff isn't all that happens. *Doctor Who* is a real industry around here. There's the Doctor Who Expo in Cardiff Bay, about a five-minute walk from Mermaid Quay, which is essentially a museum for props complete with gift shop. We've also got several SF and comic shops, all of which have prominent displays of *Who*-related merchandise and, whenever there's a signing event for DVDs, audiobooks or other media, they're generally held in two places: London and Cardiff. Between that and the increase in tourism from fans coming to visit the main filming locations – yes, my friends all ask for tours – it's a big source of income.

We also get a lot of people cosplaying: in most cities, if you see someone in a long brown coat and a brown suit and you think to yourself that "it's the Doctor!" you might shake your head slightly and laugh. In Cardiff, it may well actually be someone dressed as the tenth Doctor. I've lost track of the number of grey RAF greatcoats I've seen lurking around Roald Dahl Plass and elsewhere, not to mention getting a tiny, tiny flutter every time a black SUV passes by. I've actually been seeing one quite regularly, the last little while; I'm sure it's nothing. Again, though, it adds to the surrealism. Some people are lucky enough to end up passing the actors, writers and other members of the production teams of the three series in the streets, though I haven't been so fortunate.

On a typical Monday, I might take a trip to my research project site, a run to a library and some long walks. I won't really start seeing anything all that interesting until I get from Roath to Cathays, though I frequently find myself wondering if the metal mannequins in some of the shop windows that I pass are meant as a way of preventing the Nestene from taking them over. Walking down Park Place, I go by the Psychology School, where part of one of the later episodes of *Torchwood* Series Two was filmed (I haven't been able to find out which) and the Cardiff University Students' Union, within which the tenth Doctor met Joan Redfern's great-granddaughter, Verity Newman. I work in that building as well, though, sadly, not the filming location itself. Still, a girl can dream.

A little further down the road, I walk by City Hall, upon which Jack stood in *Greeks Bearing Gifts*, within which Blon Fel Fotch killed a scientist (*Boom Town*) and Jack made his series debut in an officers' club (*The Empty Child*). Just next door is the National Museum which has featured in various episodes of all three series, including *Dalek*, *Random Shoes* and *Mona Lisa's Revenge*. Every now and then I'll walk by and see the circus – that's the fleet of trucks and such that bring set decoration and props and lights and so on – sitting in the carpark. I've even stepped over an electrical cord that was hooked up to some sort of electrical device being used whilst filming an episode of the 2010 season. Just past there is a gorgeous little park called Gorsedd Gardens, where Martha gave flowers to Dr Docherty in *Last of the Time Lords*. (In that scene, look for a woman in a white cardigan in the background; that's a former classmate of mine.) After that, it's past Oceana, the club in which Jack found the recently deceased Owen and just outside of which they were arrested (*Dead Man Walking*). Then it's the New Theatre on your right, said to be "in East Acton, Ealing" in *The Sarah Jane Adventures* but really just before Queen Street in Cardiff. This is actually the one bit of filming I saw live; the circle of people possessed by The Ancient Lights in *Secrets of the Stars* was being shot as I was passing by. I was in a hurry, alas, and couldn't stop. The interior of the theatre was also used in *Evolution of the Daleks*.

After this, it's Queen Street, home of rampaging Cybermen, the shadow of Abaddon, the chase scene that began *Torchwood*'s *Ghost Machine*, and, quite nearby on side streets, where Jack, Martha and the Doctor found out that the Master was PM (*The Sound of Drums*), Jackie Tyler was attacked by Autons (*Rose*) and where Tosh first tried out telepathy alone in a crowd (*Greeks Bearing Gifts*). Thanks to the three series, it's one of the most instantly recognisable places in Cardiff.

Once I leave Queen Street, I'm on Adam Street or Bute Terrace (it changes its name). Just down the road from me is Hope Street, a featured location in *Torchwood*'s *From Out of the Rain*; just a little ways along is the car park with a bit of Rift activity (*Kiss Kiss, Bang Bang*) and a Weevil infestation (*Dead Man Walking*). Whenever I'm in that area, I do check for Weevils, though I've yet to see one. I walk right by the Altolusso building, which is a block of flats where Jack stood in *Everything Changes*, and where a friend was living at the time. (I've probably seen at least three people in long coats and a couple of black SUVs by this point, and smiled to myself about it.) Then it's over to Lloyd George Avenue and straight down to Roald Dahl Plass.

Let me take a moment to talk about the Plass. First of all, despite what you saw in *Children of Earth*, it's fine. I admit I had to go and check for myself during that week. But standing tall in the Plass, just opposite the Millennium Centre – which will be doubling for the Louvre in the 2010 season and was already the hospital in *New Earth* (yes, they do have a little shop) – is the silvery plinth that marks the "tourist entrance" to the Torchwood Hub. If the weather is nice, it reflects the sunlight, sometimes little rainbows if the water droplets catch it just right. But even when it's rather dull and grey – this is Cardiff, after all – shrouding the place in mist, it's still beautiful. Even when they plaster big strawberry decals on it – symbol of one of the summer festivals, and a great shock to me when I first saw it – there is just something about that sculpture that defies any attempt to minimise it. In a way, that's quite metaphorical for the Torchwood team itself.

Every time I can, I do step on the invisible lift... which does sort of defeat the purpose of having an invisible lift, but never mind. I still do it each time and I almost always see visitors doing so as well. Adults, kids, men, women, cosplayers and not, there's just something special about standing on that one spot and imagining, just for a second, that it might actually move.

Of course it doesn't move, so I move on to the final spot in my itinerary: my research project, which is at the "tourist information centre" on the lowest level of Mermaid Quay which is, of course, a front for Torchwood. Even before it became an impromptu memorial – cataloging it is my research project, or one of them, anyway – it was a place for fans to gather and take photos and just generally enjoy the atmosphere. Whenever I lead locations tours, everyone always has photos taken of themselves here and on the invisible lift. If you're wondering, the door is a real door: an access door to the pipes that run under the main level of Mermaid Quay (or so the maintenance and construction workers tell me).

After some time spent cataloging, it's time for the journey to the library. There are two university ones that I frequent, but today, let's say I'm going to the Bute building. I retrace all my steps and then to get to the library I walk a little ways down the road to King Edward VII Avenue. The Temple of Peace features frequently, both exterior (*End of Days*) and interior (*The End of the World*). But the street itself doubled for London in *Children of Earth*, as you saw officials arriving at "Downing Street" – that is, the Glamorgan building – which means that it can be rather upsetting heading toward an area my brain still sort of thinks might contain the 456.

My library needs completed, I head home. I don't pass any other locations that I know of, but give them time; no block will be left unfilmed soon. Of course, this itinerary doesn't even talk about St Mary's Street, which shows up in *Everything Changes*, when Gwen reacts to seeing the dead resurrected, plus it pretends to be Oxford Street in London in several episodes of *Doctor Who*. There's also the bus station and the rail station next door, where we saw Mickey arriving in *Boom Town* and Gwen jumping a barrier and having a spectral encounter in *The Ghost Machine*. Also Cardiff Castle, whose keep – a tower on top of a purpose-built hill at the centre of the grounds within the castle walls – was where Captains Jack and John watched various parts of Cardiff being destroyed by explosives in *Exit Wounds*. (I should point out I was living within one of those blast zones at the time, which was a little disconcerting.) The "server building" from that episode is actually the British Gas building and it also stands tall in the Cardiff skyline, visible on my walk; in *Kiss Kiss, Bang Bang*, it's the building Jack was thrown off. There is also the Cardiff Central Market just down from the Castle, as seen in *Small Worlds*, and Bute Park, which has been everything from Hooverville (*Daleks in Manhattan / Evolution of the Daleks*) to a nice park in *Adrift* to the mystical stone circle in "Roundstone Wood" (*Small Worlds*), as well as where Jack was buried as a foundation offering in *Exit Wounds*. I have sat on those stones, though nothing mystical happened. Perhaps it was the ice cream I was eating?

One thing I should say, though, is that, as compact as Cardiff is, the shows do skew the geography of the city quite a bit. This is the case even when *Torchwood* is showing the city as itself, rather than London. Do not, under any circumstances, attempt to use anything you see as a map or even vague guide to where things are in relation to each other, and definitely don't trust the time estimates! I'm pretty well convinced that Brian Minchin worked in references to the various modifications of the Torchwood SUV in his audiobook *The Sin Eaters* purely to account for such impossibilities as getting from the Hub to the carpark discussed above in under about six minutes in *Kiss Kiss, Bang Bang*, or running to that car park from Oceana in a scene, like in *Dead Man Walking*.

Still, the fact that the shows are shot here seems to be a real source of pride, occasional mutterings about fandom aside. Open the door to any office and you'll undoubtedly find a poster or magazine cover or other picture from one of the shows placed in a prominent position in the coffee room, in cubicles, or on the backs of doors. Any building or room or other item that is bigger than it seems gets analogised to a TARDIS. I see children clutching bookbags shaped like Daleks and once I even saw one with a laser screwdriver; my first instinct was to tell the parents they shouldn't let the child play with weapons! People do order pizza in Cardiff Bay under the name of Torchwood, and the restaurants are perfectly happy with that. There is even a pub near the university called "Mr Smith's", which I'm dying to check out just to see if it might look at all like Sarah Jane's attic on the inside. I'm half-hoping they serve house specialty drinks called "sonic screwdrivers" or "laser screwdrivers" or maybe even something called "Retcon". Then again, maybe they do and I've just forgotten.

So, that's a bit about what it's like living in Cardiff as a fan of *Doctor Who, Torchwood* and *The Sarah Jane Adventures*. It's surreal and strange and occasionally worrying when various sorts of aliens seem bent on taking out the local shopping areas. But it's also beautiful and wonderful, and very much like coming home, especially when you find yourself out in the Bay area, striking up conversations with people from all over the world because you speak the common language of *Doctor Who*.

Now, you'll have to excuse me. A black SUV has just pulled up and I think there are some people coming up to the door. I wonder what they want? And why do they have a small white pill...?

The Downloading FAQ

by Arnold T Blumberg

I'm a big fan of Doctor Who, but I live in the US. Is there any way I can see the new episodes on the same day of transmission in the UK?

No.

I thought they were also put online.

Yes, through the BBC's iPlayer, but that's region restricted for the moment, so if you're outside the UK you're out of luck.

Well, isn't there any other option?

Sure, you can wait until the episode airs on BBC America, which is only a couple weeks these days, or you can wait even longer until the DVDs come out in Region 1 format and then buy those.

I don't want to wait! Fans in the UK get to see the show the day it debuts, why shouldn't I? Isn't there anything else I can do?

No, that's it.

What about downloading them? Can't I download the episodes from somewhere?

Sure, there are lots of places where you can do that: torrents, RapidShare and other file-hosting services, newsgroups. Copies of each episode turn up within hours of their broadcast and can be downloaded and viewed easily through a variety of freeware and shareware applications...

Great!
... but that's illegal.

What?
If you download those copies, you're breaking the law.

You're kidding.
Nope. It's illegal.

That's it? That's the big helpful FAQ? "It's illegal." That's all you have left to say?
What do you want me to say?

Hey, I'm the one that asks the questions!
Sorry.

But is it really that simple? "It's illegal" and that's it?
No, it's not that simple. It's much more complex.

How so?
OK, let's get this out of the way right at the start: yes, we can all agree that if you're a US fan downloading an episode of *Doctor Who* to watch on the day of transmission or at least well before a legal broadcast on BBC America or release on DVD, you are breaking the law. According to the strict letter of the law as it stands today, you are a criminal.

But if that sounds excessive and silly to you, it is. There are murderers, car thieves, bank robbers and mortgage lenders out there. You download a TV show you want to watch on the day that it airs and you're in the same class with those guys?

Yeah, that's crazy!
Well, at least we know where we stand emotionally. Now let's talk about what's really going on here and how the archaic legal system needs to catch up because the future is here. With a vengeance.

The future?
Yes, of content consumption. We're on the cusp of a major transition in so many ways, from local to global media, physical to virtual formats

and the law refuses to change... at least, so far. In the past, this was all so easy to figure out. Whether it was a TV show airing in a certain country or even a physical media format like a videotape or DVD region-coded for a particular geographic location, our corporate media structure was based on the idea that ownership of intellectual property also meant ownership of the means and extent of distribution. But now that the walls of Jericho are falling, and digital technology has enabled anyone, anywhere with certain technical knowledge and equipment to have access to whatever they want to see or hear, the old laws and ethics don't apply. Even the attitudes of viewers have shifted forever.

Some UK fans even yell at me because they think I shouldn't even have the right to see the show when they do.

That's legacy thinking. UK residents pay a licence fee that entitles them to the BBC home service, and therefore – some argue – US fans of a show like *Doctor Who* should not be entitled to the same viewing rights since they haven't bought into that system, nor are they in a position to do so. For them, they can only wait until the show has been purchased by an American-based broadcaster (PBS in the old days, Sci-Fi and now BBC America today) or released on a home video format (VHS and now DVD).

That was fine when the world was different, when we weren't interconnected with cable and modems and wireless networks that allowed us global access to media on a near-instantaneous basis. But now that we are – now that a US fan can theoretically obtain a digital copy of a show from the UK as readily as a UK fan can grab a file of a US show on the day of broadcast or shortly thereafter – the old paradigm makes no sense. Why should anyone have to wait, licence fee or no licence fee? Simple answer: they don't have to, they often don't choose to, and that holds true for either side.

The fact is that the technology to stream content globally has existed for a long time and broadcasters have chosen not to implement it, leaving the very international audiences they crave for lucrative aftermarket dollars feeling like forgotten relatives or second-rate citizens who have to sit at the back and wait their turn. In this day and age, waiting doesn't come naturally to many people and, since our technology now tells us waiting is a sucker's game, it's time for the rest of the world to catch up and acknowledge that the old way is no longer viable.

Kids don't even understand copyright anymore.

That's true, there are young people growing up today who have had access to all this technology their entire lives and therefore feel completely entitled to whatever entertainment they wish at any time. It's not that they want to break any laws or that they're inherently an unethical or immoral generation; it's that they genuinely don't see their relationship with media in the same way that their parents and grandparents did, because their relationship with media is now different. It's evolved.

Are you telling me I should just go ahead and download the episodes and not feel bad about it?

If you don't want to listen to me, a humble little FAQ, how about renowned ethicist Randy Cohen?

Who's that?

He's a renowned ethicist. He recently said, in a column published by *The New York Times*, that if you already purchased the hard copy of a novel, for example, it was ethical to "pirate" an e-version for your digital use even if that's still technically illegal: "Author and publisher are entitled to be paid for their work, and by purchasing the hardcover, you did so. Your subsequent downloading is akin to buying a CD, then copying it to your iPod. Buying a book or a piece of music should be regarded as a license to enjoy it on any platform."

Look at it this way. You're a fan, right?

Sure!

And you intend to buy the DVDs when they come out, don't you?

Of course!

Then the situation is the same.

No, it's not! If I'm pirating an e-version of a television episode before I purchase the DVD version, that's putting the cart before the horse! Cohen's example involved purchasing a legal copy first. Why should the intellectual property owners trust that I'm ever going to buy a copy of the show if I've already stolen one?

Let me answer you with another question: how is it any less ethical to reverse the process if the purchase of a legal copy that makes it ethical is inevitable anyway? You're a fan, you're far more likely to follow through than a casual viewer. We now seem to live in an age where ethical and legal matters have not only taken up residence on different levels of reality but operate outside the normal boundaries of linear time. How appropriate for *Doctor Who* fans.

Not everyone who pirates stuff is going to buy a legitimate copy.
Yes, that's true.

In fact, lots of fans distribute material illegally because they feel they're helping to promote their favourite show or music or whatever. Isn't that exactly what these content creators are most afraid of?
Ah yes, the "promotion" argument. A silly one, but it does happen a lot. In fan circles, this kind of behaviour is much more ingrained. After all, fans can be evangelical in their desire to share their beloved TV series with others. In the past, this may have meant making VHS videotaped copies of episodes and mailing them to other fans or sharing them locally with friends. Shows like *Mystery Science Theater 3000* made a virtue of this practice by featuring the slogan "Keep circulating the tapes" at the end of every episode. And long before the RIAA (the Recording Industry Association of America) was suing old ladies and knocking down doors with the help of law enforcement authorities, devotees of every band under the sun were trading cassette tapes of live performances and copied CDs.

Now, however, it's a different story. Fans haven't changed in their passion for sharing the things they love, but the ease of their ability to share them and the sheer volume in which they can distribute material has multiplied beyond anyone's expectations. Instead of making a couple of cassette dupes of a CD or a few videotapes of TV episodes, a mildly tech-savvy fan with a laptop and an internet connection can upload a high-def season's worth of television or several perfect CD copies to a newsgroup or P2P site for tens if not hundreds of thousands of others to access. And even the original founders of *MST3K,* now producing a similar series on DVD called *Cinematic Titanic,* have said that their philosophy has definitely changed and they hope fans will not "circulate the ripped DVD files".

I don't think your friend Cohen would support that kind of behaviour now, would he?
Certainly not, but he's not my friend.

And even if I'm just pirating that one copy of the show and then buying the DVD, Cohen's word doesn't change the fact that I'm still considered a criminal and it won't stop someone from prosecuting me.
That's true, technically. But, for one thing, that doesn't happen very often, because the effort required to pursue you for grabbing a few *Doctor Who* episodes here in the US is too disproportionate for the BBC to bother. Also, Cohen's view of the matter illuminates a larger issue.

Which is?

That we now live in an era where the ethicality of an action no longer equates with its illegality.

This is hardly the first time in human history that something ethically right or at least acceptable has been made illegal.

I know, but there's such logical dissonance here. The insanity of attempting to preserve outmoded notions of regionality in media has led to a world in which fans across an ocean can access a website for a favourite show, read text and look at still photos but are prevented from viewing a video clip because for some reason that's a step too far. But since there are always tech-savvy folks with the ability to circumvent such limitations, those clips turn up on YouTube and a million other websites within hours anyway, so nothing is being accomplished; except perhaps the broadcaster making it clear that they have no real interest in including the audience they will later depend on for their dollars when the DVDs arrive. Our convenience culture has outgrown this view of the world as a collection of regions because it simply doesn't see the lines of demarcation.

It sounds to me like everyone has a reason to be scared: the piraters, the content creators, everyone!

Yes.

Okay then, you're the all-knowing FAQ. What happens next?

Things have to change. Maybe it'll involve content creators selling their material directly to consumers via micro-payment or subscription models. Maybe the iTunes method will work in the end and everything will be pumped through those channels. It's already been proven that people do tend to use those options when they're offered. Remember, it's about convenience and if it's more convenient to get a copy of a TV show via a modestly priced legitimate system, people tend to choose that avenue.

You're saying people really like to do the right thing?

Oh, hell no! It's not about doing the right thing; it's about doing the easy thing. If it's cheap and easy, they'll do it. And if they can pay a few dollars for something or sit down and try to figure out how to install a torrent client, a viewer, a decoder or whatever they have to use to access or reassemble all those pirated files, they'll tend to go with the legal choice. Because it's easier. But it's still not that simple. Pirating can still be very easy, and we still have those generations of young people growing up with a very different idea about what should be free and available to them at all times. So it's hard to say how it's all going to work out.

Wait a minute. After all this, you're telling me that you have no answers?
No, it's worse than that.

What do you mean?
I'm not just telling you that I don't have answers, I'm telling you that right now, there aren't any answers. No one has them. Not me, not the big entertainment companies, governments, leading legal thinkers or Randy Cohen. Everyone is lost... for now. The rapid progress of our technology and the ensuing shift in culture that has convinced generations of young people that everything should be available to them instantly and for free at all times has forever altered our relationship to our media content. That will not change back; the path lies forward. Are we really going to brand those generations of kids filling their iPods and computers with television, movies and music as criminals in need of jail time? Or are we going to take a long, hard look at our legal system, our media distribution methods and our corporate culture in order to begin the difficult work of evolving to meet our technology?

You're asking me the questions again.
Sorry, but that's the way it is these days. Life in the twenty-first century as an American *Doctor Who* fan is an ethical minefield trickier than the one the Doctor navigated in *The Sea Devils* and we have no sonic screwdriver.

You've been no help at all.
What are you going to do now?

There's a new episode of Doctor Who *on BBC1 today. I'm going to wait a couple of hours, download and watch it. In a couple of weeks I'm going to watch it again on BBC America and, in a few months, I'll buy the DVD box set and the Character Options action figures based on it.*
Will you feel guilty about it?

Probably. But I'll also be hoping that one day the world will catch up to me and I won't have to.
Until then, I have only one last answer for you.

What's that?
Enjoy the show.

HOORAY!

Before 2005, *Doctor Who* was probably the single finest defense against the auteur theory, or the idea that a film or television production was "authored" by a single person. The classic series was always a glorious example of television by committee: stories had the handprints of writer, producer, script editor, even the actors, all over them. The series was even created out of a vague, woolly collaborative process.

That changed, forever, with Russell T Davies.

Television, or at least good television, had been moving into auteur territory: *The West Wing, Mad Men, The Sopranos, Breaking Bad, Buffy the Vampire Slayer, Coupling*... these were shows where, even if an individual episode was given over to a staff writer, it still reflected the voice of its head writer or showrunner. This tradition had been well ensconced in British television for decades thanks to the Dennis Potters and the Alan Bennetts and the Paul Abbotts. Fans who think that the BBC chose Russell T Davies to produce *Doctor Who* as some kind of a fluke are deluding themselves: in 2003, the BBC did not greenlight a revival of *Doctor Who*; they greenlighted Russell T Davies' revamp of *Doctor Who.* Davies – already one of the best known writers in television in Britain – was the draw, not *Who*.

As a result, the first four years of New *Who* reflects the spirit of a dominant author for the first time ever. And it reflects it from script to screen, with Davies polishing most other scripts and presiding over the all-important tone meeting to determine how the story will feel onscreen.

If *Doctor Who* was going to become an auteur production, it picked the best possible auteur. Russell T Davies, as a writer, producer and pundit, is larger than life, containing contradictions and complexities. He's driven to make television that's exciting, challenging and popular, and he's a man of distinct convictions. He's also a huge fan of both *Doctor* Who and television. He understands both intimately

Naturally, such an idiosyncratic approach will, by its very nature, polarise opinion. The great thing about Russell T Davies is that he's bigger than all that, looming above the fray, just getting on with the Herculean (and frankly rare) task of creating television that's watched by nine million people.

In so many ways, the Doctor from 2005 to 2009 was neither

Christopher Eccleston nor David Tennant. It was Russell T Davies, a larger-than-life figure who turned everything upside down, emerging triumphant in the end. How perfect is that?

Wasn't It Glorious?

by Scott Clarke
From Enlightenment #146, July 2008

"He's fire and ice and rage. He's like the night, and the storm in the heart of the sun."

—*The Family of Blood*

Paul Cornell was writing about the Doctor, but would I be overstating the case if I said there was a little of the Doctor in Russell T Davies' larger-than-life influence over the phenomenal return of everyone's favourite Time Lord?

There is something of a magical touch to the program's success. And, while he's certainly in control, Davies is enabled by an incredibly talented team in front of and behind the camera. Sometimes he leaves the spotlight for others to shine (*Human Nature, Dalek, The Empty Child*). He ups the ante with each season finale, displaying the glee of child and fan alike. And no, he doesn't always make the right choices (Gollum Doctor in *Last of the Time Lords*). But neither does the Doctor. Neither do we.

*

Only now [the Doctor] looks at [Jabe]. And he's wild, hollow, wretched.

—*From the stage directions in* The End of the World

It seems popular for people to say, "We're eternally grateful that he's brought the series back and made it incredibly successful, but..."

How about "and"?

*

"Turns out I've had the most terrible things happen. And the most brilliant things. And sometimes... well, I can't tell the difference."

—Elton Pope, *Love & Monsters*

Mind you, it feels a tad premature to make an assessment of Russell T Davies' tenure as show runner of *Doctor Who*, what with four more specials to come in 2009, but I can't help but feel that an era has truly come to an end. Sure, he's coming back to perform a couple of encores, but the concert is at an end.

Davies has been able to put his stamp on the programme in a way that is unparalleled in its history. Even strong personalities like Barry Letts and John Nathan-Turner, who had their fingerprints all over the show, never achieved the level of influence that Davies has.

A well-respected writer of such dramas as *Queer as Folk, Bob and Rose, The Second Coming* and *Casanova,* Davies often claimed that only a chance to revive *Doctor Who* would bring him back to the BBC. Yes, the ground was fertile with many sympathetic supporters such as BBC1 Controller Lorraine Heggessey and Head of Drama Jane Tranter, but it's impossible to say how history would have unfolded if Davies had been uninterested or unavailable to helm the revival. The ghost of the show's past still hung uneasily in the air, with a mix of fondness and embarrassment like Benny Hill, Nehru jackets and toad-in-the-hole.

Any doubts were dispelled when *Rose* hit the airwaves in 2005. The frenetic crash-zoom into the Earth and the time-lapsed depiction of a day in the life of a working-class shop girl was pitch perfect. Here was a writer who knew how to communicate a great deal of exposition with elegant economy (a major plus for a 45 minute drama that had oodles to set up). Perhaps one of the most incredible feats Russell performed was giving *Doctor Who* the immediacy of contemporary television. We forget what a shock it was to see *Doctor Who* begin and complete an adventure in a mere 45 minutes.

*

"Let me tell you something about those who get left behind. Because it's hard. And that's what you become. Hard. But if there's one thing I've learned, it's that I will never let her down. And I'll protect them both, until the end of my life."

—Jackie Tyler, *Love & Monsters*

Some fans of the 40-year-plus programme were hot to trot and eager to get right back into the swing of things. Davies had other plans; he was clearly focussed on reintroducing the concept in an accessible way to a mainstream audience: in particular, the nation's children. A burping wheelie bin may have seemed rubbish to some forty year olds, but Russell could still see into the minds of ten year olds.

Of course, making the programme accessible also meant making the characters and situations identifiable and the themes universal. Rose Tyler had a family, as did Martha Jones and Donna Noble after her. While the characters were whizzing off on adventures, they were always rooted and responsible to their relationships. In some cases, we saw the consequences of not attending to those relationships: Jackie's loneliness, Mickey's inability to let go of Rose or Martha's mother jumping to the wrong conclusions with disastrous results.

Those who were familiar with Davies' previous work weren't surprised. Dramas such as *The Second Coming* or *Bob and Rose* are about regular people caught in extraordinary circumstances, whether it be grappling with your friend's revelation that he's the son of God or a couple who break sexual and political taboos by falling in love.

*

"The ripe old smell of humans. You survive. Oh, you might have spent a million years evolving into clouds of gas and another million as downloads, but you always revert to the same basic shape. The fundamental human. End of the universe and here you are. Indomitable, that's the word. Indomitable!"

—The Doctor, *Utopia*

Davies returns to his favourite themes as often as he does to his favourite names. There's a warm streak of optimistic humanism through all of Davies' work, and indeed the entire programme under his tenure.

Time and again Davies explored unrequited love (*Boom Town,* Martha's entire character arc), empowerment of the ordinary person (*The Long Game, Parting of the Ways,* Donna's entire character arc), the strength of solidarity (*Last of the Time Lords, The Stolen Earth*), loneliness / loss (*Gridlock / Doomsday*) and self-sacrifice (*Voyage of the Damned*). These themes echoed in the scripts of the other writers too. There was a cohesion to the programme that it rarely had in the past (somewhat let down in the 2006 season as Davies struggled to work out Rose and the tenth Doctor's relationship).

And yes, conversely, I suppose one has to acknowledge that Davies put a strong rewriting hand to the scripts of the other writers (Steven Moffat notwithstanding). But who could blame him? His name and reputation was at stake, particularly in the early years. But then, he had an innate ability to capture what other writers did so well. Russell, it has been said, wrote most of *The Impossible Planet* and *The Satan Pit.* And "Street corner, two in the morning, getting in a taxi home; I've never had a life like that" in *Father's Day*? That was Russell.

*

"Britain, Britain, Britain. What extraordinary times we've had. Just a few years ago this world was so small. And then they came. Out of the unknown. Falling from the sky. You've seen it happen. Big Ben, destroyed. A spaceship over London. All those ghosts and metal men."

—Harold Saxon (The Master), *The Sound of Drums*

Davies gave us some of the most memorable and iconic moments of the new series. Rose and the Doctor running hand in hand across the bridge in *Rose*; the famous "chips" scene in *The End of the World*; the equally powerful scene at the end of *Gridlock*; the heartbreaking finale to *Doomsday*, the Doctor and Rose divided by a wall and a universe. Who else would conceive of the potential of horror from Lesley Sharp as Sky Silvestry simply repeating words, or devise that heart-stopping return for the Master in *Utopia*? And, just when you think he may have run out of juice, he serves up that brilliant miming scene between the Doctor and Donna in *Partners in Crime*.

His ideas have been big and brash and sometimes illogical, but they've been inventive and sublime too. A self-proclaimed atheist, he nevertheless understood the truth of having his characters sing old-time gospel hymns in *Gridlock*, keeping the faith (so to speak). And if the Doctor just can't seem to let go of his "little shop", there are simple understated moments like those between Jabe and the ninth Doctor that are pitch perfect.

Watching Davies talk about the series in interviews or on *Doctor Who Confidential*, one is struck by the obvious glee he takes in devising the big *Who* moments. One oft-levelled criticism of Davies is that he writes himself into a corner as a result of his huge enthusiasm and love for shocks and spectacle. Another is that he sacrifices logic and plot for character moments or even for a joke. I suppose whether one feels cheated from a piece of writing is ultimately subjective, no matter how much we try to convince ourselves otherwise. When Rose consumes the time vortex and puts the Daleks out to pasture, it doesn't ring true because that's what we'd do in real life, but rather because that's what we'd do in our greatest fantasies. It's the force of character that led her to that moment that contains the power. The Daleks are incidental. Good fun. Threatening when they need to be, and funny when they're called upon.

*

"Don't be so daft. I'm nothing special."
"Yes you are, you're brilliant!"
—The Doctor and Donna, *Turn Left*

Russell T Davies has created a storm over the past three years. He's changed the landscape for *Doctor Who* and leaves the endless possibilities for creation and destruction as fertile and as behind-the-couch frightening as they ever were.

Love him or hate him, the man brought us *Doctor Who*.

And wasn't it glorious?

Reaching Total Dominance

by Simon Kinnear
From Shockeye's Kitchen (online version), June 2005

You can pinpoint, virtually to the minute, the moment when fandom finally fell in love with Russell T Davies. At 7.40 (or thereabouts) on Saturday, 11th June, 2005, the Doctor finally made his stand against the forces of evil – "I'm coming to get you, Rose" – and a hundred thousand jaws hit the floor in unison.

Had you told me a year ago that it would take such a crowd-pleasing rallying cry to reconcile a petulant flock with their televisual saviour, I would have been convinced you'd gone crazy. *Doctor Who* is coming back, I'd have replied, with a decent budget, a high-profile lead and, best of all, one of Britain's leading writers at the helm. This is the beginning of a beautiful friendship; what could turn it sour?

Even a mere three months ago, there was barely a batsqueak of dissent about the direction he might take the programme in. When the series debuted, we were too busy celebrating to find cause for complaint (dare I say it was viewed through Rose-tinted glasses?) and RTD was the most popular man in fandom.

Of course, it didn't last. I've come to the opinion that *Doctor Who* fandom has some sick compunction to find a hate figure, someone to blame when things aren't as perfect as we want them to be. Call it JN-T Syndrome. We'd all assumed that the new series' weak link would be Billie Piper, but when it transpired how good she was, we needed a new scapegoat and (despite briefly alighting on turncoat Christopher Eccleston) there was only going to be one candidate for the position.

Since that first week, an increasingly vocal minority have pilloried RTD for his populism, his emphasis of character over plot, his perceived "gay agenda" and, in general, for shattering the stone tablets that some fans would like to think govern the parameters of what's allowed in *Doctor Who*. As the season has wound on, the arrival of RTD-scripted stories has been greeted with increasing derision and sullenness, which just shows that some people can never be happy.

To be fair, *Who* 2005 is as radical a concept as they come, so it's perhaps unsurprising if we've sometimes run scared; I must admit it's caught me off-guard several times. The boldest step RTD has taken is to establish the show's core traditional values by grounding the fantasy in emotional realism. The trick may have been stolen wholesale from *Buffy*, but it's a durable one, allowing Russell to pre-empt the public's scepticism of the dusty clichés we take for granted with wit, compassion and intelligence.

Episodes like *Aliens of London* and *Boom Town* are conscious "what if?" dramatisations of the inner lives of the Doctor and his companions. Viewed strictly in terms of the classic "base under siege" thriller, they're arguably unsatisfying, but they offer a thematic and emotional weight, season-wide, that's never been attempted in *Doctor Who*.

The inspiration, clearly, is the pioneering US dramas of the last decade or so: a "long game" approach rarely allows for a stand-out individual episode, preferring the cumulative impact of a wider, progressive vision. As *Who* fans, raised on the portmanteau structure of the classic series, we're unused to seeing such consistency; we've been trained by decades of let-downs to believe that every classic must have its corresponding clanger.

In this season, RTD's scripts were the easiest target. In retrospect, it was incredibly brave of RTD to commission other writers to pen the episodes the fans were most looking forward to – the Hinchcliffe-style horror stories, the Dalek comeback, the time-travel paradox – leaving him solely with the more experimental (and, therefore, controversial) adventures.

The strategy paid off handsomely in giving us instant classics like *Dalek* and *The Empty Child*, but left RTD to face the backlash alone. His scripts were either too Hollyoaks, too comedic or too camp. The latter complaint smacked of homophobia, with the really militant moaners clutching at every straw of dialogue or action to persuade us that the show was a hotbed of same-sex propaganda.

Yet the unspoken fear common to all of his objections was the realisation that, after being pandered to by years of books and Big Finish, we were suddenly surplus to requirements; the series simply isn't geared towards the pre-existing audience of fans. RTD's target is the everyday viewer, the person who sits on the sofa and wants to be transported by the television, to laugh and cry and be amazed. The element mistaken for "camp" is an infectious sense of fun, a sense of warmth and optimism that's largely absent in classic *Who*. Face it, Robert Holmes – the official postholder of best *Who* writer – is a grumpy cynic whose stories tend to involve supremely dumb, ineffectual societies incapable of transformation without the Doctor's help. Whereas RTD, even when attacking corruption, greed and indolence, is backed by an unshakeable belief in the possibility of change...

... a belief that extends even to *Doctor Who* fans. For, little did we know, RTD had a plan all along. Just as the Doctor was gradually being drawn into the machinations of the Bad Wolf, so fandom was being prepared for its final immersion into one man's vision of how good the show could be. He'd won the public over with Britney Spears and farting aliens, kept the fans' brickbats at bay with a chained-up Dalek, pushed the show's boundaries with a Doctor / monster dinner date and then, finally, just as we were preparing to rewrite our All Time Worst lists, has delivered what looks set to be British TV's boldest, most talked-about piece of sci-fi since Professor Quatermass' ill-fated experiment. And we fell for it.

It's ironic, really, that *Bad Wolf* would be the episode to silence the haters. It's whimsical (the "reality TV bites" satire is a gnat's whisker away from Cartmel era silliness), it's camp (see Jack's innuendo-strewn encounter with Trinny and Susannah) and, with its high-concept storyline and stunt casting, it's aimed squarely at the British public's tabloid instincts. In the week leading up to its broadcast, many were quick to pronounce it as the death knell of *Doctor Who*.

Instead, what happened was that, miraculously, the dissenters were silenced. The anti-RTD jokes were hastily rewritten as hymns to his majesty. And fandom, finally, learned to stop worrying and love RTD.

I tell you what, though; I feel sorry for David Tennant. Little does he realise that the position of fandom's Most Hated has just become vacant.

You Must Have Been Like God

by Lloyd Rose

Russell T Davies' prankishness – his sly, mischievous glee – is the heart and soul of New *Who*. If there's a moment of pure self-expression in the show, it's when that impish id the Master twirls through the door and dances across the bridge of the *Valiant*: *Doctor Who* is all his! YES! And he is going to do astounding things with it!

And Davies did. Five years ago, I would have said reviving *Doctor Who* was impossible. Just maybe, Joss Whedon (who spent several of his school years in England and obviously knew the show) could have done it. But then again, maybe not. The show's colour, that peculiar mix of wit, whimsy and terror, wasn't in what you think of as the normal creative palette. And it was hard to see how the charms of its tinfoil-footed robots and shag-carpet monsters could be redone for the Oughts. In hindsight, considering how successful some of the New Adventures and Eighth Doctor Adventures were, my concern was kind of beside the point. And Davies didn't even write one of the more successful NAs; *Damaged Goods* was fascinating and dark, but his humour and energy and, well, sass were missing. Television, not staid grey print, is his medium, and he can make television seem like a form of dance.

As a choreographer, Davies goes in for flash, kineticism and surprise, including unexpected bursts of wit and energy, and startling shifts of mood. These traits can be found in every aspect of the show, from its art design to its sound, costuming, direction. Disappointingly – with reliable exceptions like Moffat and Cornell – not so often in the scripts. From a producer / writer, weak scripts are the last thing you'd think would be a problem, but this is where New *Who* has suffered most while continuing to look and sound smashing.

Some of the weaknesses have been downright weird for a show that prides itself on its political savvy, such as the statement in *Daleks in Manhattan* informing the audience that there was no racism in America during the Depression because the working class achieved solidarity in the face of the collapse of capitalism (tell that to the black victims of white vigilantes; an anti-lynching bill was defeated in Congress in 1935). This sort of political blunder is, unfortunately, not atypical.

I still can't work out what Davies thought he was doing in *The Sound of Drums* when he destroyed Japan. We'd had the shot of the Lenin-style statue of the Master, so I suppose that scored (lightly) off the Soviet Union. Time to smack America for Hiroshima and Nagasaki? By doing it all over again in fiction?! Wasn't once in reality enough? Couldn't he have blown up Canada or California or someplace? Not that anyone in the episode pays much attention to this genocide; certainly there's no character of Japanese heritage to miss cousin Yasunari – though possibly Toshiko, if she heard about it in the Himalayas, might have had a twinge or two. I guess it was just all in fun.

The trilogy that ends the 2007 season – *Utopia, The Sound of Drums, The Last of the Time Lords* – is full of these bewildering, semi-ludicrous missteps; it's also amazing television. I can't think of anything else on the small screen that achieves in so little time (two hours and fifteen minutes) such an epic sweep. Part political satire, part love story, part fairy tale, part *Doctor-Who*-old-enemy episode and all crazy ambition, the finale is misshapen and impossible to the point of embarrassment, yet inexplicably and disturbingly powerful, like a nightmare that, however silly its remembered details, retains its staining dread. Moods swing near-pharmaceutically, tone shifts with a screech, jokes bounce around like ping-pong balls, and there are periodic lurches into swamps of grandiosity and sorrow. Davies unabashedly casts the story on a Wagnerian scale as, in the twilight of their destroyed civilisation, the only two surviving gods battle over the fate of the Earth.

It's preposterous, it's laughable, it's too much, it's a mess, it's brilliant.

Davies' writing here is wry and tragic, silly and doomed, sentimental and grotesque, cruel and naive. As with fairy-tales, he touches on primal elements while telling a story for children. The antagonists' grand challenging meeting, where they throw down their respective gauntlets, plays like some sort of phone sex. The unfairness of Jack's "wrongness" separating him from the man he loves is a miserable comment on the plight of a gay man in love with a straight one. We're shown the wretched end of the human race. Despised and hopeless love underpins everything: Jack and Martha's futile yearning, Lucy's broken dreams, the impossibility of the Doctor and the Master ever uniting, as survivors, as friends, as lovers, as symbols of life and death, as anything.

Frissons of creepiness worthy of the Brothers Grimm slither by. Ever since William Hartnell turned into Patrick Troughton, *Doctor Who* has had a built-in, rather eerie sensitivity to the body: our hero changes his, which saves him not only from death but from ageing. In a move arguably more shocking than any sexual use of the character could have been, Davies strips Tennant of his beauty and strength, lays him bare in the humiliation not of nakedness but of withered old age. He smears the all-but-immortal's face in coming death, as if it were filth. When the shrunken creature the Doctor becomes (unfortunately, an unsuccessful CGI design) is locked in a cage, he's like Hansel waiting for the oven. The Master works from the microcosm – the Doctor – out: he'll deform and obliterate the universe. He isn't just a bad guy; he's Death itself. To conquer him, the Doctor has to be cornily, embarrassingly, in a lavender-lit special effect out of a video game, reborn. And so Death is swallowed up in victory.

Davies is an atheist, but these specifically Christian overtones can hardly be accidental. The Doctor forgives his enemy. He himself is rescued and transformed by the power of love. In his eyes, the meek, with their humble chops and gravy, are the rightful inheritors of the Earth. (Admittedly, this is solid leftwing theology too.) The character was already into that dying-and-resurrecting thing; in his tenth incarnation, he claimed absolute authority for moral decisions. But without genuine religious underpinning, this attitude isn't much more than one man's ego-trip. The Doctor's ability to play god comes to rest in the fact that he's simply the most powerful person in the game: he's got the lightning bolts and might makes right.

Of course, all that power extracts a terrible price; he also suffers for our sins, saving us from our follies again and again, a sacrifice that the show presents as mostly unacknowledged. Though the Doctor is there for everyone; no one, finally, is there for him. It's one poignant moment of loss after another: his home, Rose, the Master, his daughter, Madame de Pompadour, River Song, Donna. Give the guy a break – and the audience too. How much sorrier for him can we feel? Fortunately, Tennant is such an unmaudlin actor that he drains most of the infection from this repetitive whininess, but it still smells. He's lonely, God he's lonely, he's all alone, everyone else is dead because he had to kill them to save the universe and nobody seems to understand how hard that was on him, and now he's so, so lonely; oh, and unappreciated too. Where is all this whinging coming from? Tom Baker, Peter Davison and Sylvester McCoy each suggested a core of melancholy in the Doctor, but Davies' *Who* insists on it.

In interviews, Davies has said that when he made up his own *Doctor Who* adventures as a child, he was always the companion. Some fan critics have pounced on this – with surprising prejudices for a community that prides itself on sophistication and tolerance – as proof that Davies wants to see himself as a hot blonde like Rose or a hunk like Captain Jack and indulge his secret fantasies about the sexy actors he's cast as the Doctor. My guess is it's a rare producer who casts a gorgeous lead without some fantasising about her or him: often this gives the show a spark; it certainly has with *Who*. I don't think Davies has been secretive or coy about the matter. But neither do I think his surrogate is any of the hangers-on. A genius who plays God to make everything all right and sometimes has to do awful things that aren't understood by the very people to whom he brings such a wondrous gift. What is that if not the self-portrait of a television producer?

Morality Play

by Jonathan Blum

Doctor Who used to be happy to give us characters who fit neatly onto the Good List or the Bad List. Which one someone belonged to was usually visible at a glance; maybe a secondary figure on the Bad List could work their way onto the Good List, but usually only through a determined self-sacrifice around episode four. If they didn't go the redemption route, they could usually be guaranteed a death by poetic justice, as the storytelling universe paid off their transgressions. There are exceptions but, in many ways, *Who*'s morality was an exercise in well-delivered blame.

On the occasions when it did present us with a deliberately murky moral situation, the arguments about it still polarised quickly into black and white. And usually white was whatever square the Doctor was standing on. Even in *Genesis of the Daleks,* there's very little sense that the Doctor could be wrong not to destroy the Daleks; never mind that his closing benediction, about how through their violence the Daleks will be a force not for evil but for good, is an echo of what Davros said earlier in the story. *Remembrance of the Daleks* later showed a Doctor who could premeditate genocide of a monstrous race; this was clearly meant to introduce a sense of ambiguity, but the number of people on both sides of the argument who insisted that there wasn't anything really grey about it – that the Doctor was now an irredeemable monster, or that there wasn't actually anything disturbing about mass-murder for the greater good – still amazes me. Perhaps it's because the argument could easily become abstract; something to be viewed in the nice comforting black and white of a chessboard.

But in the new series? Things are just a little bit funkier, not least because the moral questions are personal. From the moment the tenth Doctor turned the same dismissive vengeance on Harriet Jones that he did on the Sycorax leader, or Rose ran roughshod over Mickey's feelings while saving the world, Russell Davies has made it progressively harder to view *Doctor Who* without acknowledging more than one side to how his people behave. He's shown us characters, and stories, which plant their feet firmly in both Good and Bad categories at once.

Harriet Jones in *The Christmas Invasion* is a classic example of moral ambiguity for the post-*Buffy* age: take a sympathetic and loved character, and have her do something drastic and heinous for absolutely the right reasons. Then have both her and the Doctor push each other's buttons in a fit of pique until he does something drastic right back. This is the argument which the show didn't dare let the Brigadier and the Doctor have after *The Silurians,* because it would have had to end either with one of them backing down, or with something irrevocable like the Doctor leaving UNIT. But the new show goes there, and keeps going there, with the consequences of this event: both plot-related, with Harold Saxon's rise to power being a direct consequence of Harriet Jones' downfall, and in terms of the argument itself being revisited when Harriet reappears in *The Stolen Earth.*

The difference is, in most earlier moral arguments, the show in some way signposted whose side it was on; the Brigadier may have a fair point in *Silurians*, but the script ensures our emotional reactions are with the Doctor: we're shown his despair and sense of injustice, while the Brigadier is kept completely off screen till the following story. *The Christmas Invasion* doesn't just give us the Doctor's emotional reaction, of righteous fury at the slaughter of a defeated enemy; it also shows us the full range of Harriet's emotions in the space of a few minutes: her joy at hugging "my Doctor", then her conviction that humanity needs to be able to protect itself, and her moment of heartbreak and panic when the Doctor turns his back on her and ends her career. Imagine how the *Genesis* argument would have gone if Sarah or Harry had lived through their world being conquered by the Daleks, had lost co-workers and loved ones to them, and brought those emotions to bear on the Doctor; that's what Harriet brings to the table in those scenes. We're made to feel for both sides of the moral argument, as never before. And so we can't rely on our emotions to lead our intellectual judgement, or even to clue us in to which side the story is taking.

Of course, that made for wildly contradictory readings of the scene. How dare Russell Davies make the Doctor look like such a self-righteous idiot as to disagree with Harriet! How dare Russell make Harriet into such a monster! How dare he say that the *Belgrano* incident which inspired Harriet's actions was justified? How dare he say that it wasn't?

Well, what the hell is Russell Davies saying, then? Precious little. He's letting Harriet Jones and the Doctor each say the things they would say. What the story does, what Russell Davies' writing regularly does, is depict rather than judge: it sets up characters with clear, usually admirable, traits, winds them up, lets them collide head-on and shows us where the pieces fall. It's not a morality play, it's a depiction of cause and effect. A strangely neutral picture of how the things which make characters strong and admirable, taken in the wrong combination, can also be their tragic flaws. Rose's devotion to the Doctor and determination are literally enough to save the entire universe in *The Parting of the Ways* – and those are the exact traits which lead her to dismiss Mickey in that story, a dismissal which leads to her heartbreak half a season later. Or *Midnight*, in which the very things that make the Doctor feel Doctorish – his belief in his own intellect, his gift of gab, his wandering outsider nature – are the exact things which make him the least likely person to be trusted.

Rather than presenting every action of his heroes as justified, Davies keeps putting in little touches which point directly to the difficult bits. It bothers some fans that the new show diminishes the Doctor's moral authority, but they seem to think this is just creeping in by accident without the writer being aware of it. When the Doctor declares that there's no higher authority than him in *New Earth,* isn't that pretty arrogant? It's partly just a reflection of there not being any other Time Lords about, but who elected them, for that matter? Who does this guy think he is, especially given that he can get things wrong? Well, that's exactly the question which stories like *Midnight* and *The Christmas Invasion* put in the spotlight.

Davies lets the impact of the moral conflict keep unfolding over later episodes. By *The Sound of Drums,* it turns out that the Doctor's unseating of Harriet eventually allows the Master to come to power. So was he wrong to overthrow her? Erm, maybe not... because the same story shows us doing exactly what he accused her of starting: we see the human race unleashed as monsters on the universe. In another delightful moral irony, our transformation into the Toclafane is in a way the ultimate vindication of the Doctor's classic description of humanity, as reiterated the week before in *Utopia*: our indomitability, our refusal to accept that everything dies, is what leads us to discard our bodies and merge our minds in the name of survival, and wreak havoc across the universe. Again, our best features are also our worst ones; at the end of the story, our ability to come together with one mind and one purpose for a great aim – to defeat the Master – is exactly the same trait which, trillions of years in the future, turns us into the Toclafane. (See also *Gridlock,* in which humanity's religious faith both allows them to bear the unbearable and lets them accept the unacceptable.)

When Harriet Jones finally reappears in *The Stolen Earth,* this time she gets all the emotions on her side. She's shown with unflinching bravery and dignity, as she sacrifices herself in order to lead the Doctor back to Earth. The same woman who provoked the Doctor's "get ready for the real monsters, the human race" becomes the ultimate example of a human standing up to help the Doctor, simply because it's the right thing to do. She even gets to justify her stance, with no one to contradict her: she did what she did because she knew a day like this would come when the Doctor wasn't around and humanity would have to stand on its own two feet. Is the show saying that Harriet was right and the Doctor was wrong? No, because by calling for the Doctor she's accepting that humanity can't stand on its own two feet. Is she conceding that the Doctor was right? No, because she still believes it was right to try. Most tellingly, Harriet Jones may think the Doctor was wrong on that point, but she doesn't think that makes him the enemy.

It's that difference, between emotionally connecting us to one side and vilifying the other, which is fairly new territory for *Doctor Who*. The show can now allow a couple of grownups to continue to disagree, without having to make either one look like a fool. But you have to look at the whole of the content presented on the subject to recognise this. When Martha is upset at the Doctor's lack of romantic interest, the show arrays our emotions against him: we remember the Doctor obliviously going on about Rose while Martha is lying in bed with him in *The Shakespeare Code* and he looks like an insensitive cad. That moment can blind us to the way he behaves in the rest of the season: after that point, he never brings Rose up to Martha again. (He only mentions her when other characters, including Martha, raise the subject.) The series also contains a number of scenes where Martha talks to other people about her feelings, in stories like *Gridlock* and *Daleks In Manhattan*, but doesn't say it directly to the Doctor, tying in with a character trait of hers which Davies alludes to in *The Writer's Tale*, which is Martha's unwillingness to be direct about what she's feeling. It's a multifaceted view of unrequited love, in which it's not just his fault for missing clues but also hers for only giving clues. Rather than showing the Doctor taking Martha for granted, he repeatedly thanks her and states his appreciation of her, at the ends of *42*, *Human Nature* and *Last of the Time Lords*; the stronger emotions attached to his earlier moment of bad behaviour can make that one incident eclipse the others.

That's the trap of truthiness: evidence which supports the things we feel, we remember; evidence which goes against them, we tend to overlook. Look at how Christopher Eccleston's Doctor is regularly painted as thoroughly scarred and angsty, even though in fact he spent about as much time grinning "Hullo!", fanboying to Charles Dickens and bopping about to Soft Cell as he did shouting about the Time War. The intensity of feeling obscures how much time is spent on other shades.

If anything, being extremely familiar with the way *Doctor Who* works can skew how we perceive the characters' moral qualities. It can lead us to dismiss stupendous bravery and amazing devotion to the welfare of others, as the sort of thing that happens all the time. The Doctor singlehandedly leads an infiltration of a Cyberman headquarters in the midst of a London warzone, shouts down a mechanical tyrant, and sleight-of-hands a security code into the system to destroy his army? Just another day at the office. But if the Doctor is thoughtless and rude to Mickey Smith in the process? Oh, that's reprehensible. And if there are several of these moments over time – which of course there will be, because the Doctor has always been a bit of a knob; just ask Harry Sullivan – then those moments, not the huge actions in between, get seen as the dominant pattern. Just like the way the Doctor's imperfections as a hero attract far more attention from fans than his ability; in *Rose*, he may have singlehandedly tracked down a Nestene invasion, blown up their transmitter, brewed up a chemical weapon to destroy them, tracked them to their lair, and faced down the big writhing monster to demand that they cease and desist, but that's not as new-and-noteworthy as the fact that it took Rose swinging in on a chain to win the day, which therefore means that the Doctor's obviously a helpless waste of space who needs someone else to cover for him.

Over the years, the TV industry has shifted across the board in its approach to drama, emphasising the characters' emotional reactions to events far more than in the largely plot-centered days of *Gunsmoke* and original-series *Star Trek* – and this shift can skew the needle when a viewer tries to read a moral compass. (Especially within fandom, which focussed intently on moments of character reaction even in the old days; they loom even larger now.) In *The Long Game*, the Doctor grabs Adam by the ear and throws him out of the TARDIS; because we've been led to sympathise with the kid, this can feel like the Doctor's suddenly developed a deep judgemental streak. Then again, if you look back over all those years of the old show, you realise he's always been quite happy to decide whether various people or monsters should live or die. (Of course, those were all baddies, right? Erm, not exactly free from judgementalism there.) Beyond that, there's everything from his dismissal of those savages Ian and Barbara at the start of the series to his repeated contempt for the Brigadier and Harry Sullivan to the sixth Doctor's attitude towards the universe in general. But because of the different emphasis at the time, these events were more easy to overlook – and allowed people to assume that, because the Doctor's a good guy, he must be a nice guy.

I have to wonder how much of this idealisation stems from our collective childhood as fans, when we all felt the Doctor was our favourite mad uncle. We knew he'd be nice to us; yes, he was rude, but only to people who were the equivalent of the ones who picked on us in school. It's only as grownups that we can look at his abuse of people like Ralph Cornish or Sir Colin Thackeray who were just doing their jobs and see that maybe they don't deserve it, that he's rude to ordinary people too. So his rejection of Adam or his insensitivity towards Martha or Mickey triggers an unimagined sort of primal terror: what if we met the Doctor and he didn't like us?

Davies has explicitly focussed on this blind spot as well; in *Love & Monsters*, his fan surrogate Elton is on the receiving end of the Doctor's dismissal, and Davies practically has the Doctor turn to the audience as he tells Elton "Don't ever mistake me for nice." However, Elton doesn't hate or punish the Doctor for it either; in his closing musings, he can still see how wonderful the Doctor is even after this, though he directly wonders how long the Doctor and Rose have before they get burnt.

They do get hit with consequences, just a few episodes later in *Doomsday* but, interestingly, while Davies is entirely willing to hit the Doctor with serious blowback for his attitude, from his dressings-down by Queen Victoria and Joan Redfern to the rise of Torchwood and Harold Saxon, he generally doesn't show the Doctor learning a valuable moral lesson and changing his ways as a result. There's a flicker of realisation in *Partners in Crime* about how things got "complicated" between him and Martha, but other than that? He just goes on as he always does. Even if he's aware he's "destroyed half (Martha's) life", he blatantly hasn't learned the "right" lesson, that he shouldn't behave in the self-isolating ways which drove her away; rather, his way of coping is to isolate himself further.

This can produce an odd sense that the comeuppance doesn't quite count. In a series where having your sins paid off was usually both permanent and / or fatal, having characters go on more or less as they were even after paying a price is disconcerting. While Rose is heartbroken at the end of *Rise of the Cybermen* because she's lost Mickey forever, because of the way she treated him, she doesn't stay heartbroken the next week. Although that kind of story-by-story character development is far more common now than in the old show, when it was almost nonexistent – look at the end of *The Curse of Fenric,* where the Doctor's actions are brushed aside even before the final scene – it still doesn't sit quite right.

Part of this is probably because modern genre expectations have been shaped by shows like *Buffy the Vampire Slayer*, which follow every major development with several episodes' worth of dwelling on the consequences. With this as SF and fantasy's major model for continuing storytelling, it can feel like this is the only way to handle drama: any significant event has to be referred to in major ways the following week. And when those *Buffy* episodes are usually set days, or at most a few weeks, apart, that makes story-world sense as well. However, when you're dealing with a show like *Doctor Who,* which treats its episodes much more individually – where there could be months between *Rise of the Cybermen* and *The Idiot's Lantern* – maybe the dramatic need for such links isn't so compelling. In the larger world, *Who,* unlike *Buffy,* is consciously designed to be as accessible to casual viewers as possible; something like five-sixths of *Who's* audience, many times *Buffy*'s entire viewership in the UK, only watch occasionally. So everything that's featured within a particular episode is made to serve that episode, not necessarily a previous one. If there are going to be moral consequences, they're largely going to be concentrated in a story that's designed for that purpose, like *Doomsday* or *Journey's End.*

Perhaps the underlying question is: why does RTD go there in the first place? If he doesn't think his characters are right to act this way, and he doesn't want to play out the consequences of their behaviour for weeks on end, and if he's not interested in making them know better, why does he put so much emphasis on how his heroes can act like gits?

Well... Russell Davies doesn't write role models. It's not about right or wrong. He tells the story of how he tried, once, to write a socially responsible story about gay men behaving the way they ought to – and felt completely hamstrung, threw in the towel and came out with *Queer As Folk* instead. He's an observational writer, trying to capture the complexities of life as it is or could be, not a moralist showing how it should be. His heroes are people like the thrillingly irresponsible manchild Stuart in *Queer As Folk*, or Bob from *Bob & Rose*, who annoyed RTD's gay fanbase by falling for a woman. Or the Doctor, who has never been a well-behaved character in any sense. All these figures are fascinating and courageous and selfish and caring and flawed. However, the flaws aren't enough to make the writer hate them; as with the Toclafane, these failings are different expressions of the same traits which form their strengths.

The Doctor's pride and arrogance in Davies' stories are part and parcel of his Doctorishness. If there's one underlying theme in this era of *Who*, it's that being proud of yourself is the exact opposite of a sin. Rather, it's a lack of a sense of what they're capable of which keeps Rose stuck in an unfulfilling job, which leaves Donna shouting at the world because she doesn't think she's worth listening to. And when Rose clearly starts thinking she's hot stuff, towards the end of the 2006 season? Well, by then, she's singlehandedly wiped out an entire Dalek army and saved the Earth, and, for an encore, she killed Satan. Isn't that enough to entitle a girl to feel good about herself?

This is not a series about teaching people to be humble and know their place. It's about bursting triumphantly out of your place. About celebrating your accomplishments and having pride in what you do. Modesty is not a virtue in this show – and, for the Doctor, it never has been. Putting him down for thinking he's so great is a bit like accusing Louis Armstrong of blowing his own trumpet. Of course he thinks he's wonderful: he's the Doctor, he's saved more lives and civilisations than he or you can count, you'd have to be mad to overlook that. He and Rose lay this on the line in so many words in *Rose*: "You think you're so impressive!" "I am so impressive!"

He's also a git about it sometimes. And gets slapped down by reality once in a while. That word "and" is a keynote of the series: arguments about morality are usually expressed in terms of "but", as if one element cancels another out. However, Davies' *Who* bypasses "but" in favour of "and". It's like Douglas Adams' intelligence test, from the *Hitchhiker's* computer game: the ability to accept two contradictory thoughts in your head at the same time. Which is partly just Douglas being a bit Zen, but is also a fundamental truth about the world; having tea and no tea at once is like being both happy and sad, or seeing someone as both wise and immature in one. But that's exactly what Davies sets out to do: he writes Rose as brave and courageous *and* selfish, the Doctor as brilliant and compassionate *and* emotionally clueless *and* ruthless *and* a hyperactive child *and* a tremendous hero *and* a bit of a bastard.

What's more, he doesn't connect the dots between these traits and the action in such clear-cut terms. The show expresses a deep-seated separation between doing the right thing and behaving well – and between what you do and whether the universe rewards you for it. Look at *Voyage of the Damned,* which plays with the conventions of the disaster-movie genre: characters like Midshipman Frame and Mr Copper who are blatantly marked for a heroic sacrifice make it through, so does Rickston the complete bastard, but the top-billed female star plummets to her death, and even what looks like a last-minute twist saving her life doesn't pan out. Davies explicitly makes the point that it's not about whether you deserve to live or die, that someone who meted out that sort of simplistic justice would be as monstrous as Mr Copper's vision of Santa Claus. (A comment which seems even more pointed in the religious context of Christmas.)

Instead, in Davies' Whoniverse, the only moral judgement is cause and effect. If you step into the Doctor's world, you will be amazed, your life will be turned upside down, you may do things you never dreamed of, but you will get burned. Whether you deserve it or not. Whether you do the right thing or not. It will just happen. If anything, it's a consequence of a life fully lived.

The result is a no-hugging, no-learning kind of *Doctor Who,* but it still makes its points. Rose doesn't realise in *Doomsday* that she's been handed a cosmic comeuppance for being smug about her place in the universe; she isn't standing there explicitly tracing the threads through time and space which viewers can see, showing that her smart remark to Queen Victoria directly led to the founding of Torchwood, which directly led to Canary Wharf, countless deaths, and her being separated from the Doctor forever. She's not looking back at the teaser scene of the first episode of the season, where Mickey says "I love you" and she just buggers off with the Doctor without a reply, and weighing that against her own unanswered declaration on the beach at Bad Wolf Bay at the other end of the season. The character doesn't realise any of this consciously; she shouldn't have to, any more than Colonel Skinsale in *Horror of Fang*

Rock has to spend his final moments realising, "Oh good heavens, my confounded greed got me into this, oh the iro*bzzzzzapp*." The point is still made. And, unlike old-*Who*'s victims of the Wheel of Morality, she has to live with the consequences.

However, that can still leave some people in the audience itching for the final definitive moral word on the subject. Its absence may be the most disconcerting feature of some of Russell's scripts. At the end of *The Parting of the Ways*, it's disturbing that the Doctor doesn't really make his case for not triggering the Delta Wave; instead it treats the argument against a kill-em-all-let-God-sort-em-out approach as obvious. But the episode has done a serious job of making it not feel obvious. Throughout the episode, our sympathies have been with the people who have fought and died to get the Doctor to that point. For him to decide after all that it's better for him to give up and do nothing, with no plan left to save the day, feels deeply unsettling. As before, our emotions aren't enough to guide us in this situation. The story doesn't really emphasise that none of the people sacrificing themselves know that the Doctor won't have time to calibrate the weapon, and that it will destroy all their loved ones on the planet below; if one of them had objected, it might have put a different complexion on the situation. It also doesn't emphasise its point that he'd be killing something like sixty times as many innocent civilians as Daleks, or the danger of the rationalisation that they're as good as dead anyway. The story seems to rely on the audience having an equally strong visceral reaction against mass slaughter for the greater good, even after emotionally doing its utmost to celebrate being willing to fight to the death. (Your own death, not everyone's.) I'm not sure whether this is a clever subtlety or a flaw. However, what this story is really showing us is the sharp end of "while there's life, there's hope". The Doctor decides that for people to live through a Dalek harvest is better than opting for a nihilistic total destruction; even when you want to make deaths worthwhile, no matter how much you feel you have to do something, some weapons really are too terrible to use.

To pack all this into the one line "Coward, every time" isn't enough to reassure us. Not when the Doctor has done something unprecedented, and taken the sort of principled decision he never quite had to in *Genesis* or *Resurrection*. *Genesis* had the Doctor hesitate over the chance to destroy the Daleks forever, but come out with a rationale for why this was for the best; *Resurrection* had him lose the chance to execute Davros, but didn't have him repudiate trying; this time he actually did decide to pass up bloodlust, but without a soliloquy to justify it. And so the story caught flak both from people who genuinely thought mass death would be better and those who couldn't see the worth of the Doctor's principles in the matter. All because it didn't make its case in words.

In fandom, we have a bias in favour of the pretty speech. This is probably a holdover from the days when dialogue was all the show could afford: we learned to love the well-spoken word because we certainly weren't going to get that kind of impact out of glorious visuals. However, it means we underrate what it's possible to say through how the characters act, if there isn't a quotable line to go along with it. *Journey's End* overtly kicks against this, by having the Doctor repeatedly reject the chance for old-school verbal fencing with Davros ("I have one thing to say to you... Bye!"; "We're not doing the nostalgia tour"); as usual, the Doctor is more concerned with getting on with things than with reflecting on them. This does mean that when Davros does unleash a killer lecture, it appears to go unanswered; the Doctor never makes a counterargument to Davros' claim that he turns his friends into killers. The thing is, the answer to Davros' case isn't brought across in clever lines nor in spectacular visuals, but in actions: in Martha not blindly obeying orders, but bending them to follow what she's learned from the Doctor; in the way his friends united to make saving the day possible; in the quite literal way in which a piece of the Doctor's essence turns Donna from an insecure temp into a gleefully efficient genius. Without a word on the subject, this last one practically double-underlines what exposure to the Doctor does to his friends – he doesn't just turn them into killers or victims, he turns them into heroes.

(It's a shame that the way Doctor-nature is expressed in the story is just through firing off technobabble while pressing lots of buttons, rather than some more expressive bit of lateral thinking or sheer determination, but you can't have everything.)

Wonderfully, the story also underlines that this too is accidental. The Doctor isn't deliberately trying to improve his friends through his example; Donna being transformed isn't a carefully planned day-saving surprise. Instead, it's the freakiest of freak occurrences, a side effect which simply springs from him doing the sort of clever and Doctorish things he does naturally. Like so much else, it just happens.

Maybe Russell Davies does believe in karma after all.

Though even then, he doesn't believe in having his characters think about it that way.

Journey's End closes with one more morally arguable act, without a word of reassurance: the Doctor wipes Donna's memory to save her life, even as she begs him not to. Again, as in *The Parting of the Ways*, it's getting into the thorny bits of while-there's-life-there's-hope; the Doctor keeps Donna alive against her own wishes, because even a mundane Doctorless life is better than dementia and death. Our last sight of

Donna, panicked and pleading, keeps it from being just a matter of principle. Davies could have had Donna reluctantly accept that he had to do this, but instead he chose to put our emotions on the other side. He makes us wonder: is the Doctor being high-handed and refusing to give Donna the right to die on her own terms? Or does the damage that's already been done to Donna's mind mean that it's not just his right but his responsibility to make the decision for her? It's a tangled, awkward and heartbreaking decision in a moment of immediate crisis, in which both sides genuinely think they're doing the right thing, but neither has a chance to make a speech settling it.

James Bradley in *The Australian Literary Review* wrote an essay about "the new television": sophisticated dramas in the vein of *Mad Men*, *Battlestar Galactica* and *The Sopranos*, which revel in their ability to suggest and imply rather than state. "These innovations remove many of the crutches TV usually uses to tell us what to think and feel; we are on our own, left to make our own decisions. [...] In part this is about the larger canvas on which such shows are painted, but it is also about a willingness to embrace the ambiguity of real life and its shifting rhythms." He's not just talking about minimal exposition, but this kind of minimal moral signposting: "It may be no coincidence that so many of the shows that have worked during the past decade [...] have done so precisely because they exploited the possibilities of the moral and imaginative space their challenges to conventional morality opened up."

Doctor Who isn't really trying to be *The Sopranos*, because it's always conscious of the fact that it still has to work on a basic level that will enthral an eight year old; on the surface, it's heavily signposted, we're left with very little doubt what we're seeing or how we're "meant" to be feeling. At a time when these high-end American dramas can let scenes peter out in a mass of open-ended implications (the way high-end British dramas used to be known for), *Who* has to hurry on to the next monster. What's remarkable about *Who* is that even though it's so determinedly mainstream and accessible on the surface – unlike all the niche dramas listed above – it still packs in all the new-television material I've talked about, lurking underneath. In fact, the very uppercasedness of *Who*, with the apparent crutches of a bold musical score and huge emotive close-ups, makes the extra nuances and meanings played against the surface readings that much more ironic. The end of *Dalek*, with its heartfelt choir, may tell us the Dalek's suicide is a moment of redemption through its touch of humanity, but the lines it speaks tell us it's killing itself out of disgust at the way its humanity has contaminated it. *Doomsday*'s ending may be huge and weepy, but that doesn't erase the scripted ironies which have led the characters to that point. There are all these acid little "and"s for sophisticated grownups to add to their picture. What's astonishing about *Doctor Who* is how much character and moral complexity it squeezes beneath the child-friendly, snap-judgement-ready surface level.

Now, maybe I've sunk into the namby-pamby relativism of middle age; maybe I'm so determined to look for my preferred 5% that I'm downplaying the clear-cut 95%. Maybe I'm even inventing some "and"s where the series isn't really establishing them. However, it's clear the show no longer tilts the moral balance in favour of where its heroes happen to be standing; it's full not just of ambiguity but ambivalence towards its characters' actions, either in the foreground or woven into the fabric. It's carefully painting in the questions about them even as it continues to celebrate the things which make those characters so wonderful.

ALLONS-Y

In the lead-up to the Christmas that saw David Tennant depart the role of the Doctor, Tennant appeared as the Doctor in a series of interstitial ads on BBC1 which featured the Doctor hooking a snow-buried TARDIS to a reindeer and flying it off into the horizon. The ads, the core of the BBC's promotion of their Christmas programming that year, were instantly iconic.

Now, take a step back and think: in 2005, David Tennant was an up-and-coming character actor best known as the third-billed lead in *Blackpool* and soon to star in *Casanova.*

It's easy to forget these days – with the tenth Doctor now regarded as a pinstriped icon and Tennant himself poised to conquer Hollywood (it's just a matter of time) – that, like just about everything else that happened in that topsy-turvy year known as 2005, the casting of David Tennant as the Doctor at the end of the season was a giant gamble. Christopher Eccleston was a heavyweight actor, widely known and regarded. Tennant might as well have been a total unknown. It was easily the most dangerous, the most risky regeneration since Patrick Troughton emerged from a dodgy-vision-mixer effect wearing William Hartnell's opera cloak in 1966.

The amazing thing about David Tennant's tenure as the Doctor isn't that he caught on with the public; it's that he became a superstar doing so. No Doctor has taken the public by storm like this since the days of Tom Baker.

And Tennant was the new frontman for a band that was already tight. The bold experiment of 2005 became a brand during 2006-2009. These years saw a honing the format, upping the stakes, and bringing the series to new places and new heights.

The popularity of the series under David Tennant brought out a complex emotional response in *Doctor Who* fans. On the one hand, fans revelled in the show's newfound popularity as it climbed to the top of the British TV charts, overturning viewing figures untouched since 1964 when there were only two channels; on the other hand, fans were concerned the series was becoming addicted to spectacle at the expense of plot and were worried that the lonely god character of the Doctor was becoming an über-emo.

Whatever the response, it was, if nothing else, passionate. And that seems appropriate as the tenth Doctor was a passionate Time Lord with sticky-uppy hair, a motor mouth and the intense charm of a sentient sun.

It is, in a word, brilliant.

Counting To Ten

by Graeme Burk

David Tennant was my Doctor.

I never intended that to be the case. I'm an old-school fan. Until 2005, I would have said Tom Baker was my Doctor, on the off days when Peter Davison wasn't. This late in my life, I wasn't expecting to find a Doctor that I would love and feel a connection to as a character. That's the sort of silly, soppy, sentimental thing that happens when you're young.

And yet, it happened to me. When David Tennant regenerated in a blaze of TARDIS-trashing glory in the final minutes of *The End of Time*, I felt, for the first time ever, that my era of *Doctor Who* had come to a close.

What was it about David Tennant that elicited this loyalty? This excitement? Let me count the ways...

One: It was the final scene of *The Girl in the Fireplace* that did it for me. The digital copy I had... stumbled across... had a flaw in it. After discovering Reinette had died having missed him, Rose asks the Doctor if he's all right. The copy I had skipped a second or so over the Doctor's response "I'm always all right", leaving me with the Doctor wordlessly fiddling with the TARDIS console, ignoring Rose altogether, living in a world of his own pain. An episode before, the Doctor had a lengthy monologue of the curse of being a Time Lord where the Doctor (self-indulgently, I felt) bemoaned the fact that his kind watches the people he love die in the space of a moment to him. Here we saw it happen, and the pain the Doctor felt was palpable. It was an astonishing scene, and David Tennant managed to convey so much just looking at a prop and absently flicking a switch. Even when I finally saw the scene properly with the line of dialogue included, it had the same impact (though I could have done without that line, or the Doctor repeating it in *Forest of the Dead*).

And that's when I suddenly realised we were onto something special with David Tennant's Doctor.

Two: The thing is, I should have seen it coming. A couple of weeks before *The Christmas Invasion* aired, David Tennant appeared in a two-part series called *Secret Smile*. *Secret Smile* is a typical ITV potboiler, pure and simple. But Tennant is stunning, playing what can only be termed a cockroach. In it, Tennant is someone who, having been dumped by one woman for creepy behaviour, romances the woman's sister, infiltrates her family, drives her mentally ill brother to suicide, eventually kills the sister – and makes the woman seem like a paranoid nutter all the while for suspecting him. And Tennant makes it all believable, creepy and dark. It's a performance that is way better than the source material.

People like to point to *Blackpool* and *Casanova* when noting David Tennant's bona fides for playing the Doctor but I think they're wrong, as good as those performances are. My theory has always been that the way to see how good an actor will be as the Doctor is to picture them in the darkest role they've ever played and then picture them using that intensity playing a 900-year-old Time Lord. It works remarkably well (try it sometime with Tom Baker as Rasputin or Paul McGann in *Paper Mask*) and here it gives a good indication of what was to come.

Three: The thing I love about David Tennant is his range. He plays a character with many facets ranging from the comic to the tragic, from the quiet to the totally overblown. And, really, that's the character of the Doctor as he's written right from the start of the Russell T Davies era. The Doctor in the first production block of 2005 (*Rose, Aliens of London / World War Three*) is pretty much the tenth Doctor: garrulous, chipper, excitable and romantic, with moments of darkness that show signs of something more dangerous. As great as an actor as Christopher Eccleston is, you can see, as the 2005 season develops, that's not a character he's interested in playing. Subsequent production blocks during 2005 ditch the early characterisation in favour of a Doctor that's darker and broodier and frankly, more in keeping with the dark, broody material that's Eccleston's comfort zone and expertise as an actor.

Tennant, on the other hand, is pretty much happy to play the character as Russell T Davies originally envisioned him. (In many respects, *New Earth* is a soft reboot back to the Doctor of the first production block of 2005.) He loves – nay, relishes – the range this affords. This is a man who does the camp version of Cassandra-as-the-Doctor, the passionate plea that he will save everyone and the quiet sad man watching Cassandra die, all in the same episode.

Four: If anything, I think Russell T Davies did Tennant a disservice for much of the 2006 season. The two great scenes in *The Christmas Invasion* are the scenes where Tennant's Doctor babbles about seeing a great big button and the scene where the Doctor takes down Harriet Jones with six words. Most of the 2006 season, had lots of "great big button" manic monologues. There were precious few scenes of quiet emotional intensity. The scene in the pool with Finch in *School Reunion* was a great reminder of that aspect of Tennant's Doctor, as was the aforementioned scene in *The Girl in the Fireplace* and the Doctor's quiet conversion from an atheist to an agnostic as he abseils into the darkness in *The Satan Pit*. But mostly it was all Big Red Button all the time.

In some ways, I think that was deliberate. Because it made the emotional punch of *Doomsday* all that more powerful. *Doomsday* was, for me, the moment when David Tennant finally came into his own as the Doctor. Billie Piper is astonishing at capturing the reality of someone whose world suddenly, finally collapses. David Tennant does that too, but he does it without histrionics, just intense silence, putting his head to a wall. It conveys the emotion, the humanity and yet the alienness of the Doctor all at once.

The thing about *Doomsday* is that it takes the Doctor to a place where we've never seen him before. No Doctor has ever been brought to that precipice where he's been brought to tears. Some might have thought it couldn't have been done, given the nature of the Doctor's character as aloof outsider. But David Tennant made it happen and never made it seem out of character.

Five: All this, I think illustrates the best quality of Tennant's Doctor. He's probably the most human Doctor. He's passionate, full of emotion. He weeps for the loss of a once-friend and the only other person of his kind when the Master dies out of spite, but he also knows and experiences the joy of just larking about with a friend somewhere. He's a Doctor you feel empathy toward. He's a Doctor who's easy to get along with, who knows how to flirt, who can be charming. He's completely and totally fallible. He can be hurt – he's probably the first Doctor to stop travelling with companions because he was tired of having his heart broken – and you can see him emotionally naked, like with Wilf in the café in *The End of Time*.

He's human, but we're also aware that he's bigger than human as well. Tennant is careful when walking that tightrope, being emotionally accessible and yet bringing an alien perspective. *The Fires of Pompeii* and *The Waters of Mars* show the Doctor in the centre of that conflict: facing facts the way a Time Lord must view immoveable events and yet with a human anguish of how awful that knowledge must be. And Tennant, as always, sells it.

In many respects, Matt Smith's Doctor is the best possible reaction against that: by *The End of Time* there really was no way to take the Doctor in that direction further. Tennant had really exhausted the possibilities of that approach. Gloriously so.

Six: The thing about Tennant that I still marvel at is that he was never satistfied with letting his Doctor descend into a schtick. Admittedly, his Doctor yelled almost as a lifestyle choice, but it could have been so easy to let it descend even further into a series of facial tics and cries of

"Maaartha!" / "Donnnnna!" as so many good actors playing a continuing role often do. (Hugh Laurie in *House* suddenly springs to mind.) That Tennant didn't is to his credit. Furthermore, Tennant remained happy to be taken out of his comfort zone. Smith in *Human Nature* could have just been the Doctor by a more human name, but Tennant creates a totally different character with ramrod-straight posture, perfect Edwardian diction and yet virginal awkwardness. *Midnight* puts the Doctor in a situation where it becomes impossible to be the Doctor and Tennant is wonderful conveying at the fear of being in that place. And when the Doctor becomes completely helpless, it's totally chilling.

Seven: He makes John Barrowman and Freema Agyeman – lovely actors but, bless them, not exactly heavyweights – seem amazing. I'm just putting that out there.

Eight: His double act with Catherine Tate, though, is nothing short of incredible. Part of that is the genius of the pairing: with Donna, the Doctor has found an equal, of sorts: someone just as passionate, just as quirky and just as lonely. Catherine Tate and David Tennant build on that though, creating a relationship that is wonderfully nuanced, full of good-natured bickering and disagreeing but also full of trust. The scene where Donna begs for the life of Caecilius' family in *The Fires of Pompeii* is pure, raw drama; Tennant and Tate just collide with each other with equal intensity.

The thing is, they do that every episode. Tate and Tennant just bring out the best in each other, whether it's doing full-on comedy in *Partners in Crime* and *The Unicorn and the Wasp* or coming to terms with the horror of *Planet of the Ood* or nudging the Doctor to try being a dad in *The Doctor's Daughter*. The two characters are so tight – and Tennant and Tate are so good at playing them – that how the Doctor saves her in *Journey's End* seems truly obscene.

Nine: The great thing about Tennant's Doctor is he went out on top. *The Waters of Mars* sees the Doctor starting out as his cheery, motormouth self and ends in the worst possible place mentally and spiritually. In *The End of Time*, Tennant is wonderful at showing us a man who is desperate to avoid his end but then takes us to the next place: a man coming to accept that.

That's David Tennant's performance all over. There's always something surprising, something under the surface. It's why David Tennant's Doctor has become my Doctor.

Ten: There's no denying it, David Tennant is a very pretty boy. But I'm not going to say anything else about that.

The Importance of Being Brilliant

By Julie Chaston
From Enlightenment #156, March 2010

David Tennant. The tenth Doctor. David Tennant *as* the tenth Doctor. It's probably impossible to try and say something that hasn't already been said. But you know what? I'm going to say it anyway. This actor – this Doctor – deserves every bit of praise that's been bestowed.

In 2005, when Tennant was announced as taking over the role, there were some – including me – who were already fans. We'd seen him in productions like *Blackpool* and *Casanova* but, as engaging as he was, we still wondered how he'd "fit" as a Doctor. After all, we'd only just become used to Christopher Eccleston's somewhat dark portrayal and now he was going to change into someone who, frankly, didn't seem all that Doctorish.

Well, five years later and all the worry and chatter seems almost laughable. The tenth Doctor had me transfixed right from the moment he stepped out of the TARDIS in *The Christmas Invasion* asking "Did you miss me?" David Tennant was the Doctor. My Doctor. The one. The only.

That says it all, really. Tennant didn't just play the Doctor; every time he put on that brown (or blue) suit, he became the Doctor – and we loved it. We laughed and cried with him. We felt his wonder when he saw a new planet, or his fascination with every little blob of goo. If he let his anger or frustration show, we were angry and frustrated too. And when he was heartsbroken, then our hearts (collectively) broke a little as well.

None of this could have happened to the extent it did without Tennant in the role. The fact that he's a self-admitted *Who* fan allowed for an innate understanding of how to play the tenth Doctor. The fact that he's a brilliant actor allowed that Doctor to become real.

It didn't matter if the script he was given was *Midnight* or *Daleks in Manhattan*. *Human Nature* or *The Idiot's Lantern*. *The Waters of Mars* or *The Poison Sky*. I could go on. The point is, it made no difference. David Tennant gave his all to every single scene. Much has been said by fellow actors, directors and just about everyone associated with *Doctor Who* about his professionalism and dedication, both on and off set, and I think that came through loud and clear to the audience. Even when something didn't really make sense, at the moment the Doctor was saying it, we believed it, because David Tennant believed it. We tend to assume that's a given for an actor, but it's only when you see superlative performances like those we were treated to during the past four years, that you realise how important it is. Every single story, be it a barnstormer or only so-so, had at least one or two lines where Tennant – because of his skill – moved the character of the Doctor forward or gave us a moment that will be remembered again and again. It didn't have to be an earthshaking, heartrending scene. It might simply have been a raised eyebrow or sideways glance reacting to something another character said. They could be equally powerful.

That being said, it's probably true that the biggest change for the Doctor in the new series, primarily once David Tennant came on board, was that for the first time we met a Doctor who was willing to acknowledge the consequences of his actions, a Doctor who had a full range of emotions and was not afraid to show them. We had a Doctor who said he was scared (*42*). A Doctor suddenly faced with self-doubt (*Midnight*). A Doctor trying to deal with confusion and uncertainty about his own future (*Silence in the Library*; *The Waters of Mars*). A Doctor who actually cried! For me, the final scene of *Gridlock* where he finally told Martha the truth about Gallifrey tugged at the heartstrings just as much as the final scenes of *Doomsday* or *Journey's End*. The Doctor's love story with Rose (and yes, I do believe and will always believe that he loved her), his different but equally strong love for Donna, his trust and friendship with Martha that could never be as much as she wanted, even the respect and camaraderie he had with Wilf at the end; none of these relationships would have had the same audience impact with another actor in the role.

*

For pure, raw emotion, nothing touches *Human Nature*. Obviously, during most of the story, David Tennant wasn't the Doctor, he was John Smith. Yet, being able to play two distinctly different characters who were actually the same man, and still make us care just as much about John Smith as we did our Doctor, is something very few actors could do as convincingly. The performance was sheer brilliance. Even though it was actually Smith who had to make the difficult choice, when the Doctor went to the book signing and came face to face with Joan Redfern's great-granddaughter in *The End of Time*, we finally saw how much that choice had affected him. A tiny moment, but the expression on his face said everything the audience needed to know.

Similarly, the scenes in *Midnight* where the Doctor was taken over by the entity were another amazing achievement and, for me, just as compelling. Tennant had to show utter terror in his eyes but keep the rest of his performance measured and emotionless. It worked.

During David Tennant's reign, there are those who have complained that the emotional aspect was not true to the character. I strongly disagree. In the original series, he simply wasn't written that way. The focus was always on the plot instead of the "humanity" of the Doctor. There were occasional moments, to be sure, but none of them ever really had any lasting impact on the stories to follow. To be completely honest, would any of the previous actors have been able to carry off that kind of performance? With the possible exception of Peter Davison, I doubt it. This is not a knock against the abilities of any of the others; they just had different strengths and played the role as it was written for them at the time. Even Eccleston, although definitely accomplished and able to show us the turmoil boiling beneath the surface of the ninth Doctor, would have given the tenth Doctor's stories an entirely different spin.

Of course, it wasn't all doom and gloom. The last few years gave us countless opportunities to smile. Be it a one-liner tossed out in a most unlikely situation, being put in his place by one of his companions, our amusement at the Doctor trying to find his way out of a silly predicament, or a completely tongue-in-cheek episode like *The Unicorn and the Wasp*, we laughed. There was some good writing, to be sure, but it was David Tennant's masterful comedic timing that took it a step higher.

Sadly though, nothing lasts forever. The announcement by David over a year prior that he was leaving made all of 2010 seem like a prolonged period of mourning and was understandably rife with speculation about how he'd go out. But the end of the tenth Doctor's era, whether you agreed with *The Waters of Mars* and *The End of Time* or not, was perfect. The audience was able to see even more facets of the character and Tennant was allowed to extend his acting chops that little bit further. We'd seen the Doctor frustrated and tempted before, but never to the point of a Master-like ego trip. We'd seen him despondent, but never seriously contemplating just giving up. And we'd seen him angry and annoyed by injustice, but never had those feelings turned inward and made him sorry for himself. But it all made complete sense for the character. Everything that the tenth Doctor had been through and the way that David Tennant had played him, full of gusto and anguish, meant it couldn't have ended any other way. "I don't want to go": that's exactly what it was all about. The inevitability of regeneration was always there, lurking in the shadows, but it came too soon, for our Doctor and for us.

*

Having had an actor like David Tennant who was willing to take his Doctor to the next level, someone we came to love as a fully rounded being instead of just a limited character, is something we should cherish. We cheer for our heroes and root for our underdogs; with the tenth Doctor, David made it possible for us to do both. It's something we may not truly appreciate until we realise it's not there anymore. With Steven Moffat's ability to pull on the heartstrings and a talented actor like Matt Smith coming in, the eleventh Doctor will no doubt bring us continued joy and sorrow and everything else that comes with it. But it won't be the same. The tenth Doctor did it first, and that's special.

So thank you David. You drew us in, you made us want to believe. And we did.

Savage Who

by Scott Clarke

From Enlightenment #134, July 2006

Every year around Easter, I succumb to the temptations of Cecil B DeMille's *The Ten Commandments*. Sure, there's more ham on display than on my grandmother's holiday table; yes, Chuck Heston has rather dubious political leanings; and by God, it goes on and on, but I can't help myself. Big overblown spectacle, I am thy slave. Watching all those bloated camels and endless extras dressed in Edith-Head-designed bathrobes crossing a pre-CGI Red Sea gives me goose pimples every time.

And then the complaining starts. Moses led them out of slavery and these people can't stop bitching (sure Edward G Robinson eggs them on in true moustache-twirling style, but really). I want to hurl my remote at the TV every single time.

Doctor Who fandom elicits a similar reaction in me. It's not that people aren't entitled to their opinions, but the level of discourse seems to lie somewhere between legal brain death and downright maliciousness.

And so it is that I have decided to borrow a page from my favourite sex columnist, Dan Savage, and answer some annoying questions that just can't be ignored any more:

"I was thrilled when Doctor Who came back last year. But what's with all the focus on his companion, Rose? I paid my license fees to see the Doctor and he doesn't seem to "do" anything anymore. What gives?"

—Doctor U Do Everything

Yo DUDE, check out season one of the original series (most of the good stuff is now available on DVD). Barbara (and to a lesser extent Ian) was clearly the focus of those early stories. While Hartnell spent most of his time whacking cavemen, hiding fluid links and playing enigmatic, Barbara, like Rose, was designed as a character the audience could identify with and without her the series likely wouldn't have made it out of Totter's Lane. She was the moral compass for the programme, grappling with the complexities of time travel or convincing us of the terror of the Daleks. She even had a whole story devoted to her and her dilemmas; *Father's Day* has nothing on *The Aztecs*. Without Barbara and Ian front and centre, the character of the Doctor would have been saddled with all the boring stuff like kissing girls and applying left hooks to a Voord.

In Season Twenty-Six, Ace was similarly charged with all the major dramatic beats in stories such as *Ghost Light* or *The Curse of Fenric*, effectively creating a unique character arc in the program's history. By deflecting some of the attention away from the Doctor, the writers were better able to restore some of the mystery that had been lost in the show. It's called fresh storytelling.

Russell T Davies, like his predecessors, is exploring new ways to present *Doctor Who* for a modern audience. Having been through the Time War and suffered the consequences of his actions, the ninth Doctor is hesitant to act by himself. Instead, he chooses to inspire others, most notably Rose, but also Cathica, Nancy and Lynda with a "y". Sounds a hell of a lot more interesting than simply reversing the polarity of the neutron flow (not that there's anything wrong with that).

If you want to complain about a sidelined, ineffectual Doctor, postmark your letters to Eric Saward!

"Boom Town *was pants; finally the Doctor has to deal with a serious ethical question and RTD cops out by opening up a magic root cellar full of pixie dust. Then he does it again in* The Parting of the Ways *with super-shiny Rose! He's clearly side-stepping moral dilemmas in favour of lame* deus ex machina."

—Boomtown Lost Integrity: Needless Drivel

Was I dreaming that whole sequence in *Genesis of the Daleks* where a fledging pepperpot blew up the mutant embryo tank, neatly side-stepping the Doctor's need to take care of business himself? And is not the aforementioned story actually frequently voted as one of the top ten stories of all time? Ditto on the faulty door that kept Davison from lobotomising Davros in *Resurrection of the Daleks*. And what to do about integrating the Silurians into society? Nah, let's have the Brigadier blow it up.

Look BLIND, *Doctor Who* isn't the new *Battlestar Galactica* and never will be. If you want *Galactica*, go watch *Galactica*.

"Every week the Doctor and Rose seem to show up somewhere on Earth. It's a huge universe out there (despite a good portion of it being devoured by the entropy field). Why don't they ever visit alien planets? Seems to me like a serious lack of imagination on the part of the production team."

—Put Earth Drivel Away, Need Time In Cosmos

So if I understand you right, PEDANTIC, you're not getting enough gravel pits and polystyrene rocks? But seriously, much of *Doctor Who* is about the hero's connection to planet Earth and its brilliant, resilient, dumb-ape inhabitants. In fact, three of the most classic seasons of *Who* – and I'm not talking about the Pertwee years – rarely left Terra Firma. Season Twenty-Six saw the Doctor wearing his "I heart heart Earth" T-shirt at every opportunity and still managed to be one of the most original seasons in years. The Doctor and Sarah Jane spent a great deal of time hanging around the home counties in Season Thirteen (even when they were dressed up to look like Scotland). And Season Five, that classic monster year that gave us the Yeti, the Ice Warriors and the Weed Creature, was surprising earthbound with only a single side trip to wallop the Cybermen on Telos. And no, the wheel in space does not constitute an alien planet.

"I'm getting sick and tired of the Doctor making pop-culture references all the time. It cheapens my favourite programme and turns it into an inter-galactic version of Family Guy or Seinfeld."

—Doctor Uses Language Lazily

First of all, I should declare right up front that I'm a fan of both the aforementioned shows. Secondly, what kind of pre-Raphaelite, vacuum-packed fantasy world are you living in, DULL? *Doctor Who* has always been a product of its time. Verity Lambert shamelessly flaunted the Beatles before us and Barry Letts hit us over the head with ecology, feminism-lite, and pop-Buddism. And let's not pretend the Doctor doesn't name drop every opportunity he gets. One must also consider that the current tendency to weave pop culture through television programs is something that has only really come into vogue post-*Simpsons* (hence post-Season-Twenty-Six). Why *wouldn't* the Doctor drop a reference to *The Muppet Movie* as casually as he would Beau Brummell?

"What are you anyway, a Russell T Davies apologist?"

—Davies Envies Verity, Innes, Letts

Yes, I receive a cheque for 50 quid on the 15th of every month and I have a Slitheen tattooed on my left butt cheek. Okay, I thought RTD made some questionable choices in *New Earth* and, while the story is quite watchable, it's a bit too cluttered with ideas and would have benefited from another draft. However, I appreciate the difficulty of cutting a good idea. *Boom Town* is still one of my favourite stories though, and if that causes you to retch on the page, please be advised that the editor of this fanzine does not bear any responsibility for replacing your copy.

Evolution of the Christmas Special

by Robert Smith?
From Enlightenment #144, March 2008

The past three years have seen an extra-length *Doctor Who* episode aired each Christmas. All three have featured David Tennant, the Earth being aware of aliens, fake snow generated by alien intervention and at least one incredibly iconic moment for the Doctor. Furthermore, against all expectations, all three have also featured a different companion.

The Christmas Invasion is still the defining special. It's got it all: Robot Santas, a proper, honest-to-goodness alien invasion, Christmas dinner, edge-of-the-seat tension (the A-positives on the roof), UNIT, Torchwood, the Powell Estate, Harriet-Jones-Prime-Minister, a post-regenerative Doctor, hand-to-hand combat and a twist in the tail so delightful that they haven't even tried to top it since, knowing they probably couldn't.

Then there's the iconography surrounding the Doctor. Taking him out of the picture is a brilliant move, as it allows us to see the sheer power of what he does by his absence. Which, like the pictures on radio, is always going to be more powerful than his presence. Harriet Jones' plea, via television of all things, for the Doctor to come save us all, is just heartbreaking. It underpins so much of what happens, from Rose's breakdown that destroyed her character in one fell swoop, to Harriet's actions at the end – and, indeed, the whole Torchwood arc of the forthcoming season.

Indeed, the only odd thing about *The Christmas Invasion* is the pacing. It's immediately obvious that this wasn't designed to be a 60-minute special and has had the pilot-fish subplot grafted on like an extra limb. Indeed, all the references to Christmas bar one happen either here or at the very end, bookending an otherwise entirely Christmas-free 45 minute episode that was almost certainly written for the 2006 season.

In some ways, it's a bit of a pity, because "The Sycorax Invasion" would have been a far stronger season opener than *New Earth* was, probably disguising many of that year's faults for longer. On the other hand, the Christmas specials have a bigger role to play: they're the year's showstoppers, the spectacle event to grab the viewers that isn't accompanied by an ongoing season. They're *Doctor Who* for people who don't watch *Doctor Who*. It works too: with 10.3 million viewers, *The Christmas Invasion* beat every episode from the seasons either side of it, except for the two highly publicised season openers.

The only real problem with *The Christmas Invasion*, from the general public's point of view, is that it's too intricate. It's great for us fans, but the casual viewer and her family doesn't want to figure out who Harriet Jones or UNIT are. Indeed, they probably don't even want the heavy backstory that is Rose and her family.

And so, next time around – and the time after that – we get almost entirely link-free stories, with big-name stars, playing characters no one's seen before and featuring broad brushstrokes of a plot that anyone can get a handle on. The Doctor has to get a bride to her wedding and there are spiders at the centre of the Earth. Got it. Spaceship *Titanic* is going to crash into the Earth because Donald Trump plans to collect the insurance. Check. Next Christmas, expect a floating island in space, where the contestants have to survive or be eliminated. Yeah!

The Runaway Bride isn't the best television ever made, but... actually, no, there isn't really a "but". It's not very good, is it? Okay, it has one and half redeeming features: Donna is utterly superb and the pacing in the first half is excellent. It runs like greased lightning, moving so fast that you don't stop to question what's going on – and nor should you, because this ride might not be the best one ever built, but it's determined to be the fastest!

Donna is fantastic, in both her personas (the abrasive one and the subtler, more sensitive one she only lets show at the end); she's easily the best thing about the story. First time around, her nails-on-chalkboard persona is a bit of a shock to the system, but on subsequent viewings it's one of the highlights of the show. She's Tegan Jovanka for the twenty-first century and that's exactly what the show needs. Her softer side is magnificent too: Tate gives us someone who's abrasive because she's protecting something vulnerable within. Not unlike a certain ninth Doctor we're not supposed to refer to any more. The upcoming season has the potential to be something quite amazing, given her energy and ability. Plus, isn't is great to see a companion who isn't waif-thin, for once?

The Doctor has his iconic moment of the year, when he stands calm amid the flames after announcing "Gallifrey!" as though that solves all his problems. It should be a shocking, disturbing image, but it's not quite there. It needs the right reaction and Donna's response is a muted one. She should be disgusted and terrified, but instead she's... slightly disconcerted. It robs the moment of the power it needs by shying away from drastic consequences. Because it's Christmas and we need fake snow and a bit of a smile for the ending, right?

The other thing that *The Runaway Bride* succeeds at is that it allows the Doctor his chance to grieve for Rose. This is quite necessary, but is also something that could very easily get in the way of story progression... as it essentially did, right through Martha's tenure. *The Runaway Bride* should have been the end of it, as it does what it needs to and then moves on. Instead, Martha gets sacrificed at the altar of being not Rose, for no reason whatsoever.

You can really see how they've learned from *The Christmas Invasion*. World in peril, good. (Although *Voyage of the Damned* only has to mention people on the roof to reference *The Christmas Invasion*; to refer to *The Runaway Bride*, it has to actually show us the Racnoss star on television, as it's not nearly as memorable.) Robot Santas, okay. (Well, they were there last time, why not?) Surprise at alien invasion, funny. (Donna's excuses for not knowing about aliens are hilarious). Iconic-looking villain, er...

Well, okay, a great big spider should be fairly memorable, but the Empress of the Racnoss is memorable for all the wrong reasons. The entire thing grounds to a halt the minute Sarah Parish appears on the screen and stays there for the remainder of the story. It's the kiss of a spider woman of death, destroying the energy of the first half and turning something that could have been fluffy and amusing fun into something to mock for its badness. Oh well, it's not like *Doctor Who* hasn't survived that before...

Still, it may not matter, in the eyes of the general public. Tate and Parish are big, big stars and they're in the episode to get bums on seats and for no other reason. Kylie Minogue's performing the exact same function in *Voyage of the Damned*. Indeed, given that Parish is the only one to disappoint, we actually have a pretty good hit rate. Considering that this list includes an in-yer-face, "shit-ache mushrooms? I ask you!" comedienne and a pop singer so kitchsy she became a gay icon, it's a wonder that we get any acting at all, let alone the quality of what these women produce. True, we've had a former pop singer who turned out to be an acting tour de force in *Doctor Who* once before, but you'd think that'd make it all the more difficult for lightning to strike again.

Voyage of the Damned isn't light on other name stars either: Geoffrey Palmer gets a cameo and Clive Swift gets a supporting role. These aren't just cameos by classic-era *Doctor Who* actors, these are recognisable name actors in the UK. Still, if you're looking for Classic-era *Doctor Who* allusions you can find them: *Enlightenment, The Robots of Death* and *Frontios* all get a fairly overt nod... but you'd never know it if you're the casual viewer on Christmas Day, having just eaten the Turkey people. *The Christmas Invasion* and its multiple backstories this ain't.

Once again, we've got a moments of such iconography that you wonder why the Christian coalition isn't complaining. Oh, wait, they did. The Doctor being lifted up by angels, having just calmly walked through the flames, is almost too powerful an image for the show. Any more and you're teetering on self parody. There's also the Doctor's "I'm 903 years old" speech, which was written either entirely as an excerpt to be used in the promos, or entirely to piss off the fanboys, I'm not sure which. I'm hoping the latter.

However, where *Voyage* beats the other two hands down is in the pacing. Like *The Christmas Invasion,* it has a longer running time thrust upon it... but this time around, you'd never know, because it's so smooth. The whole thing unfolds gloriously, with just the right amount of setup and jokes at the beginning, extended tension once disaster hits, surprise deaths of sympathetic characters and a plot that culminates in an unexpected, but very satisfying, reveal of the villain. Indeed, if anything, the confrontation with Max Capricorn seems to be over too quickly, but leaving us wanting more is by no means a crime against drama.

Voyage of the Damned is a supremely polished production, with amusing jokes (the Christmas misconceptions might not be the wittiest one-liners ever devised, but I heard people repeating them down the pub at Christmas), well-defined characters (and isn't Bannakaffalatta the best alien name, like, ever?), stalking robots who look like angels, unexpected outcomes (those who survive, which defies all expectations, but punctures the Doctor's pomposity brilliantly; not a single promise he makes in the episode turns out to be one he can keep) and, best of all, a sense of joie de vivre that makes you want to stand up and cheer when it's all over, even though the ending isn't actually trying for that response.

The Christmas specials have come a long way in a short time. They've moved from being an extended episode of the series, using all the tropes and characters inherent in the ongoing show, to one-off "event" episodes that use big name stars and simple, broad storylines to attract simple, broad audiences. They might not be what we as fans want, but – at least for the next year – we fans largely have what we want in the ongoing series. There are 13 million reasons why we won't see the likes of *The Christmas Invasion* again. But if they can go the way of *Voyage of the Damned,* rather than *The Runaway Bride,* then we shouldn't complain.

After all, Christmas is a time for giving, so maybe it's okay, once a year, to give our show over to the general public so they can enjoy it too. Either that, or cash in on the Christmas sales...

How Do You Kill A Wasp?

by Nina Kolunovsky
From Enlightenment #147, October 2008

"I have asked you to come here," said the Great Detective ponderously, "to discuss The Case of the Unicorn and the Wasp."

He looked around the drawing room at the gathered suspects. They all knew it was the seventh episode of the fourth season of the best TV series ever... but how many of them knew the whole truth about it? How many could look beyond the obvious to discover what made it really special?

Outside the French window, the night was dark and stormy. Inside, the young gentleman in cricket whites began speaking.

"Obviously, if you are a connoisseur of traditional British cozy mysteries, you would appreciate the classic inter-war country house party setting. The tea on the lawn, the upstairs-downstairs romance, the old family secrets as twisted as the hallways..." He trailed off, lost in a world of Christie, Dorothy L Sayers, Margery Allingham, Josephine Tey, Georgette Heyer and Patricia Wentworth.

A tanned man with military bearing picked up the thread of conversation. "The episode borrowed a lot more from Christie and similar authors than just the setting. From the plentiful red herrings to the drawing room resolution, the story borrows the conventions of a traditional mystery and then revs them up a notch. Some might say that the conventions are turned on their head, but I wouldn't." The military man's limp began to be more noticeable as he started pacing around the room. "Gareth Roberts might poke gentle fun at the standard drawing-room mystery, but he also uses its structure. He adds more humour, more romance, more action..."

"And more aliens," murmured the elderly lady in the corner, without lifting her head from her knitting.

"He does add more of these things but, aside from the alien influences, he just adds more of what's already there. Christie's fans know that her books often have a romantic side and gentle humour. And, later in her life, her mysteries moved away from country houses and into mountain-top lairs of international criminal masterminds. Writing in the twenty-first century, she may have added more car chases herself."

The vicar coughed delicately. "But, Colonel, being an Agatha Christie fan is definitely not required to appreciate either the hijinks in the episode or the new aspects to the Doctor's and Donna's relationship." He sipped the tea again and continued, "Of course, the avid Agatha Christie reader would definitely get a kick out of the sneaky name-checking of her books, from 'Why didn't they ask...? Heavens!' to 'Murder at the Vicar's rage'. And I was just appalled at the lack of reference to 'The Man in the Brown Suit'."

"I am glad you mentioned the hijinks, Vicar," drawled the short-haired flapper reclining on a chesterfield. "I like my mysteries with tongue planted firmly in cheek..."

"No just the mysteries, I hear," mumbled the uniformed lady's maid entering the room.

"...tongue planted firmly in cheek," continued the flapper, "so I had a lot of fun with the episode. How about the moving finger, pointing at every possible suspect but the guilty one? Or those cheeky breaks through the fourth wall, via the recursive and overlapping flashbacks? And, of course, the highlight of the episode, Tennant's frenetic 'detox' set-piece, as classic an example of physical *Doctor Who* humour as you are likely to find anywhere. The charades, the anchovies, the 'shock'... it's certainly a lot more fun than wheatgrass juice!"

The lady's maid was walking around the room, re-filling delicate china cups. The great detective nodded towards her. "As Abby reminded us, there were also a couple of minor scenes, completely ignored by 98% of viewers, but causing great hubbub among the Great Gay Agenda proponents and antagonists."

The Great Detective considered the suspects around him. They had all pointed out the many aspects of *The Unicorn and the Wasp*, but they missed the dog that did not bark in the nighttime. He would need to question them further to discover what made this episode stand out.

"How does this episode fit into the season?" he asked, almost rhetorically.

"Well, this episode did air following four episodes full of tragic planet-wide slaughter, real or potential," the gentleman in cricket whites said ponderously.

"That simply won't do. The only slaughter I prefer involves gin, tonic and my liver," replied the flapper, idly playing with her pearls.

"Be that as it may," the young master continued, undeterred, "there have been a great deal of implacable foes, poison gas, bottomless mud pits, scary foreshadowing and the need to make impressive speeches."

"Always with the impressive speeches," the flapper harrumphed.

The Colonel picked up the recital. "After this episode, we are off to more of the same: wholesale slaughter, planetary collapse, impressive oration... This season, it seems that the Doctor is not the Doctor unless he is being chased by a Sontaran brandishing a Dalek in one hand and a Pyrovile in the other. And a *Doctor Who* episode is not a real *Doctor Who* episode unless the Doctor gives a long, intense speech about the pain of being a Time Lord or Donna gives a short, even more intense speech about the need for taking a humane attitude towards every non-human they encounter."

"But, in between, we get tea and crumpets!" announced Abby.

The vicar nodded. "Here we have the Doctor and Donna at a house party in the 1920s, enjoying the cocktails and the local lingo, investigating a murder with house guest Agatha Christie. It's all about 'Will they be able to catch the killer and keep the others safe?' That is all. The universe was not coming to a tragic end. An entire species of alien isn't about to be exterminated. Neither the Doctor nor his companions are in mortal danger. There is no deep political point hitting the viewers over the head."

"This season," the flapper pointed out, "I already learned that slavery is not nice and that war is less fun than one might imagine."

"Thank you, *Doctor Who*!" exclaimed the child, with doubtful sincerity.

The knitting lady put down her needles. "There is something about living under continuous existential threat that defies suspension of disbelief. I am willing to accept the existence of Daleks. I am not willing accept the fact that the Doctor seems to annihilate them every couple of months, using some chewing gum and a piece of string, and then appears terrified the next time it turns out that the reports of their the annihilation were premature. The Doctor in end-of-the-world mode is supposed to be impressive; he is meant to terrify his enemies and even scare his friends. This does not work if the end of the world comes five times a season, when we have no fun, easy-going Doctor to contrast him with."

She picked up her knitting again and continued, "This episode clearly shows that, even without death threats, the Doctor can still be the Doctor. He is charming, determined and funny. With endless energy and insatiable curiosity, he almost bounces off the screen. Donna can still be Donna. Between charming the locals and playing dress-up, she can help the Doctor to focus on the human aspects of the case without a 15-minute lecture on 'Humanity for Gallifreyans: Advanced.' Their relationship can still develop as they argue, discuss and connect with each other, all without dodging bullets. Watching them uncovering the problems and working out a solution kept me involved and fascinated, even when there were just a couple of lives at stake. Donna and the Doctor sharing a sotto voce aside makes them both more real than yet another scene of them running for their lives."

The Great Detective lifted his finger ponderously. "Looking at Donna twirling in her flapper dress or trying out her 20s slang, I remembered something obvious: travelling with the Doctor is meant to be fun. There is a reason why we all want to be his companions, and it's not because we like breathing in poison gas or drowning in mud. We want to experience different times and different places, not just different ways to narrowly escape gruesome death."

"So the episode brings fun to an otherwise too-serious season!" the vicar gasped.

"It's probably more fun than hanging around this silly review," the flapper muttered to herself.

Re-Mastered

by Lloyd Rose

From Enlightenment #141, October 2007

Back in 1990, in *House of Cards,* Ian Richardson cocked a knowing eyebrow at the audience and invited us to come along on his Machiavellian journey to 10 Downing Street. A splendid time was guaranteed for all. I can't think of a worthier successor as PM than John Simm's reincarnated Master (aka Harold Saxon), pop star charismatic in a sublimely cut suit and madder than a barrel of hatters. Simm has the contained, silky elegance down pat, but even when he's standing quietly, observing the fools around him with tolerant irony, he's dancing. His whole character is there in that first, manic whirl around the console of the TARDIS he's about to steal: this is a man who loves, loves, *loves* getting what he wants.

Russell Davies, who wrote the role for Simm (how did he know what was in there?), is up there dancing with him, his words partnering the actor, bringing out all his charm and menace, his gift for comedy, his innocence and vulnerability. Simm responds by catching every nuance, taking lines that were already terrific and putting an extra spin on them, continually surprising us (see, for example, the look on his face when, for an instant, he isn't sure whether he's aged the Doctor several more centuries, or, oops, killed him: an embarrassed, uncertain half-smile with just a tinge of worry). Forget whatever's going on between the Master and the Doctor. This is the real love story, the romance between writer and actor, a fusion of shared exploration and delight.

By his own account, Davies spent two years trying to work out how to bring the Master back as something other than a played-out embarrassment before inspiration hit and he realised that the contemporary equivalent of the Mephistophelean villain – seducer, pretender, deceiver is...

the politician. The Bad Guy In A Great Suit (and who designed Saxon's outfit, anyway – Louise Page? Hugo Boss? Credit must be paid!) has been around for years, but generally he's a CEO or the head of some nefarious secret agency, taking over the world behind closed doors. Making him a public servant adds that intoxicating fizz of hypocrisy. Spinning us towards destruction, he sighs that he feels our pain.

Davies' writing has always shown considerable political wit ("Six words") and making the Master Prime Minister was satirical genius. The more you think about the idea, the richer and funnier it gets. In *Heroes*, the villain becoming President was treated as grim and frightening, a Serious Matter. But Simm's PM is, at least at first, his country's id. Gassing the fatuous Cabinet. Blowing up the arrogant American president. In your dreams, Britain! But wait: the young, energetic saviour turns out to be a scoundrel and horrible bloodshed ensues. In your reality, UK! The joke just keeps twisting, like a knife.

For someone who's only seen Simm as the earnest, anxious Sam Tyler in *Life on Mars*, his Master is as surprising as a firecracker under your chair. As far as I can tell, Simm's background is mostly in gritty, realistic roles but he plays in a band and his stylised, alarming, comic Master is a musical comedy star turn, even before he cranks up the volume on "I Can't Decide". There's a giddy release in his acting, as if he'd been waiting for this role: turned loose and told to run, he leaves the track, bolts the fences, and lights out for the territory. Yet he's never out of control. Like Richardson – and like Alan Rickman in *Die Hard* and *Robin Hood: Prince of Thieves* – he projects, even in his wildest moments, a sense of held-in power, the possibility of more, and much worse, to come. Also like them, he's a deliciously witty fiend, amused and almost surprised by the easy success of his plots.

Not that Simm has Richardson or Rickman's aristocratic air. Where they're all cheekbone, he's round-faced and impish. And, in spite of the suit, Saxon is a bit of a prole, easily imagined heading down the pub of a Saturday night to happily bang some heads together. Simm isn't exactly pugnacious, but he's scrappy and a good part of the Master's contempt for his rival seems provoked by Ten's resolute niceness; when Saxon rolls his eyes at some example of decency, you can practically hear his mental sneer: "So bloody bourgeois." Fans postulate that the Master was the Doctor's boyhood friend (if not something closer); I think he beat him up in the playground.

Certainly, the playground is this Master's home turf. Both Davies and Simm zero in on the career-politician's desperate need for attention and admiration, his essential childishness. This is the best Mad-Child-In-Charge-of-the-Universe television since Billy Mumy sent his neighbors to the cornfield in *The Twilight Zone*'s "It's A Good Life" 46 years ago. (It's possible, though I wouldn't take bets, that the Master's repeated "It's good, isn't it?" is a nod to that episode.) Bright-eyed and bouncy, with a great little-boy's pout, Simm is a mischievous monster, less Mr Hyde than Bart Simpson's hyperactive evil twin. He's not so much immoral as pre-moral, a hideous innocent. "I thought it would be fun to run a newspaper," the young Orson Welles confesses in *Citizen Kane,* all baby-faced guilelessness as the tyrant-in-embryo Charles Foster Kane. Clearly, the Master thought it would be fun to run the world and – how about that? – it is! So much to blow up! So many people to kill! All the candy you want (though you're nice and share with Lucy)! It's playtime – and a sense of play, of uninhibited discovery and enjoyment, is the sparkling soul of Simm's performance.

Amazingly, Simm is never camp. The Master has always been a moustache-twirling role – elegantly for Delgado, ludicrously for Ainley and Roberts – and it's not as if Harold Saxon isn't aware of what a bad boy he is. But he's too impatient to pose and sneer; a moment spent laughing evilly would only be one more moment of not getting his latest desire. What's the point? Grab the prize. Enjoy, enjoy, enjoy. Having taken over the world in 18 months, Saxon must be a meticulous planner, but the man we see on screen has the attention span of a tachyon. He's always in motion, always on to the next thing, one pleasure after another seized and drained. Until finally we perceive that the antic performance is haunted by exhaustion. Under the exuberance pounds a rhythm of futility: the sound of drums.

Where to Next?

by Richard Salter
From Enlightenment #144, March 2008

I've been told (mostly by my wife) that I'm something of a pessimist and a cynic. She has other, less complimentary names for me too, but they're pretty much unprintable. I have a pretty good life and I'm very lucky in many ways, but I can't help but wonder when it's all going to come crashing down around me.

Russell Davies must be thinking something similar; if not at the forefront of his mind then lingering somewhere at the back like a man whose daughters have dragged him along to a Miley Cyrus concert. In many ways, things could not be better for *Doctor Who* right now. The ratings are still strong after three years since the relaunch, with the 2007 Christmas special achieving viewing figures not seen by this show since Tom Baker scrawled "This is a fake" on a bunch of canvases of the Mona Lisa during an ITV strike. The show is hugely popular with a broad spectrum of the British public and has been sold all over the world. It's garnered acclaim, overwhelmingly positive press reviews, Hugo, People's Choice and all manner of other awards. It's made a genuine star out of David Tennant and forced British folks to banish all memories of "Because We Want To" when they look at Billie Piper. Oh yeah, then there's the small matter of two highly successful spinoff series (and whatever you think of *Torchwood*, it is a success), something the original series never managed to do.

So the pessimist in me starts asking himself, what happens next? What's left to conquer? Surely the only way to go now is down? Right? The inevitable ratings slide. The falling out with the press. The run of poor scripts that put off more and more people. The sudden resurgence in viewership for Ant and Dec causing the BBC to start losing the ratings war. The realisation that this show everyone now seems to love once starred Matthew Waterhouse. It's got to happen soon, surely.

Part of me almost wants Davies to call it a day right now. Go out on a high. Having conquered Saturday night TV and introduced a whole new generation to *Doctor Who* (and a few older ones), you could forgive the man for exiting stage left while the crowd is still applauding. So far, he's not done that, a fact that drives some old-time fans barmy and delights the rest of us who think he's turned *Doctor Who* into one of the most successful and entertaining programmes on television without stomping all over what made it so great in the first place.

Any signs of the impending apocalypse yet? Well, there are a few territories as yet unruffled. Apparently the show didn't do that well in Germany. Hardly a disaster but a chink in the armour nonetheless. There is still a vocal minority of fans who believe Davies is the antichrist and get uncontrollably upset whenever he does exactly what producers on the classic series would have loved to do if they'd had the budget and the balls. The biggest disappointment for me is probably the lack of mainstream success in the US. Granted, the unique way American television is set up isn't exactly conducive to a quirky British sci-fi import, but it's hardly been a runaway success even by *Galactica* standards. (That said, *Torchwood* is the best-rated show on BBC America.) I'm at a loss as to why *Doctor Who* wasn't nominated for a Golden Globe. If the British version of *The Office* can win such a major award, why not *Doctor Who*? A Globe for the Doctor would bring the show to the attention of a much larger audience. It might even lead to a US remake, though perhaps that's not something we should be hoping for. Unfortunately, if it hasn't happened already, it probably won't happen at all.

Is *Doctor Who* the Robbie Williams of the television world? Stunning success and myriad accolades at home, only middling success in the States. Is *Who* about to hit the Williams slump, with disappointing sales on the latest album and a critical drubbing to boot? Perhaps the Doctor should go into rehab, as seems to be the trend these days. It keeps you in the public eye and does wonders for your career.

I shouldn't really worry. Each season of *Doctor Who* has taken a risk or three, and so far it's come through with flying colours. For the 2005 season, the risk was obvious. Spending a fortune on a glossy relaunch of a programme that had become a national punchline; well, you can't get much more risky than that. Davies may be the hottest writer in the UK right now, but that didn't stop *Mine All Mine* or *Bob and Rose* from being largely ignored by the viewers. And then there's the casting of Piper, most famous for marrying DJ and TV presenter Chris Evans very young and then divorcing him, and for being the British Britney of her day (minus the head shaving and the meth addiction). The whole thing could have been instantly rejected by both press and public, resulting in a costly mistake for the BBC and the final nail in the coffin for this Time Lord.

Then came the 2006 season. Having established Chris Eccleston as the Doctor, he promptly changes into relative unknown David Tennant. The risk-o-meter is flashing on Orange Alert now. Billie's still there, Russell is still at the helm, but the leading man has gone off in a huff and has been replaced by a skinny Scotsman who was brilliant in *Blackpool* and *Casanova* (according to the five people who watched those mini-series) but has yet to prove himself in a really big role.

2007's big risk? No more Billie. Having terrified fanboys with her original casting in the role of Rose, she went on to prove everyone wrong, becoming the cornerstone of the series and a huge draw for many new demographics that had proved elusive to the series in the past. Would all these new viewers keep watching without her? Too right they would.

And so onto the 2008 season. The risk this time? Catherine Tate. Never has a more polarising actor been cast in a lead role in *Doctor Who*. She'll either prove to be a huge ratings draw, or a massive turnoff. Time will tell.

And beyond that? 2009 sees several specials and no fifth season until 2010. Will audiences decide that the lack of full season next year means this show is on the way out? Will they turn their attention to the next big thing?

Post-2010, or even before, it's reasonably safe to assume that both Davies and Tennant will move on, and then we'll be hitting Red Alert on the risk-o-meter. Tennant is a hugely popular Doctor, but this is a show that can survive losing its stars and often thrive as a result, thanks to its unique format. No, what raises the risk to Defcon Five is the inevitable departure of Davies. Say what you like about him, without this man's enthusiasm, drive, creativity and willingness to take risks, the series could very quickly fall into decline. Is Davies the only person who can produce modern *Who*? Of course not. But choosing a replacement is a critical decision that could dictate whether *Doctor Who* continues to be successful for another five years and beyond, or not.

However, maybe that's the key to all this: *Doctor Who*'s ability to not only change, but take massive risks while changing is what makes it unique in all of television. It can withstand – indeed, right now it thrives on – changing the leads. Historically, during the best years, it was able to change with the tastes of the public, changing its tone, its focus. And during the wilderness years, it proved flexible in adapting to other media.

Perhaps that flexibility is what might inoculate the series, if you like, from the threats facing it as it continues into a fifth and a sixth year and hopefully more down the road. *Doctor Who* has proven to be bigger than Christopher Eccleston and Billie Piper; perhaps it's bigger than David Tennant and Russell T Davies as well.

A Review of Planet of the Dead

by Jim Mortimore

I loathe and pity the 2009 Easter Special as if the damn thing crawled out of the drain of Dr Moreau's abortion clinic.

Special Blend

by Graeme Burk

From Enlightenment #158, July 2010

During the 372 days between Christmas 2008 and New Year's Day 2010, *Doctor Who* only existed as five hour-or-so special episodes that marked the end of both David Tennant and Russell T Davies' respective eras. Given that this was roughly 35% of normal output, and interspersed throughout the year no less, there were a lot of expectations riding on these specials. Expectations which, if we were fair, there was no way they could meet.

Watching these all together on DVD, a different view of the 2008-10 specials takes shape. The specials are almost a diet version of a regular season of new *Doctor Who*: a high-gloss Christmas special and fun season opener, a pacey potboiler and two separate stories that form an epic finale. All that's missing are the children's monster two-parter and the disappointing story by Stephen Greenhorn.

Watched as a whole, it works remarkably well. *The Next Doctor* probably improved the most in esteem. It's a lot funnier and more poignant. David Morrisey is charming playing a man who believes himself to be the Doctor and it's lovely the way Russell T Davies deconstructs the character of the Doctor through Jackson Lake: Jackson looks and acts the part the viewing public largely believe the Doctor to be (right down to the Victorian outfit he hasn't worn since 2005) and it's only when we get to the heart and emotion of the character that he suddenly comes to life.

And yet, it's Dervla Kirwan who steals the show as Miss Hartigan; she's probably the best villain New *Who* has ever seen. It's a shame the story doesn't do more with her. Typical of an RTD Christmas special, the plot scrambles quite a bit to justify the cool visuals: why on earth were the children needed? How would parallel-earth Cybermen create a weapon like the Cyber King? (Davies, along with Steven Moffat in *The Pandorica Opens*, seems to have confused the old Cybermen and new Cybermen.) And how would the Doctor know what it was? Nevertheless, it's a rousing adventure that's only bittersweet because you know it's the last time this Doctor will have such a thing.

Watching the specials together makes me more kindly disposed to *Planet of the Dead* as well. Not watching it as the only New *Who* for an eight-month stretch makes it easier to accept the story for what it is: a silly, inconsequential change-of-pace runaround. David Tennant is clearly having a ball with the script, milking way more laughs out of any scene than it rightfully deserves. (The same is true for Lee Evans'

Malcolm, only multipled by a factor of 50 Bernards.) Alas, the DVD boxset didn't CG in a better actress than Michelle Ryan to play the role of Lady Christina. The problem with Ryan's portrayal is that it's just one-note – smug – and she lacks any charisma or chemistry with David Tennant. Worse, thanks to the costume design, she's not even sexy. (Here's the thing about Lara Croft: no one would possibly dress like her, but that's not the point!) One also wishes there was a little more substance. Even by the standard of *Who*'s frothy Christmas fare, this is remarkably lacking in jeopardy. In a story that should be a cross between *Midnight* and *Voyage of the Damned*, it studiously avoids all the things that made both these stories great.

The Waters of Mars, on the other hand, has substance and jeopardy to spare. That's why it's not only the best story of this shortened season of specials; it's one of the best stories of David Tennant's tenure as the Doctor. The genius of Davies' and Phil Ford's script is that it plays on multiple levels: it's a brilliant base-under-siege thriller with a creepy monster, but it's also a dark meditation on power and responsibility in the *Doctor Who* universe. It's also a wonderful character piece for the tenth Doctor, as he starts out as his cheery, motormouth self and ends in the worst possible place mentally and spiritually.

The great thing about David Tennant is that you don't even worry anymore that such a range is beyond him. He's that good. Lindsay Duncan proves *Planet of the Dead* false by showing the casting of the female lead is indeed crucial to the success of the episode. Duncan, as Adelaide, is strong, grim and determined but never – take note, Ms Ryan – one-note. The moment when she finally lets herself be swept up with the adventure and agrees with the Doctor that bikes are a good idea is wonderful, as is her dramatic confrontation with the Doctor after his sin against the laws of time. As expected for anything with the credit "directed by Graeme Harper", the rest of the cast is just as great. You care for the plight of Bowie Base One because of all the vividly depicted characters on screen.

The only thing that seems wrong with *Waters* is the use of location. The corridors between the biodomes seem too large for credibility (and it drains any tension out of the chase sequences, because not even Graeme Harper can make it seem as claustrophobic as the studio sets for the bridge and the airlocks). However, that's a small quibble, which I'll tolerate. I'll even tolerate the cute robot with flaming tire tracks.

Oh, there's one other problem with *The Waters of Mars*: quite frankly, it eclipses *The End of Time* in every way. As great as David Tennant is in his swansong, as stunning as Bernard Cribbins is, and as lovely as the last 20 minutes are, *Waters* shows the benefit of tight plotting and thoughtful merging of themes to dramatic situations. *The End of Time* is a disjointed assemblage of set pieces.

Fortunately, most of the set pieces range from great fun (the Master while hungry) to painstakingly beautiful (the Doctor and Wilf talking in the café) to really exciting (the Doctor facing down Rassilon). But there are far too many "what were they thinking?" moments for comfort (the Vinvocci, the Naismiths – who must have the creepiest father / daughter relationship ever shown before the 9 pm watershed). And, as with *The Next Doctor* and so many stories over the past five years, there are a lot of scenes that are there because it looked cool, as opposed to making dramatic sense (the Doctor's 100 foot drop, the Master's super powers, the involvement of President Obama, I could go on and on...).

But what's wonderful about *The End of Time,* taken as a whole, is how much it keeps changing the game (the impact is somewhat blunted on repeat viewings, but then, the same is true with *Blink*). It starts out like a bonkers John Simm Master story and then the Time Lords come in... only they're villains. The Time Lords, it turns out, have been manipulating the Master all along in order to bring themselves back. Then, when the Doctor defeats the Master and the Time Lords and stops the destruction of the time itself, there's the knocking four times. And the Doctor has to die not because of the cosmic sturm and drang, but to save someone he cares about – someone who accidentally locked himself in a cupboard about to be flooded with deadly radiation.

And isn't that like death? It's random. The person who knocks four times isn't the (literal) James Bond villain or the Master but an unhappy, fluky accident. The Doctor's raging against his inevitable fate seems a bit too much on the nose, a bit too human and unheroic – but there's something profoundly honest about it too.

Even on repeat viewings, the Doctor's reward and regeneration is still one of the most beautiful sequences in an incarnation's finale. The extended epilogue may cause the story to have more endings than *Lord of the Rings* (or even *The Family of Blood*), but it's absolutely beautiful, as the Doctor says goodbye to all of his friends. It's a sort of *Doctor Who* version of the Canadian film *One Week* as the Doctor makes peace with the life he's led. And, while I could have done without Mickey and Martha as the ultimate rebound relationship, the others were quite affecting; particularly the Doctor's wave goodbye to Sarah Jane that said everything with a single gesture and the Doctor's conversation with Joan Redfern's granddaughter. And how wonderful is it that as his last goodbye, he gets to, in his own way, say farewell to Rose? It seems so beautifully appropriate that the Doctor's last moments before his regeneration were in the council estate where New *Who* started.

I'm still amazed that a family show airing on Christmas and New Year's Day would air a secular, pop-culture fable about coming to terms with one's own death. And, make no mistake, *The End of Time* is about death and dying, grieving and letting go. The scene in Part One where the Doctor sits in a café and talks to Wilf may be perhaps the best scene in the tenth Doctor's final year. In it, he talks in stark, scary terms about the truth of regeneration. It is a death: the obliteration of a personality, a particular soul inhabiting a man. *The End of Time* is about the process of coming to terms with that.

It's an unusual approach for a final story of an era: a story where you care (and grieve) more for the loss of the departing Doctor than for the arrival of the new incarnation. Which is only fitting as, in his time as the Doctor, David Tennant not only took us to new adventures in time and space, he took us to unseen places in the Doctor's soul. In *The End of Time,* he took us even further than we thought he could, as we witness a Time Lord having to face the death of his personality. It's only fitting that his Doctor's last words should be "I don't want to go."

What's incredible is that Russell T Davies makes such a sobering message so downright entertaining by putting it within a story with the Master and Time Lords and everything else. It may be disjointed and overblown, but it's also bold and gutsy and heartfelt in all the right ways. And that's the incredible genius of Russell T Davies all over. But, then, re-watching the 2009 specials reminds me how much the previous regime is missed. All five episodes show some of the worst excesses of this era of *Doctor Who* – spectacle before plot, Tennant shouting as a lifestyle choice rather than dramatic need – but mostly it shows how exciting, thrilling and fun new *Doctor Who* was for its first five years, and how brilliant the man playing the Doctor's tenth incarnation was.

INTERLUDE

Journey's End - 2

by Scott Clarke
From Enlightenment #155, December 2009

So where were we? Ah yes, editor in the snow, calling to me, "Where's that second article?" I didn't exactly go directly for my keyboard. Kind of procrastinated about. This and that. Cleaning out the prosperous carrot gel of the great fridge-smellin' uber-rot. Saved some tupperware from the blue carnivorous mould. Named a houseplant Allison. Anyway, I must not delay further...

Part Two: Mythology

When I watched *The Stolen Earth* for the first time, I was alone and I entered right into the story. There was no one else in the room rolling their eyes or passing judgement. If you'd been a fly on the wall you'd have heard more than a few omigods, or perhaps seen me rocking the couch a few times. Torchwood, Sarah Jane, Davros (with cool prosthetics for a change), Harriet Jones, regeneration and more portents of doom for poor old Donna. Squee time, cause I'm up to my neck in mythology. It's a different experience from watching *Blink, The Unicorn and the Wasp* or *Midnight*, all excellent examples of standalone *Doctor Who* (and in many ways wholly representative of the spirit of the programme). There's a sense of purpose in mythology episodes, of great forces moving towards something bigger.

Mythology is central to the human psyche. It's the way we make sense of the world around us. Creating order from seeming randomness. It also juxtaposes what is knowable and familiar (stories of human experience) with what is larger than our understanding (mysteries of the universe, concepts of god). And from this juxtaposition we discern patterns.

Back before "new" *Doctor Who* finally arrived on our television screens, there was much speculation with regards to the shape the returning classic would take. Would it be a complete re-boot of the original (taking the character back to basics and ignoring existing continuity) like the deliciously revitalised *Battlestar Galactica*? Or would it be a direct continuation of the original, more like *Star Trek: The Next Generation*?

Fast forward to Spring 2008. *The Stolen Earth / Journey's End* is a feast of mythology both classic and newly conceived. Witness the moment when Davros recognises Sarah Jane Smith and remarks that the "circle of time is closing" as she was there at the beginning on Skaro. Truly the circle has closed. In that one moment, the Time War (Davies' own masterstroke of mythology) and the classic 1974 episode *Genesis of the Daleks* are merged into a moment of epic scale. In plot terms, it was a throwaway exchange, but the added value is phenomenal. Davies sees these moments as essential (in *The Doctor Who Annual 2006*, Davies himself acknowledged that the origins of the Time War stretch back to Genesis).

When mapping out how New *Who* would look, Russell T Davies was obviously very sensitive to the needs of modern audiences. Television viewers today expect a lot more in terms of characterisation and sophistication of storytelling than they did in the past (shows like *The X-Files* and *Buffy* balanced nuanced characterisation with complex mythology). At the same time, he was keenly aware that *Doctor Who* has a sense of mystery at its core. How do you reinvent a character like the Doctor so that he contains both mystery and expected characterisation? So much is known about our favourite Time Lord.

Davies creates a Time War in the Doctor's recent past and then doles out fragments of info to tantalise, but never shedding too much light on the mystery. What we do know is that the Doctor had to make a horrible choice, which resulted in the destruction of both the Daleks and his own people, the Time Lords. The mythology of the Time War informs almost every aspect of the new series. The ninth Doctor was battle-scarred and angry, afraid to act through most of his time. Instead, he enabled others to be heroic. The tenth Doctor is portrayed more as the "lonely god", craving companionship on the one hand, struggling with massive responsibility on the other.

If we "reverse engineer" *The Stolen Earth / Journey's End*, it's fascinating to trace back the threads of the mythology that have been woven together. Paramount is the idea that the Doctor cannot go back in time and save his people juxtaposed against the actions of a desperate Dalek Caan who somehow was able to re-enter the Time War and rescue Davros, the creator of the malevolent pepperpots. Here's a man who resisted Donna's attempts to save the inhabitants of Pompeii from being wiped out, who was consumed with pain over the demise of the only other member of his race (even though that person was evil beyond measure), and was tempted by the Krillitanes with the possibility of a Time Lord resurrection. It seems clear when watching the episodes that Davies is taking us on an epic journey that has a past, present and future.

Dip into the future for a moment, and the events of *The Waters of Mars* clearly illustrate that the Doctor's actions as last of the Time Lords will have even greater consequences.

Rose's return is played out parallel to the return of the Daleks. Planned by the production team since *Doomsday*, her arrival on the scene has been slowly seeded over the course of the 2008 season, beginning with a mysterious appearance at the end of *Partners in Crime* and growing to the "bad wolf" crescendo at the end of *Turn Left*. I've noted before that the Doctor and Rose's resolution is unsatisfying and flawed, but I'll certainly give Davies credit for the epic scope of it. It strives to reach the level of Homer's Odysseus.

Davies' gives us crossovers with *Torchwood* and *The Sarah Jane Adventures* (even retrieving K9 from a black hole), and throws in UNIT, Harriet Jones and Mr Copper. The missing planets include Klom (homeworld of the Abzorbaloff), the Adipose breeding planet and even Callufrax Minor (presumably a relation of the world eaten in *The Pirate Planet*). Each is given its small place in the larger story. Harriet Jones is allowed to be heroically redeemed without back-pedalling on who she is. Jack "dies" and is mourned by the woman who is unknowingly the cause of why he will momentarily be resurrected! Delicious irony.

And we get the culmination of the story of the Doctor's Hand. Honestly, what once seemed like a cool mishap in *The Christmas Invasion* has spiraled into its own epic arc, spanning two television series. Yes, it seemed like a humorous curiosity in the clutter of the Torchwood Hub, but subsequently acted as a divining stick for the Doctor, a source of genetic coding for the Master's anti-anti-aging plan, an omen of the Doctor's clone daughter and finally a makeshift life partner for Rose. If Davies is to be believed, he had it all planned out from the beginning. Each of these represents dividends paid out from a carefully laid mythology.

Typically, mythology is created either by design or out of plot necessity. Some of *Doctor Who*'s most cherished mythology was created as a way to simply make an individual story work. Regeneration was a way to facilitate a rapid casting change. UNIT was a budgetary consideration. Robert Holmes originated the concept that Time Lords can only regenerate 12 times to add gravitas the Master's desperation in *The Deadly Assassin*. Successive writers and production teams then either incorporate the new mythology or ignore it.

One of the things I most appreciate about Davies' take on mythology is how he continually makes it work to his advantage in his storytelling. To Davies, the difference between "continuity" and "mythology" is purposefulness. He isn't asking himself "How do I fit the hand into my story?" but rather "How can the hand assist me in telling the story?"

Does Davies ever go too far with the mythology of the *Doctor Who* universe? Certainly, the answer to that question boils down to respect and a sense of stewardship. A self-confessed fanboy, Davies never hesitates to mine the history of *Doctor Who* for story ideas. Inserting something as obscure as the Macra (from the Troughton era's *The Macra Terror*) into *Gridlock* does no harm to the story but allows a fun callout to long-term fans and probably tickles some spot in Davies as well. Of course, fan opinion is diverse and not everyone is going to be happy. The growing emphasis of the Doctor's godlike qualities is offputting to some. Seeing him ascend into the air with "angels" (*Voyage of the Damned*) or revive through the power of "prayer" (*Last of the Time Lords*) makes some viewers uncomfortable. Others are content to get a bee in their bonnet over why Sarah Jane doesn't seem to remember the events of *The Five Doctors*. (Although they're quite ready to make up an answer for themselves, and hey, that's great!)

Ultimately, I love that Russell T Davies has brought back the mystery and awe to *Doctor Who*. Like when two schoolteachers followed an enigmatic young girl home on a cold November night, I thrilled when that hand reached through the door and urged a beleaguered young shop girl to run. Autons, Nestene and a mysterious Time War.

What did it all mean?

Stay tuned.

THE 21ST CENTURY IS WHEN IT ALL HAPPENS...

Doctor Who is as much a franchise as a TV programme. Longtime fans, especially the ones who stuck around during the inter-war period between TV series, know this from the sheer amount of spinoffs the tie-in product generated. In the 1990s and early 2000s, the books gave us the adventures of *Bernice Summerfield, Faction Paradox* and *Time Hunter,* while the audios gave us *Dalek Empire, Cybermen* and *Doctor Who Unbound.*

It was only a matter of time before the new TV series realised its spin-off-making potential. By the early twenty-first century, it had become *de rigeur* for a popular series to spin off into new series: *Law and Order, CSI, Buffy the Vampire Slayer, Grey's Anatomy* and more have spawned spinoffs. Surprisingly few British series go this route (they tend to have sequel series, which continue the ongoing story and characters), which makes *Doctor Who* and its post-2006 offspring something of a trailblazer.

Doctor Who's spinoff strategy is also unique. It relegated the spinoffs to specialty slots or minority channels like BBC3 or CBBC. It also played with the demographics, aging up and down from the family audience watching *Doctor Who*. Thus, *Torchwood* skews more "adult" while *The Sarah Jane Adventures* is firmly established as a children's series.

What makes this strategy fascinating is how quickly it didn't work: both spinoffs made it to the mainstream anyway. *Torchwood,* in particular, went from BBC3 to BBC2 to BBC1, even throwing in cleaned-up "airline" versions to show kids before the watershed. There was no need to explain who anyone was when the characters from *Torchwood* and *Sarah Jane* showed up in *The Stolen Earth* because both spinoffs had rooted themselves in the public consciousness.

The success of these spinoffs is subject to lively debate. Do they stand in their own right as dramas? Do they demonstrate the same exciting, inventive DNA as *Doctor Who*? Are the characters well-drawn? There is, as you can see from these essays, a plurality of opinion on the subject.

One thing that is clear is that these spinoffs are popular. *Torchwood* was the breakout hit on BBC1 in the summer of 2009 and it was BBC

America's most popular show (until they started showing *Doctor Who*!). *The Sarah Jane Adventures* far outstrips the ratings of the other CBBC shows. And there's a new season of *Torchwood* being made in America as a BBC / Starz co-production. It seems that *Doctor Who* and its spinoffs have made the Doctor's pronouncement in *New Earth* of going "further than we've ever gone" a mission statement.

Barrowmania

by Richard Salter

From Enlightenment #130, October / November 2005

Brace yourselves. Captain Jack Harkness is back. You know, Captain Jack: sometime companion of the ninth Doctor, con-artist extraordinaire who plays for both teams, smooth-talking space adventurer with a sonic gun thingy and a penchant for innuendo. You remember him, right?

But, I hear you cry (but not too loudly please, you'll wake my wife who slumbers peacefully, dreaming of Captain Jack in Lycra), we were told he wouldn't be back for the 2006 season. Well, he won't be. Instead, we're going to get 13 new episodes of Barrowmany goodness in 45-minute chunks of something called *Torchwood.* And, get this, it's a spinoff of *Doctor Who.* It doesn't just star Barrowman in the lead role, it actually stars Captain Jack.

So here, then, is my hastily cobbled together FAQ on *Torchwood* for the benefit of those who after all this time still don't know how to get Internet Explorer working long enough to type the phrase "Outpost Gallifrey" into a search engine.

Q: Who's writing it?

A: It's a Russell T Davies series. Does it matter who's actually writing the individual episodes? Davies will just rewrite them all anyway. And it'll be brilliant, so who cares? Oh fine then, that Sapphire and Steel guy and some newbie nobody's heard of. Go read the Doctor Who News Page or something, jeez. Ask me something useful.

Q: What's a Torchwood then?

A: I'm not entirely sure what the title means. I know it's an anagram of *Doctor Who,* but what exactly is a Torchwood? Is it a deliberate misspelling of Touch Wood (which would be appropriate for a series featuring Captain Jack, I'm sure)? Will there be a big bonfire at the end of each episode where they burn the remains of the villain of the week? Does it just sound good? You decide.

Q: Wait a minute, this is a spinoff of *Doctor Who*?
A: Yeah, hard to believe eh? The last time that happened was in the ultra-groovy *K9 and Company*, which went on to enjoy 15 top-rated seasons before the show's star died and Liz Sladen suffered a particularly virulent case of split ends. Or not.

Q: So will the title sequence to *Torchwood* be some funky 80's retro dance mix that goes "do-do-do-du-do HARK-NESS", with Captain Jack sitting on a wall, jogging down a road and sprawling over the hood of a 1960's Morris Minor?
A: Probably not, but I'll pass on the suggestion to Russell T, how does that sound?

Q: So *Torchwood* is supposed to be a more, er, adult show, am I right?
A: Yeeeees.

Q: So, that scene in *Bad Wolf*, where Captain Jack has all his clothes disintegrated...
A: Where are you going with this?

Q: Oh nowhere really. Just wondering. You know, since it's an adult show...
A: Uh huh, I see. Well I'm guessing there won't be much full frontal, but the odd butt cheek might be on display.

Q: Good enough for me. So this is a sort of *X-Files* meets *This Life* thing, right?
A: Think *Supernatural* meets *Ultraviolet* (the British vampire series).

Q: Sexy and thrilling, and mysterious and cool, right?
A: Yes.

Q: Set in Cardiff.
A: That's right.

Q: Cardiff, Wales.
A: Yes, what's your point?

Q: Oh nothing. So Captain Jack will be joined by an ensemble cast?
A: Absolutely. Here's what we know so far about the cast and the characters they play. Brian Blessed will play Prince Vultan, who flew too close to Captain Jack's charisma and singed a wing. He's now stuck on Earth

and forced to help solve crimes and shoot aliens and stuff. Richard O'Brien plays Fico; we don't know what he'll be doing, but apparently he'll also be in a crossover episode with *Doctor Who* where the Doctor and Rose get trapped in the Crystal Maze. Then there's Max Von Sydow as Emporer Ming, who will be the Torchwood organisation's main enemy; think The Hood from *Thunderbirds* or Baron Greenback from *Danger Mouse*. That's all we know so far.

Q: Isn't that just the cast list from *Flash Gordon*?
A: Why, er, so it is.

Q: You don't actually know who's in *Torchwood* at all, do you?
A: Er, John Barrowman's in it. But, er, other than that, no I have no clue. Sorry.

Q: Useless. Can you tell me when and where it will show in Britain?
A: Ah, now this I do know. BBC3 sometime in 2006.

Q: BBC3? Nobody watches that, do they?
A: No, they don't. But if the ratings are good, BBC1 might show it too.

Q: Are you going to coin a new phrase for Captain Jack fandom now?
A: Yes I am, and it's Barrowmania. You heard it here first.

Q: That's not very good.
A: Yeah, well FAQ you, buddy.

Q: So did Angel still love Buffy even after he moved to LA?
A: Wrong spinoff.

Q: Bear with me, I'm going somewhere with this line of questioning.
A: Fine. Yes, he probably did.

Q: And does Captain Jack still desire a threesome with the Doctor and Rose even after he returns to Earth?
A: I expect so. Am I fuelling your weird-ass slash fiction fantasies here?

Q: Um, no, no, I was writing a letter to my mother.
A: Uh huh.

Q: No really. She's a big Captain Jack fan.
A: Twisted.

Q: My point is, just as Angel came back to the *Buffy* series, will Captain Jack come back to *Doctor Who* and vice versa?

A: Possibly. Nobody's ruling out Jack popping up in the 2007 season. But the BBC has stated that for the 2006 season of *Doctor Who* and the first season of *Torchwood,* there'll be no crossover episodes. There will, however, be the odd mention of the Torchwood organisation in *Doctor Who.*

Q: Will it be like, "Hey, Rose, have you seen that new TV show on BBC3 called *Torchwood*?" "No, Doctor, I have not. Is it any good?" "Yeah it's brill!" Like that?

A: Sure, if you like.

Q: Will it be any good?

A: You're seriously asking me if a series produced by Russell T Davies, starring Captain Jack and without the restrictions of a family audience, that purports to merge the best elements of US-made sci-fi series with all their mood lighting and special effects and stuff, with the best, funniest British TV drama... you're asking me if this will be any good?

Q: Yes I am.

A: Let me put it this way. I can say right now, with absolute conviction, that *Torchwood* will be much better than *K9 and Company.*

Q: Last question then. The moment *Enlightenment* goes to press, what other *Torchwood*-related announcements will be made?

A: Oh all sorts. Here's just a few I predict:

- John Barrowman breaks a hip doing pantomime, Chris Eccleston will now play Captain Jack.
- The *Sun* launches a campaign after Anthony Read's estate refuses to allow Russell Davies use of the Nimon in an episode of *Torchwood.*
- A second spinoff of *Doctor Who* is announced called *Raxacoricofallapatorius Nights.*
- Big Finish is to produce a series of *Torchwood* audio dramas starring Bonnie Langford and David Warner.
- The BBC announces six hundred new seasons of *Doctor Who.*
- Sylvester McCoy snags a lead role in *Torchwood* as the Ferret King.
- David Tennant quits after filming just ten minutes of *The Christmas Invasion.*

Q: Thank you, that was all very informative.

A: Liar.

The Ten Commandments of Doctor Who Spinoffs

by Graeme Burk
From Enlightenment #143, December 2007

I love *Doctor Who*, and in a perfect world you'd think that more spinoffs would equal more *Who*, which in turn would equal more love.

If only it were that simple.

The trouble any spinoff faces – whether it be *Torchwood, Star Trek: Deep Space Nine, Law & Order: Special Victims Unit* or *Private Practice* – is to develop its own distinctive identity while, at the same time, not alienating the audience it brought from the parent programme.

In *Doctor Who*'s case, it's a more interesting dilemma. *Doctor Who* isn't your ordinary TV programme with a set format. In fact, with minor changes, *Doctor Who* could theoretically be rejigged to be either *Torchwood* or *The Sarah Jane Adventures* (the Doctor as the weird maiden aunt across the road; hmmm...) or any other format, just as easily as it had been earthbound military adventure, Hammer horror or hard SF in the past.

What *Doctor Who* does have, though, is a certain tone, a certain style which is hard to define but easy to mess up. Any show spinning off from it needs to be mindful of this style.

Thus far, we've had an initial season for both *Torchwood* and *The Sarah Jane Adventures*. Two very different series, two very different target audiences – and yet both have strengths and weakness not only as a *Doctor Who* spinoff but as a TV show. As we get ready for the next season of *Torchwood* in January, I thought it would be fun to outline what I think are some of the things the *Doctor Who* spinoffs should be doing. And since fans like to think they're bringing their own wisdom from on high, I would like to descend from the Mount and give you the Ten Commandments of Making *Doctor Who* Spinoffs.

I. Thou shalt honour thy parent programme

Actually, in terms of the letter of the law, *Torchwood* and *The Sarah Jane Adventures* do this fairly well. *Torchwood* has some lovely subtle references to the "mothership" series and *The Sarah Jane Adventures* seem to have made it its mission to activate the fan gene in the pre-teen, *Doctor-Who-Adventures*-reading audience by making explicit references to both classic and new versions of *Doctor Who*.

But the problem is that it can't just be teases and references to

Sontarans and UNIT. Honouring the parent programme is about honouring the spirit of it as well. And, as the ancient scholars used to say, the rest of this is commentary.

II. Thou shalt at all times possess a sense of humour

No one wants *Torchwood* or *Sarah Jane* to become a laugh factory, but one of the things that separates *Doctor Who* from its military-jump-suit-wearing contemporaries in genre television is that it has a healthy sense of the absurd and the ridiculous. Or, as Steven Moffat put it in his *Enlightenment* interview, "*Doctor Who* isn't a comedy, but it has the grace of one."

Which is the main reason for me that the first season of *Torchwood* didn't work a lot of the time. Russell T Davies himself made a similar assessment when he said in a recent *Doctor Who Magazine* interview: "It became a very dark series. If you watch my first episode, it's got a pterodactyl, and an invisible lift, and a very witty Captain Jack... but we lost some of that because of the speed of production." *Torchwood,* often times, seems obsessed with being as dark and miserable as humanly possible. Moments of comic relief, often scattershot, in episodes like *Greeks Bearing Gifts, They Keep Killing Suzie* or *Random Shoes* seem few and far between. In stark contrast, *The Sarah Jane Adventures'* genius is in the brilliant light touch that knows how to flit between the serious and the dramatic and the totally frothy; one only has to see stories like *Whatever Happened to Sarah Jane?* or *Eye of the Gorgon* for proof.

Again, I don't think *Torchwood* needs to give up its "adult" trappings, but there are loads of adult shows that have a total sense of humour about themselves. I'm cautiously optimistic that things might be different in the new year.

III. Thou shalt use the charm of thy lead actor

If there is one thing *The Sarah Jane Adventures* does hands-down better than its post-watershed contemporary, it's that they've made its star absolutely and totally compelling. Lis Sladen is funny, charming, vivacious, vulnerable and heroic. I'm an old-school fan: Sarah is my favourite companion and I don't feel out of place watching her here. She's just as charismatic now as she was in 1975. The scripts know how to play to her strengths.

Which brings me to Captain Jack. I love Jack. Jack enabled me to forgive so many problems I had with the Series Three finale for *Doctor Who* just because of the way he flirted with the Doctor throughout. And yet I feel totally out of place watching him in *Torchwood*. All his charm and charisma have been obliterated. He's dull, brooding and ineffective. I still don't get how, in a programme which is supposed to be more "sexed up" than *Doctor Who*, Jack isn't shagging men, women and vending machines every episode, but Owen is. (Seriously. The man's mouth wraps round his face. What is the appeal? Eww.) The best Jack does the whole year is an off-screen romance with Ianto, the tea-boy who wanted to kill him. Okay...

Seriously, John Barrowman is a 50,000-watt beacon of intensity and he's wasted playing a cut-rate version of Angel. I seriously think Russell T Davies wrote Jack in *Utopia* to show up the writing staff on *Torchwood* and remind himself of the incredible charisma this character has. I hope the Series Two *Torchwood* writers take up that challenge.

IV. Thou shalt steal, only so long as thou shalt create stories that bring new life to old ideas

Doctor Who has been filching from different genres, archetypes, and high and low literature since that beat-up Police Box wound up in 100,000 BC back in 1963. It's a part of the basic DNA of the programme, and it should be a part of the DNA of its spinoffs. But it should be in the spirit of *The Robots of Death* or *Pyramids of Mars* and make something new and different out of something that's familiar.

That's precisely what *Torchwood* did with the episode *Out of Time*. On paper, *Out of Time* is approximately five episodes of *Star Trek*: people from the past wind up in the present / future; culture shock, comedy and drama ensue before the characters eventually adjust to their circumstances. And yet, *Out of Time* subverts the formula by having all but one of the people from the past deciding to abandon this new world and their lives as the future is ultimately too much for them. (The scene where a man visits his Alzheimer's-afflicted son in an old-age home is heartbreaking.) Consequently, it's the only truly "adult" episode during the first season.

The genius of *Out of Time* is that it takes an old idea and looks at it from a different angle. *Combat* and *Countrycide* ape *Fight Club* and *The Texas Chainsaw Massacre* and just look like pale copies of the original. The same is true of the *Sarah Jane* episode *Warriors of Kudlak*, which freely borrows from *The Last Starfighter* but doesn't do enough with the concept to make it new or compelling.

V. Thou Shalt Not Bore The Viewer

You would think this would be obvious but I thought it was worth mentioning. So far neither spinoff, even at their worst, has done that, but neither should it start happening any time soon.

VI. Thou Shalt Show A Sense of Wonder

The trouble with *Torchwood* is that in many ways it's been designed to be the antithesis of *Doctor Who*. While *Doctor Who* is about optimism and the triumph of life in the universe, *Torchwood* is obsessed with death – virtually every episode ends with the solution of "kill the bastard" – and deals with characters living amidst horror and detritus.

How much more wonderful it was to watch even a mediocre episode of *Sarah Jane* like *Warriors of Kudlak* and witness Sarah Jane and Maria looking over the Earth in a spaceship. In an episode featuring child kidnappings and war-weary aliens, there was this beautiful serene moment.

One of the things I think Russell T Davies intended to set up when he created *Torchwood* was the dichotomy between *Doctor Who*'s optimism and *Torchwood*'s reality. As Suzie says in *Everything Changes*, "You do this job for long enough and you end up thinking, how come we get all the Weevils and bollocks and shit? Is that what alien life is, filth? Maybe there's better stuff out there. Brilliant stuff. Beautiful stuff. Just, they don't come here. This planet's so dirty, that's all we get, the shit." But I think the reality of the season was that the focus shifted to the filth, without any sense of the aspiration for something better. I'm hoping the balance shifts in future.

VII. Thou Shalt Not Be Afraid To Recast

The one thing that didn't work in *Sarah Jane*'s pilot was the annoying and useless character of Kelsey. It's to the series' credit that they saw the problem with Kelsey and recast Porshe Lawrence-Mavour in favour of Daniel Anthony's much more interesting Clyde. Suffice it to say, my heart sank when I saw that Toshiko and Ianto, who were deadweight characters played by lightweight actors, managed to survive to the second season of *Torchwood*. Hell, on *Doctor Who* these days, they recast one of the leads every bloody season because they feel like it. But we're stuck with Gareth David-Lloyd for another 13 episodes. There is no justice...

VIII. Thou shalt not insult the viewer's intelligence

Again, you would think this would be a no-brainer, and yet *The Sarah Jane Adventures* gave us *Revenge of the Slitheen*, which had a plot that could stunt growth. *Torchwood* is far from exempt. *Countrycide* shows the characters as being totally inept: they completely self-destruct when their car gets stolen. That's not even mentioning the atrocity known as *Cyberwoman*, where a character can keep a WMD in the basement that kills three people and not get fired. And then there's *End of Days*, where the characters are totally lobotomised, the villain makes no sense whatsoever (in spite of a brilliant setup in the story before) and, once again, we have a story where there are absolutely no consequences for anyone's actions.

IX. Thou shalt be consistent.

My main complaint about the first season of *Torchwood* is that, in spite of it having the illusion of continuity, none of the writers appear to be actually working on the same show. Every episode has a completely different set of assumptions on how secret Torchwood is, what the team does and how the characters interact with each other. Leaving aside the pig's ear *End of Days* made of *Captain Jack Harkness,* Chris Chibnall's own individual scripts don't really jibe with each other. *Sarah Jane* may have been a kids' show, but the production team worked hard at making all five stories in the first season seem like they were all from the same programme (even a story that broke all the rules like *Whatever Happened to Sarah Jane?*). All the stories were furthering the same goals for the characters and building on them so that the finale was rewarding for the viewer. Hopefully, *Torchwood* will learn from that in the coming season.

X. Thou shalt connect big emotions with big events and create big drama

At their best, both *Torchwood* and *The Sarah Jane Adventures* exemplify what I think might be called the Russell T Davies method of writing television but frankly is pretty much how all television is done nowadays. Episodes like *Captain Jack Harkness, End of Days* and *Everything Changes* get that all-important conjunction of scary events and powerful personal emotion, while *Eye of the Gorgon* may be the best episode of any *Who*-related spinoff for taking the character's emotional arc in a completely different direction thanks to the supernatural menace they encounter. If they can make more episodes like these, we have a lot of things to look forward to in 2008.

Death, Corpses and Un-death in Torchwood

by Helen Kang

High art and popular culture in the Western world have had a morbid curiosity with the body suspended in death. The vampire "undead" of Bram Stoker, the zombies of George A. Romero and even the puppet corpse in *Weekend at Bernie's* are part of the eclectic history of this motif. *Torchwood,* the darker and more macabre spawn of *Doctor Who,* joins in these ranks with its own unique twist on this age-old theme. After all, with Captain Jack Harkness suspended in indefinite living, it is not such a far jump to the other side of the spectrum. But the candidate for the body trapped in death is probably the unlikeliest character in the cast. It's not the brooding and tragic Ianto, nor the shy and self-pitying Toshiko, nor the thrill-seeking ex-cop Gwen. It is Owen Harper, played by Burn Gorman, the cocky, self-centered "bad boy" philanderer of Torchwood.

Owen is a curious juxtaposition of high passion (in his sexual conquests) and high reason (in his profession and role in the team) that would have outraged Decartes. Owen is also another curious juxtaposition of life and death: he is a medical doctor who spends more time examining various manifestations of death than tending to matters of life, executing an endless series of autopsies of human and non-human corpses, including chunks of alien flesh in *Meat*. This inherent contradiction in Owen's persona makes him an unexpected and yet interesting candidate for the body suspended in death. In some ways, death has surrounded Owen from the very beginning.

Owen's transformation in the second season of *Torchwood* explores three different aspects of the theme of life and death: personification of Death, the joining of death and life during the autopsy and the absence of a sense of time in death. While the first is a familiar motif, the latter two are rather unconventional and out of this world in just the kind of way that gives *Torchwood* its unique identity from *Doctor Who*.

Wrestling Death

At the end of the episode *Reset* in Series Two, Owen is fatally wounded by a bullet which was originally aimed at Martha Jones. In the subsequent episode, *Dead Man Walking*, Jack is unable to accept Owen's sudden death and uses the Resurrection Glove (twin of the original in *They Keep Killing Suzie* from Series One) to revive Owen at the autopsy table. The team hurriedly bids Owen goodbye, including Toshiko Sato, who professes her secret love for him. But this glove is unlike its pair and Owen remains conscious (though dead) long after 30 seconds are up. Owen's inexplicable state of living death is intertwined with the episode's central narrative: when Owen returned from death, he brought Death with him.

In *Dead Man Walking*, Death is a personification, the taker of life, in the manner of medieval depiction of the Bubonic plague: a skeletal form in a hooded tunic, carrying a terrifying sickle. Death is a menacing figure, an opponent and foe to be overcome by Torchwood who are protectors of the living. What we thus see are themes of defeating or cheating death and, indeed, wrestling death, as in the case of Owen, whose sparring with Death is reminiscent of the Biblical account of Isaac who wrestled an angel.

The personification of an abstract idea into a visible and tangible form, particularly one that is semi-human, is not new to the viewers of New *Doctor Who* and its spinoffs. We saw the Vashta Nerada, microscopic beings that gorge on flesh, as the personification of the Dark in *Silence in the Library / Forest of the Dead*. In *The Impossible Planet / The Satan Pit*, Evil takes the shape of a minotaur-like figure of Satan but also a force or an "idea" that possesses Tobias Zed, the archaeologist. Similar to the latter, Death uses Owen as the portal to enter the world of the living and our unlikely hero becomes the gatekeeper, risking his own "life" by wrestling Death in its tracks.

In *Dead Man Walking*, Death is a force with a tangible manifestation that must be kept out of the realm of the living. It is identifiable as the antithesis and threat to life. Martha is "poisoned" by the ghostly figure of Death, which sucks years of life from her, leaving her as a 70-year-old woman. The aged Martha looks at herself in the mirror and utters, "It must be Death because it took my life." The figure of Death concretises something that is elusive and abstract.

Meaning of Death

Torchwood takes an unusual and exciting look at the familiar theme of death, doing what it does best and distinguishing itself from *Doctor Who*. It takes the relative common theme of the living dead, or the undead, and reimagines it through human drama, asking: What does it mean to live in death? Is Owen a dead man whose body has somehow managed to retain its motor function? Is he frozen in the moment where one transitions from living to dead? If so, is he dead, alive or perpetually dying?

Ironically, death, life and dying are the domain of Owen's trained knowledge and practice of medicine. The viewers witness countless scenes of Owen poring over cadavers as unsavoury sound-effects accompany his surgical manoevres. Yet, when he is at the other end of the scalpel, Owen's lifelong training as a doctor fails him. He cannot comprehend what is happening to him. Medicine has no explanation for his condition.

In *Birth of the Clinic*, twentieth century historian and philosopher Michel Foucault argues that prior to the development of pathological anatomy – the very subject of Owen's expertise – Western medicine perceived death as an absolute, the end point of life. In death, eighteenth-century medicine lost access to any knowledge or understanding of matters of life, including disease.

Pathological anatomy vitalised the concept of "death" for Western medicine. Death was no longer the pitch-black pit of unknown. Corpses were now seen to hold valuable meaning for medicine with respect to the life of disease. Thus, opening corpses also opened up new possibilities for medicine to claim knowledge and expertise. Death was not the end, the absolute and finite point at the end of life, but it, too, offered its own timeline and continuities which are related to life. Foucault describes the practice of post-mortem autopsy as having practically conjoined the last stages of life and the beginnings of death, or what he calls "pathological time" and "cadaveric time". The autopsy table is symbolic of the at-times ambiguous and uncertain distinction between life and death: it is a place where the dead object (corpse) tells the story of what happened in life (details of disease and circumstances of death).

Foucault's notion of conjoined time between life and death takes several different imageries in *Dead Man Walking*. Foremost, the episode opens with an eight-minute scene at the autopsy table where Owen comes to a rude awakening from death with the aide of the Resurrection Glove. Owen's cadaveric time overlaps with his pathological time as the victim of a gunshot wound. However, the scene also symbolises Owen's transition from the observer of death to the object of the pathological gaze. Indeed, we see that his body becomes slowly overtaken by an unknown foreign substance, like a disease, that is eventually identified as Death.

The autopsy table is a place of control and power, in Foucault's sense of the terms, as a way to understand and master something that is unknown and whose potential for chaos can be a source of anxiety. While death is a valuable source of meaning for pathological anatomy, such close interaction with death can at times come with too high a price. If the temporal distinction between life and death become less certain and less rigid through the moment of autopsy, then where does life end and death begin? Is there really a sure way to distinguish one from the other? Owen's body as living death symbolises this anxiety. His body is the site of a dangerous impossibility: a bridge between life and death, which should both remain as two distinct worlds.

Doing Time in Death

In philosophical, theological and cultural ideas of life, "death" is often conceptualised in spatial terms, as a place you go to when you are no longer living. The explanation for these places usually falls under the domain of religion and spirituality; Christianity, in particular, tends to focus on notions of heaven and hell, death and resurrection. The emphasis is on the idea that life and after-life are separate places, the latter full of mystery and reverence that invites curiosity, yet to know it is forbidden and impossible.

But what happens when we consider how time can be experienced in death? Is there even time in death?

After Owen conquers Death in a wrestling match, the Torchwood team is left to deal with his seemingly impossible state of living death. Weary of what other dangerous mysteries reside in his inexplicable body, Jack places Owen under moratorium from work until the team can figure out what to do with him. Owen resents being demoted to making coffee for the crew and demands to be reinstated to his position as physician. At Owen's angered requests, Jack orders him to "go home and watch TV" instead of brooding at work.

The viewer had previously seen Owen's flat, the love nest that witnessed countless passionate affairs. But when he returns to the same flat in *A Day in the Death,* we see an entirely different place. The minimalist modern furnishing suddenly appears stark and sterile. It is no longer a space that breathes wantonness and sexuality. It is a dead space. Owen purges all evidence of life from his flat, emptying the refrigerator of all food and drink that he can no longer consume and the medicine cabinet of all toiletries that he no longer needs. Owen doesn't breathe, he doesn't drink, he doesn't shave, he doesn't eat, he doesn't expel excrement and he doesn't have sex. All the daily activities of the body that mark the passage of time, including embarrassing bodily functions, no longer pertain to him. The living body is defined in terms of its relation to time, through imperceptible cycles of cell death and division, and the ability of the body to heal itself. Owen is now removed from this cycle of continuity. A combination of hauntingly repetitive electronic music and uncomfortably long shots of Owen's blank expression add to the smothering feeling of stillness.

In social and linguistic theories, post-structuralism blasted the stability of the individual as a unique, coherent and fully rational subject. The post-structural subject is fluid, shifting, unstable and constantly changing. We may believe ourselves to be unique, individual and in rational control of our thoughts and actions, but we are much more affected by language, cultural norms and social institutions than we think. Quite often, this understanding of the subject and identity have been met with significant antagonism, discomfort and fear. If our identity and our sense of ourselves are always shifting, changing and uncertain, then we have no point of reference. The celebration of the individual as a creature of reason and whole spirit is at the heart of humanism and liberalism, which are deeply engrained in our contemporary cultural fabric.

But Owen is the polar opposite of the post-structural subject: he never changes, never shifts and never fluctuates. He has absolutely no choice in the matter. He is the extreme exaggeration of the stable humanist and liberalist individual to the point of horrifying stagnancy and, indeed, deadly stillness. How do you feel time when your body no longer changes according to its passage? Can you even feel anything? If you can't feel, then what does this mean for your humanity?

Death and Thereafter

The theme of after-death in science fiction and fantasy is often filtered through Christian imageries of heaven, hell, resurrection and self-sacrifice. Death can be a rite of passage to a higher existence, it can lead to retribution for ill-doings, or it can be the cause of grief and loss. *Torchwood* is saturated with death of all kinds, yet it does not try to rationalise death through spiritual ideas of divine purpose or design. It is decidedly unspiritual, particularly evident in the events surrounding Owen's death, yet it isn't exactly atheist, either. *Torchwood* altogether avoids the spiritual or religious questions of death, as though it wants to claim that there are more important and interesting stories to tell. It asks, at the moment of death, how vulnerable and desperate do we allow ourselves to become? And, in these moments, we discover shameful weaknesses and unexpected strengths that escape the narratives offered by religion. Therein lies the unique allure of *Torchwood*.

Camp Noir

by Lynne M Thomas

When *Torchwood* was announced by the *Doctor Who* production team as the "adult" spinoff, there was rampant speculation and a bit of confusion as to how, exactly, one makes *Doctor Who* "adult" – especially given that *Torchwood* centers around Captain Jack Harkness, the rogue time agent introduced in *The Empty Child / The Doctor Dances*. "Adult" series like *Battlestar Galactica* or *Dollhouse* tend to feature decidedly dark themes and characters. Captain Jack is a lot of fun: he's cheeky, he's brash, he hits on everything that moves. I had serious doubts that anyone having that much fun sleeping his way across the universe could come across as dark. I expected to see *Doctor Who* without the Doctor, but with more violence, swearing and sex, rather like the *Sarah Jane Adventures* for grown-ups.

Torchwood spent some time finding its feet, which made for an uneven first season. There are some truly great episodes (*Small Worlds, Out of Time* and *Captain Jack Harkness*). There are also episodes that use profanity, sex and violence rather gratuitously just to prove that this is an "adult" show (*Countrycide* comes to mind) and the occasional outright clunker (*Cyberwoman*), as well as episodes that fans either love or hate (*Random Shoes*), rounded out by adventures that fall somewhere in between (*They Keep Killing Suzie*).

Never have I yelled "I cannot believe that they just did that!" at the television when watching a series as often as I did with the first season of *Torchwood*. Any time I thought that I could predict what would happen next, they stuck out their tongue and did something else completely. I didn't want to miss a single moment. I tuned in week after week, dying to see what the hell they were going to do next to top the previous week's episode. Although I was occasionally disappointed with the execution of some episodes, I was still always surprised, fascinated and greedy for more. Even when it was bad, it was never boring.

Torchwood is, frankly, a bit bent. It's the particular way in which it is bent that I find so fascinating. It begins as science fiction noir: corrupt and corruptible characters solve science fictional crimes in an urban setting, with style. (It would be urban fantasy, like the *Dresden Files*, if the alien technology were magic.) But that science fiction noir is presented through the very queer point of view of Captain Jack Harkness, Big Gay Superhero. Jack's character is a fifty-first century omnisexual, of course. (The Doctor described Jack's sexuality in *The Doctor Dances* as "Just a bit more flexible when it comes to 'dancing'... So many species, so little time.") John Barrowman's portrayal of Jack incorporates a lot of specifically twenty-first century recognisably gay mannerisms. Jack's story (and *Torchwood*'s, by association) is one of a camp response to noir challenges. While definitions of camp vary, it is, roughly, queers satirising heterosexual culture through exaggeration. This re-envisioning of science fiction noir through a queer sensibility creates an entirely new genre, *camp noir*, and gives *Torchwood* its unique tone.

Scratch *Torchwood*'s surface and you will find a bunch of queer humans performing an impossible job with a great deal of relish. Team Torchwood survives their deep, dark existential science fictional noir pain by reminding us that often, the most effective way to fight off the darkness is to laugh at it, or shag right in its face. These powerful, empowering, and utterly human acts raise a defiant middle finger to both the unrelenting darkness of the universe and those who try to perpetuate it as the best possible way to tell the story.

Torchwood Noir: More than Jack's Swoopy Coat

Michael L. Stevens describes noir as "A contemporary crime movie in which the characters are corrupt or corruptible. Generally the milieu is urban and middle class. The overall feel is one of repression and fatalism. Finally, style, whether expressed in black and white or colour, reinforces these themes." *Torchwood* has all three elements. Corruption is rampant. Jack can't police his own team on simple safety rules, like "no alien tech leaves the Hub". Owen arguably date-rapes a couple, using an alien spray to make himself irresistible to them (*Everything Changes*). Ianto builds a lair in the basement for maintaining his cybernised girlfriend and doesn't tell the team, putting them all in danger (*Cyberwoman*). Toshiko gets so caught up in using an alien artefact to hear what people are saying about her that she forgets to mention its rather dangerous existence to her colleagues, along with the presence of the giver (*Greeks Bearing Gifts*). Suzie uses the gauntlet to practice bringing the people that she has killed back to life (*Everything Changes*).

Team members consistently betray one another. Suzie shoots Jack and then herself after killing three people for practice with the resurrection glove (*Everything Changes*). Gwen and Owen's uncharitable thoughts about Tosh become known to her when she uses her amulet (*Greeks Bearing Gifts*). Ianto betrays the whole team in his bid to keep Lisa alive and they all betray him by killing her (*Cyberwoman*). Jack slips Retcon into Gwen's drink after her initial discovery of Torchwood (*Everything Changes*) and betrays the team by leaving them for the Doctor without a word at the end of the season (*End of Days*). His decision to let the Faeries have the little girl at the end of *Small Worlds* to save Earth from a much larger threat is not only a betrayal of the little girl's mother and Estelle (one of his exes who came to him for help), but is also a direct precursor to his sacrifice of his grandson in *Children of Earth*. He has no compunction about letting Mark die in *Combat* for his role in setting up Weevil Fight Club and his attempt to talk John out of committing suicide does more harm than good (*Out of Time*).

Even Gwen is corruptible. She is originally brought into the team as a moral center. When Gwen asks what Torchwood needs her for, Jack replies, "Because maybe you were right; we could do more to help" (*Everything Changes*). Over time, though, she loses her certainty as she gets more involved in Torchwood. Jack's overtly sexual lessons in using firearms are just the beginning of Gwen's re-examination of her own moral code (*Ghost Machine*). She cheats (by her own description) on Rhys with Owen, then doses Rhys with Retcon after telling him she has done so, absolving her own conscience without damaging her relationship with Rhys (*Countrycide, Combat*).

Cardiff is not New York, Los Angeles or Chicago, but it qualifies as urban by Welsh standards, as repeatedly pointed out by Owen in *Countrycide*, in the hopes of making you believe it. Suzie discusses the entire planet as being "dirty, so all we get is shit" when referring to alien life like weevils (*Everything Changes*). *Combat* features bored, middle-class urbanites creating their own fight club with Weevils and the alien sex gas monster in *Day One* trolls through urban dance clubs. Ianto is constantly making espressos – the ultimate urbanite, middle-class drink – for the team. Although *Torchwood*'s visual style is inconsistent from director to director, some elements reflect a noir sensibility. Cardiff is often shot at night, in the rain, with characters consistently moving in and out of shadows. Jack's vintage World War II dress sense and Ianto's snappy suits also embrace a noir aesthetic. Other noir elements and motifs incorporated into Torchwood include amnesia (the use of Retcon in *Everything Changes* and *Combat*) and the femme fatale (*Greeks Bearing Gifts, Cyberwoman*), as well as stories set during wartime (*Captain Jack Harkness*). These noir elements really come into their own, however, when they are portrayed by a bunch of queer characters.

Torchwood Queers: We are everywhere

Torchwood is overwhelmingly queer. In the Land of *Torchwood*, straight monogamy is not the default assumption, unlike nearly all other television drama. Radclyffe-Hall-style characters who die for the sin of being queer in other series are single-handedly satirised by Jack, the queer who cannot die. Bisexuality (or omnisexuality, in Jack's case) runs rampant. Granted, it could be a self-selecting group; Jack likely requires flexibility to be part of his team. Every recurring character in *Torchwood* is at least nominally bisexual, whether it is simply kissing, flirty tension or full-on sex. Consequences for those individual relationships vary, based on whether the relationship itself is healthy, not on the genders of the people involved. For instance, Toshiko's relationship with Mary in *Greeks* is not portrayed as "experimentation" or "failed lesbianism"; it's an unhealthy relationship. The lesson is: don't give in to your attraction to ex-con aliens who offer you tech, no matter how sexy they make you feel, something the team should have remembered when Captain John Hart showed up in Season Two.

While no one in Torchwood is very good at building healthy relationships, the straight, ostensibly monogamous relationships are portrayed as having the least healthy outcomes. Gwen cheats on Rhys with Owen and struggles with her feelings for Jack (*Countrycide, Ghost Machine*). Ianto is understanding of Jack's occasional outside activity (*Captain Jack Harkness*), while his feelings for Lisa led him to betray his entire team (*Cyberwoman*). The tone of the portrayal of the relationships encourages the notion that Jack and Ianto are a more "real" couple than Gwen and Rhys: Gwen and Rhys are often played for comedy, while Jack and Ianto are played as drama. Owen is a complete mess after falling in love with and being left by Diane (*Out of Time*). Toshiko can't seem to form any lasting relationships at all because of her unrequited feelings for Owen.

Captain Jack Harkness also shows the emotional impact of a queer relationship played for drama. Captain Jack dances cheek-to-cheek with the original Captain Jack in front of a crowd in 1942 and then tenderly kisses him goodbye. This subversion of the noir trope of the soldier's last dance before going off to war is written with the same emotional resonance as if the two Captain Jacks were a straight couple, rather than a soon-to-be dead guy being kissed by the guy who's about to steal his identity. "Our" Captain Jack then strolls through the Rift back to Torchwood with Tosh, as the original Captain Jack salutes him. In that moment, the original Captain Jack experiences a healthy attachment to another man, which he carries into battle. A tender moment, twisted out of its genre expectations through a purposeful anachronism (the real Captain Jack would have been court-martialled as soon as our Captain Jack disappeared), subverts our expectations of how that brief relationship would play out on any other series.

When Torchwood is not distracted by their relationship woes, however, they return to their mission of protecting the Earth from what comes through the Rift, fueled by Ianto's endless supply of freshly made espresso and Jubilee Pizza. In their caffeine-induced frenzy, they seem to consistently take their mission to eleven, protecting the Earth in the most camp manner possible.

Taking It Over The Top

The textbook example of *Torchwood* camp noir is in *Cyberwoman*. The pivotal scene in the episode combines the noir peril of Ianto putting his team in danger by keeping Lisa's secret from them (she is the ultimate femme fatale in her kinky cybernetic outfit) with the SF trope of defeating high tech through primitive means. Jack's use of barbecue sauce and a hungry pterodactyl to defeat Lisa deflates both plot elements through incredibly silly means, yet still works within the episode's structure.

In *Everything Changes*, *Torchwood* takes what should be ominous narration that sets the tone for a noir episode and deflates it by playing with gender expectations: "There you go. I can taste it. Oestrogen. Definitely oestrogen. You take the pill, flush it away, it enters the water cycle, feminises the fish. Goes all the way up into the sky, then falls all the way back down onto me. Contraceptives in the rain. Love this planet. Still, at least I won't get pregnant. Never doing that again." The assumed noir masculine heroic persona is deflated through one of the most visible signs of femininity: pregnancy.

At the end of *Countrycide*, kicking in the door is not a dramatic enough method of saving the team for Jack: he drives a tractor through it. He then shoots the cannibal villagers with a shotgun and his handgun – to disable, rather than kill them, so that they can be brought to justice. (In a truly noir universe, they would have all been dead.) The direction in this particular scene heightens the effect, slowing down Jack's shooting spree at random moments, then speeding it up again, focusing on the shells as they fall to the floor. Jack's rescue becomes a camp version of a grainy homage to noir gangster films, removing the body count so that we are focussed instead on Jack's over-the-top rescue methods.

While the camp elements of *End of Days* may be unintentional, they are decidedly present, undermining noir elements through repetition and execution. Jack, betrayed yet again by his team, must defeat Abbadon, a mythical beast from before time that saps life energy. Jack's deaths in this episode are so close together that they cannot be taken seriously. His grand heroic self-sacrifice also becomes a mockery, because the unfortunate visual effect used to show Abbadon taking Jack's life-energy makes Jack look like a Care Bear sending out beams of happiness and Jack's personal posture looks suspiciously like he is committing jazz hands while saving the world.

Deflated Emo

As consumers, we love our emo. Often, in fan communities built around genre television, movies and comics, "dark" is extrapolated to mean "good", "more valuable", "better" or "deeper" storytelling than stories that have a happy, positive, hopeful, or even ambiguous ending. *The Dark Knight* film and comics version of Batman is held up as superior to any other version. The best film in the *Star Wars* franchise is also the darkest: *The Empire Strikes Back.* The new version of *Battlestar Galactica* is considered miles better than the original series. Fans of shows like *Xena: Warrior Princess* and *Buffy The Vampire Slayer* tend to prefer the dramatic episodes to the comedies.

While I enjoy many of these particular products and properties, I disagree most vehemently with the notion that "dark" always equals "better". The key to good storytelling is to understand whether the tone fits the story that you are trying to tell. The unique genius of *Torchwood*'s first season is that you get to see what happens when the tone undercuts the storytelling. It transforms the story and its reading into something else entirely. While *Torchwood* Series One is not to everyone's taste, it does something that we don't often see: it mocks the notion that "good" science-fiction television must always be unrelentingly dark, through its camp noir presentation of its universe. It refuses to take itself or its mission too seriously, for that way lies madness.

Torchwood: fighting intergalactic crime through the power of jazz hands and really good coffee since 1879.

That's my kind of show.

What Does It Take To Get Fired From Torchwood?

by Graeme Burk

From Movement #125, Spring 2007 (revised December 2010)

I don't think I have ever been more angered by 45 minutes of television than when I watched the *Torchwood* episode *Cyberwoman*. The plot, in case you missed it, revolves around Ianto Jones, the logistics-coordinator-stroke-tea-boy for the super-secret security organisation known as Torchwood. It turns out he's secretly smuggled his girlfriend into the base, only his girlfriend is now a partially converted Cyberman from *Doctor Who*. He wants to cure her somehow, but a cure is impossible and she turns out to be the lethal killing machine everyone else in Torchwood – and the viewer – knew she would turn out to be. By the time they kill the girlfriend, two other innocent people are dead and the cybernised girlfriend has nearly succeeded in recreating the cyber race on Earth. Along the way, Ianto holds a gun to the head of Captain Jack Harkness, the head of Torchwood, and pretty much disobeys every order he's given while clinging to the belief that what he's doing is somehow going to work.

Even so, until this point, the episode in question has been just an undemanding science-fiction romp – one that was heavy on gore, and was about as dramatically interesting as an early level of *Doom*. (In its favour, it had a pterodactyl in it). But then something happens that infuriated me: Ianto gets off scot-free. The assessment of Captain Jack and Gwen Cooper, seems to be, "Well, he was in love. That he lost his girlfriend is punishment enough."

Let's recap: two people die as a result of Ianto keeping a Weapon of Mass Destruction in the basement of Torchwood, and he doesn't get disciplined or fired or arrested.

At the time I watched *Cyberwoman,* I worked for an organisation that worked with at-risk youth. It was written in my employment contract that it was a firing offense to bring alcohol on the premises, much less offer it to youth. And yet, Ianto can keep a WMD in the basement, cause the deaths of two people, hold a gun to his boss' head and risk destroying the planet, yet that's okay because he was in love. I could even live with that if the experience itself changed Ianto, but it doesn't. In fact, Ianto never seems bothered his actions led to the death of others.

I shouldn't be surprised by this. No one ever takes responsibility for anything in *Torchwood*. That's a core premise of the series. This was established in the very first episode as the Torchwood team trample through a gruesome crime scene. Not, as it turns out, to help investigate the crime but to test out a nifty alien device that can resurrect the dead for three minutes. (It also turns out one of the team is actually committing the murders in order to test it out.) The point is made: these people are above the law, above morality, above everything.

Which is a shame because, frankly, the Torchwood team suck at what they do. Again and again, throughout the series, characters do what the hell they like, creating terrible messes for the sake of their hubris and never suffer any consequences. It's a bad joke in the final episode of Series One when Owen, the team's ladies man, opens the space-time rift under Cardiff because he wants to get back a lost lover, and in doing so causes untold catastrophes ranging from the return of the bubonic plague to fractures in very fabric of time. He gets told, "There are consequences to what you do," but he still doesn't get fired. No, he gets fired *later on* for disagreeing with Captain Jack (but even this doesn't last).

It's not even as though this is just an anomaly in *Torchwood*'s first season. Dubious ethical choices reign supreme in the second season (finding another resurrection glove to resurrect Owen in order to find out the codes to the morgue) and *Children of Earth* (Jack doesn't seem to have a problem asking his daughter if he can borrow his grandson for medical experimentation).

So, then, if no one takes responsibility for their actions and no one does their job well, then what does it take to get fired from Torchwood anyway? Most reasonable causes for dismissal – incompetence, laziness, lying, dereliction of duties, failure to perform – fail to pass what I called "The WMD Test". If you can keep a WMD in the basement and kill innocents and not get fired, your job security is pretty much golden.

In the initial descriptions to come out for *Torchwood,* they talk about how they wanted to do a more "adult" take on the *Doctor Who* universe. It's not really. It's just *Doctor Who* with more gore and sex but without the compelling lead characters. If anything, I find it more childish.

By comparison, *Battlestar Galactica* is adult. It has achingly fallible characters who do things and their actions have consequences – emotional, legal, moral and spiritual – that are revisited again and again. The universe they live in is one that has no fixed compass in terms of ethics, characters can make bad choices, and they suffer for those choices through alienation, loss of power, guilt and personal suffering. But they learn from those things as well. And, occasionally, they get fired – or worse – for their screw-ups.

That, to my mind, is what *Torchwood* could have done – and it wouldn't have required much effort. There should have been consequences that the characters lived with, developed from, and then grew as a result of over time. Consequences that result in drama.

Could have. Should have. Didn't. That's the *Torchwood* experience: people doing whatever they want, skipping the results of their actions and never facing any kind of need to be adults.

Because, as near as I can tell, the only way to get fired from Torchwood is to steal office supplies or forget to bring coffee.

Captain Jackass

by Cameron Dixon

From Enlightenment #149, December / January 2008-2009

One of the first things I noticed about the Series Two *Torchwood* DVD set was that the colouring of the packaging was much lighter. The same thing happened between the first and second batches of original novels. The symbolism is obvious: the series has gone from brooding and moody to bright and raring for action. Pity that the other overriding colour in the scheme is the rusty red of dried blood, then. Our heroes are still living in a world where puppies get run over by trucks, even if they're acting like a team at last and aren't actually throwing the puppies off the overpass themselves. And if you think that's an horrific metaphor, bear in mind that I've just watched Series Two of *Torchwood* for the third time.

The opening episode is an enjoyable romp that picks up the RTD-scripted intro and runs with it, largely successfully. Unfortunately, the series then hits us with a string of episodes ending in suicide, sacrifice, euthanasia, murder and death – consecutively and occasionally concurrently. Making the characters fallible should add depth and resonance to their efforts to save the world but, when they consistently fail, it just comes across as predictable. Watching Owen being forced to kill a creature he's trying to save should be an emotionally draining moment for the viewer, but not when it's just more of the same. It should be tragic seeing Toshiko lose the man she loves, but not when it happens four times, twice to the same person. Especially not when the one person whose advances she spurns survives to the end of his episode.

The emotional manipulation isn't just predictable, it's frequently cheap. The death of the space whale is supposed to come across as a hard and painful choice, but really it's the easiest way out for the team, who would otherwise have been forced to find a way to keep the thing alive and get it home. At best, the downbeat endings are cruel and arbitrary; at worst, they're shamelessly manipulative.

Everything right and wrong about the season can be found in *Adrift*. Well-directed sequences develop a growing sense of unease, ending in some shattering revelations and an emotionally devastating climax. But look again and wonder why, if not for authorial fiat, Gwen just happened to come across Jacob in that one-sixth of the day when he wasn't screaming. Wonder why Jack didn't allow her to see Jacob's true condition before allowing her to bring in Jacob's mother and springing the horror upon them without warning. Once Gwen had found out the truth for herself, what possible reason was there not to give full disclosure?

If Gwen had known of Jacob's state and then had to decide whether to break the truth to his mother, we'd have seen an adult character making a hard adult decision; if she'd then made the wrong one, at least it would have been earned through drama. As it is, an innocent woman's hope is destroyed and Gwen is emotionally shattered, apparently just because Captain Jack wanted to tough-love her into seeing for herself that he was right and she was wrong. This isn't Captain Jack, it's Captain Jackass, and it doesn't stop there. When the Doctor forgave his arch-nemesis in his season finale, he did so for his nemesis' sake; when Jack forgives his own nemesis, he does it because he wants the same in return. Frankly, what a dick.

The same can't be said for Rhys, whose character has benefited tremendously, and not just in the obvious way, from not being killed at the end of Series One. Rhys has been the best thing about Series Two, doing for Gwen what Gwen was originally supposed to do for Torchwood: anchoring her to the real world. Even after the downbeat ending of *Meat*, he still greets the opening up of his universe with wide-eyed delight. He supports Gwen, not without question, but lovingly. His speech to her in the park is the truest thing to be found in *Adrift*, he keeps her motivated and encouraged in the season finale, and in *Something Borrowed* he has the single best use of the F-word in *Torchwood*, if not in anything ever. Give credit where it's due: Rhys is the most well-written, well-behaved and grown-up character in the entire series.

To be fair, the season is only bad when watched as a whole; the individual episodes stand up on their own, even if their combined weight wears one down. It's consistently well-directed, whether the writing supports it or not. *Sleeper* develops its story well with consistently increasing stakes, even if the alien tech seems to malfunction according to the needs of the plot. The internal logic of Owen's condition may not hold together, but *A Day in the Death* remains a strong allegory for depression and his character finally redeems himself almost as well as Richard Briers redeems himself for *Paradise Towers*. *Something Borrowed* is an absolute hoot, a perfect example of what one assumes Russell T Davies always intended the series to be.

It's an improvement over Series One, and I would cautiously recommend it, but I can't help but hope that subsequent seasons continue to improve.

What's the Point of a Spinoff?

by Robert Smith?
From Enlightenment #153, October 2009

The *Doctor Who* spinoff hasn't exactly had a long and noble history, has it? Until 2007, the entirety of televised spinoffery consisted of, erm, *K9 and Company*. That's it. A single, uber-eighties, one-off production with a theme tune so dire that it became the musical version of *Plan 9 from Outer Space*, there to be mocked – alongside "Doctor in Distress" – for all time. (Any connection between the fan-turned-producer of each musical travesty is doubtless entirely coincidental.)

Suddenly, however, the spinoffs are big business. *Torchwood* has just completed its third season, while *The Sarah Jane Adventures* has racked up two, with more coming. Each of these sees former companions to the Doctor taking on the good work of fighting prosthetic aliens when the Doctor's not around.

What's interesting is the hybrid nature of such things. Captain Jack is a poor man's Doctor in *Torchwood*, half the time wanting to be the immortal, unknowable outsider who never changes his clothes, the other half a hypersexualised teenage boy, with no leadership capabilities and an intense death wish. Say what you want about *Torchwood* (and we all do), you've got to admit, that's one hell of a setup for a TV series.

Similarly, Sarah Jane Smith has a foot in each world: half the time she's a one-woman investigation operation, with an intense dislike of weapons and the military, fighting aliens with sonic lipstick and her robot computer in the shape of a dog. The other half, she's mothering the neighbourhood kids and investigating suspicious soft-drink companies.

All this happens while, over on the main series, the good Doctor travels the universe, jetting about through time and space, having adventures and generally making himself, and his series, impervious to snappy descriptions like the ones I just provided above. *Torchwood* and *The Sarah Jane Adventures* have a definite feel. *Doctor Who* fights the idea of a "feel" with everything it's got.

In essence, as Steven Moffat once said, when the Doctor steps out of the TARDIS, you have no idea what kind of story you're going to get. It might be a present-day setting with the Doctor foiling a stealth alien invasion. It might be a far-future space epic, set amongst all manner of aliens and the death of planets. Or it could be a historical oddity featuring somebody famous set among the most detailed and accurate set designs the BBC can offer.

Make no mistake, that's very, very powerful. It's a formula that's helped *Doctor Who* survive for decades now and will do so for generations to come. Even when *Doctor Who* sometimes locks itself into a particular genre – base under siege, exile to Earth, gothic horror – the power of the series is that it won't stay there for very long. *Doctor Who*'s like the weather: if you don't like it, there's bound to be something different along shortly. And, like the weather, it's endlessly discussable.

But if that's so powerful – and it is – then what's the point of a spinoff?

Initially, a spinoff is a vehicle for familiar actors and characters. We all love Sarah Jane, but having her in *Doctor Who* every week wouldn't really work, so this is a way to get to see her again. This is a factor, of course, and part of the reason fans of one series will tune into a new one, but it's only really the hook. It's not what the spinoff is for.

Doctor Who is, at its core, a dangerous show. It portrays death and violence and unerring evil on a weekly basis. But it's also an uncomfortable show. It rips you away from your home and sends you off into the vast panoply of the universe, with only an alien for company. Almost nothing in your life thus far can prepare you for what you're going to encounter, short of your compassion. Any education, skills or experience you've amassed in your lifetime will be almost entirely useless out there. It means that you have to rely on your wits and it shows you the very stuff you're made of, but it's definitely not comfortable.

Spinoffs, instead, have a fundamental difference: they have a home base. *Doctor Who* has a home base too, but the TARDIS is never portrayed that way. Instead, it's simply a narrative vehicle for getting you to this week's exciting new locale and that's usually it. It's rarely a place of safety during the narrative and it's never a working base of operations (and nor should it be).

But there's more than just a fixed location to the power of the spinoff. With a location come residents, who we can see again and again. Is it any wonder that *Torchwood* works best not when it's focusing on Owen or Tosh, but when it features Rhys or PC Andy? These are comedy-relief figures who breathe life into the show through their very normality. They give the impression that the series is part of a larger world and that life goes on beyond the Hub. In short, they're proof that the series has consequences.

Doctor Who doesn't really do consequences. Sometimes, for dramatic effect, it might feature a few tidbits (the Doctor's interventions in *The Long Game* return to haunt him in *Bad Wolf*) or as part of a larger arc (think of Dalek Caan's various appearances throughout the last several years), but it doesn't do messy, day-to-day consequences. Sarah Jane has to deal with Maria's dad – and, when he learns the truth, the series fundamentally changes form. Luke's questionable status as her adopted son comes back to haunt her in *The Lost Boy* because of the fact that she tries to build a life with him.

Indeed, the vast majority of criticisms flung at *Torchwood*'s first two seasons were about the lack of consequences for its characters. Ianto threatens that he'll never stop until he kills Jack for what he did to Lisa in *Cyberwoman,* then they're playing stopwatch games a few episodes later. Owen's living death in season two fails because it's entirely inconsistent with the properties of the resurrection glove explained in Series One. *Torchwood*'s third season...

Ah, yes, *Children of Earth.*

What's incredible is just how different *Torchwood*'s third season is from the previous two. And how amazingly it works. This is the story that *Torchwood* was born for. It works – oh boy, how it works – precisely because of its nature as a spinoff. Everything that came before had the show in conflict with its existence as a *Doctor Who* spinoff, unsure whether to embrace or reject it. *Children of Earth* sweeps all that aside (most of it literally so, in the first episode) because it fundamentally knows what it is.

Partly it's the thinking through of the consequences in a sensible fashion. There aren't the inconsistencies that plagued the earlier series, which helps a lot. But a lack of inconsistency isn't what makes *Children of Earth* so brilliant. Instead, it's the embracing of what a spinoff does best.

And that's families.

Sarah Jane works so well because it has roots within the community. There's the conflict between the secret investigation of aliens and the mundane need for these kids to survive school and parents. Turning Sarah from a journalist into a mother was jarring at first, because initially you're still thinking of her as a *Doctor Who* companion. But she stops being one once she has a son to care about and instead becomes her own person, with much more at stake than before. Elisabeth Sladen's acting was always the ingredient which made Sarah work so well, but we actually knew very little about her life beyond the Doctor. That's no longer true.

These days, *Doctor Who* also does families. Indeed, I'd argue that this is partly why the new series feels so odd: because it's trying to be the dangerous adventure series it started as, while simultaneously becoming a spinoff in itself. By returning to Rose's, Martha's and Donna's families over and over again, *Doctor Who* is suddenly safe in a way it just never was before. (With the possible exception of the Pertwee years, which centred around the "UNIT family".) Events not only have consequences, they have an emotional core.

This is where *Children of Earth* succeeds so brilliantly. Faced with an insurmountable problem – something's wrong with the children – it's fascinating how the Torchwood crew turn to their own families. This connects Jack to Alice and Steven, which becomes crucial not only in the resolution, but in the weight of emotion attached to it and the cowardice that overwhelms Jack. Similarly, Ianto turns to his sister, bringing in not only her family, but the whole neighbourhood and hence the connection to the working class – something that becomes vital when the cabinet office make their terrifying decisions about who to sacrifice. Gwen is already connected to Rhys and Andy, but she also becomes emotionally connected to Ianto's family, culminating in her terror and sheer desperation to save just one child at the conclusion. Even the villain gets a family and the consequences for them are utterly harrowing, in a way that the Master's wife just isn't.

You can do a spinoff without families, of course, but there comes a point when you have to wonder why you're bothering. The Bernice novels and audios started with her as an academic on a university planet, but soon reintroduced her ex-husband Jason, then eventually gave her a son, an alien father to that son and reunited her romantically with Jason. This may seem soap-like, but that's because it is: it's drawing on the power that soap operas bring, in terms of their ability to connect to the audience through the power of emotion. Even *K9 and Company* gave Sarah a nephew and introduced Aunt Lavinia in the flesh.

It's no coincidence that the less-successful spinoffs – *Time Hunter*, *Faction Paradox* – are more about the sci-fi wheeze of big ideas than emotional connections. When the chips are down, you don't come back for a clever idea, but you do come back because you care about the characters and the complex interplay they've built up over years of familiarity. While it's true that *Doctor Who* itself is more about the big idea – he can go anywhere, anywhen! – this kind of simplisticly brilliant idea is a once-in-a-generation stroke of genius, so you're unlikely to hit something equally powerful with your random spinoff.

The *Doctor Who* spinoff walks a fine line between trying to be too much like its parent and finding its own way. When done badly, it can be a disconnected series of sub-*Doctor-Who* tales, that happen to feature familiar faces, but which have no emotional core (see *Torchwood*, Series One and Two). When done well, it can be utterly riveting (see *Children of Earth*). The key to believability is in the level of consequences, but the key to emotionally connecting with the material isn't in the spinoff characters, it's in their family dynamics.

After all, what's a spinoff if it isn't a child?

The Attic Inside Out

by Jon Arnold

I wasn't old enough to fall in love the first time. I was only two when the Doctor moodily abandoned Sarah Jane on the mean streets of Aberdeen in 1976. She was a companion I only knew through Terrance Dicks' novelisations and the odd repeat, no more special to me than Jo, Vicki or Zoe. We were both in the right place but, as so often with events involving the Doctor, at the wrong time. Of course, I found out more about her later, when home video made her adventures freely available but it wasn't the same; she wasn't my first love and could never be. I was a generation of fandom too late.

Of course, meeting her properly when I was older allowed me to better appreciate her charms. She may have been a borderline caricatured version of a 70s feminist, albeit one who was a damsel in distress when the script demanded, but closer inspection revealed the perfect companion figure. Her background as an investigative journalist allowed her an independent streak, a curiosity to help drive stories which often conveniently got her into trouble from which the Doctor would almost inevitably have to rescue her. She was as able as the format of the show would allow the companion to be, and an audience-identification figure that the succession of alien companions that followed her could never be. Her time with the Doctor spanned the two most successful Doctor-producer-script-editor combinations the colour era of the original show saw. If there was any companion who had the recognisability factor to carry a spinoff, it was Sarah Jane. But that didn't work the first time round, a mere five years after her initial departure. Why should it work another 25 years after that, with only 45 minutes worth of TV to remind the world outside *Doctor Who* fandom of her existence?

Well, there's the indisputable fact that the production team behind the second spinoff are far better at creating popular television than the team behind *K9 and Company*. From a cursory examination of the format, *The Sarah Jane Adventures* looks like a show conceived and powered by simple nostalgia. It's genuinely one of the most bizarrely conceived shows I can remember, although it's an infinitely more palatable proposition than CBBC's original wrong-on-so-many-levels proposal of the adventures of a teenage Doctor. I'd have loved to have been in the pitch meeting for the series: "We've got a children's show based around a character who left the original series 30 years ago, our lead hasn't acted much outside the show since leaving... oh, and did I mention that the previous spinoff she was in was strangled at birth?" You can see drama commissioners leaping on that can't you? But this was Russell T Davies at the BBC, talking to a Children's Department desperate to bask in *Doctor Who*'s reflected glory, so normal circumstances did not apply.

So why, as someone who wasn't in the original cult of Sarah Jane and has barely watched any children's television in 15 years, do I find it as addictive as Bubble Shock? Let's get the obvious one out of the way first: I'm a hardcore *Doctor Who* fanboy. Sarah Jane may not be "my" companion, but it's a *Doctor Who* spinoff from the *Doctor Who* production team with *Doctor Who* actors, monsters and writers. I went in with the promise that it was always going to at least be methadone to tide me over between series. And it wouldn't have *Torchwood*'s problem of trying to be self-consciously adult by showing off how far it could go in terms of sex and violence. It would have to rely on ideas and ingenuity, which would make it far more mature than its post-watershed counterpart and more universal in appeal. Closer to *Doctor Who* in spirit than *Torchwood*'s grimness ever lets it be.

There's a slight problem in that; closer links to a parent show mean that it's tougher for a spinoff to establish its own identity. *Torchwood*'s dark nature, its concentration on sex and violence, and almost complete recharacterisation of Jack after the first episode meant it instantly distanced itself from *Doctor Who*. Compare *Everything Changes* with *Invasion of the Bane*, and it's fairly clear as to which story could, with a touch of rewriting, be a *Doctor Who* script. Both use Russell T Davies' tried-and-tested first episode format of introducing the title characters via the eyes of a newcomer, but it's clear which series is searching to break as far from association with *Doctor Who* as possible. That's natural; *Torchwood* has to survive in the rigours of prime time and, if possible, try to find an audience beyond *Doctor Who*, whereas Sarah Jane's confined to the children's TV ghetto and can survive on an audience of junior fanboys and fangirls, as well as curious older fans.

Curiously for a twenty-first century children's television show though, it is not just modern *Doctor Who* that Sarah Jane draws inspiration from; it draws equal inspiration from the original series. And I don't mean that simply in the obvious way of the lead character being swiped straight from one of the most successful periods of the old show. No matter how far she's come in time, Sarah Jane Smith can't escape the shadow of the Pertwee era she was born into.

The Sarah Jane Adventures are formatted in a similar way as the vast bulk of the original series, 25-minute, multi-part stories with cliffhangers to hopefully retain the audience for next week. Admittedly, they're two parters rather than four, making it something of a hybrid format with stories of roughly the same length as a new-series episode. This is a best-of-both-worlds arrangement, with the series retaining the pacy story-telling of the new series whilst getting the regular benefit of the cliffhanger format. Arguably, the length of story suits Sarah Jane better as modern *Doctor Who*'s running time has to include the introduction of alien or historical settings, often not doing justice to them, whereas Sarah Jane's relatively restricted locale means little time has to be wasted on establishing settings; a present-day Earth setting already has a degree of familiarity that modern *Who* only really has in its own contemporary Earth episodes (and even then, arguably the very public alien intrusions of the modern era mean it's becoming more and more divergent from our reality). It's a welcome throwback for the older generation to the days when (at least in the UK) you'd regularly have to wait seven days to find out how the Doctor and his friend got out of that one almost every single week.

It's when you start looking at the setup of the show that the parallels with the early seventies become more apparent. By the nature of the show itself, Sarah Jane is largely earthbound and, despite being mostly filmed in Cardiff and the surrounding area, confined to foiling threats to the South East of England (and, by proxy, the world). The first episode even has echoes of *Spearhead from Space*, with a factory setting and use of a ubiquitous feature of modern day life (for plastic, read soft drink) as an invasion tool. It's the middle Pertwee years that are the strongest influence, though: a time when Letts and Dicks brought a relatively cosy atmosphere and established the "UNIT family", one where the Doctor has been described as the "mother hen". Pertwee's Doctor took on the surrogate maternal role there with the Brigadier playing the exasperated father to the clearly junior roles of the nuclear family of Jo, Yates and Benton; the end of *The Green Death* is nothing if not a parent lost and lonely as their child finally performs the ultimate act of growing up and leaves to create her own life. *The Sarah Jane Adventures* may have updated to a modern single-parent family model (albeit with support from Alan Jackson and, to a lesser extent, Haresh Chandra in the blundering father figure role), but the parallel remains. In this analogy, Sarah replaces the Doctor as the strange-but-interesting mother figure with a whole lot of cool alien technology in her geek den. She's also a direct surrogate parent to Luke and Maria. A lot of Chrissy's antagonism towards Sarah Jane fairly obviously derives from the latter's influence over her daughter.

It's almost certainly not just the *Doctor Who* of their childhood that influenced the creative forces of the early Sarah Jane stories, such as Russell T Davies and Gareth Roberts. Pertwee certainly wasn't the only guru figure around in 1970s pop culture; it's a fairly common trope in children's fiction even up to the present day. There's the likes of Albus Dumbledore in the Harry Potter series or Rupert Giles from *Buffy the Vampire Slayer*, both created by famous writers who grew up in that decade. You can trace the lineage of the wise old figure back through history (the Delphic Oracle, for instance), as it's a common feature of pop culture at the time. It's impossible to know exact influences, but it's likely that characters such as Aslan from the Narnia books, Charles Xavier or Merriman Lyon in *The Dark Is Rising* sequence were at least at the back of their minds when devising the series. This reflection of television shows familiar from 1970s childhoods probably reflects the fact that the main creative forces behind the show grew up when these adventure series and their tropes were fairly prominent in popular culture.

Those 1970s roots aren't an entirely positive influence, though. Whilst the mix of ethnicities in the cast is both commendable and believable, the show does fall prey to the old British disease of class, with middle-class children as seen here considered more useful for storytelling than those from the working class. Admittedly, Sarah Jane's based in the Ealing suburbs, so it fits, but there is often a tinge of the Blytons in the main juvenile characters: both Maria and Rani's fathers have well-paid, respectable jobs. Luke is dropped into a comfortable environment, and even though he's from a single-parent family, there's no roughness around the edges from Clyde to suggest he's from the wrong side of the tracks. Looking at it from another angle though, it pulls off the rare and difficult trick of positively portraying London's racial integration without ever being patronising. There's never the sense of Clyde or Rani being token casting; they fit in to school and Sarah's Scooby Gang (or the K9 Gang, if you prefer) without compromising their cultural identities, or even being asked to. The series rarely, if ever, resorts to cultural clichés to provide character material, avoiding the tempting writing traps provided by Clyde's single-parent family, or Rani's fairly close-knit family.

However, like *Doctor Who*, only part of the appeal of the show is rooted in nostalgia. The greater appeal is that it fuses the best of the series that crop up on nostalgia shows with the best of more modern television. Sarah Jane is defiantly a modern show, although it'd be a stretch to call it typical of modern British children's television, since production of children's drama in Britain has atrophied catastrophically over the last decade. Given it deals with schoolchildren, it's tempting to draw a comparison to the first three seasons of *Buffy*. Sarah is the Giles figure with an exciting past, battling monsters, assisting one super-powered teenager and friends, with certain episodes having problems faced by the characters as metaphors for growing up. *Day of the Clown*, for instance, would sit quite happily in any of those early *Buffy* seasons. All you'd need would be to change the SF explanation for a more mystical one. *Buffy* was often cited as a comparison point in the early days of the new series of *Doctor Who*, but the influence is far more direct and obvious here.

Like both *Buffy* and the current series of *Doctor Who*, the title's a touch misleading. Buffy and the Doctor are the central character, but they're not the story of the series. *Buffy* is as much about her Scooby Gang friends as the Slayer herself and, like the original dynamic of the Hartnell years, Russell T Davies' *Doctor Who* (and also Steven Moffat's) is more the story of how the companion is affected by the Doctor. It's the same here. The first season is really Maria's story, and how her relationship with Sarah affects and changes her, in the same way the Doctor changes his companions. Clyde even refers to Maria as "the new Sarah Jane" in *The Mad Woman in the Attic*. Similarly, her replacement, Rani, wants to be a journalist, but that somehow seems parochial in comparison to how Sarah Jane widens Maria's horizons. Rani is also a comparatively passive character, as subsequent seasons don't focus on her story, instead bringing Clyde to centre stage (as the Series Three introductory sequence makes clear; it's him at the door when Sarah Jane and Luke run out to another adventure). Moving the focus to an already established character is a clever, brave move which allows Series Two to retain a fresh feel whilst having a sense of continuity.

The fusion of old and new is also clear in the portrayal of the lead character. It would have been all too easy to have Sarah Jane reverting to the pre-new-series character type, and her curiosity and courage in investigating stories certainly hasn't changed. It's also abundantly clear the Doctor's influence on her is still incredibly strong. She can deal with alien invasions with no problems, yet still has a certain amount of difficulty with more mundane matters. What's satisfying about the characterisation here though, is that it feels like a natural development, almost a reward, for coming to terms with her past in *School Reunion*. The closure granted in that episode allows her to move on with her life and Luke's arrival gives her a late, unexpected chance at a conventional life that her Doctor fixation seemed to have denied her. That resolution, plus the arrival of Luke, gives Lis Sladen and the writers plenty of scope to flesh out the character, to move Sarah from adventure sidekick to the more complex figure needed to carry a Davies-created show.

The show's at its best when it gives Sarah an emotional stake: having Luke snatched away from her in *The Lost Boy*, meeting and then having to sacrifice her long-lost parents in *The Temptation of Sarah Jane Smith* or losing the man she loves in *The Wedding of Sarah Jane Smith*. And while she makes bad choices (as in the aforementioned *Temptation of Sarah Jane Smith*), they're understandable bad choices, human ones. She's allowed to have bad days, to be irritable and difficult, particularly from the perspective of her teenage gang. What fans fell in love with in the seventies was a shadow compared to the depth and nuance provided in this series.

It's one thing to bring an icon back, it's another thing entirely to not only change her, but change her successfully and strengthen her legend, as much for today's generation as for the original one. It's a trick Russell T Davies and company have managed to pull off on two shows now. I may have been too young the first time, but sometimes falling in love when you're older, with the supposed benefits of experience and wisdom, is just as satisfying.

WIBBLY-WOBBLY...

An American cable network has the tagline, "Story Matters Here". That may also be the pithiest distillation of what makes *Doctor Who* great.

It's telling that one of the major tomes published about *Doctor Who* in recent memory is Russell T Davies' *The Writer's Tale*. The first edition, in particular, is probably one of the best articulations of the writing process ever written. It perfectly describes the sometimes arduous, sometimes joyous process of finding solutions to puzzles created by the confluence of plot and character; working out the best way to create a scene or character; and figuring out how to go around external demands such as budget or timing.

Ultimately, this is the world of *Doctor Who*. The world of words that create a simulated, and immediate, reality. How those words are wielded – how one writer uses them instead of another, whether they're influenced by other sources, what the intended audience is and whether they create new worlds or expand on the one we live in – is all part of the excitement of creating that world.

It's writing that sparks our imagination, whether it's the last of humanity clinging to survival at the end of the universe, time shenanigans recorded in a series of DVD Easter Eggs or the emotional power of the first world war, wrapped around an iconic love story. These aspects engage our brains, our hearts and our souls. They're the engine that drives *Doctor Who* forward.

Make no mistake. In *Doctor Who*, story matters here. Every word on a page that becomes a line of dialogue, an action for a character to perform or a CGI spaceship is part of a hard-fought battle won and lost even as the writer types "INT. TARDIS – DAY".

A Letter from Zog to Doctor Who Magazine

by Paul Magrs

From Doctor Who Magazine #375, November 2006

Greetings from the Desk of Supreme Ruler Zog
of the Fantastically Exotic Planet of Zog.

In the space year twelve.
Monday.

We the Supreme Ruler Zog of Zog would very much like to drop a quick line to all you people of Earth. To you delightfully humdrum council-estate-dwelling Earthlings of Earth: hulloo from Zog and everyone on the exotically alien planet of Zog!

Oh, how we've missed you! I really can't tell you how much we have missed you.

Things have been very exciting here recently on Zog, believe it or not. We were just talking about this, me and Chancellor Zeg, my trusty companion and helpmeet. We were up on my balcony overlooking the vast plains of the desert of Zog. The shifting scarlet sands of the desert of Zog surround the ineffably alien and wondrously futuristic city of Zog, of course, as you probably remember. Anyway, Chancellor Zeg was standing there in his copperplate britches and his silver cloak, and he was blinking his three livid lime-green eyes at me with an almost unbearably pathos-filled deliquescence and he warbled: "Why, what with the Robot Slaves' Revolution, the Uprising of Our Ancestral Wraiths from The Golden Sepulchres of Doom, and the Surprise Invasion by the Rabid Lice-Gods of Niff, I'd have thought the people of Earth would have been a bit more interested, wouldn't you, Supreme Commander Zog? Oh wonderful Supremo of Exotic Zog?"

I flung out my own silver cape and marched up and down the wide balcony of my palace throne room, gazing out at the inscrutable skies of beloved Zog. Our three moons were rising just as the four suns were going down. Oh marvellous and multi-hued skies of Zog! And the flying elephants of Vish were swooping about in the far, cloud-curdled distances, and needlelike spacecraft were streaking up into the empyrean pink, on their way to new star-spanning adventures beyond time and space.

"I agree, Chancellor Zeg," I sighed, and clapped my deputy heavily on his third shoulder. He started to weep blue crystal tears and they spilled down his tight tunic front. "Perhaps one day they will learn to care about us again."

What did we do?? Did we do something to offend you?

What's wrong with fantastically exotic Zog? Don't you give a monkey's any more?

Yours,

Zog of Zog.

A Tale of Two Writers

by Scott Clarke

From Enlightenment #152, August 2009 (revised July 2010)

The last six years has been a tale of two cities of sorts: Daviesville and Moffaton. For a time, the glowing metropolis of Daviesville loomed high and mighty, dictating the economy of the land while the hip little Moffaton stood as the preferred vacation getaway by the sea. Daviesville is where you did all your work; Moffaton was a treat, where you ate ice cream and strolled along the promenade, fantasising about a different life.

And then one day you said, "Chuck it. I need a change, I'm moving to Moffaton." Some of you immediately love living in that beautiful city by the sea, some of you are lactose intolerant and grow tired of dodging the condoms on the promenade.

Davies and Moffat both have a great reverence for the show's past and the core elements that constitute essential *Doctor Who*: the sense of wonder, variety of storytelling and juxtaposition of the familiar everyday with the extraordinary. Sensibility and personal style take over from there.

Typically, Russell T Davies begins with character and moves out into plot. Look at the way he roots his companions to their earthbound lives through the addition of their familial relationships (chips and kitchen sinks). The entirety of the 2005 season is fundamentally devoted to Rose (and twenty-first century viewers) getting to know the Doctor. Aliens and the end of the world serve as code for the culture shock that ensues from a young adult taking her first steps into the world. Davies isn't overly concerned with details like solar screens or how easy it is to activate them. Many fans and some critics cried foul at the *deux ex machina* of Rose saving the day as a time goddess in *The Parting of the Ways*. That wasn't Davies' point. It was Rose's loyalty to the Doctor and her desire to make a difference that compelled her to rise to the challenge of returning to help him. And both Jackie and Mickey put aside their reservations to assist her. Davies could have been writing an episode of *Bob and Rose* with similar character beats, using gay culture as his central metaphor.

Conversely, Moffat starts with the big idea and then populates it with characters, filling them out as he goes along. Meticulously crafted stories are his strength. He's a genius at placing just the right emphasis on a story point to expand our imaginations, suggesting a universe filled with so much more. In many respects, he fashions his stories like a good magician creates an illusion, directing the viewer's eye through his strong attention to detail and potent imagery.

The Eleventh Hour has the daunting task of introducing a new Doctor and companion, much as *Rose* did and, although the concept of *Doctor Who* is pretty firmly rooted in the audience's mind, the shadow of Davies' vision of the programme and David Tennant's massively popular portrayal weighs heavily going in. Moffat carefully crafts a new mythology in the first 15 minutes of his story: we're introduced to the companion as a child, encountering the eleventh Doctor for the first time in what is essentially a mini-episode. It's whimsical, funny and smart. Then Moffat has the Doctor hop back in the TARDIS and accidentally return years later. Suddenly, we have history with both the new Doctor and Amy. We immediately care about the characters, we have anxiety over what happened to little Amelia and quite cleverly a lot of time seems to have passed since the tenth Doctor departed (even though, really, it's been no time at all). It's brilliant sleight of hand on Moffat's part.

Blink is a fantastic script that unfolds like a ghost story one might have heard as a child. Watching, one is compelled by the idea of the Weeping Angels: they come with a carefully laid out set of rules with regards to how they operate. We immediately put ourselves in the place of Sally Sparrow and the other characters. What would we do in their place? Moffat's character development then flows naturally from their predicament. Sally needs to be inquisitive in order to keep going back into danger. But Moffat knows that the recurring error in such scenarios is to have characters act stupid in order to service the plot. So he fashions his illusion with more finesse. Little details make Sally exceeding likeable: she's quirky when she talks back to the DVD of the Doctor, or she makes the same embarrassing gaffes that we all make, such as calling herself Sally Shipton. The expositional plot point of establishing Kathy Nightingale in the past is made richer by having her pursued in comical fashion by her future (past?) husband.

But ultimately, for Moffat, the sweep of the story is bigger than the characters. Moffat wants to leave the viewer with that sense of awe, and the final click of a story falling into careful place. Look at the final scene of *The Girl in the Fireplace.* He takes the audience past the Doctor's emotional turmoil to the clever reveal of the ship's name, the *SS Madame de Pompadour*. It's a very interesting choice of emphasis. By comparison, if one looks at the ending of *Doomsday* (discounting the teaser for *The Runaway Bride*), the entire plot is in aid of the devastating separation of the Doctor and Rose. Davies' asked the fundamental question: what would separate these two people who love each other epically? The answer is to match that love metaphorically. Davies pulls out the holiest of holies: a legendary showdown between the two iconic monsters of the series, the Daleks and the Cybermen, and a parallel universe that must close forever. That's how devastating it has to be. Scientific logic and plot nuance come second. The audience must feel the loss deep in their bones and, as a good storyteller, Davies employs all his skill and guile to achieve it.

By comparison, Moffat takes great pains to construct compelling and airtight realities that appeal to a viewer's sense of intellect and scrutiny. It's a common science-fiction strategy: create an extraordinary world and then fill in that package of reality with carefully placed details to offer the illusion of reality. As viewers, these details catch our imaginations and greatly enhance the thrill that what we are watching could actually happen, or at least that we suspend our disbeliefs. I don't think suspension of disbelief is really a high priority for Davies. In his book, *The Writer's Tale,* he frequently explains how he scraps technical descriptions because he believes the audience will be bored by them. He's convinced that the characterisations themselves (with perhaps a little help from humour and spectacle) will hold the drama together.

Now that Moffat has completed his first full season of *Doctor Who* as showrunner, many are celebrating his tightly plotted season arc and rightly so. But while Davies tended to be rather more scattershot in terms of connective tissue from story to story (throw in a "Bad Wolf" meme here, a "Torchwood" reference there and logic-defying Rose appearances), he did present a more cohesive narrative during the 2007 season with his Saxon arc. The manipulation of Martha's mother, the Face of Boe's revelation, the introduction of the Chameleon Arch and the awakening of the Master display some strong story planning and execution. One could argue that Moffat takes his conception a step further by even shooting scenes during appropriate shooting-blocks for use in his finale. The central idea of the "cracks in time" intensifies as the story arc continues and we're always gaining a little more knowledge. To be completely stark: a Davies arc is a portent of doom in the background of escalating character crises; a Moffat arc is like an elaborate mouse trap that the characters have to react to and find their way out of.

More significantly though, is where Davies and Moffat respectively leave us at the end of a season of *Doctor Who*. As I mentioned earlier, Davies favoured a strong emotional trajectory for his characters and, regardless of whatever crazy-arsed scenarios he throws at them, there is always a huge cost: the ninth Doctor loses his life, the Doctor and Rose are parted, Martha's family is traumatised, and a version of Donna essentially dies. At the end of Moffat's first season, everything is made whole again. The Doctor, Amy, Rory and the whole universe are restored. Davies conforms to a kind of Shakespearian understanding of tragedy, while Moffat to the Bard's corresponding definition of comedy. One can't take the comparison too far: Davies rarely produces a bloodbath on the scale of *Hamlet*, and Moffat knows how to up the tension (and certainly doesn't untie all the knots; he defers that to the future). But I dare say that Moffat is aware of the comedy conceit in his work, as he actually ends the 2010 season with a wedding, a mainstay in his Shakespearian counterparts. With the exception of *The Girl in the Fireplace*, everything does tend to work out in a Moffat story.

Both Davies and Moffat have taken missteps in the furthering of their craft, exposing the weaknesses of their respective approaches. *Journey's End* illustrates where Davies overextends himself in terms of character arc, leaving some of his plotlines overexposed. Yeah, I'm talking about Rose. At its core, the 2008 season was all about Donna's journey to becoming a fully realised human being. Bringing Rose back was a hat-trick that Davies just couldn't pull off. It was nice to see her, but there was no time to give her and the Doctor any meaningful interaction, and their final parting rang rather false. The idea of a second half-human Doctor is intriguing, but without sufficient time to really develop it, it came across as a mere device (albeit one that was nearly four years in the making). We were all left groaning, "...but Rose would never do that."

Moffat's own shortcomings were seeded in the conception of *Silence in the Library / Forest of the Dead*. Yes, I mean River Song. Now, don't get me wrong, I loved Alex Kingston and her portrayal of the mysterious woman from the Doctor's past / future and there were many successful aspects to the character. Unfortunately, the character does rely heavily on the "big idea" undergirding her. Moffat really likes to explore the imaginative / thematic elements of time travel (his stories are almost always timey-wimey). Exploring an important relationship for the Doctor that happens in a non-linear fashion is extremely exciting and ripe with possibilities. But it does ask a tremendous amount of the viewer in terms of delayed emotional investment. Yes, my imagination and my intellect were definitely tickled by the concept. However, there is something slightly hollow at the centre of this relationship. To Moffat's credit, he does seem committed to further exploration of it. River's return in four key episodes of the 2010 season certainly did much to further her as an intriguing and enigmatic character, but the viewer won't tolerate deferred gratification indefinitely. River is a smart, sassy and charming character, but she has to amount to more that just cleverness. And, as Russell T Davies has already learned, when you raise expectations, you can raise them above any possible satisfaction.

I mentioned at the start the key *Doctor Who* values that Moffat and Davies share in their approach to writing for *Doctor Who*. Both have great, albeit varied, senses of humour (Moffat tends to be more wry, while Davies is often a bit more on the silly side, though they're both brilliant with a one-liner), both are incredibly inventive in their own ways, both infuse their scripts with pop-culture references, and both continue the great tradition of taking banal and ordinary objects of our world and imbuing them with danger and mystery. They are also both interested in playing with the format. And they're not afraid to dip into the other's pool, so to speak. *The Beast Below* is most certainly Moffat's take on a Davies-esque tale with the TARDIS crew getting to know each other better (a la *The End of the World*). True to form though, he began with the mystery of Starship UK and developed his characterisation from there. Davies, for his part, gave us *Turn Left*: a more structure-heavy, "what if" sci-fi story, moving out from the relationship between Donna and the Doctor to show how important moments between people affect history.

In the end, it's their similarities that represent the distilled essence of the program's success. They both seem to inherently understand what the programme needs to be about at its core, but at the same time understand the realities of drama on twenty-first century television. While we may argue over the wisdom of farting aliens, walking fat, TARDIS windows and bow ties, we can be assured that the keepership of the realm has been – and will be – in good hands.

Whoniversal Translation

by Melissa Beattie

We all know that *Doctor Who, Torchwood,* and *The Sarah Jane Adventures* all exist in the same narrative universe. But how exactly do the three shows actually express that they're all part of the "Whoniverse", as it's commonly called?

There are several different ways television series can do this. The most obvious ways are, for example, being self-referential, like the tenth Doctor in *The Fires of Pompeii* admitting to having a little to do with the

Great Fire of Rome in 64AD (something done in the first Doctor serial *The Romans*) or times when characters on one series talk about events or characters on one of the other series, such as discussing the events of *Doctor Who* episodes *The Sound of Drums* and *Last of the Time Lords* on *Torchwood,* or the events of *Planet of the Dead* in *The Sarah Jane Adventures'* episode *Mona Lisa's Revenge*. They can also be direct crossovers, as when Martha Jones appeared on *Torchwood,* the Torchwood team and various members of Sarah Jane's team appearing on *Doctor Who,* and the tenth Doctor himself appearing on *The Sarah Jane Adventures.* But something which ties them all together in a way that is not quite so blatant is by sharing a common audio-visual and thematic language, which is a formal way of saying that across all three shows things like words and phrases, camera shots or themes are repeated.

This sort of borrowing is formally called "intertextuality" and each instance of borrowing is called an "intertext". The term originally comes from literature studies, where it means a direct (or nearly) quote put into a text; it can be either someone quoting themselves or quoting someone else, with the idea being to connect with or somehow evoke the work being quoted. When moving into film and television, we can broaden out the idea a bit more to include not just spoken dialogue but also visual references, like mimicking a camera shot, the reuse of certain symbols or props, or even the reuse of themes (both musical and dramatic). So, if a word (or phrase, or camera shot, or theme) has a particular meaning or connotation in the context of *Doctor Who,* then if we notice the same word (or phrase, or camera shot, or theme) in *Torchwood* or *The Sarah Jane Adventures,* we remember the particular meaning or connotation from the first time, and apply it onto the subsequent times we see or hear it. It's a way of giving another level of depth to a line or a scene as well as tying the series together. You can have an intertext between different shows in the same narrative universe, shows in different universes (like referencing *The X-Files* in *Torchwood*) or even things outside television (like referencing the Harry Potter books in *Doctor Who).* If you're familiar with the concept of in-jokes or homages, those are other forms of intertexts.

Like any other device, however, intertexts have their pitfalls. Anything apart from a direct quote starts becoming quite subjective on the part of the interpreter. So, what I see as, for example, a reference to a classic *Doctor Who* serial, other people might see as just coincidence or as a reference to something else entirely. So, as you read this essay, keep in mind that this is by no means an all-inclusive list and that my interpretation is by no means the only valid one.

If all of that seems confusing, then fear not; the examples I'm about to discuss should make matters more clear. Let's begin with one of the best-known examples: dancing. First appearing in *The Doctor Dances,* the term has taken on the second meaning of sex, an uncommon connotation in contemporary, everyday English. This means we can call it part of the "audio-visual language" of the *Doctor Who* universe, if we're feeling formal. But the term did not stop there; Paul Cornell used the same euphemism for sex in the 2007 season episode *Human Nature,* and Catherine Tregenna used it in her *Torchwood* episode *Captain Jack Harkness.* In both later cases, as in the first instance, dancing was not just said, but shown, so that regular viewers can automatically interpret any sort of slow dancing to have this meaning. Therefore, when we see first Jack and Gwen dancing in *Something Borrowed,* it makes us think that there might be a sexual connotation; the dialogue, however, shows that Jack has in fact accepted that she prefers Rhys, giving the dance a bittersweet quality. Ianto's subsequent cutting in to dance with Jack also then reflects their growing relationship. So the term from *Doctor Who* crosses to *Torchwood,* and in both cases verbally and visually express and reinforce elements of character.

This is hardly the only instance of terms or phrases crossing between series. One of the more emotionally wrenching intertexts links the adult series *Torchwood* and the children's series *The Sarah Jane Adventures* via the Doctor himself. In *The Sarah Jane Adventures* episode *The Wedding of Sarah Jane Smith,* the Doctor, having burst in to stop Sarah Jane's wedding – and remember that Jack did the same thing to Gwen in *Something Borrowed,* so that's a visual intertext in and of itself – is integrated into the episode, though uninvolved in the climax. When the Doctor comes back at the end of the episode, in a quiet moment with Sarah Jane, he says, "Don't forget me." This scene is a reversal of the fourth Doctor's last scene with Sarah Jane in the classic series story *The Hand of Fear,* where Sarah asks the Doctor not to forget her, an intertext that connects Sarah with the fourth and tenth Doctors, which only has added pathos given that the Doctor has been told prior to his appearance here that he is going to die. (It is also one of the last things Ianto says to Jack before his death in *Children of Earth,* which only adds to the resonance.)

Doctor Who and *The Sarah Jane Adventures* both very obviously reach back to classic *Doctor Who*; their main characters, enemies and frequently their references are all drawn from the earlier serials. But *Torchwood* is also tied to classic *Doctor Who* just as much as the other two series; it merely makes these connections through more subtle intertexts. This way, anyone who only watches *Torchwood* is not confused, but fans who are familiar with the rest of the *Doctor Who* universe will pick up on the references; a quick example would be that, when Gwen refers to Jack as her "best friend" in *Children of Earth: Day Two,* a fan familiar with the fourth Doctor serials would immediately think of how Sarah Jane was called the Doctor's best friend. But the instance that I want to discuss is both one of the most subtle and is in-depth enough to illustrate just how much can be added by using these intertexts.

In *Kiss Kiss, Bang Bang,* the first episode of *Torchwood*'s second season, we are introduced to a Time Agent of Jack's prior acquaintance, a man calling himself "Captain John Hart". This is an acknowledged pseudonym, but a character of that name has appeared before. In the third Doctor serial *The Sea Devils,* the Doctor, having visited his imprisoned enemy the Master, winds up at a secret naval base commanded by one Captain John Hart. I'm not saying that these are intended to be the same character – *Torchwood's* Captain John wears a Victorian-era army jacket and jeans, not any approximation of a seventies-era Royal Navy uniform – but examining both shows just how well these intertexts can be used.

To begin, we must briefly discuss *The Sea Devils*. As I said, in this serial the Doctor has come to see the Master, who has been imprisoned by UNIT. Over the course of the six episodes the Master escapes the prison, having misled the prison commander into believing he was helping defend the country, disguises himself as an admiral and takes over the Naval base with the Sea Devils whom he intends to use as an army of conquest. The Doctor, meanwhile, is trying to negotiate peace with the Sea Devils, aided by Captain Hart and Jo Grant. The Sea Devils capture both the Doctor and the Master and they must ally to escape; this occurs but the Master ultimately escapes from the Doctor and UNIT as well.

Now, let us look at *Torchwood's* Captain John Hart. In *Kiss Kiss, Bang Bang*, he pretends to be seeking a series of bombs to gain Jack's trust and Torchwood's assistance, nearly kills Gwen, does kill Jack (temporarily), and then dangles knowledge of Jack's long-lost younger brother just as he is leaving through the Rift. This all suggests that Captain John is Captain Jack's equal and opposite, or the *Torchwood* version of the Master. Those familiar with the classic series who remember that there was a "Captain John Hart" in *The Sea Devils* would, most likely, see this as an in-joke or intertext which supports this analogy. Then, at the end of *Fragments* and the beginning of *Exit Wounds,* Captain John insists that he will destroy Jack's world and is upset that Jack is ignoring him. The revival's version of the Master, who has progressed to having a full-on obsession with the Doctor and with whom the audience would presumably be quite familiar, then acts to reinforce the audience's subconscious connection between Captain John and the Master. Because of how *Last of the Time Lords* ended, the audience is expecting (or expected to be expecting) that Captain John will cause destruction, probably do something terrible to Jack's brother and / or the Torchwood team but ultimately be forgiven by Jack; all which had been done by the Master and the Doctor.

This, of course, was not the case at all. Though having intertexts from both the classic and new series which connect Captain John and the Master, it is the classic storyline which foreshadows the ultimate twist, that Jack and Captain John will ally against a common, sympathetic enemy in Jack's brother, Gray. The exact circumstances are, of course, very different, but the basic plot twists are the same, and the intertexts were clearly used consciously by the production team to both create an analogy between Captain John and the Master, but also to offer two distinct foreshadowings, one of which was intended to mislead the audience about where the plotline was going to go. Obvious in retrospect, really, but a very effective way of keeping the viewers guessing.

At any rate, all of that is one way in which you can take a relatively simple intertext, borrowing a name from classic *Doctor Who* and using it in *Torchwood*, and turn it into something which ties together the series in a lot of different ways. But sometimes you don't even need to say a word; you can just use an object to connect things. We all know that the ninth and tenth Doctors don't like guns, actively refusing them in some cases. Yet we see the Doctor holding a gun twice in the 2008 season; three times, if you count the water pistol in *The Fires of Pompeii*. What is noteworthy about that is the fact that the gun in question in both *The Doctor's Daughter* and *The End of Time* is a Webley revolver, a weapon most associated with Jack Harkness on *Torchwood*. So this, visually, will automatically start drawing parallels for the audience. Then, once we start looking at context, it becomes even clearer. In *The Doctor's Daughter*, the Doctor takes the weapon which has just mortally wounded his artificially generated daughter and holds it on her killer; he then exclaims that he would never kill in anger and exhorts the colonists around him to build their new society upon that principle.

In *The End of Time*, the Doctor holds the weapon, given to him by Donna's grandfather Wilf, alternatively on the Master and Rassilon, before destroying a machine which will trap the Time Lords back within the time lock. We know that the Doctor had a family lost in the war – he says so in *Father's Day* – and it's implied that the unnamed Time Lady who came to Wilf may have been a relation, possibly the Doctor's granddaughter Susan, though that's not certain. At any rate, being forced to sacrifice family in order to save the Earth and losing a loved one in the process – the Master trapped himself with the Time Lords in order to save the Doctor – draws a parallel between the Doctor here and Jack in *Children of Earth*. This is also supported when we remember that the Doctor says in *The End of Time Part One* that he needs someone to travel with because he'd got things wrong; so, during the epilogue of that story, the Doctor makes sure that Jack finds a good person to travel with and, presumably, help him heal. This is an example of how you can use even a simple but recognisable object to connect characters, storylines, and series.

We talked earlier about both the Doctor and Ianto asking not to be forgotten in the context of a direct quotation of the line. But the theme of forgetting is also associated with the Doctor in that Donna was forced to forget him and all of their travels in order to save her life. This sort of thematic borrowing is yet another type of an intertext. There are several themes which can be seen running through all three series, but there are two which I will discuss as examples.

The first theme is that of guilt, both that which is felt by a character and that of which a character is culpable. The most common expression is survivor guilt, something which ties together both *Doctor Who* and *Torchwood*. By the time of the revival, the Doctor is (more or less) the last of his kind. Thanks to *The End of Time*, we know that the Doctor trapped the Time Lords and Daleks (and others) within a time lock which will lead to their inevitable destruction; judging by what we saw of the Time Lords, however, they were just as much a menace as the Daleks, so it would appear to be an act which was absolutely necessary to save the Universe. The Doctor still, understandably, holds himself responsible for their deaths and is badly affected by this throughout the series, to the point where he says in *Dalek* that his survival of the Time War was not by choice. At any rate, guilt is a strong theme throughout both the ninth and tenth Doctor's lives.

Throughout *Torchwood*, Jack suffers from increasing survivor guilt, due in large part to his extended lifespan. I want to talk, however, about one very specific cause from before he became immortal, as it also ties in with *The Sarah Jane Adventures*. As shown in the *Torchwood* episode *Adam*, when Jack was an adolescent he accidentally let go of his younger brother's hand while both were fleeing from a bombardment from above, one which appears to have massacred many if not most of the inhabitants of the Boeshane Peninsula. Jack holds himself responsible for this error – as does Gray – despite the fact that Jack was a child himself at the time.

This can be compared to the first season episode of *The Sarah Jane Adventures*, *Whatever Happened to Sarah Jane?*, in which a childhood friend of Sarah Jane's called Andrea agrees to allow the Trickster to save her from dying. Andrea is hanging from a pier, but the main difference is that she is aware that Sarah Jane will die if she accepts the Trickster's offer, whereas Jack was not aware of the consequences in his situation. Andrea also is made to forget her bargain, whereas Jack cannot. Thus, these are different examinations of the same themes: how much culpability does a child have in these cases? How much guilt should they carry with them throughout their lives? These questions, of course, do not have set answers, but they reflect the underlying theme of guilt which permeates the entirety of the *Doctor Who* universe.

Let's return to the notion that an intertext can be used to imply that two relationships are analogous. This is the case when looking at the relationship between Jack and the Doctor, especially in the 2008 season of *Doctor Who,* in comparison to the relationship between Jack and Ianto in the first season of *Torchwood*. These are mostly visual intertexts, or parallels outside dialogue and not particularly relating to theme. For example, in *Utopia,* we see Jack taking the Doctor's coat and holding onto it; we see Ianto holding Jack's coat in *Out of Time* in much the same way. We also see Jack making tea for the Doctor and Martha in *The Sound of Drums;* this function is, of course, most associated with Ianto on *Torchwood*. What this all suggests is that we can see shades of one relationship in the other. The Doctor and Jack have a strong mutual respect and friendship, implying that the same can be said between Jack and Ianto; that is, the latter relationship is not simply sexual, a fact which is borne out in later seasons of *Torchwood.* One can also, then, make the reverse argument, that the parallel suggests that there is, or was, a sexual component to Jack and the Doctor's relationship though, given the family friendly nature of *Doctor Who,* it is unlikely that this will ever be directly addressed.

As you can see, these intertexts, or instances of being self-referential or referencing other shows, can work on a lot of levels. Not everyone picks up on or even agrees about all of them – and that is the key to a successful intertext, making sure the audience can always follow the plot even if they don't understand the references. However, for people who are dedicated fans of all the series, classic and modern, and who watch episodes multiple times, they start to stand out. They act as foreshadowing, as misleads, as winks to the audience and, most of all, as a way of deepening the meaning and connecting the entire narrative universe together. This "multi-layering" effect is one of the reasons why the series of the Whoniverse are becoming such objects of study; there's a lot to be examined. So, now that we have successfully established that all three series – despite their disparate target demographics – are all integrated into a single narrative, we can start looking at them as something like a modern televisual epic.

Like A Hovercraft

by Graeme Burk
From Enlightenment #141, October 2007

Last week, I watched the pilot for the remake of *Bionic Woman*. I loved Ronald Moore and David Eick's edgy revisioning of *Battlestar Galactica*, but here all Eick has succeeded in doing is what die-hard *Galactica* fans complained they did with the updated *Galactica*: take an iconic show from the 1970s and just make it depressing and dark, stripping it of any charisma or interest.

I mention these things because it makes me glad for what we have with *Doctor Who*.

One of the greatest things Russell T Davies did when he wrote *Rose* wasn't bringing back the Doctor or the TARDIS or making Rose so compelling. No, it was the awesome and absurd scene where the Doctor is being strangled by the Nestene-animated mannequin hand while Rose is ignoring him, thinking he's joking.

Because, really, that for me was my confirmation that – no matter about the leather jacket, or Christopher Eccleston's northernness, or the poptastic soundtrack, or the lightspeed pace – this was *Doctor Who*.

During the time since the classic series went off the air (and even just before that), popular culture went through a sea change. It wasn't enough to love adventure heroes and superheroes and science-fiction heroes for what they were: characters of fantasy and imagination that entertained. No, they had to somehow make sense in the real world. They had to be grim, sombre and "adult".

Doctor Who went along with that idea for a while, with the novels published by Virgin and BBC books. I loved a lot of them – they're great books and often brilliant *Doctor Who* – but I periodically had to take sabbaticals from them (the last time was *The Adventuress of Henrietta Street*; I never went back). My friends also joked about my habit of reading the last page; not to see how the story ended, but to see if the Doctor and companions were still on speaking terms so I could prepare myself beforehand if not. Don't get me wrong, I loved these books. For me the best *Doctor Who* book ever – indeed, the best *Doctor Who* produced in the 1990s – was *Damaged Goods*, which is *Doctor Who* at its most grim, sombre and adult. Curiously, it's also written by Russell T Davies.

Which brings me back to that scene with the hand. Based on *Damaged Goods* (which has a lot of jokes, but most of them contextual to the setting) and even his other TV work, I never thought for a million years Russell T Davies would write that kind of scene. But, once I saw it, I realised he understood what made *Doctor Who* tick better than most. Because *Doctor Who* at its best is funny. There are scary bits. There are grim bits. There are even adult... um... aspects. But *Doctor Who* on TV is supposed to, first and foremost, entertain. It's meant to make you laugh and then scream. It doesn't have to be a comedyfest, but it should have a rich sense of humour.

I know a number of fans who were appalled by that scene. They wanted *Doctor Who* to come back like *Battlestar Galactica* or the books and be serious and adult. To them, scenes like that undermine the sort of real-worldness they want.

But I would argue that's not *Doctor Who*.

That's not to say the series is pretending it's the 1970s. The show is very much of its time with a sophisticated emphasis on character. And it's not that the show avoids the grim consequences of featuring a character like the Doctor; we need only see episodes like *Love & Monsters*, *The Runaway Bride* and *The Family of Blood* to be reminded of that. But it's all part of a bigger picture, one where the shade happens in the light of big thrills, laughs and scares.

The 2007 season finale for a brief moment took us to places where *Doctor Who* doesn't normally take us: a grim world where the Master wins. Where the Earth is ravaged and characters are tortured and the Doctor is kept around as a pet. It was deeply unsettling to watch. It was inevitable that the reset button would be pulled (in fairness, it was great the way they used it so that the core characters still remember all that happened – and that changes the lives of the Joneses, Jack and even the Doctor), because even that brief glimpse was too grim to bear.

And yet, in the midst of that, we have the dementedly funny scene where the Master dances to a Scissor Sisters song.

Tom Baker once wrote, "[*Doctor Who*] is like a hovercraft – on a fine line all the time. You don't dare touch the ground." That's what I think makes the show so great. It demonstrates that you don't have to be grim and drab to be relevant to today's audiences.

I think the word I'm looking for is "fun".

Little Boys, Young Farmers and Gays

by Dewi Evans
From The Tides of Time #31, November 2005

In April 2005, the internet fan community was, understandably, alive with debate about the new series of *Doctor Who*. Russell T Davies' *Aliens of London* caused particular consternation, eliciting lively debate for the inclusion of elements hitherto largely alien to the series itself: farting invaders, a realistic domestic setting, the introduction of the companion's family as a semi-regular element and the overt engagement with contemporary politics. Perhaps most surprising, however, was the 20-or-so-page debate on the fan site Outpost Gallifrey's *Aliens of London* thread regarding Rose's branding of the Doctor as "so gay!" when he complains about being slapped by Jackie.

I could fill a book with comments on the various ideological standpoints adopted by those who took part in the debate, but I have neither time nor space (no puns intended) to do so. I will only note, therefore, that the various positions of those who posted to this thread could be very broadly summarised thus:

- Those who felt that any reference to homosexuality had no place in a family programme.
- Those who feared that the use of the term as slang, though it accurately reflected the speech of a 19-year-old London girl from 2005, might seem to endorse the use of the term for young viewers. This was felt to be a bad thing because, while Rose was, presumably, using the term in a way that was not intended to be homophobic, the usage still represented the implicit homophobia of the society that had given rise to it.
- Those who thought that the line was a subtle reference to the idea that the profusion of gay fans derives from an identification with the Doctor's otherness.
- Those who felt that this was simply a throwaway line and, as such, didn't require such lengthy analysis.

The main point about this debate is that the arguments advanced are less important, I would argue, than the fact that the debate actually took place in the first place. Angry posts about Russell T Davies' "gay agenda" are not entirely unfounded. The series certainly has a moral agenda, but it is the same moral agenda that was implicit in the original show for almost all of its 26 years on air. It simply happens that RTD's own writing traits tie in rather neatly with the morality of the old show, causing it to become more overt. The fact that the new series works (mainly) in terms of 45-minute storylines also means that successful episodes must have a solid thematic basis because there isn't enough time to develop more than the simplest of plots. The main point of this article is to demonstrate the way in which the series is more concerned with raising questions for debate, rather than actually attempting to resolve those debates in any concrete way.

In terms of language, the stories (especially those by RTD) employ a technique identified by the linguist Deborah Cameron as "verbal hygiene". Cameron illustrates the term using a sentence from a hypothetical estate agent's manual: "Make sure your client understands the terms before she signs the document." Cameron argues that, by using the female generic, the writer of the document surprises readers who expect the more common male generic. In doing so, the author implicitly calls into question ideas about language and the expectations regarding its usage: why, the reader asks, was he or she so surprised by this unusual use of "she" as a generic term?

In *The End of the World*, Cassandra's line about her time on Earth as "a little boy" is an example of verbal hygiene in action. The viewer expects Cassandra to have been a little girl; in revealing that she is actually a transsexual, it reminds us that our assumptions about gender are fundamentally inadequate. Nine times out of ten they may be accurate, but such instances as these draw attention to the fact that we all too often forget about the other ten per cent of instances where the ability of our language to accurately represent the world simply isn't up to the challenge.

A further example occurs in *Aliens of London*, when one of the false MPs says that he enjoyed being Oliver – he had a wife, a mistress and "a young farmer". Fans eagerly pounced on this as a further reference to the bisexuality of the aliens, but this is verbal hygiene in reverse. Why couldn't a "young farmer" be a reference to a female farmer? While the script is structured to draw attention to the possibility that the farmer is likely to be a man (why else mention a mistress as well?), the ambiguity of gender association with the title "farmer" is still apparent, breaking down all kinds of social assumptions with one throwaway line.

Indeed, the fact that both these lines are "throwaway" is key to their success. Some of the Outpost Gallifrey posters complained that the sexuality of characters was thrust in their faces. In fact, it is quite the opposite. I would argue that the first category of posters mentioned above were actually unsettled not by the subject matter itself, but by the way in which it was presented: by the fact that the idea of alternate sexuality was not thrust in their faces, or made an issue, but was dropped casually into the script as if it were (shudder) normal. The throwaway nature of the line represents the throwaway nature of the concept to the more enlightened members of these future societies. These lines, therefore, are a linguistic representation of the idea of social ambiguity propounded in Mark Gatiss' *The Unquiet Dead*: "It's different, yeah. It's a different morality, so either deal with it or go home."

This is a common trait in Davies' series: the raising of awkward questions without the suggestion that there exists a simple answer. In *Queer as Folk,* a series which ultimately celebrates a hedonistic lifestyle, one of the characters' mothers, attending the funeral of her gay son, who dies after taking impure heroin with "a casual fuck", presents Vince with a moral dilemma: would this have happened if her son had been straight? The answer, probably, is "no". For a series which exists to celebrate gay life, it raises some awkward questions about the stereotypes many gay men would wish were not true. It confronts such questions, but does not suggest an answer; no one answer is going to cover all gay men. In the same way, *Bob & Rose* pointed out that being "gay" did not mean that one could not fall in love, marry and start a family with a woman. Once again, critical reaction from the public (gay and straight alike) demonstrated the unease at which this disruption of categories was greeted. Gay critics argued of *Queer as Folk* that the public advertisement for underage sex (as many saw it) and a lifestyle based around intoxicating substances and sexual hedonism was not a representation of gay life that the public needed to see. After all, the House of Lords was about to vote on the lowering of the gay age of consent and a series which portrayed a 30-year-old man having sex with a 15-year-old boy was not going to help matters, even if such things did occur.

Just like the Doctor, exasperated at human beings' capacity for denial of anything that occurs outside of a "cosy little world" that "could be re-written like *that*!", RTD's exasperation at such narrow-minded critics is obvious, and permeates this new series. It emulates a theory of artistic representation that confronts and attempts to understand the world as it is, not as some would like it to be. Of asking the right questions; not of obtaining, or even hoping to obtain, the right answers. A prospect that worries Dickens in Gatiss' episode is that his own understanding of the "real world" is all wrong; at the end of the episode, however, he has decided to embrace the fact that he will never understand everything.

So, to return to the issue of being "so gay!". By employing this usage in *Doctor Who* for the first time ever, Davies probably realised that he was being provocative. He also has the advantage that, because of his own sexuality, people would never be able to accuse him of straightforward homophobia, simply of representing others' feelings. If we look again at the list of categories of poster that opened the essay, we see that they represent various degrees of open-mindedness. Those who hate to see homosexuality represented at all do so because that is how they would like to see the world represented: a knowable, closed system, where we can forget that "others" ever existed at all. Those who objected to the usage of the term as an insult are more aware of the politics at stake, but their assumptions are challenged by the fact that Rose has amply demonstrated her own open-mindedness and acceptance of "others" by this point in the show. She has, after all, been deeply offended by the Doctor's "cheap shot" about the Deep South two episodes earlier, and is already complaining about the mundanity and sheer small-mindedness of the world she has returned to; clearly, she is not using the word with insulting connotations.

The way in which the word "gay" is being employed here is far more complicated than even the most open-minded of posters would like to admit; it is thus the ultimate example of verbal hygiene, of upsetting social categories by disrupting the social consensus regarding the relationship between mere words and what they actually mean to different people. Like Rose's "cosy little world", the meanings of the words used to represent that world can be "re-written like *that*". Indeed, the meaning (or, at least, the connotations of words), as with the meaning and nature of the society they represent, can never be truly pinned down, even after 20 pages of heated debate. Things just aren't that simple.

Just For Kids

by Scott Clarke

From Enlightenment #127, April / May 2005

"If ten-year-olds aren't talking about the show in the playground on Monday morning, then we'll have failed."

—Steven Moffat, in an interview with *The Scotsman*, June, 2004

"I Want To Be 10 Years Old Again"

—Mike Doran, *The Doctor Who Blog*, March 9, 2005

Doctor Who is a kid's show.

Oh, I could bore you with lots of oft-quoted research about the BBC drama department, family entertainment, Sydney Newman and educational mandates (see *How to Survive Alien Radiation and Ace Your "O" Levels*), but what's the point, really? At the end of the day, the TARDIS is basically a big cardboard box you can climb inside and pretend it's pretty much anything, going pretty much anywhere. And who understands the magic of cardboard boxes better than children?

With his magic "box", the Doctor is the magician at a kid's birthday party or the street entertainer at an open-air festival. The show does everything in its power to hold your attention. It's flexible, inclusive and full of explosive colour and vivid images.

Oh sure, *Doctor Who* can and should be watched by the whole family, but the kids are holding the car keys on this one.

Children have the ability to imagine the most ordinary of objects as being imbued with some alternative, deeper, more magical purpose. *Doctor Who* comes from the same grand British literary tradition that spawned CS Lewis, JK Rowling and Roald Dahl. The police box is the "wardrobe" that leads to the secret world of Narnia or Hogwarts. Characters like Ace, Peri and Rose are rescued from their ponderous or regimented lives and thrust into worlds of unexplainable wonders and frights. Look at the similarities between *James and the Giant Peach* and *Doctor Who*. In Dahl's classic fantasy, a little boy, James Henry Trotter, resides with his two unpleasant aunts. When a mysterious stranger appears with a bag full of magic, James is whisked off to a whimsical world where insects become real life characters and an ordinary peach grows to immense proportions. It's upon this peach that James and his new insect friends travel and make their way toward his dreamland. Sound familiar?

And, like the worlds created by Dahl or JK Rowling, *Doctor Who* could be a dark, frightening universe. Sure, there was fun and silliness, but there were very real consequences to the actions of the Doctor and his companions; the programme never sugar-coated the truth from children as Mary Whitehouse would have had it. Death and mishap were part of that package of reality. We're not talking Smurfs here, but robot mummies that crush poachers, friends who die in spaceship crashes and people who can never go home again. As Christopher Eccleston noted in an interview with Simon Mayo on BBC Radio 5, "Darkness appeals to the children because it throws up strong emotions and strong questions."

Doctor Who always treated kids with respect, though, never talking down to them. Sure, it was sophisticated enough for adults to appreciate, as they watched through the delight of their children, but – make no mistake – it was made for children. And anyone who has the ability to watch it with the eyes of a child.

Watching *Doctor Who* with other adults is an altogether different experience. A level of critique informs the viewing experience: we judge it by different standards or simply take the piss out of it. The Nimon are perfectly reasonable alien beings when viewed with an open mind and the drapes drawn. Who cares if their bodies can't possibly support the weight of their bulbous heads? Big gigantic heads are intimidating and creepy, and guaranteed to reside in your memory for the rest of your days. It's as if adults require special 3D-like glasses to get it.

People recall the wriggling maggots scattered across the Welsh countryside or the squishy talking brain that got knocked to the floor. Shop dummies transformed into figures of sinister threat and a cricket ball could propel you to safety in space. (Tip: older brothers, show your little sister *Genesis of the Daleks* and then chase her around the living room with a clam shell you picked up at the beach.) Why? Because they first experienced them through the eyes of a child.

In fact, there are a whole host of cues or codes that kids understand implicitly when playing, a kind of short-hand if you will, and the creators of *Doctor Who* could always be trusted to tap into them. Children are trying to make sense of the universe around them, and there is still far more "space" to be filled in terms of what they will and won't except. The lines between scary, silly, improbable and possible are much more fluid. Ketchup and peanut butter sandwiches are to be readily attempted, while stuffed olives could just as easily be rejected because they're too eyeball-ish. There's room for a tin-plated dog to battle aggressive weed balls or Daleks to fire on Frankenstein's monster.

And, of course, the Doctor has always been somewhat naughty, thumbing his nose at authority and solving problems in unorthodox ways. He was frequently emptying his pockets of yo-yos, candy, bits of string, and all sorts of odds and sods. Or putting some pompous civil servant in their place. Does he merely tie up Harry Sullivan in *Robot*? No, he skips with him first. Look at the way the Doctor and Romana test the true nature of the Movellans in *Destiny of the Daleks*, using the old standard Rock-Paper-Scissors. While getting the information they need, they're clearly reveling in a moment of play.

Monsters on the show were also designed to appeal to children, with a curious blend of sluggish safety and gross-out fascination. Behold the Yeti: a giant teddy bear or an overpowering, unrelenting force of fear that could smother you? Well, that's the point really. You see, kids can live with that ambiguous duality. As adults, we tend to compartmentalise expectations in our viewing experience. Either something is completely terrifying or it's silly and non-threatening. Not so in the mind of a child. Mickey's "taffy pull" encounter with the Wheelie Bin in *Rose* is ridiculous in the extreme, but in the end it does "consumes" him. The silly "belch" is code for "he's been eaten". Kids get that.

And so it would seem do the creators of the new incarnation of *Doctor Who*. But they're also aware that kids are exposed to much more media these days and the pace has quickened since the 1970s or even the 1980s. Some changes in sensibility have to be acknowledged. The hyperkinetic opening of Rose is in keeping with the hip, frenetic pace of *SpongeBob SquarePants* or *Spy Kids*. The writing and portrayal of Rose, while a tremendous leap forward in terms of *Doctor Who* companions, is also quite encouraging in terms of its appeal to girls (and women in general). Rose doesn't save the day by doing something unbelievable (which would be cheating, even for a kid). She's merely brave, and wants to help her new friend.

Judging from trailers I've seen, the aliens that the Doctor and Rose will square off against are sufficiently offbeat and fanciful to appeal to children. Not the sort of subtly-thought-out aliens one encounters in the *Star Trek* universe, but truly bizarre and fun offerings such Cassandra, the "last human" who is no more than a talking bit of stretched skin. Truly in the spirit of dog-faced giants and megalomaniacal cacti.

So where does this leave the "adults"? Good storytelling is good storytelling, whether it allows us to see the world through the eyes of a queer person, an Aboriginal person or a kid. Lots of things with appeal to kids grab adults. Book series like Harry Potter are successful across age groups, because they take their audiences seriously, weaving worlds of fancy with the very ordinary stuff of our lives. And *Doctor Who* should remind us of what that was like when we were ten.

If the kids aren't talking about it on the playground Monday morning, it isn't *Doctor Who*.

Death of the Planet

by Robert Smith?
From Enlightenment #151, June 2009

"We need to return to Earth to get an emotional focus on what's going on. If we're on Planet Zog and Zog people are being affected by a monster, we couldn't really give a toss. But if there's a human colony on Planet Zog, then that's more interesting."

—Russell T Davies, March 2005

One of the criticisms of the 2005 season was the fact that it never left Earth. Every story took place in the past, the present, the future, or on a nearby space station. Which was technically leaving Earth, but such stations always had an intimate connection to the planet, making them just an outreach. *The End of the World* has an all-alien cast, but it's still inherently about Earth, telling a hugely important piece of humanity's story: the destruction of its homeworld. *The Long Game* and *Bad Wolf* are the exact opposite: they've closed Earth's borders to the alien, but are about its salvation.

This serves multiple purposes. It keeps the budget in check, of course. But it also gives us a connection to the events, as Davies' point about the planet Zog illustrates. And the new series has really taken this to heart: alien planets visited in the two subsequent seasons included New Earth, an Earth outpost populated entirely by humans in *The Impossible Planet,* an Earth hospital on the moon, and the last-ever human colony. All of these are connected to Earth and Earthlings. Indeed, only *The Impossible Planet* satisfies the "human colony on Planet Zog" premise. The others are all intimately connected: they either involve us directly, or they tell big, crucial stories about climactic events in future history.

The 2008 season went further, showing us a human corporation on the planet of the Ood, humans at war with fish aliens, a library planet populated entirely by humans, humans on a bus in *Midnight* and a planet indistinguishable from a Chinese market in *Turn Left*. These are much more along the lines of the colony of Zog and less about the big, dynamic settings that tell us about the pivots of the future.

What the new series excels at is making these connections meaningful. The one time they didn't, in *The Doctor's Daughter,* you can really tell. And even that story still has a meaningful connection: it's just connected to the Doctor, not to us. So it's no coincidence that you just don't care about the two factions, or the alien world, or indeed anything in that story except Jenny.

Planet of the Dead is a case in point. Humans on a bus in an alien world, populated by talking flies and flying robots would have worked just fine. But they go the extra mile and link the events to Earth, via communication through the wormhole. So what appears to be a subplot involving UNIT turns out to be the crucial thing that grounds us to the story. Literally.

If you'd lost that, or just used it as a framing device at the beginning and the end of the story, it would have worked out just fine – and been entirely forgettable. But the very human interactions on Earth are what gives this story any depth at all. What's great is that they don't subtract from the action on the planet, they enhance it.

The key word in the title isn't "dead", it's "planet". "Death" is just a bogeyman, used to set the scene and lead into a cliffhanger. But "planet" involves serious thought in order to make it work. For the new series, that's much, much scarier than death. You can see why the new series mostly avoids alien planets; there's just too much required in the setup and they simply don't have time for that any more.

Science fiction is fundamentally about tackling the issues of the day, through a lens that keeps controversial topics one step removed. When no other TV series could show the effects of war during Vietnam, *Star Trek* had Kirk arming primitives against the Klingons in a misguided attempt to create peace. Mary Shelley's *Frankenstein* warned of the dangers of this new thing called electricity, disguising it as a fantastical story about reviving a cadaver. *Battlestar Galactica* shows us the effects of what we're becoming in the wake of 9/11, only setting it amongst robots and spaceships.

Doctor Who was no stranger to this. The dangers of organ transplants were expressed through the Cybermen wearing nylons on their heads. Pacifism is critiqued in the Dominators, by showing pacifists hanging around in frumpy dresses. In the midst of a miner's strike, at the height of the British labour unrest, *The Monster of Peladon* used allegory to present two sides to a mining dispute, cleverly avoiding direct parallels by doing so in a story that featured a hairy carrot and a giant phallus in a cloak.

When you couldn't talk about racism on TV, SF could show two alien factions fighting it out over minutely minor differences, in order to show us how ridiculous it was. This was an astonishingly effective tool: it makes its points insidiously, so that the viewer has certain belief systems and attitudes reaffirmed implicitly. It can undo so much of the mentality that's sent our way, equally insidiously, by most other shows.

This was utterly crucial back when there were so many things you couldn't talk about in public and when there were very few means of mass communication, all of them controlled by a select few individuals and subject to powerful lobby groups.

Much of that no longer applies. If we want to discuss the dangers of racism, anyone can start typing and send their message out to the entire world in a matter of seconds. If it's well written enough and insightful enough, it can be read by a great many people, unfiltered by editorial interference or censorship.

So, in the changing world of mass communication, we need to ask: what's science fiction for? Or, perhaps more specifically, what does *Doctor Who* get out of being science fiction?

The new series has done its fair share of allegory, of course. The 2005 season was positively rolling in it: *Aliens of London* was all about the invasion of Iraq, yet they got away with it by having farting green aliens. *The Long Game* was a critique of the media, which is always a tough message to get to the masses, given that you usually have to do it via that selfsame media, but they cleverly disguised it by having a big piece of meat in the ceiling. And *Bad Wolf* pilloried reality TV, by suggesting that they were a front for a bunch of faceless robotic exterminators, hell bent on destroying humanity as we know it. Wait, sorry, that wasn't allegory after all.

However, there's also a sense in which these allegories aren't as powerful as they would have been back in the day. They're not, for instance, the only critiques of war, the media or reality TV that you or I are likely to experience. They still have their place, but now they're only one voice among many. A voice that's still powerful, compared to the average blogger perhaps, but still not the sole critique of society.

Dissent in mainstream media is still strongly discouraged, of course. How many sitcoms have the family's son heading off to Iraq? No more than had them heading off to Vietnam in the sixties. And SF's insidiousness can be used for evil, as well as good. *Star Trek, Babylon 5, Battlestar Galactica,* etc, are glorious advertisements for the military-industrial complex. They normalise the idea of the bold, heroic soldier and gloss over the negative parts of a vast, state-sanctioned war machine. *Doctor Who* is better on this, with its defiant refusal to glorify the use of guns and its insistence upon compassion. There's still a lot of cosying up to the military, but at least it's one step removed.

Indeed, I'd argue that *Doctor Who* is no longer science fiction at all. The TARDIS is now just a time machine, not a space-time machine. All those jokes about companions not wanting to join the Doctor when they think the TARDIS only travels in space are right on the money. And the Doctor is much more of a magician with a lot of historical knowledge, than someone who is truly alien. His knowledge base has increased in proportion to the shortening of the running time, so precious screen minutes aren't wasted on figuring stuff out. And it's telling that so many stories are resolved either through *deus ex machinas,* unintelligible (to us) rewiring of circuitry or through simply pulling a plug of some sort.

Doctor Who's use of the empathetic connection to Earth could be a strength: not just for linking the story to "us" in order to make us care, but using this link to make its points and critique of society. Using its particular form of home-linked SF to make its critiques have resonance could be a powerful tool for informing and educating. The fact that – the 2005 season aside – the new series has been so disinterested in doing this only reinforces the point that it's not really SF.

Even when it does attempt some commentary, the results are so half-hearted that you wonder if they're just going through the motions. *Planet of the Ood* is a critique of corporate practices, but is so clichéd that it's hard to see it as a meaningful allegory. The very fact that we've seen this all before – evil corporation enslaves native population, uses dodgy business practices and lies to cover it up – shows how mainstream this has become and simultaneously shows how lazy this kind of thing seems. *New Earth*'s critique of the medical system is so lightweight, it's hardly even criticism. Only *Gridlock*'s commentary on traffic has any real bite.

So what's it all for, then? It's much more about telling a story that's a) entertaining and b) makes us care, by giving us a connection we can empathise with. But these don't depend on the genre being science fiction. Science fiction still has power, but *Doctor Who* largely doesn't embrace that power, either literally, in the form of travel to wondrous alien worlds, or figuratively, in the form of SF's allegorical critiques of our own society. For a series that can do anything and go anywhere, it's stuck in the past, present and future.

The space age is over. Long live the age of time.

INTERLUDE

Journey's End - 3

by Scott Clarke
From Enlightenment #156, March 2010

I wake up and stumble into the living room, sideswipe the fish tank and fall headfirst into the mid-range IKEA couch. It's 7:37 on a Wednesday, ten years later. I flip on the television. It's supposed to be Channel 50: Space, the imagination station. But they've long since stopped playing those endless repeats of Hartnell Doctor Who. *Instead, there is nothing but snow. An odd sight in this digital age. I stare dumfounded at the TV, and then I strain to hear a faint sound. It's a voice. "He will text four times." What does it mean, I ponder? "He will text four times and then it will be the end of time."*

I've been here before...

Part Three: Plot

It might have been sufficient to end *The Girl in the Fireplace* with that shot from above the TARDIS interior, looking down on a heartbroken Doctor. Viewers might have forgotten, in that wrenching moment, that earlier a group of clockwork robots were on a bloody rampage to procure the noggin of Madame de Pompadour. But Moffat lays down his final card: a shot of the ship's hull with the nom de plume *S.S. Madame de Pompadour* emblazoned across it. It's an "a-ha!" moment that invites our intellect to revisit the carefully constructed story and revel in the clues we missed and the perfect sense it all makes. In his book, *The Writer's Tale,* Russell T Davies describes Moffat's plots as being "as precise as a Swiss watch".

Steven Moffat knows he's our daddy (or mummy).

Selecting "plot" as the subject of my final article might seem a tad pedestrian for such an auspicious occasion. "Plot" sounds a bit too much like plod, you say. (Okay, most of you wouldn't say that, and you care a great deal about plot, so let's park that thought for the moment.) And yet, I must confess that there's always been a part of me that stands in awe of a carefully crafted plot. I love a good mystery novel. I love to be outwitted. I also love trying to figure out what's really going on. My favourite DVD extras are those where the writers actually talk about the challenges of making the plot work. Plot can be poetic under the right circumstances.

Oddly enough, many classic *Doctor Who* stories really sucked in the plot department. Too many stories ended with a convenient explosion (yes you, *The Seeds of Doom*) or a hard-to-swallow pseudoscience explanation (that's you, *The Pirate Planet*). Plot was never something that drew me to those stories (and more than often we got exposition, escape, capture, escape, capture and explanation disguised as plot). Mood, wit, allegory, vibrant imagery and richly drawn characterisation came much higher on the list in ye olde time *Doctor Who* story of yore. Besides, nobody expected those stories to ever be watched again and the Target novels could smooth out the rough spots.

Fast forward again. The basic story idea of *The Girl in the Fireplace* (two people sharing an unconventional relationship in a time-travel context) has a familiar sci-fi / fantasy feel to it, evoking other stories such as the book *The Time Traveller's Wife*, and yet Moffat's script evokes a sense of freshness and originality. He treads a careful line between fairytale and presenting a workable universe. We never ask why a futuristic spaceship in the thirtieth century would have clockwork robots servicing it, because their internal logic is so strong. But is it the plot I love so much about the story? Or is it where Moffat takes the Doctor's character? Perhaps it's the fairytale mood of the whole thing?

The definition of plot is a little elusive. Is a plot simply what happens? Does a good story necessarily have a good plot? And where does mystery end and a plot hole begin? Did *The Caves of Androzani* have a good plot, or just really good characters doing really interesting things? I suppose a successful plot is seamless or invisible. It allows us to maintain our suspension of disbelief (an important consideration when watching a programme like *Doctor Who*). There is a certain level of trust that is built between a storyteller and their audience. If, like a magician, a dramatist is able to deflect attention away from the "trick" and then surprise the audience, everyone is happy. But if the audience feels cheated, their acrimony can be bitter. And nobody knows how to hurl poison darts like a *Doctor Who* fan. Fans are like shareholders who expect certain dividends from their investments. And we love to be rewarded for our loyalty and attention to detail.

But exactly how important is plot to a successful *Doctor Who* story?

Television has done a one-eighty since *Doctor Who* left our screens in the 1980s. Most importantly, concerning plot structure, we now have, for all intents and purposes, a mix of 45-minute standalone and two-part stories. In the old days, the serialised format had to obey two masters: the structure constraints of the single episode, complete with cliffhanger, and the parallel structure of the overarching story (told in a mix of two or more episodes). Stories could be told in a more leisurely fashion, but they often contained a lot more padding. Telling a story in 45 minutes, while certainly the norm for a drama series, forces the writers to throw out a whole slew of preconceived ideas.

Russell T Davies, architect of modern *Doctor Who*, is the man charged with setting that tone. For that reason, it's a little hard to talk about alternative approaches to plot in the series. We all know that Davies rewrites scripts. On another show, where the house style is more solidified, this process would probably be seamless but, on a programme that is inherently eclectic in its style, sorting it all out become a bit more complicated. Davies claims that he doesn't touch a word on Moffat's pages and I think that can be taken as a given. He also claims that he doesn't rewrite a couple of the other writers. We can only judge what makes it to the screen.

Fans (and some reviewers) frequently complain that Davies writes himself into a corner, resulting in incoherent endings or resolutions that rely on some sort of *deus ex machina*; that his scripts are over-stuffed with distractions instead of getting down to business. Open your internet browser right now and type in "Russell T Davies" and "plot holes". Not only will you read line after line of teeth-gnashing frustration, but also oh-so-helpful suggestions for correcting said plot oversights. Mind you, most of them would put 90% of the mainstream audience to sleep in under two minutes.

Davies has been accused of "lazy writing", but that rather misses the point that he's a very strong personality and makes very definite choices around plot (read his book, *The Writer's Tale;* he's on record). *Tooth and Claw* was a good example of how Davies can work with more intricate plot elements if he chooses to. Mind you, there will always be those lined up to ask, "Where did the monks go?"

Russell is like a kid in a sandbox who builds something cool out of muck with bits of stuff sticking out of it. Pretty soon a crowd forms around him and there's lots of laughter and excitement. Meanwhile, Moffat is in the art class lovingly constructing a precise model right down to the itsy bitsy details. Most people won't even notice the detailed work, but those who do are thrilled.

As I've mentioned, it's so hard breaking down a *Doctor Who* story into its component parts. Great direction (read: Graeme Harper) can strengthen the sins of a weak plot (read: *Planet of the Ood*), while alternatively lacklustre direction (read: Euros Lyn) can bring down a more nuanced script (read: *Silence in the Library / Forest of the Dead*).

It's hard to know in a story like *Planet of the Dead* whether the opening sequence with armed guards facing away from the object they're guarding is plot expediency or if it's trying to be stylish. I can't believe that two intelligent writers like Russell T Davies and Gareth Roberts actually wrote it that way. It seems much more likely that it was a compromise during production. One could still argue that the writing overstretched the possibilities of the programme.

Again, the issue of trust between storyteller and audience is essential. Modern audiences scrutinise plot details much more carefully than in the past. It's a hell of a lot harder to surprise people than it used to be. And the art of misdirection is a tricky one. Moffat is careful to set up the "rules" that exist within the confines of his stories (regardless of how preposterous the underlining elements are). The time portals in *The Girl in the Fireplace* work under a certain logic (the one that eventually allows the Doctor to return to the spaceship is "offline" due to Madame de Pompadour's earlier actions). Body parts are gruesomely, yet logically, deployed as spare parts in anticipation of the big reveal (eyes are cameras, hearts are engines).

In *Silence in the Library*, we're told to count the shadows: not every shadow contains the Vashta Nerada, but any shadow can. Viewers then adjust their expectations accordingly. We hear several references to people being "saved" before the Doctor eventually puzzles out what is happening in the library. It's a clever little moment that appeals to the left part of our brains. But make no mistake, it falls under the category of "clever" and it won't register dramatically with a certain proportion of the mainstream audience.

Moffat is at his most accessible when his rules are squarely placed right in the open. I speak of course of the Weeping Angels in *Blink*. Plotwise, the story is probably the least able to stand up to deconstruction in the light of day, but it succeeds on such a gut level. The angels can't look at each other. The protagonists can't blink or look away. The rules are so simple and primal. And the resolution looks like it's going to be a *deus ex machina* involving the TARDIS, but Moffat uses that expectation to distract us. We panic when the Ship starts to dematerialise without Sally and Larry, and then the solution hits us in an immediate visual way. We don't have to think or backtrack on our knowledge of the plot.

Things become a bit trickier when considering the vast history of *Doctor Who*. If we're to feel genuine jeopardy for the Doctor and his predicaments, it's helpful to understand his powers and limitations. Watching the Doctor inexplicably fall from a great distance and survive can be seen as a cheat by some, while to others it merely underscores the poignancy of his eventual demise. (Does *The End of Time* owe anything to *Logopolis*? That's another article in itself.) Similarly, having a jet-propelled, Skeletor Master may be a very cool visual for kids suckled on Harry Potter, but many adults were left shaking their heads. I call this *The Phantom Menace* effect: no matter how hard we tear apart the structure of that movie, many kids who originally saw it will rank it higher than the original *Star Wars* trilogy.

One gets the feeling that there are two distinct approaches to plot in *Doctor Who*: let's play with the structure to make the overly familiar fresh or let's just replace the dull bits with fun, colour, wit and thrills. Moffat's solution is often to reshuffle the deck with timey-wimey goodness. For a show about time travel, it's amazing how few times it has actually played with the concept. Of course, once you start messing with the structure, the potential for plot holes increases. It's cool for Sally Sparrow to duck in 2007 after reading a message from 1969, but how does that work exactly? And do we need a complicated explanation for curing zombies when they can all just take a shower in Kool-Aid packs?

Fans will soon get a chance to see how Steven Moffat will set the tone for *Doctor Who*. It's quite likely we will see more detailed and precise plotting. More timey-whimey goodness. How will his influence be felt on the other writers? Will their scripts need to conform to a tighter structure? Or will the atmosphere be more laissez-faire? Only time will tell.

He will text four times.

Of course, it's my editor. He's looking for my article, which I couldn't seem to deliver to deadline, once again. Perhaps this time I'm dragging my feet. Perhaps if I don't hand it in, the Russell T Davies era won't end and my legacy as a full-time fanzine writer won't come to a close.

But that would be folly my friends, for change must come and – paradoxically for all Doctor Who *fans as always – with "journey's end", we can all look forward to the continuing adventures.*

The story goes on...

BOWTIES ARE COOL

The miracle has happened again.

Every time it happens, *Doctor Who* fans hold their collective breath as they ask: Will it happen again? Will it change but still keep my love? Will it be different? Will it be the same?

It's a miracle that happens every time a new actor takes to the role of the Doctor, but here there was even more riding on it. The youngest actor ever to play the title role. A new producing team and a new, though popular, head writer. A new mystery. A new stylistic direction. A new TARDIS. Even new opening titles.

Just one of these changes could spell doom, and has done so often with other television series just on the basis of recasting the central role. But with *Doctor Who*, it's the continuing miracle: *Doctor Who* not only survives change, it often becomes better as a result of it.

Is it a show about a cranky old man, a young man in an old man's body or a lonely god? Is it a show about a paramilitary organisation foiling alien invasions every Saturday at teatime, about the visceral effects of violence in an unpleasant universe or about learning to stand up and say no? Are its recurring elements bases under siege, creeping body horror or a crack in the universe? The truth is, it's all of these things and none of them. *Doctor Who* is endlessly mutable, capable of reinventing itself from the ground up, just to keep itself fresh. This is the secret of its longevity.

At the time of writing, the 2010 season is still fresh in people's minds. The excitement of the crack in everything is still palpable. The energy of Matt Smith's completely counterintuitive yet stunning debut still crackles in the air. By the time you read this (at least on first publication), there will have been a new Christmas special and a new season full of mystery, excitement and plotting via flowchart. But, even with all this, there is one reality which every fan can take to heart.

The miracle has happened again.

First Eleven

by Keith Topping

"The universe is big. It's vast and complicated and ridiculous. And sometimes, very rarely, impossible things just happen and we call them 'miracles'. That's the theory. Nine hundred years, I've never seen one yet. But this would do me."

—The Doctor, *The Pandorica Opens*

In *The Pandorica Opens,* the Doctor tells the assembled multitude of his worst enemies, ever, that whoever takes control of the Pandorica also takes control of the Universe. "But, bad news everyone." The question of the hour, he continues, is "Who's got the Pandorica?" And the answer, of course, is that he does. "Next question: 'Who's coming to take it from me?' Come on, look at me! No plan, no backup, no weapons worth a damn. Oh, and something else. I don't have anything to lose! So, if you're sitting up there in your silly little spaceships with all your silly little guns and you've got any plans on taking the Pandorica tonight, just remember who's standing in your way! Remember every black day I ever stopped you, and then, do the smart thing! Let somebody else try first."

Or, to put it another way, come and have a go if you think you're hard enough. As mission statements go, it's one of the best the Doctor's ever articulated. As he boasts to poor, dead Bob in *The Time of Angels,* "Didn't anyone ever tell you? There's one thing you never put in a trap. If you're smart, if you value your continued existence, if you have any plans about seeing tomorrow, there is one thing you never, ever put in a trap. Me."

The eleventh Doctor is a Time Lord of action. A being of astonishing energy, pace and limitless capacity for pithy one-liners. "Is this world protected?" he demands of the Atraxi in *The Eleventh Hour*. "Cos you're not the first lot to have come here. Oh, there have been *so* many. And what you've got to ask is, what happened to them? Hello. I'm the Doctor. Basically, run." Making bold declarations of your own power and abilities is something the Doctor had learned to do very well over the years. In *Victory of the Daleks,* his near-narcissistic streak almost gets the better of him: "Enemy! And I am yours! You are everything I despise. The worst thing in all creation. I've defeated you. Time and time again, I've defeated you. I sent you back into the Void! I saved the whole of reality from you! I am the Doctor! And you are the Daleks!" But he has moments of quiet introspection too. "You save everyone. You always do. That's what you do," Amy demands in *Amy's Choice* when Rory is seemingly killed by the Dream Lord's trap. "Not always. I'm sorry," replies the Doctor regretfully, in a horrible portent for realities to come two episodes later. "Then what is the point of you?" asks Amy, angrily. It's a valid question – even if in grief – and it's one that's been asked more than once previously. Occasionally, by the Doctor himself.

The eleventh Doctor is a Time Lord of profundity and wisdom. "A lot of bad stuff happened. And I'd love to forget it all. But I don't. Not ever. Because this is what I do. Every time, every day, every second. This. On five, we're bringing down the government." He shows anger at stark and manifest injustices: "Nobody talk to me! Nobody human has anything to say to me, today!" In *Amy's Choice,* he orders Amy and Rory to "Stop talking to me when I'm cross!" But he's nothing if not practical, telling Rosanna Calvierri when she proposes they become allied in more physical ways that he'd anticipated "I'm a Time Lord, you're a big fish. Think of the children!"

The eleventh Doctor is a Time Lord of humour. A witty time traveller with a pithy quip for every carnage-wishing space monster he faces and every alien invasion he encounters. "Twenty minutes to save the world and I've got a Post Office. And it's shut!" Or: "I have one of those faces. People see it and can't stop blurting out all of their plans!" And: "No tea, then?" It's something we've grown used to over the year. "You're not armed," says Vincent, horrified, when the Doctor is about to enter the church and face the invisible Krafayis. The Doctor can only tap the MacGuffin-type device he has brought with him from the TARDIS and admit "I am. With this, overconfidence and a small screwdriver!"

The eleventh Doctor is a Time Lord not blessed with an overabundance of patience, however. "Is this how time normally passes?" he asks rhetorically in *Vincent and the Doctor,* looking bored and rather disturbed. "Really slowly and in the right order?"

The eleventh Doctor is, perhaps tellingly, a sentimentalist at heart. When he sees Rory and Amy dancing at their wedding there's a lump in his throat as big as that of the collective audience when he notes "The boy who waited. Good on ya, mate." His little victory in *The Lodger* is to save not a whole universe but just two people – Craig and Sophie – who obviously belong together, he decides. His decision to show Vincent what the future has in store for his legacy is a brave one. A momentary act of kindness that will not change the course of the universe but will, for a least a short while, bring some calm to a troubled mind. But the eleventh Doctor has a dark and troubled side himself, as *Amy's Choice* demonstrates. The Doctor is given an uncomfortable look into what he soon realises to be a deep, dark and truthful mirror. "There's only one person in the universe who hates me as much as you do," takes on a quite chillingly sinister additional level with hindsight when the audience realises just who the Dream Lord really is.

The eleventh Doctor is equally at home eating fish fingers and custard with a scared seven year old girl or dancing with children at a wedding as he is conversing with monarchs, prime ministers, gun-wielding bishops or fish vampires. A creature of effortless intellect and knowledge who knows that there's little point in being a grown up if you can't act like a child every now and then. Someone who has, by his own self-aggrandising admission, saved the universe countless times and who is unable to save a companion from never having even existed. The eleventh Doctor plays the long game with Amy Pond, knowing from the start that there's something about her life that doesn't quite add up: the too-big house, the missing parents, the duck pond without ducks. Okay, he never, quite, gets around to explaining the latter but there's time yet!

The eleventh Doctor is not, however, all knowing. He possibly could be if he'd only taken a peek into the spoilers in River Song's journal. But he's too honest and too wise to do something as crass – as ordinary – as that. He is someone who can find wonder in the – literal – blink of an eye and reboot the universal with a piece of self sacrifice which, he believes, will wipe his own existence from the face of reality. "I'll be a story in your head," he tells the sleeping little Amy as he says his, supposed, final goodbye to her life. "But, that's okay. We're all stories in the end. Just make it a good one, eh? Cos it was, you know. It was the best. A daft old man who stole a magic box and ran away." That he subsequently returns from the void is down to those very stories that he, and the TARDIS, have buried deep in the memories of a newlywed. Something old, something new, something borrowed, something blue. Magic blue.

The eleventh Doctor's first season of adventures take him from a quiet, John Wyndhamesque English country village to a spaceship Britain of the far future, blitz-torn London, the distant crash of the *Byzantium*, Renaissance Venice, his own subconscious, a Silurian-threatened Welsh valley, van Gogh's Provance, suburban Essex, Roman Wiltshire, the end of the universe, and back to Leadworth in time for tea and dancing. Along the way, he's brought down a government, defeated the Daleks (twice), faced down the Weeping Angels, stopped the vampire-fish-things, battled with his own dark side, lost a companion, failed to prevent a celebrated suicide, scored a load of goals from a Sunday league football team, got back the companion he lost and saved the universe. He's shown Amy and Rory what the cosmos has to offer and that, no matter how scary or dangerous it is, it's better than staying at home and growing a mullet.

The eleventh Doctor is at home banging in the goals for the King's Arms as he is trying to broker a peace treaty between the Silurians and humanity. A Time Lord of considerable contradictions, then. One who tetchily throws his own TARDIS manual into the vortex because he disagreed with it, yet someone who understands, implicitly and with alarming clarity, the complexities of what makes psyches tick. The eleventh Doctor always has a plan, even if it isn't always a very good plan. "We've got surprise on our side. They'll never expect three people to attack twelve thousand Dalek battleships. Cos we'd be killed instantly, so it would be a fairly short surprise. Okay, forget surprise." It's easy to see why others, those who fear him, regard him as "A goblin, or a trickster, or a warrior", or, as it happens, all three. "A nameless, terrible thing soaked in the blood of a billion galaxies. The most feared being in all the cosmos. Nothing could stop it, or hold it, or reason with it. One day it would just drop out of the sky and tear down your world." That the trap they prepare for him is sprung by his own curiosity is, in a way, entirely fitting. It's got the Doctor into more than enough situations over the years as it stands.

The eleventh Doctor is a poet philosopher. A fisher king with a deep and awesome understanding of universal truths. "People fall out of the world sometimes," he tells Amy. "But they always leave traces. Little things we can't quite account for. Faces and photographs, luggage, half-eaten meals. Rings. Nothing is ever forgotten. Not completely. And, if something can be remembered, it can come back." He is amused by, and often amazed by, the capacity of those he meets for magnificence ("Why do you have to be so... human?") The eleventh Doctor knows the score, and has an idea how to get it all sorted. He can cut down over-ambitious plans using withering sarcasm ("today, just dying is a result!") but can project a need, a necessary need, for triumph, for glory, for hope and integrity and wonder and, magnificently, redemption. "You'll dream about that box. It'll never leave you. Big and little at the same time. Brand new and ancient and the bluest blue ever. And the times we had, eh? Would've had. Never had. In your dreams, they'll still be there. The Doctor and Amy Pond and the days that never came."

In one episode, Matt Smith became the eleventh Doctor. In 13, he became did something few of us could've dared to hope for. He created something extraordinary. Otherworldly and yet charmingly almost-human at the same time. Bowties, and fezzes, are cool, it would seem. Soon, he and Amy and Rory will be off again, into the unknown, searching for Christmases past, present and future. The girl who waited, the boy who waited, and the Time Lord who sailed and saved the universe. Again and again and again. What happens next could be very interesting indeed. Geronimo.

What Kind of Doctor Who Producer Are You?

by Robert Smith?
From Enlightenment #126, February / March 2005
(revised August 2010)

You've been offered the enviable task of reviving *Doctor Who* for a new decade! After all your hard work, here's the chance to take everything that was great about the world's greatest science-fiction series... and throw it away in favour of something completely different. That's a very necessary component in the overall success of *Doctor Who*, partly because any ongoing series must change and adapt, but mostly because your predecessors were a bunch of second-rate hacks. How will you fare?

How do you see the casting of the Doctor?

A. We've just managed to hire one of Britain's leading comedians, known for his funny voices, comedy lisp and hilarious hair. This will finally take the show in the comedic direction it so clearly needs to go.

B. We've inherited Tom Baker, so obviously we're going to be a smash hit ratings success just on that basis alone. He's so indelibly associated with the role that he'll probably play the part forever and we'll never get cancelled!

C. Paul's just signed a contract for the weekly television series once we get the pilot out of the way. Since we'll be seeing so much of him then, maybe we'll give Sylvester's agent a call and see if he doesn't want to fill up the first third of the movie, because you really can't have too much continuity.

D. We've decided to subvert all expectations and hired an actual actor. Sorry, everyone; it won't last long.

E. Some 26 year old kid, to capture that all-important youth market, because the age of fuddy-duddy professors wearing bowties and braces is over. Right on! Solid, dudes.

How do you see the role of the companion?

A. She must reflect the growing movement of Women's Liberation by being highly intelligent, charismatic, able to carry whole subplots on her own and, like all scientists, wear incredibly short miniskirts. And then, next year, we'll turf her out without a word and replace her with a dimwitted bimbo.

B. Holy crap, we just got rid of Romana and K9 and now Tom's leaving, so we've only got a pyjama-clad boy genius. Better offer some minor guest stars a contract, regardless of accent, experience or talent.

C. Everyone liked those "kisses to the past", so we thought we'd take it to the next level.

D. We don't want to distract viewers with any of that pesky acting or emotion, so let's go as shallow as possible. We'll hire a hot celebrity, preferably one who's put out teenybopper hits and had a high-profile divorce by her twenties. What can possibly go wrong?

E. A sexy policewoman babe! What do you mean, actual policewomen don't wear miniskirts that short? Oh, all right then, make her a kissogram for one episode and then never mention it again.

How do you imagine introducing the complex concept of Doctor Who to an audience who may be making the transition for the first time?

A. *Spearhead from Space.*

B. A two-minute panning shot across a beach and then back to business as usual, only minus the comedy. Nobody watched *Doctor Who* for that, did they?

C. *Spearhead from Space.*

D. *Spearhead from Space.*

E. Let's have the Doctor be all weird, with a kid companion who's actually a better and more convincing actress than the grown up we'll replace her with 15 minutes later.

The Doctor's costume is perhaps the most visually important brand that can immediately hook an audience. What do you consider its most important aspects?

A. An elegant coat, frilly shirt, cravat and an obligatory hat scene, in order to convey the essential "gentleman of the universe" concept that has been one of the few consistent trademarks of the character.

B. An elegant coat, waistcoat, boots and a hat, only everything in burgundy. And I'm surprised and delighted to bring back the scarf, in order to convey the essential "Tom Baker" concept that has been one of the few consistent trademarks of the character.

C. An elegant coat, waistcoat, cravat and an obligatory scarf scene, in order to convey the essential "Wild Bill Hickok" concept that has been one of the few consistent trademarks of the character.

D. Any old leather jacket and black T-shirt thing.

E. An elegant coat, braces and bowtie, and possibly a fez, in order to convey the essential "Patrick Troughton" concept that has been one of the few consistent trademarks of the character.

Tell us about your vision for redesigning the show's logo and title sequence.

A. It's the seventies and we've just got colour, so everything should be blindingly bright, with exciting swirls. That'll never date.

B. It's the eighties and we've just got computers, so everything should be in that neon font, with an exciting starscape. That'll never date.

C. It's the nineties and we've just got retro, so let's just do whatever they did in 1970, with an exciting voiceover.

D. It's the twenty-first century and we've just got Photoshop, so let's make it, um, horizontal! And... no, that's it.

E. It's 2010 and we've just realised that everything good has been done decades ago, so let's go with initials that nobody uses anyway but make it cleverly dissolve into the TARDIS. That'll never date.

How do you envision the dramatic first appearance of the TARDIS?

A. We're going to use its iconic status as one of only two returning images to inform other characters and the audience that this radical reimagining of the series is nevertheless the same show.

B. As the punchline to a two-minute sight gag.

C. Just start the action inside the console room. We don't need to bother with setting up the Doctor's home as an otherworldly mystery to be solved throughout the course of the story. Nobody wants to see that. Plus, we want to get maximum airtime for the console room. Wait till you see it, it's really expensive! I mean, good.

D. We thought we'd widen it and flatten the roof a bit. That won't upset the fans, will it?

E. How about... sideways? Oh crap, didn't they do that in the Davison era? Wait, nobody's done the St John's Ambulance thing in about 45 years! That'll look sort of original-ish. Huh? What New Adventures? For cruk's sake, it's in the opening titles, what more do you want?

Who do you see writing for the new series?

A. Pretty much the same group of professionals who wrote for it before with maybe easing one new writer in at the end. *Doctor Who*'s a complex and demanding show, you'd be insane to do anything other than rely on the experts.

B. We're open to pretty much anyone, except for the bunch of hacks who've written for it before. We wanted a fresh approach and felt that was best achieved by hiring only writers with little or no experience of television at all, let alone a show as complex and demanding as *Doctor Who*. And if it goes wrong, Chris can always give the scripts a bit of a polish in his spare time.

C. Any old bloke on staff with a laptop. Who cares about the script? Wait till you see the TARDIS console!

D. Me, mostly. Oh all right then, a bunch of my New Adventures mates can have a go too. I hope you're laughing now, rec.arts.drwho...

E. The last bloke did most of it himself and nobody really minded, did they? Sounds like a surefire route to success to me!

How do you feel about characters who appeared in previous eras?

A. We're going to pick one who appeared twice and use him to establish the new format for the show and also as the sole link to the series of the past. Returning characters are best ignored totally, unless they're members of a multinational paramilitary organisation or creations of Terry Nation.

B. We plan to have a surprise villain turn up at the end of the season – and then repeat that trick every third story until it has no impact whatsoever. Returning characters are best when used as often as possible, like the use of flashback clips, stories involving multiple Doctors and light-entertainment guest stars.

C. We plan to have a surprise villain turn up in the first few minutes. Returning characters are best introduced at the beginning, preferably with voices that sounds as much like Smurfs as possible.

D. We plan to start by pretending to revamp the show for a new generation, but will slowly dilute that in favour of more and more old monsters each season. Returning characters are best used as often as possible and preferably given their own spinoffs that will one day make me a lot of money in America.

E. We plan to start by pretending to revamp the show for a new generation, but will slowly dilute that in favour of more and more old monsters throughout the season. Returning characters are best used when redesigned in bathtub-friendly colours for maximum marketing profits.

Tell us about the guest cast you're got lined up.

A. We only intend to hire the finest thespians working in today's industry. And when the money for that has run out by the end of the season, we'll set everything in a parallel universe and simply recast our regulars.

B. We'll be filling the show with an extravaganza of yesterday's light-entertainment stars, who will be carefully handpicked for availability based on who's still alive.

C. Eric Roberts! We've got Eric Roberts! (But we'll let you take him off our hands for a very reasonable fee.)

D. Read 'em and weep.

E. Everyone who's anyone has been in it by now, but we did discover that Arthur Darvill can act, much to everyone's surprise, so let's keep him on. We'll, er, figure out the details next year.

Tell us about the publicity blitz you've got planned.

A. *Radio Times* cover and at last a leading man who's not petrified of interviews and willing to look like a big chicken in a cape. The ratings for this season are going to blow the sixties out of the water!

B. I'm telling you, these light-entertainment stunt castings will have the viewers in stitches. The ratings for this season are going to blow the seventies out of the water!

C. An occasional ad during *The X-Files* mentioning a rubber octopus. The ratings for this telemovie are going to blow the eighties out of the water!

D. A daily dose of "Who Spy" featuring online images from the production, such as ladders, banks of lights and the occasional toolbox. The ratings for this season are going to blow the nineties out of the water!

E. A 3D trailer whose punchline is a Silurian in a mask and a series of Big Questions for the main actors on things unrelated to the show that we'll nevertheless hide behind regional firewalls so no one outside the UK can access them, except for anyone with the slightest internet know-how whatsoever. The ratings for this season are going to blow the noughties out of the water!

What sort of competition are you facing?

A. That *Star Trek* show just finished. And good riddance too, I'm glad we'll never see that again.

B. A couple of minor things called *Buck Rogers* and *The A-Team*. Nothing to worry about, I'm sure.

C. We're up against *Roseanne*. *Roseanne*! Honestly, this telemovie couldn't fail if it tried!

D. Did anybody notice they just cancelled *Enterprise*? No, I thought not...

E. Competition? What's "competition"?

How would you compare the strengths of that crucial first season with what you have planned for the future?

A. We'll start with a series of intricate and demanding storylines, with an uneasy Doctor-UNIT relationship, a companion too intelligent for TV, and a plausible and logical rationale behind the weekly menaces. Then we'll junk all that for a cosy, unrealistic family of regulars, invade Britain somewhere every Saturday at teatime and have the same villain behind it all every week. Brilliant.

B. We'll reinvent the series as Proper Science Fiction, with carefully-thought-through scientific concepts, developing themes and a richness to the direction. Then we'll turn it all into a weekly soap opera, replace random villains by the Master in inexplicable disguises and show it bi-weekly. But don't worry, it's all part of our long-term plan to have the lead actor in a hideously tasteless coat, 45-minute episodes and more pointless continuity than you can shake a stick at. Genius.

C. We plan to follow up on our multi-million dollar movie with a series of novels featuring an entirely dissimilar lead character that will halve the reading audience in no time at all, a bunch of audio adventures you can't even buy in the shops and an online remake of an old Tom Baker script that'll be so dull no one will ever speak of it again. Gold.

D. We'll begin with shocking originality, a Doctor played by an actor you can't take your eyes off and a story arc so clever you'll be itching to find out just how two words can follow our time travellers around the universe. Then we'll replace our lead with a hyperactive child who costs a lot less, remove all character growth from the companion, substitute original storytelling with yet another returning monster and stick in the odd recurring phrase at random even though we don't actually care where it's going. Solid.

E. Wait till you see the episode done in split-screen. Wait, was that out loud?

If you answered:

Mostly A's. You're the kind of producer who likes to reinvent things for dramatic necessity. You believe the past is another country when it comes to storytelling, but there's no substitute for experience. You understand the importance of structure, of teasing the audience onside and intelligent drama that truly spans the entire family's tastes... You'll last about two stories.

Mostly B's. You're the kind of producer who likes to reinvent things for their own sakes. You believe that there's no higher calling than pleasing the fans with lashings of continuity. You understand casting companions "for the dads", stretching a tiny budget to unimaginable lengths and that when your lead actor says he's leaving, as he did every year, the correct response is not "Don't be silly Tom, of course everyone loves you" but rather "Right, off you go." Congratulations, the job's yours for as long as you'd like to stay!

Mostly C's. You're the kind of producer who likes to throw the entirety of the series' backstory at us in an opening voiceover. You're so obsessed with the Seal of Rassilon that you probably have it tattooed somewhere about your person. You've put years of hard work into bringing *Doctor Who* back as a love letter to the fans... who will nevertheless curse your name for the next ten years for your attempts to add something new.

Mostly D's. You're the kind of producer who can not only bring *Doctor Who* back from the dead, you can convince the BBC that their embarrassing franchise they've had all this time is actually good, and you can make an outdated children's TV series beloved of the general public and media alike. The fans will tear you to shreds.

Mostly E's. You're the kind of producer who is desperate not to live in the shadow of your predecessor, so you'll go all out to make everything intricately connected, plotting everything in advance, replace *deus ex machinas* with actual endings and recast the show as a lyrical fairytale that will nevertheless show that a time-travel series about a fuddy-duddy professor in a bowtie who speaks with Received Pronunciation and doesn't lust after his companion can be beloved by the general public and media alike. The fans will tear you to shreds.

Dear Matt Smith

by Graeme Burk

From Enlightenment #149, December 2008 / January 2009

Dear Matt Smith,

You don't know me. You probably never will. Perhaps, one day in the future, you might see a middle-aged, heavy-set Canadian in a queue for autographs at a convention. That might be me. Then again, you might never ever go to a convention so the matter is moot.

Anyway, I'm a fan of *Doctor Who*. And you, well, you're Doctor Who. Or will be soon enough. So, well, hello.

I'm writing to welcome you to this weird and wonderful world of being the Doctor. I'm sure things are absolutely mad for you right now. One day you're this actor with friends and family and flatmates and bills and auditions and roles and then... you're on national television being interviewed as the eleventh Doctor. And now I'm sure everything in your life has gone totally insane for you: your face is plastered everywhere in the press, on TV and on the internet. You have no privacy whatsoever. Middle-aged blokes from Stowe and Montreal and Des Moines and Canberra have an opinion about you. You haven't seen a script. It's several months before you even film a scene. Good grief, it's about 16 months before your first full episode as the Doctor is even broadcast.

It's madness. And it will get even madder, I'm sure.

If it's any comfort, it's mad from where I'm sitting too. I checked

Facebook last Saturday afternoon after you were cast and these were the first two status updates I saw (names changed to protect the perpetrators):

> **David Agnew** is surprised: someone called "Matt Smith" is the new Doctor. Hmm.
>
> **Robin Bland** thinks *Doctor Who* has finally jumped the shark. It was good while it lasted but now it's over.

As time wore on, I started to see status updates like these:

> **Norman Ashby** is depressed that Matt Smith was born six months after Peter Davison's first season as the Doctor.
>
> **Paula Moore** is in mourning for David Tennant.

But a lot, if not most of them, echoed the sentiments here:

> **Guy Leopold** is very impressed with the choice of Matt Smith as the new *Doctor Who* and loves that Moffat et al have continued the great tradition of from-left-field casting.

I think the good news is most people are pleased. Some are pleased but were nonetheless expecting Paterson Joseph – you can't help that – some are just cautiously optimistic and some are agnostic until 2010. But that's all good.

There are, of course, doubters. Put the announcement about your casting in front of six million people at 5:35 on a Saturday night and you'll get plenty of them. There are people who worry you're too young. Steven Moffat, I thought, did a great job of assuaging that fear, pointing out that the Doctor is a mixture of young and old and that older Doctors (like Pertwee, Tom Baker and Troughton) demonstrate younger traits while younger Doctors (like Davison and David Tennant) demonstrate older traits. I don't feel this is a cynical, after-the-fact attempt to sell you to the British populace; I know this is true because that's why I loved both Tom Baker's and Peter Davison's Doctors.

And yet, people complain. They say you look like a kid or you're appealing to the *Twilight* demographic. Personally, I think it more reflects people's own insecurities. *Doctor Who* is an old, established show and fans, particularly those of us leaving our thirties who grew up with an older Doctor – be that an uncle or a knowing middle brother – don't want to be reminded that youth is now the provenance of someone else, particularly the guy playing our older hero. I think David Tennant already started to remind them they were getting older and now you just emphasise the fact.

As for me, while I'm one of that demographic – you were a toddler when I became a fan 25 years ago – I'm not bothered. I don't see that youth should be a barrier to playing the role. Peter Davison was amazing when he was only two years older than you. And I thought you were charismatic, intense and magnetic in your *Doctor Who Confidential* interview. I think you have – and I really mean this kindly – a gloriously weird face. The fact that you're 26 is fantastically irrelevant. You impressed Steven bloody Moffat for goodness' sake.

I'm sure over the coming months people – including myself – will track down everything you've ever been in that doesn't also star Billie Piper and analyse it for hidden traits and nuances. Don't worry about that. In fact, that brings me to the reason I'm writing you today.

Stay away from us *Doctor Who* fans.

No, honestly. I'm not saying this because we don't like you. We do, or we will in Spring 2010. No, I'm saying this because I think the worst thing you can do is listen to us fans, ever. Put three of us in a room and there are four opinions. No, really, Matt. I'm confident you have it in you to be a great Doctor but... stay away from us.

Avoid the internet. For God's sake, get someone to put parental controls on your computer that block the Doctor Who Forum and anywhere else where online fans congregate. I know this is counterintuitive to any artist or performer who naturally craves feedback like breathing but... trust me. You will be saner if you do this. Russell T Davies refused to have a message board put on the BBC *Doctor Who* site. He is the smartest man in Britain.

Please understand, it's not that we fans hate you; it's that we love *Doctor Who* so much more than anything else. (As a football fan, I'm sure you understand that passion.) As a result, everything that happens in the show, from storylines and characters to casting and even a 10-minute interview with a new Doctor, is dissected and examined and discussed within an inch of its life. And sadly, these discussions are often led by the most vocal, not necessarily the most people.

With that passion – and the principle holds true for fans of football, music, baseball and theatre – fans can develop an incredible sense of entitlement, that we are personally owed something by you. But the truth is, really, what you owe us is what you owe your job: to give the best possible performance; to use your talent as an actor and your natural charisma and make *Doctor Who* the best programme to watch in 2010. Many, like me, feel they're entitled to more than that. I'm sure the press and others have already made a similar stake. But no one is entitled. Your job is to be lead actor for the most entertaining, most intelligent, most fun adventure-comedy-drama series ever made. Just go ahead and do that to the best of your ability. I have faith in you.

You don't know me. You probably never will. But I wish you the best, Matt Smith, Doctor eleven. Burn brightly and blow the doors off the TARDIS in 2010.

Yours sincerely,

Graeme Burk

A Madman With a Box

by Mike Morris

I might as well admit, right now, that by the time he left I was sick of the sight of David Tennant.

That's hard on the actor, whose performance had been generally impressive when given the right material but, from 2008 onwards, that material became harder and harder to find. This is probably because the writers began turning out episodes that were based on Things That David Is Good At, which pushed him into a comfort zone of "throwing out plot exposition by talking very fast", "gazing off moodily into the distance", and "knowing banter with people he meets that never really approaches a real conversation". It's a shame, because the best turns from Our Dave are the ones where he's pushed; I'm thinking here of his performance as John Smith in *Human Nature*, or the deconstruction of his character in *Midnight*. In many ways, the fact that Donna's brief sojourn as a Time Lord surrogate was specifically written to give her reams of technobabble to shout was an indictment of where the writing was at this stage; the Doctor had become a collection of abstractions rather than a character in his own right, with some honourable exceptions along the way.

When Tennant shuffled off to the land of Sylvester McCoy, his last words were "I don't want to go", but all I was thinking was "Tough. Sod off." It's harsh, sure, but that terribly self-indulgent rant at Wilfred Mott – I'll save your life sir, but by god I'm going to make you feel shit about it first – contrasted so unfavourably with Eccleston's simple, modest and apologetic passing (to say nothing of previous regenerations, such as Peter Davison's earnest final scenes) that I actually detested the Doctor as a character.

I'm supposedly discussing Matt Smith's debut in *The Eleventh Hour* here and, if I'm discussing it in terms of comparisons with other Doctors, I might as well go back a little further. When the new series began in 2005, from its very first shot – a zoom from the expanse of space to Billy Piper's bedroom clock – it set itself up as a drama in which people were tiny, perspective was everything and a mundane job was something that you could show in a 60-second montage. The plot of *Rose* (and no one would claim that *Rose* was perfectly made; in fact, it was badly directed and had a rather rushed alien-invasion plot) was simple: a rude, strange and untrustworthy man wanders into the life of Billie Piper, bringing untold carnage with him (the first thing he tells Rose is that her colleague is dead), and shows her the broader world, where empires rise and fall and the universe barely notices.

And yet, if you describe this as the basis for "drama", you miss the point. More than anything, *Rose* was about two people. Characters who would later get rounded out (Mickey, Jackie) were portrayed as caricatures, representative of a wider society where people sue for compensation or do silly dances to impress their girlfriends. The story was about Rose and the Doctor, and the most important and memorable scene wasn't anything to do with Autons, or killer wheelie-bins, or shopping centres being invaded; it was when Rose entered the TARDIS, and stood in front of a man who baldly admitted he was an alien. Rose burst into tears at this point, suffering from culture shock, and this was the most human reaction to anyone entering the TARDIS since... well, possibly ever, and certainly since *An Unearthly Child* aired in 1963.

Eccleston was / is the best actor ever to play the role, and was never as loved as David Tennant simply because he was more difficult to get a handle on. This was a character who would point a gun at you, nearly get your boyfriend killed, call you a stupid ape and then tell you what to do anyway. He didn't pull rank; rather than bigging-up his own mythology, he did his level best to hide it, and squarely admitted he'd have been buggered if Rose hadn't been around to save him at the end. If Tennant's Doctor might open up a window on your dusty world and show you the glorious sun outside, Eccleston would do the same even if it meant you got drenched.

In short, he was dangerous. Importantly, though, being dangerous wasn't all that defined him. Eccleston's Doctor is textured by little offhand moments: his knocking on Rose's head before he stomps off, or the gleefully sarcastic way he shouts "run for your life" while brandishing a bomb, is as important as his speech about feeling the world spinning. Both the Doctor and Rose are properly quirky, rough-around-the-edges people with foibles and inconsistencies.

It's an interesting comparison with the current Proper Show We're All Supposed To Like, *True Blood,* which has an opening that follows all the same lines: a mysterious stranger walks into the life of an ordinary, working-class girl and promptly starts buggering it up as soon as she gets too close. And yet, *True Blood* is killingly banal when compared to *Rose,* for the simple reason that neither of its central characters ever do or say anything interesting; indeed, for the duration of the first episode, they barely have a conversation worthy of the name. They're a shorthand version of people with all the knots and nooks and crannies sanded off; televisual constructs that comply with the rules of demographically targeted cult television Dark Moody Stranger and Aspirational Girl, who never take the time to behave like actual people. We're supposed to accept their attraction because, y'know, that's what characters in these dramas do.

Davies-era *Who* was one of the few television programmes that could just show people relaxing, chatting, and being funny, likeable, ordinary and vibrant. This was always part of the narrative, even if it was seldom part of the plot. *42*'s only worthwhile moment is when the Doctor openly says how scared he is; it's incidental, a moment that just occurs and then lets the audience process it. And yet, the more time went by, the fewer characters we saw who felt like real people rather than agents of this week's plot – something that culminated with *The End of Time*'s villainous Naismiths, who are given no discernible character at all. New *Who* opened up with a single, council-estate raised, uneducated girl saving the hero's life armed only with guts and a bronze in the school gymnastics tournament; she would save the Doctor again, from destruction in *The Parting of the Ways*, and from himself in *Dalek*. Yet it culminated with a story in which the only human character worthy of mention, Wilfred Mott, has a role which centres on him talking to the Doctor as an impromptu representative of the Little People – and really, it's only Bernard Cribbins' charm that prevents those scenes from being godawful.

Time for change, then. Time for a new production team, a new aesthetic, a new beginning. I'm writing this after episode ten of the new series and it's been thoroughly enjoyable, if uneven. The greatest triumph is the character of the Doctor himself, though; even in the poor stories, he's managed to redeem something from the episode (I'm thinking most notably of *The Vampires of Venice* here). Having said that... how new is the new season, exactly? It's got the standard-issue young-attractive-companion format, it's got an ongoing season arc tying the episodes together, it's stuck with the three two-parters format (and kept them in the same place), and even the structure is remarkably similar to previous seasons: *The Beast Below* is doing more or less exactly the same job as *The End of the World* did, while *The Eleventh Hour* is not wildly dissimilar in format to *Rose* or *Smith and Jones* (albeit with some added temporal niftiness). *The Eleventh Hour* begins with exactly the same zoom-from-space that opened *Rose* and the rest of the pre-titles sequence seems to have been inserted at a later date to give an RTD-esque TARDIS stunt (upping the bar set by *The Runaway Bride* for Entirely Ludicrous Action

Sequences).

As for the new Doctor, he's young, he's acquired a suitably attractive companion and he gets as grandiose a background as the lonely god who came before him; the postscript to the story, in which the Doc warns off the Atraxi by saying "don't you know who I am?" is exactly the same adolescent cod-grandiose rubbish that blighted Tennant's last couple of years. The look is hardly breaking new ground either: Smith's Doctor couldn't be more generic-geography-school-chic if he tried (although you do get the impression with Smith's Doctor that he really would dress that way because he likes Indiana Jones and thinks bowties are cool). And yet...

And yet, even if we accept that this Doc is never going to run the risk of being uncool and comes with more than a whiff of bland demographic engineering, then what's the first thing we actually see him doing once he's left the skies of London?

He's having a conversation.

This shouldn't be shocking in the context of contemporary television, and yet two people talking is no longer the sort of thing that televised drama does. Certainly, cast your mind back and try and remember the last time *Doctor Who* did anything as natural as just letting its main character have a chat. Only the Doctor's aforementioned conversations with Wilfred come to mind, but whereas that was sodden with backstory and Big Decisions, Smith charms his way into Amy Pond's life just because he seems genuinely interested in her as a person. His working through the contents of her kitchen is genuinely funny and charming, but throughout he talks to her instead of at her; the single sentence, "she sounds good, your mum", is more real and empathic than anything we ever saw from David Tennant, certainly in the last two years. When Tennant grinned wildly, it was because he wanted people to know how good-humoured he was; when Smith grins wildly, it's because he's delighted. He's persuasive (the scene where he convinces Amy to let him go is wonderful, harking back to the "I can make your dream come true today" scene from McGann's telemovie), happy, witty, genuine and self-deprecating. This is no longer a godlike figure condescending to lower himself to our level.

In short, I'd fallen in love with the Doctor well before the hour was over. Almost single-handed, Matt Smith has made the programme palatable again.

This is the main reason that *The Eleventh Hour* feels fresh and new, and is at least the most exciting *Doctor Who* story since *Utopia*. The changes we do get are subtle. Non-urban *Doctor Who* based around the village green is genuinely unseen in the new series to date, something fans forget due to their grounding in stories like *The Daemons*. *The Eleventh Hour* also has a lot more going on in terms of narrative than the broadbrush half-story we got in *Rose*, although the flipside is that none of the supporting characters are anywhere near as well-developed (indulging Moffat's tendency towards sneeriness; the shy one lives with his mother and watches porn, for example).

As for the plot itself... we've seen that Steven Moffat has no objection to reusing old ideas that worked, and this story contains many of his old staples. Amy's relationship with the Doctor is similar to *The Girl in the Fireplace*; the perception filter is treated similarly to the statues in *Blink*; the aliens repeat the same phrase over and over (*The Empty Child*), and its meaning is obscured by wordplay (*Forest of the Dead*); Amy's boyfriend Rory bears a distinct resemblance to Lawrence from *Blink*. There are even some rather too-cosy nods to the audience, such as the reusing of the lines from *Blink* ("Duck") and *The Girl in the Fireplace* ("You've had some cowboys in here"), neither of which really make sense on their own merits.

Amelia Pond is the Doctor's new companion, but there's a 14-year break between their meetings; the final shot is a nice hook and the character as a whole is successful. It's nice to see a character who's slightly damaged, and the notion that she's run away with her imaginary friend is clever. Moffat has made it clear that he sees *Doctor Who* as a fairytale, and this is very much a continuation of that desire. Sitcom characterisation is something of a quirk with Moffat and there are times when the character comes across as a bunch of mannerisms rather than a real person; Amy nonetheless works well, in spite of the rather over-lascivious shots of her in full kissogram gear and the glib edge given to her relationship with the rest of the villagers.

Overall, *The Eleventh Hour* is a roaring success. It's not as raw or spiky or unexpected as *Rose*, or even *Smith and Jones*, but it knows that and wants us to like it anyway. And, whereas the RTD series deteriorated from its early genius to a smug project that constantly aggrandised its lead character, this was fun and earnest and wanted to be liked. Smith didn't even bother checking what he looked like until the end of the episode; even if the season is concerned by how it's perceived, Smith's Doctor clearly isn't. Forget all the backstory, forget the lonely god; this Doctor is, well, definitely a madman with a box. Matt Smith is the Doctor, and Amy Pond has run away from home with her childhood hero.

Here's to the future.

Squee-mendous

by Robert Smith?

From Enlightenment #158, July 2010 (revised August 2010)

Excuse me for a minute while I just squee.

How good is Matt Smith? The eleventh Doctor is electrifying. I cannot take my eyes off him. People have complained about some not-quite-there stories like *Victory of the Daleks* or *The Beast Below*, but they clearly aren't watching the same show I'm watching. Shows where the Doctor holds off a Dalek attack with a biscuit or that deal with the consequences of Amy knowing this newly regenerated Doctor far better than he does, solely due to the time travel of the previous story. I am loving this.

Apparently, when they cast Matt Smith, they wanted him to be yet another hip young Doctor, someone who talked and acted like a sexy guy you met at a nightclub, only with a bit of an alien tweak. A guy much like the last two. Only they sent him away to do some research on this 45-year-old show and he took one look at Patrick Troughton and went "That's who I want to be!" An eccentric professor-type, who talks with Received Pronunciation and who exudes a sense of alienness and disconnect, but with an immensely likeable human warmth. Right down to the costume, which Smith reportedly chose himself.

Steven Moffat talks about having been blown away by Smith's audition and it's not hard to see why. He's phenomenal. Everything he does on screen is adding to the action, providing extra layers that aren't in the script or the dialogue. He's fluid and yet awkward, mildly camp and yet authoritative, unusual-looking and yet appealing. Indeed, despite the Troughtonesque nature of his Doctor, there's more than a smattering of Tom Baker about him.

What's more, his Doctor is a problem-solver. I thought that was a function of twentieth-century *Who*, because New *Who* moved at such speed that the Doctor now had to be a know-it-all or else the plot would never get out of the gate before the opening credits. In the eleventh Doctor, we see a man who figures things out, who attempts to understand and who doesn't come with all the answers pre-prepared.

Best of all, he's often wrong. He can't save everyone and he can't always keep his promises. What's brilliant is that this makes him more human, at the same time as his personality makes him more alien. *Doctor Who* succeeds best when it strikes that balance, but it's a very, very difficult one to get right. Impressively, the eleventh Doctor's mistakes don't undermine the character, probably because he didn't start with enormous hubris that was just waiting to be taken down a peg.

Look at the way he sets himself on the problem of Amy's memory at the end of *Flesh and Stone*. Despite the, er, distraction, he treats it like a particularly interesting problem that a student has raised in his classroom. Or his buildup to the word "tongue" in *The Beast Below*, where he's trying to coax Amy into thinking before just revealing. The way he mediates between opposing parties at the start of *Cold Blood*, setting himself up as cautious, optimistic and yet slightly above it all. He's an educator, leading others to the same place he's already arrived at – not to show off how brilliant he is, but because he genuinely wants them to learn.

The climax to *The Eleventh Hour* is astonishing, with a standoff actually occurring in the middle of a costume change. The "Basically, run!" denouement is amazing; even though the same writer used the same resolution in his immediately previous story, you don't mind, because 26-year-old Matt Smith has enough gravitas to make it powerful. What's great is that the writers seem to know just what they have on their hands. When he wants to pretend to be Amy's Dad in *The Vampires of Venice*, you don't realise how ridiculous this sounds until Amy points it out, because he has such natural authority.

Look at the way he walks like a bow-legged old man or flirts with the museum curator in *Vincent and the Doctor*. This is a complex individual, embodying so many layers of experience and identity simultaneously. It's a startling take on the Doctor, who usually just picks an identity and sticks with it for the rest of his regeneration. The eleventh Doctor is like a carapaced insect, revealing a multitude of emotions and levels, and yet somehow maintaining a consistent identity.

From the comedy head in a cake in *The Vampires of Venice* to the "element of surprise" scene in *The Pandorica Opens*, Smith can pull off scenes that would fall flat with almost any other actor. Indeed, perhaps what's so impressive about his first season is the speed with which the gimmicks were dropped, because this Doctor doesn't need them. (How often does he actually say "Geronimo"?) He brings so much more to the role than any contrived gimmick could impose that the writers can set him down a more straightforward path. Because seeing where he takes that is somehow even more fascinating.

What this means is that otherwise run-of-the-mill stories are much better than they have any right to be. And really good stories become fantastic, because the leading man is raising the bar so high. Look at *The Hungry Earth / Cold Blood*, which should be a simple runaround with a twee political message like the Pertwee era it's trying so desperately to emulate. The eleventh Doctor makes this into unmissable viewing, framing the moral questions at every turn and providing something riveting to watch so you're not distracted by any flaws in the tale. And that's without the arc-related ending, which is both heartbreaking and sublime.

Time of the Angels / Flesh and Stone has witty direction, scary monsters and important arc developments, but Smith makes it phenomenal. Whether he's accidentally ripping pieces of the set or facing down Angels from a comfy chair, you're in for the ride because he makes it so appealing. And his chemistry with River Song is excellent, making the character work in a way she simply didn't last time she appeared.

Then there's *The Lodger*, an episode seemingly written around Smith's personal charm. It's a joy of an experience, watching the Doctor try to live a normal life, play football, work in a call centre and attempt to use an actual screwdriver, because everything he does is so adorable. It's the episode of the season that should be its biggest failure – "The Doctor has to live in a house! And go to work! And... no, that's it!" – but it's the surprise hit of the year, solely due to the lead actor's charisma.

He's also amazing in the two-part season finale. The scene on top of Stonehenge, with his speech to the ships, is incredible. In retrospect, you know intellectually that the real reason the ships didn't attack was because they had something else in mind all along... but the speech is delivered so powerfully that you suspect it gave some of them cold feet anyway. If David Tennant had made this speech, it would have been a moment of icy acting, fixing the camera with a steel gaze, as he delivered his speech in a heart-pounding oratory. Which would have been great, but you know from the get-go exactly how he'd deliver it.

Against all expectations, Matt Smith delivers it like a man who's had too much to drink – and it works! By all that's Rassilony it shouldn't, but it does. He slurs his words, he staggers around like he's lost his balance and he basically shouts out to the assembled armies of the universe, "Come and have a go if you think you're hard enough!" – and my little fanboy heart was pounding like a demon. This is like Christopher Eccleston's "It means no" speech in *Bad Wolf*. Indeed, it almost is precisely that speech, complete with the "no weapons" line, but it's saved from the repetition by Smith's incredible acting.

He's once again excellent in the season's final episode. His fez antics are hilarious and his physical acting continues to inspire. Look at the way his legs instantly splay sideways when the TARDIS is jolted. He's not going for the usual choices and simply jerking against the console, but is instead doing some sort of Bee Gees move. His "radish" dance with the kids at the wedding is infectious. And the way he says "It's a fez, I wear a fez now" in a tone full of dramatic gravitas is laugh-out-loud funny. Nothing he does should work, and yet everything does. He's spent the entire season making the uncool cool, which is really a gift to all of us at home. I love this man.

In short, Matt Smith is nothing short of stupendous. For a while, I felt as though *Doctor Who* had moved away from me and I was reluctantly okay with that, since millions of viewers seemed to love it that way. Now, however, *Doctor Who* is once again the show I fell in love with and it's an utterly incredible feeling. The fact that it's popular is just icing on the cake. You could give me an entire episode where the regulars were stuck in the TARDIS or in some sort of dream sequence and I would love it. Oh, wait, they already did. And I do!

Matt Smith is the Doctor. OMG, like, *Squee*!

Visionary

by Anthony Wilson

"There is more to the world than the average eye is allowed to see. I believe, if you look hard, there are more wonders in this universe than you could ever have dreamed of."

—Vincent van Gogh, *Vincent and the Doctor*

Like any good work of literature, the 2010 season of *Doctor Who* has levels and a depth which – other than allegories from Peladon to *Paradise Towers* – the show has not always possessed. This absence is perhaps surprising, as good children's literature – which, of course, *Doctor Who* is – has always been notable for having different levels. *Harry Potter* is about wizards, or it's about growing up. *Peter Pan* is about staying young forever, the childlike belief that you can fix the world by clapping your hands and wishing it so, or it's about relationships with parents. *The Chronicles of Narnia* is the most heavy-handed allegory for Christianity ever written, but it's also about the childlike wonder of discovering a world that adults can't see. Indeed, this idea of believing in something that you can't see riddles its way through children's stories and, perhaps not coincidentally, given the "fairy story" aspects which are also evident, is the underlying theme of Matt Smith's first season. Yes, beyond the Mighty Morphin Daleks, the frog "vampires" and the visually impaired Silurians, the whole season is rooted around how we interpret what we see.

It's not obvious, at first. The design of the Atraxi is very powerful in itself, and it's only in retrospect that you realise the relevance of the first image we see in the crack: an eye, looking, searching, seeking. Later in the episode, we observe not the Doctor's thought-processes, but his pattern of vision: the things that he has seen and, from there, how he interprets them. Furthermore, the clue he gleans is itself based around what someone else is looking at and how they, in turn, are unable to interpret what they are seeing. A similar sequence happens in *The Beast Below* for Amy, which not only demonstrates that she and the Doctor approach visual interpretation in the same way, but also serves to reinforce the very importance of making that effort: it's not enough just to look, but you also have to perceive (meaning "see within context and with thought"). At the start of that episode, the Doctor takes Amy, and us, through this process. Look at the child, he says, but look at everything around her as well. Only then can you truly understand the surrounding context. Meanwhile, back in *The Eleventh Hour*, the Atraxi have to have their vision focussed; the Doctor makes them see things as they really are.

And once you start looking for it, you realise the season is riddled with sight and perception imagery. The whole premise of *Amy's Choice* is interpreting which of two different presented scenarios, both of which look and feel real, is actually truth. As it turns out, neither is. At the end of this story, the Doctor looks into a reflective surface and sees an image that we, as the observers, know is only in his mind. This hadn't happened often in *Who* before (*Ghost Light* is the main contender, with *The Power of the Daleks* the direct forerunner), but you'll notice that it's already becoming more frequent. Meanwhile, *The Lodger* is predicated on a level of a house that isn't actually there, whilst the Silurian story is built on a race of people who were always there, but no one could see them. In Amy's first appearance, she's disguised as a 1960s policewoman. Even the Doctor is an old, wise man who appears to be about nine.

In *The Vampires of Venice*, there are frog things disguised as vampires and that, too, is about perception. Vampires are what the denizens of Venice might have expected; it's within their realms of perception. Frog creatures are not and so a perception filter is employed to give people what they expect, but not what is real. Similarly, the multi-coloured Daleks, which appear to be a shameless marketing ploy, actually make a lot of sense in this context, because the Daleks are now colour / function related. In fact, it makes so much sense that the most obsessively literal beings in the galaxy should represent their purpose so strictly by their outward appearance; it's amazing that, beyond the odd gold or black Dalek, it hadn't already been done. Daleks have no subtlety, no need to interpret beyond the superficial and the basic. They need no understanding of thoughtful purpose – indeed the question "Why?" (as in "What is my motivation?") has brought them down before – and they have no need to think about perception, interpretation or shades of grey, in order to exterminate.

All of the above, though, could just be a series of coincidences. To really see how this theme runs through the metaplot of the season, one must to look to the angels. And, yes, even the very opening scene of *The Time of Angels* is a play on perception: we see a glorious summer's day in the park which, we quickly learn, is not actually there because it's the result of hallucinogenic lipstick. As it continues, it turns out that practically everything in this story is about perception and sight. From the seemingly contradictory safety procedure of looking at the angel to keep you safe but not looking at its eyes for the same reason, from the fact that Amy spends half of the adventure with her eyes shut, from the perception filter that stops the Doctor noticing the anomaly of the statues and makes Amy think that her arm is made of stone, and from the angel in the recording, the whole adventure is hinged upon the idea that once you start accepting what you see, then you're wrong. Or possibly dead. Lines of dialogue hint at this throughout: perception is defined as "a virtual screen within your mind", whilst the angels' "image is their power". There's a clue in the book with no pictures, because the image of the angel becomes the angel itself. Even in less angel-based scenes, the Doctor's angry "Yes, if we lie to her, she'll get all better" is as much about perception as anything else.

Eventually, the words themselves join in. Twice, the Doctor takes something that someone says – "Time's running out" and "Get a grip" – and takes it to mean something other than the intent. And it's only on this latter line that we realise that Moffat has pulled the ultimate perceptual trick on all of us. Because the key to story, quite simply, is that everything we've been watching since the second episode began has been at a 90 (or, briefly, 180) degree angle to reality. We were shown and told this at the beginning but, by the time we get the payoff – the reminder of the actual direction of gravity – our perceptions have been altered; we're just too used to "down" meaning "what you're standing on".

And, because the angels missed this too, they fall into the crack. Ah yes, the crack. We learn here that, if the crack eats you, "You'll never have been born; it will erase every moment of your existence." Notwithstanding that the cracks don't always seem to work in the same way, the one thing that seems almost totally consistent is that you can define their nature with six words: "Out of sight, out of mind." If there is a running theme to the season, it is that, on a superficial level, that's how people function. But not everyone, and that, too, is the point.

It is *Vincent and the Doctor* that begins to pull all these disparate strands of sight and perception into a coherent statement on the topic. If it can be summarised at all, it is that seeing isn't necessarily believing; conversely, if you don't see something, it isn't necessarily not there. As with the angels, this theme forms the bedrock upon which the plot of the episode is written. From the very obvious "Vincent can see the monster and no one else can" to the far less obvious points of Vincent being unable to understand his own abilities in context; "I know it's terrible," he says of one of his paintings but, "It's the best I can do." Even the ridiculous moment when Vincent tells the Doctor to move left, forgetting that his left and the Doctor's are different directions is about how we only perceive from our own point of view. It is also suggested that van Gogh suffers from synesthesia ("I can hear the colours; nature is shouting at me!") and can see across the timelines to an Amy who remembers losing Rory, even when Amy can't see it herself. And a Scottish accent sounds Dutch.

The dual keys to the story are the Krafayis' blindness and Vincent's ultra-perception. Neither can properly interpret the world in which they find themselves. The Krafayis dies as a result, lost and alone; tragically, despite the Doctor's best efforts, so does Vincent. In many ways, they are a reflection of each other. And yet, Vincent's way of looking at the world is powerful and beautiful. We look at the night sky and, through Vincent, it turns into *The Starry Night*. Nothing, Vincent tells us, is quite as wonderful as the things we see.

And, of course, there is a payoff. At the season's conclusion, the Doctor has vanished behind the crack in the bedroom wall, and Amy has returned to a timeline where she has been ridiculed – indeed even psychoanalysed – as a result of her belief in this strange man and his magic box. But, by this point, Amy is different to everyone else. To round off a season which has been about how we interpret and view what we see, it is now the other way around: Amy's perceptions of what should be true actually change the nature of reality. On her wedding day, Amy stands up and, to all intents and purposes, announces to everyone that she is a *Doctor Who* fan, despite all the disapprobation that this kind of public declaration so frequently earns. In essence, she claps her hands and believes in fairies and, because of who she is, Peter Pan, in his magic box all the way from the crack on the other side of the wall and the other side of the universe, is suddenly there. For Amy, believing is now seeing.

And then we realise that Amy is us. Here is a girl who spent her childhood with an imaginary friend who saves the universe and, more tellingly, refused to give him up in her adolescence. She played games with her friend and made the real people around her dress up and play the part, and everyone around her thought she was mad. She wrote stories about him, believed in him even when no one else had the chance or opportunity to see him. And then, gloriously, after she's given – how could it be anything else? – a visual clue, she gets him back. Compared to the conclusion of the first Davies series, which pilloried fandom's reaction to the McGann movie, this is quite a different beast. Indeed, the 2010 season, revelling in its memories of a 40-year-old children's story about a daft old man who stole a magic box and ran away, ends as a paean to the fandom of exile. It is a tale of those who believed when they could not see.

It's Not You, It's Me

by Deborah Stanish

From Enlightenment #158, July 2010 (revised August 2010)

I'm an American, so all that I know about soccer / football is that no one has ambiguous feelings about Manchester United and that Tom Cruise has a big ol' man crush on David Beckham. But on June 9, 2007, I was watching the results of the Manchester United vs. Watford game on a streaming bookie site just to make sure the game didn't go into overtime and cause the cancellation of that week's *Doctor Who*. This year, it took me until Tuesday to get around to watching *Cold Blood*.

So what's changed?

It's certainly not that the 2010 season hasn't been excellent. Moff time is upon us and lo, it is good. Very good. Matt Smith, as the eleventh Doctor, had me at hello. *The Eleventh Hour* is probably my very favourite Doctor introduction of any season, new or classic. Smith was a brilliant bit of casting and every week I delight in watching him physically fill the screen. He's all awkward moves and gangly elbows and feels so very Doctorish. Karen Gillan is simply gorgeous and her enthusiasm for the role shines through every moment. I can't wait to see how she develops and where her character is going.

The season, for all its whizz-bang effects and shiny new sets, has a very classic feel. The emotional highs and lows have been toned down, and we have the delicious addition of a season-long mystery, the likes of which we haven't seen since Bad Wolf. I don't have to worry week from week as to whether I need to add Prozac to my pre-watching ritual, or wonder where the roller coaster of Doctor-torture was going to crash.

Moffat consistently gave us some of the most brilliant episodes of the Davies years. By the time *Forest of the Dead* aired, I was making internet posts proclaiming that if we closed our eyes and clicked our heels together three times that maybe, just maybe, Uncle Steven would come and lead us gently into the future. I couldn't wait.

The problem is, as good as it all was, I think I was, well, a little broken. See, the ugly truth is that the Davies years were the bad boy, the bad boyfriend who flirted with your friends, never showed up when he said he would, and promised you the world before he danced off with a wink and grin to do his own thing. As much as we hated the bad boyfriend, there was no denying he was exciting. It's all fighting and making up and kissing in the rain... wait, sorry, that's Taylor Swift. But my point stands.

The 2010 season, on the other hand, for all its scary stories and dark fairytales, is the nice guy. He's the one who adores you, says all the right things, holds open your door and gets along with parents. He's the guy your friends all tell you is great and what a cute couple you make. As much as you might agree, there is a little part of you that misses the thrill, and you have to face facts that 2010 is... (dramatic pause)... the transition guy.

See, I trust Moffat. At the conclusion of *Cold Blood,* Rory had been erased from time, but I wasn't particularly worried that he'd been lost forever. I knew that the season finale would wrap up the loose ends; the Doctor would vanquish the darkness and adventure on with Amy at his side. With Davies, there were no guarantees except that the Doctor would be walking through the TARDIS doors alone, wrapped in the mantle of his epic loneliness.

Sure, people died in the 2010 season, but it's not been the manipulative shot through the heart that Davies delighted in. In Davies' world, people weren't just killed; they were decimated by cute little boys from the future who had been turned into horrific monsters, or mauled by werewolves after saving their beloved wife, or driven to suicide to fix the mistakes made by the Doctor. Davies went for the pain every time. Moffat goes for the story.

I hate that I've been conditioned to take the pain and that it's become my default. Even more, I hate that, by comparison, the 2010 season was coming across as, well, kind of nice. It's certainly a healthier viewing experience and I really don't miss the emotional hangovers. So why was a little corner of my heart holding out?

I blame *Grease 2*.

Remember *Grease 2*? It was an awful, cheesy schlock-fest starring a baby-faced Michelle Pfeiffer. It was *Grease* Mary-Sue fanfic brought to life. With music and motorcycles. And I loved it with all my childish heart. Our heroine, the tough, gum-cracking Pfeiffer, is tired of her bad-boy greaser boyfriend. She meets the smart, intelligent nice guy but, as much as she likes him, she still has a thing for the bad boy. It's only when the nice guy suits up in leather and becomes the mysterious Cool Rider that her heart falls.

My hope was that, once I got used the pace and the subtlety, there would be more than a good chance that I'd look back on 2010 with love and adoration. Moffat might even pull something wild and dynamic in the finale that would have me serving this column on toast with a side order of humble pie. The better chance is that I'd be able to put the spectre of the bad boy away, as you do with childish things. Don't feel bad, Mr Moffat. It really wasn't you, it's me.

There was always the chance, of course, that the season finale would come roaring in on a motorcycle and jump over the pool at the end-of-the-year luau. Hey, it could happen! And if it did, my heart would be yours, Mr Moffat!

What actually happened was something more subtle and insidious: a happy ending. A happy ending with dancing and evening wear and a hint of mystery to tease us into 2011. It wasn't the flaming tiki torches or choreographed dance numbers sort of story more akin to a Davies finale (although I still believe the Busby-Berkeley-every-alien-and-spaceship-ever moment in *The Pandorica Opens* was gently mocking the Davies trope), but it was ultimately much more satisfying. I think I actually felt something shift. The adrenalin rush may be missing, but a strange fluttering in my chest has taken its place. I think it might be hope.

Well played, Mr Moffat. Well played.

Five By Five

by Sean Twist

I thought I was done.

As the 2008 season of *Doctor Who* came to a planet-towing, guest-stars-chock-a-block finale, I felt something fade in me. A fire, that had once burned bright enough to fuel stars – or at least many a late night, table-pounding discussion – had gently subsided. My favourite show of all time, it seemed, no longer needed me. My Fan Dial – once set to *Inferno* – had now been turned down to a mere glow, a comforting wisp of *Ghost Light*.

It was odd. *Doctor Who* was clearly as popular as it had ever been, having returned with a phoenix's grace, blazing once again across pop culture in a way that seemed impossible in the gloomy 90s. This had been a dream of mine, and here it was now, realised in front of me.

It was clear the Doctor was cool again.

Newspapers in England proudly put *Doctor Who* stories on the front page, written in a spirit of celebration and not in the irony-drenched, poke-the-anorak tone of years past. In North America, the Doctor was on the Sci-Fi Network, the CBC, and then BBC America and Space. The Doctor also returned to North American comics, a sure sign of arrival in geek culture. In the mutable currents of social media, the Doctor was making a virtual splash. Our runaway Gallifreyan was all over Facebook, with fans punching keyboards to comment on the show seconds after the credits ended, slapping together groups and generating memes. The Twitterverse had hashtags of #doctorwho flashing across it like reliable comets. And that's not mentioning the podcasts, dedicated blogs, raging forums and those misguided souls who even went so far as to publish actual paper fanzines.

And yet, I felt somewhat saddened by it all. Part of this may be laid at the feet of the fan Gollum inside me: for years, *Doctor Who* had been my precious cult show, something I felt protective towards, something I wanted to return but conversely enjoyed the fact that it was mine. The fact that most normal people don't spend their workdays like I do, wondering about divergent Dalek timelines or what separates a Type 39 TARDIS from a Type 40, cheered me immensely. It made me feel – dare I say it? – special, like the curator of a long-forgotten museum of dusty wonder. Now, with the show's success, that museum was getting crowded, the artefacts were well lit and newfound experts were coming out of the tapestries. Having waited so long for this party, I found myself suddenly wanting to find the exit.

Aside from that introvert's nightmare, I also felt like *Doctor Who* had grown past me.

It was no longer a cult show, something only Dedicated Fans sat around watching on old VHS tapes and well-worn DVDs. Everyone knew about it. David Tennant was a pinup idol and producer Russell T Davies was a household name. Not only was *Doctor Who* back but, by 2008, it was actually comfortable in its success. And, while I still loved the show, little things began to niggle at me. I began to dread the season finales, which seemed not to be written for actual fans but for people who liked lots of explosions, for people who were doing something else while the show was on, glancing over when the music became loud or someone shouted something dramatic. The continuity gnome inside me began to grind its teeth at the fast and loose "interpretations" of things like the Doctor's biology (he becomes a puppet when he's old!), the aforementioned ability of the TARDIS to tow planets (proof that there is a pressure limit to the suspension of disbelief) and the sleight of hand at play with the once-sacrosanct act of regeneration.

Yes, each season had new gems I adored, but when Davies opted for pantomime to bring in the punters, thus wisely guaranteeing the show's success, it was like seeing your best friend decide to get her MBA. Yes, it's probably the best decision, it will help ensure financial success and sometimes you have to do things by the numbers, but there's no denying that you've kind of grown apart.

By 2008, I felt *Doctor Who* and I had grown apart.

Yes, the Doctor was cool again, but it wasn't my type of cool.

Time to get out of its way, I thought.

By the time the 2010 season – Series Five – was announced, I had resigned from being an active fan. For years, I had promoted the show, written fanzine articles, did everything I could to ensure the show's return. But no more. *Doctor Who* no longer needed me.

Of course I would watch the new season, excited by one of my favourite writers, Steven Moffat, taking over the role of showrunner, but that's all I would do. I had carried the torch long enough, and looked forward to just watching. Not getting emotionally involved, not worrying over budget cuts, not spending hours reading forum posts, not even learning beforehand what the episode titles would be.

But then I watched *The Eleventh Hour*.

This wasn't really Series Five of *Doctor Who* at all. This was a brand new show. Yes, it had the Doctor, it had the TARDIS, and it had the plucky, oh-so-beautiful companion. But it felt new, it felt special, it felt like it needed to be protected, cherished and written about. And so, despite my best intentions, I was drawn back in. So much for just being a surface fan; I was fully back into the gravity well of fandom again.

But how? Why? I thought I was done. Just what did Series Five have that could re-ignite the fire I thought wouldn't get past the level of Fanboy Space Heater again? What strange alchemy has the Doctor wrought this time?

Well, there are five reasons Five got me. And here they are.

1. Matt Smith

Expected, I know. Everyone has praised Smith's portrayal of the eleventh Doctor, and deservedly so. But what truly elevates Smith's interpretation is his bravery. David Tennant, as wonderful and iconic as he was, was a pinup Doctor, shining with sartorial excellence, damnable good looks and, always helpful with the ladies, a large dose of Tragic Hero. He was a Doctor tailor made for staring off into the sunset, his jacket flowing majestically behind him while women (and men) swooned.

Matt Smith is not that Doctor.

He's rude. He's very much in his own head, paying very little attention to social mores. He's confused by everyday manners. And his clothes are the antithesis of pinup material: tweed jacket, braces and a bowtie. (And, occasionally, a fez.) In fact, the only thing he seems to have inherited from Tennant is hair that seems to have an agenda of its own.

"The old man in a young man's body" is a take on the Doctor we've seen emphasised before, most notably with Peter Davison's fifth Doctor, but it took Smith and Steven Moffat to perfect it. A man – nay, a boy of

26 – who is able to convince us that he is close to 1,000 years old, who can appear to be carrying a millennium of tears and loss behind his eyes one second, then smile with glee at the fact he can run and jump over fences the next, is truly an achievement, if not a work of art.

Shades of Troughton, shades of Davison, but the eleventh Doctor is truly Matt Smith perfecting a theme that started way, way back in 1963.

2. A New TARDIS

That damned green light is gone. Watch the first season of New *Who*, and whenever anyone is inside the TARDIS, they look like Kermit the Frog. Yes, that light did appear to be switched off in later seasons but, with the old interior, there was always the chance it might come back.

With the new TARDIS, gone is both the green light and that sense of claustrophobia. The living coral idea design was interesting, but for a time machine that is forever proclaimed to be bigger on the inside than out, we never really saw much past the welcome mat.

We haven't seen much beyond the TARDIS console area in Series Five either, but the redesign – with its emphasis on brightness and attendant visual clarity, along with the addition of a second floor – have given the TARDIS a much-needed feeling of space and warmth. Gone is the gloom and duct tape, replaced by a Boys' Own console composed of a mish-mash of kitchen appliances and pinball machines. Contrast the interior with a throwback to the original TARDIS – complete with the St John's Ambulance crest on the right door panel – and the TARDIS now truly reflects the character of its new Doctor: old yet new, new yet old.

3. Amy Pond

Companions are often love letters to the viewers, primarily those of the male variety, written in curving, voluptuous script. But never has there been a love letter like Amy, written in code for we, the longtime *Doctor Who* fans. Or maybe just me. I mean, I do like to feel special, you know.

Sure, Amy satisfies the requirement of most new companions to be achingly beautiful. For most viewers, that's enough. But there's more, tying her to fandom more than any other companion in the show's history.

How is Amy like us?

Met the Doctor at an early age? *Check.*

Have this meeting overshadow her life from that moment onwards, with thoughts of the TARDIS, time travelling and eccentric alien weirdos never far from her thoughts? *Check.*

Written fan fiction? *Check.*

Delivered singing telegrams dressed as a sexy cop? *Well, not yet, but with this economy, who can say?*

Amy is us. If she wasn't travelling with the Doctor, she'd be posting on forums and breaking hearts at conventions dressed as Romana. Just imagine her wearing Lalla Ward's costume from *State of Decay*. You're welcome.

4. Time Travel as Mystery, Not Just a Plot Device

For a show about time travel, *Doctor Who* rarely uses it as more than a temporal subway. It's because time travel can get very tricky very fast, with minefields of paradoxes and recursions popping up like virus alarms the second you whisper "What if...?"

This season, *Doctor Who* shouted the question.

Steven Moffat knows that time travel is too cool to just use as a narrative device to get from Point A to a million years and three days before Point A. He's imbued time travel with the same level of mystery usually seen only in written fiction, letting the fascination and questions with Time drift across the entirety of Series Five (and, apparently, beyond). Instead of playing to the crowd, Moffat has asked the crowd to keep up, to pay attention, to remember and to think about what they've seen.

Instead of fireworks across the screen, Moffat is giving us fireworks in the mind, little bursts of *omigodthat'scool* as you put the temporal puzzle pieces together.

I'll take that over a thousand exploding spaceships any day.

5. The New Cool

If Russell T Davies' run on *Doctor Who* can be compared to a master showman drawing the crowds back into the tent, Series Five would be akin to Steven Moffat sitting down in front of the crowd and saying, "Right, now that I have you here, let's talk."

While still undeniably *Doctor Who*, there is a different level of engagement being approached here. More is being asked of the viewer more often, with visual themes and clues being seeded across every episode, rewarding that most rare creature, the loyal viewer. (Eyes and the question of perception, anyone? From the first trailer, the clues are already being laid before us.)

Most notably, Series Five brought a new cool to the show. In fact, the idea of what is "cool" is a running thread through the season. On a purely narrative level, we have the eleventh Doctor forever proclaiming himself and his sartorial choices – however ill-advised – to be cool, something his undeniably cooler and handsomer previous self never did. In fact, it becomes clear that either the Doctor doesn't know what "cool" means, or he just uses it to describe things that interest him. Cool isn't about looks, then. It's about perception, about how things we're used to seeing are now presented in a different light.

Instead of the handsome and heroic tenth Doctor who never acted like he was anything other than 35, we now have a younger-looking Doctor who acts like an erratic old man, albeit one who happens to look like he's just learning to shave. That's kind of cool. And, while we still have the beautiful companion in Amy, the show focuses more on her spirit and wit than her bodily dimensions. She epitomises the Nerd Girl in much the same way the eleventh Doctor does the Basic Nerd. And if that doesn't speak to this particular choir, then I will never hear again.

So, this new cool is... well, kind of nerdy. It's kind of clever. It's kind of courageous. It's more my type of *Doctor Who.* And it's brought me back to being an active fan, which is why you're reading this.

But I'm still not going to look and see what next season's episode titles are. Because being surprised?

That's cool. And that never gets old.

Back To The Classic

by Shaun Lyon

"You are not of this world."
"No, but I've put a lot of work into it."

—*The Eleventh Hour*

Let's say for a moment that you're what we call a "new" fan of *Doctor Who*. You've spent countless time poring over Christopher Eccleston and David Tennant episodes with glee, marvelling at the special effects, grinning over the double entendres and one-liners, and swooning over the Doctor's relationship with the ladies. Maybe you're what fandom calls a "shipper": a relationship-minded fan whose interest lies purely in the emotional bonds between lead characters, often between the Doctor and his young female companion. Right now, it's the end of the 2008 series, and while you're mystified (and possibly dismayed) by the sudden platonic bond between the Doctor and Donna Noble, you take heart in the fact that it's still tremendously exciting. And then, out of the blue, somebody sits you down to watch *The Keys of Marinus*, or *The Daemons*, or *City of Death* and expects the outcome to be positive.

As recently as two years ago, this might have seemed a daunting, if not impossible, task. *Doctor Who* fans have never been shy about their disdain for the foibles of the "classic" series, even when professing their undying love. The criticisms have always been there: the rudimentary effects, which might have been groundbreaking in their day but too often look like a small plastic model on a string against a starry background; the lack of depth in the supporting characters, quite often ciphers, sometimes amounting to no more than a sounding board from which a well-timed "What is it, Doctor?" could lead to pages of exposition; and stories that, while often exciting, seemed to relegate their characters to running up and down corridors, often the same one several times in the same scene. As fans, we look upon days of yore with rose-coloured glasses, dismissing the faux pas and embarrassments as distinctive parts of the show's charm, cringing at all the right moments but somehow loving it all the same. There's nothing inherently wrong with this; its charm is what brought us to the fold.

But through the eyes of the "new" fan? No lavish effects, no shouty bits, no shipping. There's nothing there that would suggest anything more than a casual relationship between the two shows: the nomenclature is the same, the police box looks... somewhat similar (though recently it's much, much bigger on the inside than the out) and the lead character might have two hearts, you seem to recall. But, man, the lead in this so-called classic stuff is much older, and – heaven forfend – parts of it are in black and white!

There is something intrinsically wrong with this viewpoint, because here we are two years later, and it's all fallen by the wayside. Let me explain, though we need to go back in time...

Here in Los Angeles, where you'd never expect this sort of thing to occur, we've run an annual *Doctor Who* convention, Gallifrey One, since 1990. Perhaps you've heard of us; we've had our share of publicity over the years. Since its inception, I've been Gallifrey One's programme director, which means I run the parts of the event the public actually sees: the events, the special functions, the guests, the autographs. I mention this purely as someone with a unique vantage point, the ability to see the subtle intricacies of the microcosm that is organised *Doctor Who* convention fandom in its prime. I've borne witness to high times and low times dating back to the end of the Sylvester McCoy era, back when any mention of the programme in the UK broadsheets was indication that the show was just, just, *just* this close to making its sparkling return. There were moments of exultation over the years (trust me, you've never experienced anything like the heady days of early 1996 when *oh god we're about to get a movie on FOX Television!*) and they invariably led to days of anguish (we all know what happened later that year). We had our substitutes and we had the cherished treasures of youth we could hold onto because others shared our passions. We had our books, which we could debate backwards and forwards about where they belonged, whether they were as good as the TV show and whether they were as good as they were two years before. We had our audio adventures and debates about whether they were as good as the TV show and whether they were as good as the books. (And if you were a true fan – and you'd really like to be a true fan, wouldn't you? – they weren't, dammit!)

I'm very fond of those days, actually; sure, our numbers weren't great, but what we lacked in attendee count, we made up for with sheer gusto. "The Big Finish Year in Review" or "BBC Books Versus Virgin: A Canon Debate" made for great moments, even if they weren't exactly mass consumable. Come on, admit it, being a fan of something in its latter days makes you a survivor.

Jump forward a bit to 2005, as Russell T Davies' lavish new production of *Doctor Who* has been realised in all its glory. The wilderness years come to a crashing halt as the Doctor faces off against the Daleks, and the triumphant fans of years gone by are jumping for joy. (Most of them, anyway; we don't like to talk about the holdouts, because they're all a bit mad. Ostensibly.) Of course, no one in the USA could possibly have seen the new show because there's no broadcaster – forget about the internet, we don't do that sort of thing – but it all worked out in the end. After a false start on the Sci-Fi Channel (or whatever they're calling it these days), it ended up – along with its sister series *Torchwood* – on BBC America where it belonged.

And fandom sighed, contentedly. Defeat and desperation led to splendour and joy, and legions of those "new" fans started paying attention.

We're now back to two years ago, near the end of the David Tennant era; he's announced he'll be moving on after the end of the next season of specials and, despite the massive outcry that the shouty Doctor's soon to move to greener pastures, the new fans are rejoicing. A quick trip to LiveJournal, the online personal blogging tool, gives a startling insight the nature of this "new" *Doctor Who* fandom: photos of David Tennant and Billie Piper, airbrushed with care, gentle phrases of devotion laid across them in pink, cursive lettering. I say this with the proviso that there is nothing inherently wrong with this; it's simply startling to discover that "shipper" fandom has hit the *Doctor Who* community, because it's never been there before. You never saw these depictions of love and tenderness between the seventh Doctor and Ace, or the fourth Doctor and Sarah Jane, or between the first Doctor and Dodo (okay, I'm stretching it a bit there). "Shipper" fandom is something we'd only encountered in other, slightly more grounded television programs, usually science fiction and fantasy shows, with strong female characters, dating back to the heady days of *Beauty and the Beast* and *Forever Knight*.

Torchwood fans, meanwhile, are swooning over Gwen and Owen,

Gwen and Jack, Gwen and Rhys, Jack and Ianto... you get the idea. *Torchwood,* it seems, lends itself more to this sort of thing; its unabashed sexuality and raw imagery is ready made for the modern fan interested in more than just visual effects and car chases. Simply put, fandom grew up in the past decade and, while there is still plenty of room for discussions of continuity, we were taught throughout the 1990s by shows like *Buffy the Vampire Slayer* that it's quite acceptable to devote ourselves to the characters and relationships, too.

But still, there is that one impasse: the natural barrier between *Doctor Who* of today and yesterday. It's somewhat akin to growing up; when you live through a musical era, that's your music and, while you might really enjoy the modern stuff, there's no way your children will; that's just wrong.

Jump forward again, this time from two years ago to today, and everything I've just said is bunk.

When you attend a *Doctor Who* convention, you see and hear a lot of strange and wonderful things. It's the only place you're going to hear people debating the merits of sonic screwdrivers (bar the internet, but everyone has an opinion on the internet). You might turn a corner and see a life-sized Dalek rushing toward you and then a few hours later you'll hear the very same Dalek performing karaoke. (I'm not kidding.) You can have your picture taken in front of the TARDIS and, if you're clever and talented like many fans today, you and all your friends dressed as different incarnations of the Doctor can do so in full costume. You can marvel at swathes of fabric used by a *Doctor Who* costume designer on the show, or meet comic book legends who have become dedicated *Doctor Who* viewers, or have water pistol fights with the young male star of *The Sarah Jane Adventures*. I've seen every one of these up close and in person; if you haven't, then you're missing out on something special.

But it's the little moments that crystallise everything for you. You get to know people and you think you understand them. They're fans of the "new" *Doctor Who* and *Torchwood*. They're young, hip, in touch with their geek sides but in the way modern-era geeks are the new cool. Then they startle you by saying that the event they're most looking forward to is seeing Frazer Hines and Debbie Watling, and they're off to the next panel with glee.

Frazer Hines and Deborah Watling are, of course, the actors who portrayed Jamie McCrimmon and Victoria Waterfield in the late 1960s. The late sixties. Patrick Troughton's era. Black and white. What is this strangeness that has overtaken two young people who have no business watching our beloved classic programme?

The lines have blurred. The barriers are breaking. Now, there is likely no evidence to suggest that this is a widespread phenomenon amongst the population at large, but something has happened the past couple of years within *Doctor Who* fandom itself: the embrace of the "classic". Perhaps nothing more than a simple curiosity at its inception, it's recently achieved critical mass and appears to be spreading.

Part of this can be credited to Davies and the writers of the new series. Take, for example, *School Reunion*, the one where the Doctor is reunited with his former travelling companion Sarah Jane Smith and her robot dog, K9. It is absolutely possible to enjoy *School Reunion* to the fullest without any knowledge of what has come before; as a standalone episode, it excels both emotionally as well as logically. But human nature is inquisitive, it craves answers to questions; it makes perfect sense, when confronted by backstory, to investigate. There are treasures and dangers to be had here, with the unabashed sense of wonder highlighted by Tom Baker (as the Doctor) and Elisabeth Sladen (as Sarah Jane) countered with the 1970s sensibility and technical know-how. After all, we live in a world of media in which immediate gratification is a pre-requisite to any experience and visual effects continually outdo each other to raise the excitement threshold of an audience with rapidly diminishing attention spans.

Doctor Who has never shied from its past, even in the modern era, and it's more than just the *School Reunion* affair that proves it. Daleks, Cybermen, Sontarans, Silurians, the Master... all villains with rich histories. The TARDIS, the sonic screwdriver, Gallifrey, the Time Lords, the Doctor himself, carrying with him the baggage of centuries. It's almost impossible to hear David Tennant speak as a 900-year-old adventurer and not be curious about what has gone before. The new series wasn't a reboot or reimagining, as so many other shows had recently undertaken. Yet it was moving forward, always forward, creating its own mythology, its own recurring villains and stories and trappings (such as psychic paper, unique to the modern programme). Strictly speaking, this is exactly what any revival of a popular but faded television series should do.

No stranger to outlandish characters and situations (witness the offbeat, over-the-top characterisations from his drama series *Queer as Folk*, where the *Doctor Who* fan is the most normal of the bunch), Russell T Davies spent the better part of five years outdoing himself. From the faux vagina mouth of the evil monster in *The Long Game* to the hundreds-year-old Cassandra, we were given names and places and situations that barely rooted themselves in standard *Doctor Who* mythology. Say it out loud: "The Mighty Jagrafess of the Holy Hadrojassic Maxarodenfoe".

The changes more recently, however, have grounded the series in a bit of reality. In fact, under new executive producer Steven Moffat, there seems to be a more dedicated return to the trappings and comforts of the classic era. Far from playing it like the shouty, over-the-top tenth incarnation, Matt Smith's new take on the Doctor is far more subtle. The youngest actor to portray the title character, Smith instead plays it almost in reverse: the quirks, the mannerisms all driving at the centuries of history this man has endured. While Tennant's Doctor related to his companions much as an older brother or similarly aged counterpart – or, in the case of the 2006 season alongside Billie Piper, a romantic foil – Smith's never ceases to be the mentor figure, the wise older traveller who knows so much more than the viewer. This is clarified early on in the action in *The Eleventh Hour*, as Smith's first encounter with another character (the delightful Caitlin Blackwood, as the eight-year-old Amelia Pond) clearly signifies the wide-eyed, innocence of youth trustfully accepting the enigmatic older man from the upturned police box. Even in the final scenes of *Flesh and Stone*, where Karen Gillan (as the older Amy) sets out to seduce the Doctor, Smith plays it like a professor brushing off the advances of the young, naive student.

There are moments throughout the 2010 season of *Doctor Who* that mark this rather pointed return to the "classic" forms of the series. *The Hungry Earth* and *Cold Blood* are, perhaps, the most crucial: the rather safe storytelling forms, with a base under siege and a lot of running around and shouting. (One wonders if you could truly build an entire surveillance system out of wiring left around a church, but something had to take the place of the running up and down corridors and that was a comfortable sleight of hand.) *Vincent and the Doctor* leaves one with a sense of wonder and wish-fulfillment, not unlike the early *Doctor Who* serials of wide-eyed, innocent explorers meeting the heroes from their history books. (Apart from Billie Piper's effusiveness at meeting Queen Victoria in *Tooth and Claw*, which served as nothing more than the setup to an episode-long joke, the encounter between van Gogh and the Doctor / Amy is probably the most pointed case of hero worship in the series to date.) *Amy's Choice*, far from being atypical, harkens back to the classic series' first season – it's a different journey to the one taken entirely in the TARDIS in *The Edge of Destruction*, but as similar a morality play as the earlier story; it's a journey through the heart and mind, with the unity of the TARDIS crew in the balance.

Of course, this return to a more classic form – away from the nonsensical, or at least the camp sensibilities that ran through the Davies years – is not without its share of groundbreaking, envelope-pushing storytelling methods. *The Lodger* is quite unlike anything we've seen in the series to date, with the Doctor breaking out of his comfort zone (resigned to the loss of the TARDIS) to explore the nature of modern humanity – and, let's face it, how best to do so but to take a flat with a roommate and live as the commoners do! Yet it's also the very same choice the series' producers made back in 1969, moving the show out of its own comfort zone (zooming through space and time) and grounding it very much in reality (the Doctor's exile to Earth and inability to travel). The entire first half of the 1970s were, in fact, rather akin to *The Lodger*: an earthbound Doctor's examination of humanity through the nature of the alien threats it faced.

I've seen firsthand the reactions people have to glimpses of the classic series. Introducing viewers to the series with what we generally consider to be the top-of-the-line serials is in fact a double-edged sword: they bear witness to the best parts of *Doctor Who*, all the while expecting it to remain just as good for the rest of its run. I've often regretted giving my long-suffering partner (who has endured my *Doctor Who* fandom, and most especially the months of fannish immersement I undertake each year for the Gallifrey One convention, for 15 years) his first glimpse of classic *Who* by sitting him down and making him watch *City of Death*. For examples of classic *Doctor Who* at its finest, I can't think of any better example for the non-fan: it's bold, fast-paced, extraordinarily amusing (written as it is by the legendary Douglas Adams) and shot on location in Paris. On the other hand, American science-fiction fandom at large is full of people who remember the series for nothing more than the "guy in the scarf" (Tom Baker) or the "guy with the celery" (Peter Davison) who is "travelling in the phone booth". Ask someone who made the choice to take in the series and was unlucky enough to catch, say, the most monotonous moments of *The Mutants* or, heaven forfend, any episode of *The Horns of Nimon* or *The Creature from the Pit* and you see what hurdles we have to face.

Yet, there they are. Fans of the new series, fans of *Torchwood*, barely out of their teens, excited about seeing Frazer Hines and Deborah Watling. Now, I've worked with Debbie several times and I know Frazer fairly well (having spent a drunken week on a cruise ship with him; you've never truly experienced time with a *Doctor Who* celebrity until you've gotten drunk with them, repeatedly), and they're both wonderful people. I'm not shocked that anyone would want to see them; they're wonderful convention speakers. But – gasp! – they're from the Patrick Troughton era. That's 1966 to 1969. That's our fathers' *Doctor Who* and ours from when we were young (or, in the case of us poor Americans, our *Doctor Who* from extraordinarily bad videotape conversions and old public television pledge drives). Our kids aren't supposed to like that sort of thing! That's like our children loving disco, or vinyl LPs. It's a product of a bygone era, our past, our history.

I find myself watching Matt Smith and Karen Gillan and, despite the relatively young ages of the characters, I see Patrick Troughton and Deborah Watling in them. Or Tom Baker and Louise Jameson. Classic combinations, the legendary Doctor and the innocent companion travelling together in the TARDIS. I see the wizened Time Lord, the weight of nine hundred years upon him, saving the Earth yet one more time, the Earth he loves and has sworn to protect. Over the years, the story has changed... but, then, it hasn't, has it? Still the enigmatic wanderer in the mythical blue box. Still the champion of good facing off against evil. Still walking the fine line between protecting history and rushing in to change it.

Has anything truly changed? Not really, and I think this is why the classic series is finding itself picking up new fans. From a monumental return in 2005 that glorified new directions and new methods of production, through outlandish and often-farfetched chases through time and space with space-cop rhinoceroses and human heads inside silver globes to now finally settling down a bit under a new producer to tell very quiet, very subtle tales of the human condition, the series has continued to progress. It reminds me of the procession from the heady days of the William Hartnell era and its new methods of television storytelling to Patrick Troughton's monster-of-the-week faceoffs and finally the TARDIS returning to Earth permanently under Jon Pertwee. The story changes, yet stays the same...

So when I see the excitement younger fans have for the "new" actors and writers and producers carrying over so well to their "classic" counterparts at panels and interviews, I'm quite heartened. Case in point: the fan who set out to find a lifelike replica of the sonic screwdriver. He was, perhaps, 17 years old. It was his first *Doctor Who* convention, and he'd been watching the "new" series all his teenaged life. He found one of the screwdrivers on sale at one of our merchandise tables, a rather accurate replica of the blue-tinted screwdriver David Tennant often sported throughout his tenure. But the fan, on very limited funds, instead found a different model: the model used by Tom Baker in his early years. This fan, quite excited, bought the old model. His reason? The Tennant one was nice, but the Baker model was a classic.

Eccleston, Tennant and Smith never wore a scarf. Yet scarves even today are a very American representation of fondness for *Doctor Who*. Think I'm wrong? Sit in on one of the knitting circles that have taken refuge in the TARDIS photo studio at our convention, populated by classic fans introducing new ones to the pleasures of ownership.

Disco came and went, the vinyl LP had its day and moved on. Yet almost everything has its due again, someday, whether kitschy or practical; everything somehow goes back to the classic. Disco found its new fans, as did vinyl. And so does *Doctor Who*. From repeats on UK broadband channels to video releases and the loving care given to the programme on DVD, the opportunities are there for new fans to discover the classic series again. Perhaps that's the most touching part of it all: the battle between new versus classic that only exists in the mind, and is slowly, incontrovertibly settling into nothingness. Five years ago it was the "new" series; now, like its predecessor, it's just the series. Then or now, it's just *Doctor Who*. And we're *Doctor Who* fans, no matter the era.

Which is exactly how it should be.

ACKNOWLEDGEMENTS

Let the thanking begin!

If it takes a village to raise a child, it takes a global village these days to raise a book. We're very grateful to all the authors, who come from around the world, for their input and assistance. We are, as ever, grateful to Mad Norwegian Press publisher Lars Pearson for his enthusiasm for this project and for his keen insight. We are also grateful to MNP designer Christa Dickson for tolerating us so decently!

The executive of the Doctor Who Information Network was very gracious in allowing us to reprint articles from *Enlightenment* and we'd like to thank them for that. The people behind *Shockeye's Kitchen* were enormously helpful and we'd like to thank especially Simon Kinnear and Steve Hatcher for hooking us up with the diaspora of authors for that zine. Matthew Kilburn continues to astonish us with his keen knowledge of the fanzine publishing world and we appreciate all his help. This volume would have been much less interesting without the cooperation of all involved.

We would also like to thank Emily Monaghan, Richard Salter, Scott Clarke, Sarah Groenewegen, Jack Graham, Laurel Brown, Matthew Harris, Jennifer Picker, Colin Wilson, Katy Shuttleworth, Eoghann Renfroe, Kate Orman, Vince Stadon and Oliver Wake. We would like to apologise to a number of contributors we would have loved to have included but couldn't find in spite of the power of Google and Facebook.

On a personal note, both editors would like to thank Julie Hopkins and Shoshana Magnet for their support and patience while the editors muttered things like "Why do they keep calling it *The Stolen Planet* and not *The Stolen Earth*?" and other, sometimes much stronger, things.

Lastly, we want to thank you for reading this. All of us behind *Time, Unincorporated* believe that, even in this internet age, there's still a place for fans to talk intelligently and articulately about *Doctor Who*. We're glad you agree. We hope that you'll seek out the fanzines that are out there and continue to support thoughtful discussion of our favourite television series. Wherever it might be.

enlightenment
THE OFFICIAL FANZINE OF THE DOCTOR WHO INFORMATION NETWORK
ISSUE DEC/JAN 2008-09
WHO AT 45
The Legend Continues
PLUS:
VOTE SAXON
We look at the new Master
ISSUE OCTOBER 2007
SPIN-OFF DOCTOR
How to make a good Doctor Who spin-off

Graeme Burk

... is a writer and *Doctor Who* fan. From 2000 to 2010, he was the editor of *Enlightenment*, the fanzine of Doctor Who Information Network, North America's oldest and largest *Doctor Who* fan club. He is the author of three *Doctor Who* short stories in the *Short Trips* anthologies, and was also a contributing reviewer for the first two volumes of Telos Publishing's *Back to the Vortex* guides to the new series of *Doctor Who*. A finalist for a new screenwriting prize with the Writers Guild of Canada, he has had his work published by magazines, websites and small presses throughout North America. He lives, sometimes, in Ottawa.

Robert Smith?

...is, scientifically speaking, the world's foremost expert on mathematical modelling of zombies. Pretty much by default. Google this if you don't believe us. His books include *Modelling Disease Ecology with Mathematics* (American Institute for Mathematical Sciences), *Time Unincorporated 2* (Mad Norwegian Press), *Braaaiiinnnsss: From Academics to Zombies* (University of Ottawa press) and the forthcoming *Who Is The Doctor* (ECW Press; co-written with Graeme Burk). He's hoping to collect some sort of award for the most diverse bookshelf in existence.

Publisher / Editor-in-Chief
Lars Pearson

Senior Editor / Design Manager
Christa Dickson

Associate Editor
Joshua Wilson

The publisher wishes to thank...
Graeme and Robert, for their tireless devotion to *Enlightenment*, and for editing this collection so adeptly; the wide range of contributors to this volume; Christa; Josh (a "Wilson" to my "House" – not that he supplies me with lunches and call girls); Michael and Lynne Thomas; Shawne Kleckner; Jeremy Bement; Jim Boyd; and that nice lady who sends me newspaper articles.

1150 46th Street
Des Moines, Iowa 50311
info@madnorwegian.com
www.madnorwegian.com